PATRIOT'S
REWARD

PATRIOT'S REWARD

Compliments of:

The Black Heritage Trail of New Hampshire

www.blackheritagetrailnh.org

STEPHEN CLARKSON

Peter E. Randall Publisher LLC
Portsmouth, New Hampshire
2007

Although, as indicated in the Notes, *Patriot's Reward* is based in part on historical record and refers to real events and actual historical figures, the work as a whole is a work of fiction and the dialogue and characterizations of individuals reflect the author's interpretation. As also stated in the Notes, some names, characters, and incidents are the product of the author's imagination, and are used fictitiously; in these respects, any resemblance to actual events or persons, living or dead, is coincidental.

Peter E. Randall Publisher LLC
Box 4726, Portsmouth, NH 03802
www.perpublisher.com

ISBN: 1-931807-56-6
ISBN13: 978-1-931807-56-2
Library of Congress Control Number: 2006940222

Book design: Grace Peirce

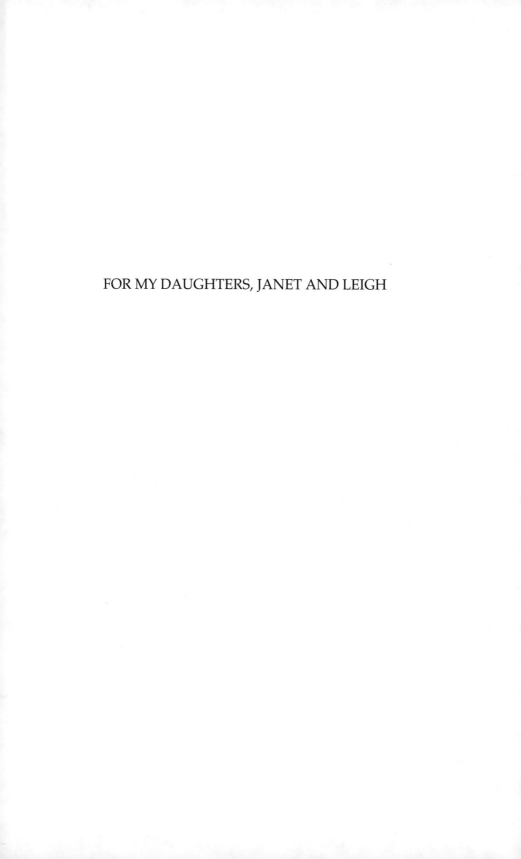

FOR MY DAUGHTERS, JANET AND LEIGH

April is the cruelest month, breeding
Lilacs out of the dead land, mixing
Memory and desire, stirring
Dull roots with spring rain. . .

What are the roots that clutch, what branches grow
Out of this stony rubbish?. . .

Unreal City
Under the brown fog of a winter dawn. . .

Here is no water but only rock
Rock and no water and the sandy road

T. S. Eliot, *The Waste Land* (1922)

Contents

Preface

In 2002, I discovered that my ancestors in America had owned a slave named Will.

Will Clarkson was born about 1739 in Africa, probably in what is now Senegal. He was captured by slave traders when he was sixteen and brought to Portsmouth, New Hampshire, where he was sold at auction to a local white tanner, James Clarkson, and acquired his English name. All we actually know about him are a few fragments.

This fictional tale takes place between the years 1755 and 1789, woven through actual historical events of those years of the American Revolution and the lives of the other real people, both black and white, who made it happen.

For those who are interested, my notes at the end provide further insight into what was real then and imagined now.

Rye, New Hampshire
January 15, 2007

PART ONE

New World: 1755–1775

1

*M*aybe it was a mistake. But that big one alone should bring enough to make the voyage break even.

John Martin stood mast-straight at the helm of his brig, the *Exeter*, as she rounded the Isles of Shoals six miles off the New Hampshire coast. Expertly he brought the ship off her northwest course and headed her west for the mouth of the Piscataqua River, toward Portsmouth, the thriving English settlement on the river's south bank.

This stretch of the North Atlantic seacoast had been discovered in 1603 by the British sea Captain Martin Pring. In 1623, a group from Plymouth, England, settled at a spot, now in Rye, called Odiorne's Point. In 1630, a larger site called Strawbery Banke was established a few miles farther into the Piscatqua. Fishing was the settlers' main occupation. The entire area adopted the name Portsmouth in 1653, and in 1679 New Hampshire was made a separate royal colony. Rye was established as an independent parish in 1726.

Over the intervening years, to the mid–1750s, despite continued pillaging by the local Abenaqui Indians during the infamous King Philip's War, Portsmouth had prospered. Indeed, by the time of the American Revolution it was one of the largest cities in the colonies. Shipbuilding, shipping, and trade were its staples. The English targeted New Hampshire's great forests for timber for both commercial and military vessels. Local sea captains and merchants exported a wide variety of indigenous products and brought back more sophisticated goods from all parts of the world.

John Martin was a product of that prosperity, and worked hard to perpetuate it. He had started in the fishing business as a young man. He still owned and operated two boats for that purpose. Later he expanded, buying three sloops that carried timber and timber products to England, France, and Spain.

The *Exeter,* his newest ship, was a two-masted brigantine weighing one hundred tons. She measured ninety-five feet in length at the lower deck, with a fourteen-foot-deep hold. She was twenty-seven feet across at the beam. Martin was rightly proud of her, the largest ship registered in New Hampshire.

The new ship's voyage had been long and arduous. On the outgoing sail to London, the *Exeter* had been packed tight with nails, rope, lumber, and furniture. In London, Martin used part of his profits to buy a variety of English finery—clothes, trinkets, pottery—and set forth to the western coast of Africa, specifically the island of Goree, east of Gambia, and south of what is now known as Senegal. There he traded the English goods for tobacco, wine, beef, rice, corn, rum, pitch, tar, and turpentine. But most important, he purchased sixty-one Africans, listed in an inventory:

Twenty Men Slaves
Seven More Boy Do (Ditto)
Ten Boy Do
Fifteen Women Do
Two Women Girl Do
Seven Girl Do
    —Sixty-one Slaves

"Shouldna bought so many," said Jacob Moulton, Martin's first mate, beside him at the ship's wheel. "Never let us sell anywhere neah that numbuh in Pawtsmuth."

"Stop worryin," Martin said. "We're going to make a lot of money on these Negroes."

The purchase of such a large number of slaves for resale in the northern colonies did represent a major financial gamble for Martin. Up to now, he and other merchant ship captains, such as his friend Pierse Long, had brought only one or two slaves at a time into Portsmouth, usually on special order from one of their best customers for other goods. Even the wealthier families owned at most five but usually just one or two Negro "servants," as they were called. If Martin was able to sell only a few, he'd have to turn back down the colonial coast to get rid of the rest—at substantial additional cost for the second voyage, and in areas where the prices he'd get would be much lower.

As the ship beat into the stiff offshore breeze on that clear day— October 21, 1755—Martin focused on the bright red and orange foliage on the shoreline. He looked forward to being home.

In near total darkness in the hold, the Africans had no more awareness that it was autumn than they had any indication of what lay ahead. Jammed into shelves on the sides of the hold and chained to the posts holding the shelf boards, many were sick with dysentery and all suffered from malnutrition. They had lived in fear ever since their capture in Gambia by a raiding party of slave traders who had overrun and burned their villages.

Rumors back in the African port had led them to believe they would suffer death by cannibalism at the hands of the white men. Some of the captives had already concluded that such an end would be preferable to continued confinement in the putrid conditions of the hold, which was, between biweekly mucking out, usually two inches deep in vomit and excrement. Already eleven captives had died en route, and three had committed suicide by jumping overboard when they were brought up on deck for a few moments of fresh air and a chance to stretch their limbs.

The ship turned quickly by Odiorne's Point on the south and moved into the mouth of the Piscataqua, where His Majesty's castle of Fort William and Mary and a lighthouse stood on the Great Island, also on the south. Martin then guided her past Long's Island to starboard and toward Puddle Dock, where the original Strawbery Banke settlement had been. Just short of the Swing Bridge over the entrance to the dock he brought the *Exeter* about, toward a row of warehouses that lined Gravesend Street, fronted on the waterside by Betts' Wharf.

The ship hit the wharf with a thud that terrified the captives belowdecks and sent some of them sprawling into the slime on the floor of the hold. They could hear shouting and felt the ship being secured to something solid.

"Bring em up!" Martin yelled to his first mate.

"Aye." Moulton threw back the main hatch and disappeared below with two of his men.

After a moment the African captives, one by one, emerged from the hold—first the men and boys, then the women and girls. They covered their eyes against the bright sun and shivered in the fall chill. Many were emaciated. Others bore the scars of whippings administered during the three-month-long voyage. Terror filled many eyes, rage others.

Moulton led them off the deck and lined them up in three rows on the wharf, prodding the men with his stick and pushing the women into the back row.

One young man Moulton did not attempt to prod or push. Six feet tall, about sixteen, with ebony skin and muscles that appeared about to burst, this man made up his own mind where he would stand. Then he strode there, to the left end of the front row. He turned and stood, calmer and more erect than the others, and his burning brown eyes resumed their intent focus on Moulton's every move.

This was Kwamba, of the Mandinka tribe. He was a direct descendant of King Sundiata Keita, of the Mali kingdom, a celebrated warrior killed in battle in the thirteenth century. In the generations since, the Mandinka people had dominated their African region and become legendary for their triumphs in battle. In Africa, Kwamba's father had very early taught the young boy about his ancestry. The teenager was fiercely proud of his heritage.

As Martin herded the captives into the warehouse, the first mate scurried off to post notices throughout town. He read the words on one of the stack of hand-written leaflets as he went:

Forty-seven likely Negro men, women, boys, and girls just imported from Africa, to be sold at the pier in front of Sheafe's Warehouse on Tuesday, October 22nd at eight in the morning.

Enquire of Captain Martin or Mr. Moulton.

The leaflets continued with a description of the subgroups from the list in the inventory.

Suddenly an imposing figure dressed in black coat and breeches, followed closely by a cluster of other townspeople, turned the corner on to the pier and charged toward Martin.

"What in God's name do you think you're doing?" William Bannister, Portsmouth's chairman of the selectmen, said.

"What are you—"

"You can't bring sixty Africans in here all at once, all knowing each other, speaking the same language."

"So?" Martin said.

"You fool! They'll plot to escape. With that many from the same tribes, they could even revolt or start a series of runaways to Boston or New York or west. We can't risk that. I'm telling you, the most you can sell here is ten. We'll allow you that many only because some of our merchants are sorely in need of labor."

Martin sighed. He knew it was no use to argue with Bannister, who ruled the town. His neighbors' apparent solidarity made matters worse.

"Aye, ten it'll be, then," he said.

⚓

These white men can't be that much smarter. I'll figure out a plan.

Kwamba lay chained on the cold dirt floor of the warehouse, trying to clear his mind and collect his thoughts in preparation for whatever would happen next. He willed himself to suppress his fury, to analyze his situation rationally.

He'd talked with some of the other captives. He knew he'd soon be sold, but he had no idea how that would happen. Escape beforehand looked impossible. His future would come down to what his new owner was like.

Baleem, one of his Mandinka tribesmen, said, "Hope I'm bought by a poor man. More likely to treat me good."

"Not me," Kwamba said. "I hope the person who buys me is a big man here so I can find out who rules this place and how they do it." He thought about the man in the black clothes. Needed to find out who he was. First he had to learn what they were saying, speak their language.

Interesting place. Busy people. Prosperous-looking people. Strong wooden buildings. Ships much bigger than our boats. He wondered what all the people were doing.

His thoughts turned back to Africa. His home, his parents, his three brothers and two sisters. It all seemed so long ago, so far away. Their games together. Tribeswomen dancing and drumming to drive the evil spirits from a sick patient. The hunting of swift animals for food. His mother and sisters working hard in the fields. His father and older brothers returning from victorious battles against neighboring tribes. Their strong love for each other. Never to see them again?

As he fell asleep, his face was wet.

2

On Tuesday a gray dawn broke over a rainy windswept harbor. John Martin and his mates were at the warehouse early, preparing for the auction. Based on the captives' physical condition and their likely ability to perform the jobs Portsmouth residents would be needing them for—housemaids, farmhands, shipwrights, coopers, rope-makers—Martin carefully selected the ones he would sell in Portsmouth: four men, one woman, three boys, and two girls. He decided to bring them out to be auctioned one at a time; the rest would stay in the warehouse awaiting their turns. He also decided that the strapping young man, Kwamba, would be put up last, after the earlier bidding had warmed up the buyers. In the warehouse, Moulton splashed the slaves with cold water to clean them up for sale. Martin then spoke with Ebenezer Trefethen, whom he'd hired to conduct the auction. Trefethen did all the auctioneering for the farmers in the area whether it was for cattle, horses, or hogs. To him, black humans were no different.

"Ben," Martin said to the auctioneer, "I don't want any of these to go for less than ten pounds. I'll stop a sale if final bids aren't that much."

"Don't worry. It's a good lot—we'll do fine."

As the hands on the clock on the Anglican church steeple approached eight, everything was ready. A crowd of about thirty people—mostly men and a handful of women, including two

African maids to provide bidding advice to their mistresses—had gathered at the end of the pier.

James Clarkson, Portsmouth's leading tanner, was there. His principal concern on this dreary fall day was the situation at his tannery. One of his long-time employees had died of throat distemper the previous winter. During the summer, Clarkson had rented a slave named Pomp from John Langdon, together with a team of oxen. Pomp was rather lazy, but he had a pleasant disposition, and Clarkson found him easy to teach and direct. All well enough as an interim solution. But now, with winter bearing down, the Clarksons needed help fast to meet the next spring's demands for finished leather. With the unskilled workers in town fully employed, James believed he had to turn to the only available permanent resource—slave labor.

Clarkson was surprised to see that Walter Abbott, the other major tanner in town, had also arrived. The two men had not spoken to each other for some ten years, ever since Abbott had lied to one of Clarkson's customers about the quality of his rival's saddles. Clarkson had responded by upbraiding Abbott at a church meeting. He knew that Abbott, shamed publicly, had not forgotten it.

The first African Moulton led out was a thin little girl who could not have been more than seven years old. She was wearing a makeshift dress of two burlap bags tied together. She held up the bag-dress by clutching the top under her chin. Her eyes darted back and forth as she tried to figure out what was going to happen. When she reached a center spot on the wharf, where Trefethen had placed an inverted wooden box, Moulton gestured that she stand up on it, but as she stepped up she slipped and fell into the mud. Some of the onlookers gasped or called out.

"Help her!" a woman cried.

The girl's bag-dress came off, and she stood back up naked. Moulton grabbed the bags and roughly pushed her up on the box as she was.

Trefethen had trouble getting a satisfactory opening bid for the girl, and he quickly settled for a final bid of ten pounds from Abraham Dearborn. Dearborn was handicapped by a wooden leg, the result of a wound received in 1748 when he'd fought for the British during the first phase of the French and Indian War. James Clarkson figured Dearborn needed someone like this girl as a domestic helper. Dearborn retrieved the girl's bag-dress from Moulton, gave it to her, and, after she'd pulled it on, gently led her away by the hand. He was already trying to explain to her his name and that he was going to call her Violet. Much of the crowd applauded.

Second on the box was Timbu, about twenty, who became the object of spirited bidding between Walter Abbott and Elijah Hall. Clarkson made a couple of bids at the lower levels but then stopped. Hall, who needed another man to work in his blacksmith shop and to help make rigging and sails in his shipping-supplies business, was bidding rapidly. He succeeded as Trefethen knocked down the sale for him at twenty-two pounds. Abbott slapped his fist.

The young Mandinka girl Aiku, twelve years old, followed Timbu. Clarkson was surprised to see Frances Wentworth, the wife of the British Tory leader John Wentworth, bidding aggressively for Aiku. She prevailed at eighteen pounds. Clarkson surmised that Mrs. Wentworth wanted another maidservant to help with the maintenance of the family's mansion on Pleasant Street.

Next came Baleem, a healthy eighteen-year-old boy. Daniel Rindge, a local merchant who maintained a countinghouse that provided accounting and banking services to other businessmen throughout the province, led the bidding. A member of the Queen's Chapel Anglican Church of England, Ringe was a well-known ally of the king, who in turn saw to it that Rindge received appropriate financial support. This day he had competition for Baleem from half a dozen other leading members of the city's business community. At the end, Rindge happily paid Captain Martin twenty-five pounds, his final bid for the young African who would provide much needed janitorial services for Rindge's places of business.

The fifth captive brought forward was a relatively older woman, about thirty. Hall Jackson, the town's physician, stood with his hands in the pockets of his long raincoat as he watched the proceedings. The doctor had told Clarkson that he needed somebody to help him in his two new projects: expanding the midwife capabilities of the females in the Portsmouth area and embarking on a broad program of inoculating the town's citizens against small-pox. He made several bids for this woman, ultimately buying her for seventeen pounds. Hall's purchase was also greeted by warm applause from the onlookers. Clarkson noticed how quickly Hall set off for his office with the woman. Not wasting any time in start-ing her training.

Three more captives were sold very quickly, all above Martin's minimum. At last it was time for the final offering of the day. Moulton pulled Kwamba out of the warehouse and pushed him onto the small box in front of the crowd. The African, wearing only a skimpy burlap loincloth, could not help shivering as a cold drizzle began to fall. He was still chained but stood straight. The rain bouncing off his shoulders and arms and the rivulets flowing down his chest emphasized his muscular physique. At Trefethen's urging, potential bidders approached him, feeling and poking him. Abbott was among them, but Clarkson stayed in the rear. Kwamba, his hands clenched behind his back, didn't move.

"Gentlemen and ladies," shouted the auctioneer. "As you can see, this young man is a fine specimen, strong, in good health. He can handle any kind of work. Do I hear an opening bid of ten pounds for this magnificent Negro?"

"Fifteen," Abbott called out. Clarkson groaned, though he wasn't surprised; he had hoped to avoid a bidding war.

"All right, gentlemen, that's still very low. We have a long way to go for this one. Do I hear twenty?"

"Twenty," said James Stoodley, the tavern owner.

"I have twenty. Do I hear twenty-five? Twenty, I need twenty-five."

"Twenty-five," said Abbott, smiling at Stoodley.

"I have twenty-five from Mr. Abbott. Will you go to thirty, Mr. Stoodley?" said Trefethen.

Stoodley paused. Then, as the auctioneer was about to speak, he shouted, "Thirty!"

Abbott stroked his chin.

Kwamba couldn't understand any of the white men's words, but he quickly figured out that his future rested on which of these two men shouting at the auctioneer proved successful. He kept looking back and forth between the two of them, searching for any indications as to which one he'd rather be owned by. He simply couldn't tell.

—※—

The crowd inched forward, eager to see not only who would win, but also how high the price would go.

Unnoticed, Clarkson tensed as he calculated what to do.

"Going once at thirty, going twice . . ." said the auctioneer

"Thirty-one," Clarkson yelled from the rear.

"Thirty-two" came immediately from Abbott.

"Three," Clarkson said.

Abbott paused, stroking his chin again. "Thirty-five," he said finally.

Clarkson didn't hesitate. "Forty."

Abbott scowled, but he had reached his limit.

Trefethen knocked down the sale to Clarkson, who stepped forward to pay his money and claim his purchase. The crowd cheered the record sale price.

Moulton unlocked the chains at the African's ankle. Clarkson had a pistol under his belt. He threw a rope noose over Kwamba's head and led him away by the neck. They walked past a number of jeering young onlookers who poked at Kwamba with sticks as he followed his new master. Neither responded to the heckling as they made their way to a house at the corner of South Road and South School Street.

—※—

As they walked, Kwamba looked the big white man up and down closely but could tell little about him. The man looked directly and silently ahead up the street and paid no attention to his new possession. His manner made Kwamba even more curious. *What's he like?*

3

*T*he handsome Clarkson house was set back from the road, with two rows of lush oak and maple trees leading across a long green lawn to the front portico. It had thirteen rooms, easily accommodating not only James, who was a widower, but also his son Andrew, Andrew's wife Lydia, and their four children—James, Elizabeth, Lydia, and Sarah. James's other two sons, James Jr. and Walter, lived in separate houses, also owned by James Sr., farther down South Road toward Rye.

Behind the white clapboard house was an unpainted barn with its weathered gray boards hung vertically. Inside, three horses kicked at their stalls while four brown-and-white cows lazily chewed their cud. Two pigs squealed as they ran for the back door. A large black-and-red rooster guarded a bevy of chickens. Adjoining the barn was a small hut with red paint peeling off, its door banging in the wind.

Pointing with his gun, Clarkson marched his new slave toward that hut and pulled open the door. Inside were a wooden bunk with two moth-eaten blankets on it, a chair, and a box with some old clothes and a worn pair of boots.

Clarkson gestured to the African to sit on the edge of the bunk. For himself he pulled up the chair, turned it around, and sat down. He dropped the rope, which still dangled from Kwamba's neck. He began to speak across the top of the slats of the chair, looking intently into the boy's eyes.

12

Kwamba looked straight back with no fear. Is this a good or a bad man? Can I trust him? He hesitated. Then, finally, he followed his captor's lead, repeating the words "Will" and "Master Clarkson" slowly, as the big white man pointed at Kwamba and then back to himself.

Kwamba, now Will, was becoming intrigued by the man's tone, earnestness, and interest.

Will watched as Clarkson picked up the heavy wool shirt and leather breeches from the box. He gave them to Will and showed him how to put them on. Will followed him out to the barn, where Clarkson pointed to each type of animal and called out its name. He then showed Will the feeding process and how the stalls were to be cleaned. Will watched and listened attentively.

Clarkson now grabbed hold of the rope on Will's neck and indicated that the African follow him back up "South Road." They walked over what he said was the South Bridge, with Pickering's Mille Pond on the left and the Piscataqua on the right, again back on Water Street, which led to the Strawbery Banke area, where the *Exeter* was still docked. But this time, about halfway down Water Street, they turned right on a path Clarkson called out as Hunkings Lane and followed it to the river's edge.

Will bridled at being pulled along like a cow. He considered tackling and subduing Clarkson, but let the thought go almost as quickly as it came. He wasn't sure how strong the big man was. And he was determined to analyze the situation before starting trouble with his new owner.

Along the way he glanced through the windows of the houses that were built right at the road's edge. He marveled at the transparent glass and strained to see what was inside each building. Sometimes he could see a woman sweeping the floor or washing dishes. There were no men inside.

At the end of the lane, on the left, they came to a small open shed in which hemlock bark was piled. Beside and behind the shed was a most curious contraption—a circular area about twenty feet in diameter, its perimeter bound by a foot-high wooden ridge, with a high pole in the middle connected to the shed by other poles with gears. Around the outside of the circle a horse pulled stone cylinders that ground the bark being spewed from the shed by the gear/pole arrangement.

A white man oversaw the operation, controlling the horse and periodically stopping the process to smooth and test the fine tanbark powder being created within the circle.

Beyond this contraption, right against the river, Will saw a two-story log building, about sixty-five feet long and forty feet wide, with two rows of windows, one above the other. Smoke plumed from a central chimney. A board ramp along the right was piled high with animal hides. Another ramp, covered with an awning roof but open on the sides, ran the full length of the river side of the building, with a wharf in the middle that extended about thirty feet over the river. Two men worked there, scraping the hair from animal hides on slanting beams. Two other beams were unattended. On the wharf a third man used a knife and hatchet to clean bones and flesh from newly arrived hides, scraping the refuse into the river, then washing the hides in the running water.

The two men stepped into the building from the wharf. Will winced at the stench in the single open room.

Directly in the center was a large two-way stone fireplace with a brick chimney extending up through the roof. On the immediate right were three round lime or "leaching" vats, each five feet high. On the left were two slightly smaller vats, one a bate vat containing hen dung, salt, and water, the other a clear-water bath vat. Across the room, sunk into the floor, were three huge tanning vats in which the hides were soaked in a mixture of the bark powder and water. Along the right end of the building was an open second floor. The upstairs room, reached by a stairway, was the drying area; beneath it, on the first floor, the leather was finally finished and cut and sewn into various products.

Will followed Clarkson through the process, repeating after his new owner as Clarkson named each element and demonstrated what had to be done at each step. Again, Will did not understand the words, but he could see the general process that was being described. As to each operation, he had many questions he couldn't communicate.

Clarkson next introduced Will to his sons. Will observed that while all three had pale skin, they were each quite different in appearance. James Jr. was the same height as his father, with a head full of reddish brown hair. He was the man who'd been directing the horse at the bark mill out front as Will came down the lane. Andrew was about four inches shorter than his father, and bald and portly. Walter was as short as Andrew but slim and wiry, with a thin mustache. Andrew and Walter were both working inside, turning the hides that were soaking in the vats.

Will saw three other men working at the tanyard. Two white men were scraping the hair from hides in the outside beaming shed and another was cleaning the new hides. Will was captivated by the deep copper skin of the third man. This "injun," as James Sr. referred to him without introduction, quickly looked away from Will. He seemed hostile, and Will wondered why.

By this time the sun, which had emerged in the early afternoon, had disappeared beneath the forest line in the west. Andrew locked up the tannery and everyone headed east, back to the house on South School Street. Even in his New England clothes, Will was cold in the darkness by the time they reached their destination.

The house was warm and well lit with kerosene lanterns and candles. Andrew's wife—Miss Lydia—met her Clarkson men with strong hugs at the front door. Will saw that she seemed to tense as she looked at him. She nevertheless extended her hand, and James Sr. took Will's hand and placed it in hers. He wondered if he was being shown how to greet another person. Did people do this every time they saw each other? He hadn't noticed that to be the case.

He was taken immediately to the kitchen, located in the ell at the left rear of the house, where he was introduced to a Mrs. Haven. Clarkson asked Will to repeat the name. The African was perplexed by the status of this white woman, who seemed to be respected yet was nonetheless a servant. She smiled at him and took him to a small pantry area at the very back, where she gave him a dish of food that didn't smell like anything he'd ever eaten. He felt safer when he noticed that Mrs. Haven had prepared the same meal for the family. She pointed to the three items on the plate and said they were potatoes, chicken, and squash. At her urging, Will repeated the words as she pointed to each item. He hadn't had anything to eat for two days and not a decent meal for months. Despite the unusual taste, the food felt good. When he finished, James led him, again by the rope, back to the hut by the barn. James locked the padlock on the door when he left.

Alone for the first time in months, Will lay on his wooden bunk and took stock. This place was colder than anything he'd experienced back home in his village. He thought about trying to escape, to run, get to a ship, and somehow return to his home—and freedom. He soon realized that this would be stupid. Although he might be able to evade his owners and disappear into the surrounding wilderness, he had no idea where he was or where to go. He didn't even know what had happened to the other captives on the ship. Were they still in the area? How could he, an easily identified man, get aboard a vessel for the long trip home? And if he succeeded, he'd have to eat, which meant he'd be discovered.

The men here weren't cannibals. The family didn't appear to be cruel. The eldest man seemed to be genuinely interested in helping him learn the words of the white man's language. Will was certain that once he learned that language, he could deal with his situation. He had to find out as much as he could as fast as he could about what was going on.

For now, sleep was important. He was exhausted, inside and out. Tomorrow he'd be stronger, then he'd figure out what to do.

4

Andrew Clarkson waved a lantern in front of Will's face. Will winced, disoriented at being jerked from a pleasant dream of sitting with his family at the fireside back in his village. He jumped up, pulled on the warm clothing as Andrew indicated, including a heavy cloth jacket, the old leather boots, and some gloves, and trudged after Andrew toward the house in the cold black air. After a quick bite of brown bread and a hot liquid Mrs. Haven called coffee, he was led back to the tanyard by the Clarkson sons.

Andrew took charge of Will, walking him through the tanning process step by step and patiently repeating *hides, vat, bate* and many other new words. At each location he demonstrated what he wanted Will to do, bringing him through to the soft, finished leather a currier on the Clarkson staff cut and sewed into gloves, harnesses, saddles, and like items.

Much of the work was difficult and smelly, but Will was fascinated. He wanted to learn the entire process quickly so he could gain the Clarksons' confidence and more responsibility.

The raw hides were purchased from nearby farms, from local hunters, occasionally from a ship dispensing cargo from elsewhere on the Atlantic coast. Tanners like the Clarksons would buy these green hides for two and a half pence per pound and sell the finished leather for fourteen pence per pound. After labor and administrative costs, tanners retained a fifty percent profit. The high demand for finished leather products such as shoes, boots, saddles, bridles and harnesses, carriage upholstery, gloves, breeches, and various military equipment led the country's first Treasury secretary, Alexander Hamilton, to observe later in the century that there were "scarcely any manufactories of greater importance" than the tanneries.

Andrew first showed Will how to choose a hide from the pile on the side of the log building and take it out to the wharf to chop off any remaining horns, ears, tail, bones, fat, and flesh. These were thrown into the river, and the hide was fixed to the dock, where it was washed by the river for up to thirty hours. Will eyed the knife, but Andrew didn't hand it to him to do any of the chopping himself.

The second step could take up to eighteen months. It consisted of loosening, or "raising," the hair in a series of lime vats and then scraping it off on a beam. A hide cleaned in step one would be placed in a very weak, or "dead," lime pit overnight, then drained for three to four days on the edge of the pit. This procedure was repeated for lengthening periods using fresher, stronger lime pits, for up to six weeks. After liming and de-hairing, the hide was immersed in the so-called bate pit to restore its pliability, then washed in a second vat of clean water. Then the hide would be "beamed" with a specially designed knife outside on the covered beaming shed, on a rounded wooden "horse" or "leg," in a continuing scraping and smoothing process that could take more than a year.

—※—

After a final washing in the river, the third step was the actual tanning process, of immersing the de-haired hides in a bath of oak bark and water. The principal element in this stage was the tanbark powder that had been ground, at a rate of about half a cord per day, in the bark mill in front of the tannery. The three sunken tanning pits were filled with alternating layers of powder, hides, and water, then covered. Each hide required twice its weight in bark and twelve gallons of water. The hides at the bottom were subject to the strongest effect of the tanning solution, and each vat had a different concentration. During this twelve- to eighteen-month immersion, the hides would be "handled" frequently in the pits with special tongs to ensure that the chemical process was proceeding evenly on all of them. When a hide was macerated to the point that the tanbark "ooze" had fully penetrated it, the "manufacture" of the leather was complete.

The last step was to dry and finish the leather. In the drying area on the second floor in the Clarkson tannery, the leather hung in the air as it was stretched by weights to keep it tight and straight. The tan was then cleaned off and the leather smoothed and rubbed until it shone with the desired texture and color. Lampblack or oil was used in this final dressing of the leather.

During the balance of the afternoon and for the next few days, Will spent an hour with Andrew at each station, actually performing the tasks himself. But most of the time he carried loads of hides from the ramp on the side of the building out to the wharf, picked up the ones ready to go inside to the vats, and carried finished hides up to the drying area.

Will could see that Andrew was amazed at his ability to learn each job quickly. Andrew even seemed suspicious of his enthusiasm. Will realized that he was probably very different from other slaves Andrew had dealt with.

Will was pleased. The first step in his strategy was on schedule.

5

*O*n the fifth morning, when Clarkson came to Will's hut to wake him, he repeated several times that there would be no work that day because it was Sunday, but that the whole family would be going to church. He handed over an old black shirt and a pair of used black trousers for Will to wear to the service. Will did not understand *Sunday, church* or the words for the clothes, but he put them on and followed his owner to the house to join the family.

He noticed that everyone was there except Walter. The mood was happy but subdued as the group headed up South Road, across the bridge, and onto Water Street for three blocks to a large white structure with a sign Andrew read aloud: "South Meeting House." The imposing building had a tall tower, with the main entrance at the bottom. Openings on all four sides at the top of the tower revealed a large bell, which was ringing as the Clarkson family approached.

Standing at the entrance to the church, greeting the parishioners, was a balding man of medium height dressed in a long black robe. He met and shook the hand of every person who entered, smiling and saying something to each. Will was startled when the man shook his hand too and said something to him, but he understood only some of it. The man's name was Mr. Haven, next to him was Mrs. Haven, and both of them called Will by *his* name. There was no mistaking the welcome in the man's eyes as he looked at Will, or the warmth of his tone.

The Clarkson family, after entering the church, proceeded to one of the polished, curved wooden benches toward the right front. Will was shunted off, then up a flight of stairs to the left, to one of three benches along the second-floor level on the side, where he rejoiced to see some two dozen Africans already sitting. The young white man apparently standing guard over the Africans motioned for Will to sit with them.

He pushed his way down the back row, smiling and accepting greetings as he went, until he saw a familiar face. It was Moto, one of his Mandinka tribesmen and a close boyhood friend. He'd disappeared from Gambia three years ago, presumed at that time to be dead or to have been captured into slavery. The two men hugged each other.

"Moto! Thought I'd never see you again. How'd you get here?" Will whispered in their boyhood Mandinka male-only dialect.

"My owner brought me across the ocean in his ship. Were you on the *Exeter*? Who bought you? What's your new name over here? I'm Jack."

"James Clarkson. He calls me Will."

"What's he got you doing?"

"I work in his tanyard. Nasty, but interesting. How about you?"

"Working on my owner's farm over in Rye, just south of here. His name's Odiorne."

"Think we'll ever get out of here and see home again?"

"Not so much getting out as no way to get there if we do. We're way outnumbered."

"Where are the others from the *Exeter*?"

"Only ten auctioned off, the rest taken down the coast. Timbu's here. His new English name's Seneca Hall. Rest are with families that go to the other churches, North Church and Queen's Chapel."

"Where's that young girl, Aiku?"

"Wife of an Englishman named Wentworth bought her. They go to Queen's Chapel, the English church."

The white monitor suddenly shushed Will and Jack as a small musical instrument that sounded like more than one began to play from the back of the church and a group of robed singers behind it started singing. Mr. Haven now strode down the center aisle and stood behind a wooden structure in the center front on the main floor. The white congregation below rose and joined in the singing, as did some of the Africans on the upper level. The newly arrived Africans remained seated.

Mr. Haven carefully positioned a pair of bridged lenses across his large nose and began, slowly at first, to speak words Will could not yet understand. As he solemnly read from bound pages open in front of him, a shaft of white morning sunlight broke through the high east window, wrapping him and the wooden structure in a warm glow.

Will was mesmerized. He noticed that the attention of the parishioners was focused. The big room was quiet.

On the polished bench directly in front of the pulpit sat Mrs. Haven. He guessed that the ten children ranging in ages from about one to twelve lined up beside her in the pew were also Havens.

The white monitor was trying not to yawn. Reverend Haven was making it clearer and clearer to the congregation that the combination of the Roman pope, French Catholic Canada, and Indian savages made up a scourge this Protestant parish and its protective ally, the king of England, must resist and defeat. As he warmed to his theme, Haven's voice grew louder and more emphatic. His face reddened and his eyes behind the magnifying lenses appeared to be on the verge of popping out of his head. Not only that, he went on. . . . and on. For nearly two hours he railed against the pope, the French, and the Indians.

Will watched him, open-mouthed at first though he had no idea what Haven was saying. The people remained silent, even impassive, despite the man's animation. Will was used to tribal religious services in which the attendees became active, vocal participants. Though he sensed the passion without knowing the meaning, after the first hour Will joined the other Africans in nodding off time and again.

At last, after a recessional hymn, it was over. The white people filed out, each complimenting the minister and chatting briefly as he or she left. The Africans went last in a group, without speaking to Haven, to join their respective families for the walk home.

In the churchyard, Moto came up to James Clarkson and asked if Will could go with him to meet the members of the Negro Court. The court was a city-sanctioned organization that provided both judicial and executive functions for the African community. It was to meet in mid-afternoon near the town pump on the Parade, the town's main street, that is, if the Clarksons and the Odiornes weren't planning to attend the second service of the day at the meeting-house. Clarkson hesitated but then agreed.

Fortunately both families chose not to go, so Will hurried over to the center of town just as Moto was trotting up the Parade from the west. He followed Moto behind the church to the corner of Fleet Street and Pond Lane, where stood the blocklong public barn and stable. As they entered, Will caught sight of six other Africans gathered at the far end of the building, behind the horse stalls.

As he looked at the group, a tan-skinned man of medium build stepped forward to meet them, speaking in the Mandinka tongue, which they all understood.

"Kwamba," he said, "I'm Pharaoh Shores, African sheriff here in Portsmouth. You already know Timbu and Baleem. These others are Primus Fowle, Prince Whipple, and Caesar Bannister."

After all had nodded hello, Shores began again. "Listen good. This is how things work here. We abide white man's law here. No shenanigans, no fighting or stealing. Any of that and you'll feel my whip at the town pump. Go and kill someone, we'll turn you right over to the white law officers. Understand me?"

The three newcomers nodded. But Will wondered what Shores's real motive was.

The sheriff continued. "You're thinking how to escape from here and get back to Africa. Don't. We know what happens to runaways. Nobody gets away. You get caught and whipped or you end up being owned by someone worse. Or you die in the woods."

Will began to seethe. *Sounds like he just wants to keep things going the way they are.*

Shores finished up. "Caesar'll tell you best way to make life here a little easier. Caesar's king of the Africans, head of the Negro Court in this town."

King Caesar Bannister was over six feet tall and weighed more than two hundred pounds—not someone Will wanted to be on the wrong side of. The king took a lengthy puff on his corncob pipe and began to speak, also in the Mandinka language, in a deep and resonant voice.

"We got it hard here. Some owners are reasonable, but putting up with it day after day is tough. We're better off here than in the South, but slavery is slavery. Can't argue with them. Can't talk back or they'll hurt you real bad. They think you're dumb, and you feel dumb. Can't fight back. Patience and silence we endure worse than you ever imagined."

Caesar looked around the group and caught Will's eye before moving on. "What do we do? Keep quiet and work hard. Sooner or later we'll get freed. Patience and time. Won't stand bad treatment. I'll go to the white leaders and object. More and more whites'll become embarrassed by it. Whites who don't have slaves will pressure owners to give it up. We help our people having trouble dealing with the situation."

At this point Will couldn't help interjecting. "I'm Will, King Caesar. What makes you think patience and time will work? No reason for my owner to free me."

Sheriff Shores pulled back noticeably at Will's questioning the king's reasoning.

"Just call me Caesar, Will," the king said. "Reminds me. Always use the English names our white owners call us. Makes them more comfortable, even part of their family. Yes, whites have no reason to set us free. But we're in the right. Most people here are religious. Church is the main thing in their lives. The churches don't support slavery. Their pastors are our best allies. Many of these white folks or their parents and grandparents came here themselves to be free."

Will knew he looked as skeptical as he felt. As Caesar moved on to answer questions from the other newcomers, Will took the opportunity to look him over. Easy to see why he was the leader. Heavy black complexion like Will's, and a confident, easygoing manner. Talked easily and well. But what riveted Will was the man's eyes— as dark and cold as the Piscataqua River. This contrast with his other outward demeanor puzzled Will. Maybe captivity had hardened him. Something had made the king calculating and determined.

Caesar was finishing up now. "That's it. You get the idea. Think it over. We meet here most Sunday afternoons after church to talk about problems. Come when you want."

As Will made his way back to the Clarkson house, he felt both better and troubled. He was happy to have met these other African men, captives like himself, he could talk to. But it bothered him that they didn't seem to be concentrating on getting their freedom. Well, that was *his* most important thing. And he was going to go after it, hard.

6

*T*wo weeks later, as Will emerged from the tannery to get some more tan powder, he saw the Clarkson dray in the lane next to the ramp. The dray, which had no wheels, just two shafts attached to the sides of the horse with the ends dragging on the ground, was piled high with leather products that had just been finished inside and covered with a canvas cloth. Walter Clarkson was sitting in the seat mounted across the shafts behind the horse.

Andrew pointed to the seat. "Get up there with him."

Will climbed in, and off they went at a fast clip out Hunkings Lane. Will hung on tight, jounced first one way and then the other. Walter seemed accustomed to the balancing act and anticipated which way to lean. He was chomping down heavily on a cigar as he tried to control the horse with tight reins, veins and muscles bulging on his thin arms.

He did nothing to acknowledge Will's presence. Will felt Walter pull away from him, as though embarrassed to be seen by his side in public.

After driving up Water Street past Puddle Dock, they stopped at a small stable on Horse Lane between Pitt and Jefferson Streets, where they dropped off some saddles. Then they rounded the corner to Colonel Theodore Atkinson's much grander stable, on the corner of Court and Atkinson Streets, to deliver some harnesses. At both places Walter pointed back to Will on the dray and referred to him as "the family's new servant." The proprietors glanced at him and looked away.

Next they proceeded to Pleasant Street, then turned past a tall brick church into the wide road designated by a sign that Walter pointed to and said "Parade." Will's eyes opened wide when he looked to the left as they passed through this area. There, next to a large pump, a crowd of about twenty-five black people had gathered. Next to the pump, tied between two fence posts, was an African man who was being whipped by another African. Each time the whip cracked the man cried out, but the spectators remained silent, watching intently. White people passing by barely stopped long enough to register what was happening.

Walter looked and said only two words: "Negro Court."

What was going on over there? And why?

At this point they turned off Market Street onto Ladd and pulled up abruptly in front of a building that Walter said was "Ladd's Clothing Shoppe." Through its window, Will could see all types of clothing in many colors, for both men and women. Walter jumped down and carried an armful of leather gloves through the door.

Will was startled at what he saw next. Out of the store, following a large white woman with a severe expression, stepped the African girl Aiku, who had been aboard the *Exeter*. She was also of the Mandinka tribe. Although only twelve, she was already a very pretty girl, with wide full lips and big eyes. But he barely recognized her in a white woman's clothes—a full-length black garment with a matching hat. Will thought she looked a little foolish in the strange outfit.

As he sat waiting for Walter to return, Aiku looked up, recognized him, and smiled, but said nothing as she hurried after her new mistress, who set off down the street at a determined pace.

Walter came out of the store and climbed back up on the dray, turning it toward Bow Street. They stopped there at a three-story brick building. A red flag with blue and white diagonal crosses on it flew above the front door.

"English garrison," Walter said, and waved Will down.

Will helped him carry saddles and harnesses inside. Behind the desk in the middle of the big room sat a thin man with a pointed nose on which rested what Will had heard were called spectacles. He wore a red jacket. On either side of the desk were two other men in red jackets and blue trousers, each standing straight and holding a long metal pipe with a knife clamped at one end and a shiny wooden handle at the other.

The man behind the desk said something and paid Walter for the leather. Will didn't understand the words, but the man's tone was ugly and the accent was different from the Clarksons'. That must be because he was English.

He followed Walter out the door after a careful look at the men's uniforms, with their shiny brass buttons. He noted also the tension and atmosphere of distrust between them and his American master. Might be something there he could take advantage of.

The final delivery was farther out toward the edge of town, at a carriage assembly factory on the corner of Deer and High Streets. Here it was heavy leather to become the roofs, sides and interior upholstery of new carriages.

They then made three pickups. The first took them past a field with stone markers that Will thought must be a burying ground. Beyond that they came to a gristmill, flanked by a sawmill with a timber dock on the river. They crossed a bridge over a wide creek to the west and continued on to a farmhouse. Here they loaded up a number of cowhides and horsehides from the farmer. Walter paid him on the spot.

After a long ride back to town, they stopped at a house where a man had twenty deer hides for sale. The last stop was at a ship tied up at Shapley's Wharf, at the end of Pitt Street. The big hides there were of moose—"from Maine," Walter said. Will wondered where Maine was. Darkness descended as the two men finished loading and headed back to the tanyard.

Most of the time Will stayed all day at the tannery, taking cleaned hides from the wharf to the lime vats and carrying limed hides to their next stations in the process. As he worked, Will recorded in his mind the schedules of each of the Clarkson employees and their habits. On the weekends he met with Jack and peppered him with questions:

"Have the slaves here ever tried to rise up against the whites?"

"How many have run away? What happened to them?"

"How many have been freed by their owners?"

"Why doesn't Caesar lead a rebellion?"

"Who's in charge of the white government?"

"Why don't they do anything to help us?"

"What do we really know about the whites, what they're thinking and doing?"

"Has anyone talked to them about ending slavery? Why not?"

"How many slaves can speak English? How many can read or write?"

"How can we get ourselves educated so we can be equal to the whites?"

In the meantime, there was his own plan. From his masters he was learning many more words than street names and the names of tanning processes. And Jack had told him that Clarkson had been a teacher before marrying into ownership of the tannery.

It was time for him to take the next step.

7

*T*he days were becoming shorter and colder. Even with his two blankets, Will couldn't stay warm during the long nights in his drafty hut. Then one morning, as he rose to feed the animals and muck the stalls before going to work at the tannery, Will was surprised to find he could hardly push open the door of the hut. When he finally did, the ground was covered with more than a foot of white, fluffy flakes that froze his fingers on touch.

"This is snow, Will." Andrew Clarkson laughed as he pushed his way through it from the house to the hut, carrying two poles with broad boards fixed on the ends. He showed Will how to shovel a pathway first to the barn, then back to the house, and finally from the front door of the house out to South School Street.

After taking care of his barn chores, Will went to the kitchen for Mrs. Haven's morning offering of a hard bun and coffee. This day at her request Andrew and James had agreed to let Will move to the main house for the winter, into a back room of the ell behind the kitchen. She beckoned him to follow her to the hut, where they scooped up his few belongings and then carried them into the house.

The walk to the tannery that morning took twice as long as usual through fresh snow two feet deep. The warmth inside the building was welcome despite the smell. Andrew didn't require that Will work outside over the swollen, windswept river that day. Instead he was assigned to monitor the bate.

That evening, Will approached James Clarkson.

"Master James," he said, "you teachuh. You teach me read, write, numbuhs. I learn say English faster. I help you better at tannery. Please, Master James. I learn good. Good for business."

Clarkson looked at Will—how in hell had the slave picked up so many words? He'd never heard of anyone else attempting to educate a Negro to any meaningful degree. But Clarkson was a teacher, and he knew Will to be a quick learner. The experiment might work. Walter said, "You'd be wasting your time, Father," but Reverend Haven and Andrew's wife, Lydia, encouraged him.

When he mentioned it to William Bannister the next day, the city chairman said, "Damn it, James, bad precedent. Only cause trouble. Don't do it."

At the tannery Clarkson spied Will moving some hides around in the bate vat. He shook his head and said, "Will, your idea won't work. I don't have the time."

"But Master Clarkson, I make time for you. Do some your work here. Work harduh. Work all Sat'day."

Well, now. The thought that he could have more time to himself on Saturdays was certainly appealing. And getting even better productivity from Will would be an added bonus. Bannister always responded favorably to business advantage.

"All right, Will. I'll do it."

The following evening after supper he came back to Will's room in the ell with an oil lamp, three books, and a couple of other items in his hand.

Will's formal education in this new land began.

The books, which Clarkson had obtained while teaching school, were the classic tools of the trade of that day for primary education—*The New England Primer, A B C,* and *The Spelling Book.* In addition he had with him the *Horn Book,* not a book in the usual sense but rather a single sheet of parchment stretched over the blade of a pinewood paddle. On it were written the alphabet, numerals, the Lord's Prayer, and a few phrases. It was covered with a thin, transparent piece of horn, hence the name. Clarkson also brought a piece of slate, chalk, and some dried beans for counting. He would use his Bible later, after Will mastered the basics of reading.

The starting point was the usual—numbers up to ten and the first half of the alphabet. These were set forth in the primer, which also included lists of vowels, consonants, and one-, two-, three-, and four-syllable words as a student progressed.

That first night Clarkson sat on the floor with Will facing him. He pushed a single bean across the floor and said, "One," which Will repeated clearly after him. Similarly up to ten beans. Then Clarkson moved the numbers around until Will got the idea and began to memorize the numbers and say their names. The process was repeated with the letters on the face of the hornbook.

The work continued through the winter. The other Clarksons and Mrs. Haven sometimes had to suppress laughter as James Sr. jumped about in the living room to demonstrate words like hop, run, and fall while his pupil looked on, eager to figure out what the teacher was trying to make him understand.

Reverend Haven often dropped by to watch this nightly scene. One evening he smiled and said, "James, I must say I'm very impressed by all this hard work—on your part and Will's. But hasn't it occurred to you as somewhat ironic that after all this effort you're both expending, you should not be willing then to grant Will his freedom? By the time you're done, you'll indeed have prepared him quite well for the role of full citizenship. He—"

"Two different issues," Clarkson said. "The purpose is to increase Will's value to us. If I grant him freedom when we're done, it would undercut my purpose and effort. Negate it, in fact."

Haven had smiled as he put the question, but he was silenced by Clarkson's emphatic reply.

—⁂—

Will overheard and understood the thrust of this conversation. It made him angry—and it made him work even harder at his lessons. He would achieve his freedom with his new knowledge and skill in spite of what Clarkson thought.

Will picked up the pace, not difficult to do, as he figured out how to learn in parallel during his workdays and how to integrate that real-life education with his formal training in the evenings. He made no effort to hide his facility with words and sums.

James Sr. seemed startled by his progress. He probably wondered what was driving Will.

The weather grew colder and more harsh as they worked their way from January through March of the following year. Many mornings, as he leaned into a driving wind and snow on the road toward the tannery, Will's face was stung by darts of sleet. The roar of the storms seemed to envelop him in a solitary remoteness that was almost otherworldly. For several weeks a shiny, crusted topping lay over the seacoast landscape. No one ventured outside into the cold unless he had to.

Will began to run special errands for Mrs. Haven, who made sure he was always well fed and warmly clothed. On one such trip in late February he went to Randall & Caswell's fish store on Ceres Street to purchase some cod. When he entered, he leaned over to knock the snow off his boots. Standing up, he rang the bell for service, and two teenagers—Samuel Caswell and Elizabeth Randall, children of the owners—emerged from the back room blushing and giggling. Will could not suppress a smile, which made them blush even more deeply, as he placed his order. As he left, he felt a twinge of jealousy.

8

As March merged into April, New England put its worst face forward. Rain fell incessantly, and the deep snow turned to miserable slush. Mud filled with rocks was everywhere, the enduring constant. The Piscataqua was shrouded in brown fog.

One night, just after supper, there was a loud banging on the Clarkson front door. The person knocking was a Rye resident, quite out of breath, his mount also panting heavily behind him.

"Shipwreck on the rocks off Odiorne's Point," he gasped. "Need as many men and women as possible to help with a rescue." Immediately six Clarksons, including Will, and five Havens pulled on heavy outer clothing and clambered into two wagons for the four-mile ride.

When they reached the point, the rain had stopped, but the sea was still raging. A break in the clouds allowed a flash of moonlight to shine through, revealing a huge ship foundering on a rock ledge two hundred yards offshore. Half a dozen oil lamps flickered from the hull, and sailors could be seen clinging to the masts and yardarms. Others were huddled on the rocks.

About a hundred townspeople had already arrived and were clustered at the edge of the shore. As the Haven and Clarkson wagons drove up, George Philbrick, Portsmouth's harbormaster, walked over to the minister and James Sr.

"She's the *Ormonde*, a merchant schooner registered in Provincetown, under Captain William Hughes. Bout a hundred and thirty

34

tons. Coming in from the West Indies with a valuable cargo. Rum, sugar, molasses. Maybe some gold and silver. Total of crew and passengers on board is about fifty people."

"What are the chances for a rescue?" Reverend Haven shouted over the roar of the ocean. His intensity echoed the desperation being voiced by many others standing by helplessly.

"Well, we've got three surfboats. Each can carry up to twenty. The problem right now is, we don't dare put a boat into that monstrous sea. Apparently the ship's own lifeboats are damaged. Or they figure they'd be smashed to pieces against the rocks or the ship itself."

"I go," Will said, pointing to himself as he looked at Andrew. "Get more men."

"Good man, Will," Andrew said. "George, we can't just stand here and watch them die. Let's try and get four volunteers to man each boat and give it a try. Walter and I will go with Will."

"All right, if you're up for it," Philbrick said.

Andrew went through the crowd and gathered nine other willing citizens. The dozen men proceeded to drag the surfboats, each containing several long lengths of rope and four oars, to the water's edge.

Will, Andrew, and Walter were to row the same surfboat, along with James Brown from Rye. Even as they shoved off, Will was fearful. Wave after wave, some eight feet high, crashed against the beach within seconds of one another. The bow of the boat swooped up with each one and slammed down in the swell behind it.

As the boat hit each swell, Andrew called out, "Pull, men, pull! Keep her straight into the sea—if a wave hits us broadside, we're goners." The boat advanced thirty yards between each wave and lost ten when the next one came. Spray flew over the gunnels, soon soaking Will, who was sweating even in the cold. But Andrew, in the stern, guided the boat forward. After forty minutes they were abreast of the ship and ledge but bobbing this way and that, maneuvering to come about safely to pick up the terrified people on the rocks.

Andrew told Will to be ready to throw the rope line when he gave the word that a swell was carrying them near enough.

"Now!"

Will threw the rope, but it fell short. He pulled the line back in and twice again made a throw. On the fourth attempt he was successful. Two men on the ledge grabbed it and pulled the boat carefully toward them until it could be grappled to a large stone. Quickly seventeen people climbed aboard. The last person was an overweight elderly man. As he stepped feebly to the boat, he lost his balance and fell into the sea.

Instantly Will plunged into the water. He grabbed the man about the chest with one arm and swam toward the boat with the other. Several times the waves pushed him back. Finally he got close enough for Andrew's outstretched hand to grasp his arm. Seconds later Andrew and another man had pulled both of them over the side and into the bottom of the boat, coughing, soaking wet, and very cold.

Andrew immediately pushed away the boat. They only narrowly avoided being smashed hard against the rock by the next wave. After a faster ride back to shore, this time with the waves assisting rather than pushing them back, the surfboat drove onto the sand, and all twenty-two people stumbled out as onlookers secured the boat. Mrs. Haven and Lydia rushed up, wrapped Will and the old man in dry blankets, and guided them to the warm bonfire nearby.

A dozen townspeople came over and congratulated Will for his daring rescue. William Bannister walked up and praised Andrew effusively but turned away quickly from Will, who was standing right next to Andrew. *That man's a problem.*

Theirs was the first boat back. The other two had a harder time, particularly in reaching the crewmen hanging from the ship's rigging high above the hull, which was beginning to break up. Those watching from the shore could see some sailors plunge into the ocean to try to reach the surfboat. It did not appear that all were successful.

Finally, almost two hours later, the other two boats had pulled in everyone they could find and beaten their way back to shore. Just as they arrived, the ship's masts tumbled into the ocean, and amid great groans of timber the hull broke in two and settled against the far side of the ledge. Kegs and boxes popped out on the surface of the sea and began to float to the shore.

In all, forty-seven people were saved. Only eight were lost: Captain Hughes and three of his officers had stayed and gone down with the ship; the other four were sailors who hadn't been able to swim to the last two surfboats.

By the bonfires the women served up hot food. Soon the towns-people piled into the waiting wagons and headed back to their houses. Each family took at least one of the passengers or crew members into its home for the night.

The Havens took two passengers on their wagon, and the Clark-sons took the old man Will had saved. James Sr. consoled the poor soul, who was in shock.

Will, Andrew, and Walter were unable to get warm again until they reached the house on South School Street, changed clothes, and sat before the fireplace for a while. They went to bed, exhausted, at three o'clock in the morning. As Will and Walter separated, Andrew slapped each in turn on the back and said, "Thank you both. A good night's work!"

Will lay in his bed before dropping off to sleep, warm at last, with some long hoped for satisfaction. At least some of these white men had seemed to recognize, however briefly, that he was a worthy human being. Whether or not any saw the irony of his trying to save the lives of people who held him captive, some of them might realize that he deserved his freedom. He believed his plan had taken a big step forward. But Bannister! With that man in charge in this town, gaining any recognition or getting his freedom was going to be more difficult and take longer than he'd hoped.

The next morning brought a surprise for Will and the other Clarksons. At breakfast they were joined by the man Will had plucked from the sea. He turned out to be the lieutenant governor of the royal province of Massachusetts, Thomas Hutchinson, who'd boarded at Provincetown to visit his daughter in Portsmouth. The man insisted on paying James Sr. for his hospitality and lavished praise on Will for saving his life. As he left, he walked over to Will and pressed three English pounds into his hand as he shook it. Will was not just pleased; he was overwhelmed. He knew that in Africa being a warrior or an ancestral aristocrat determined a man's position; he'd already learned that here a person also had to have money to succeed. Getting it would be part of his plan. This was a start.

—※—

Later in the afternoon, at the tannery, Will heard that some townspeople had gone back to the shipwreck scene in the morning and recovered kegs of rum and molasses that had floated ashore. No one had seen any chests of silver or gold, but many planned to search the area around the ledge when the sea became calmer. Will intended to do the same thing.

—※—

Eventually, toward the middle of May, spring began to show her face. Saffron crocuses sprouted by the edges of snow patches. These were followed by daffodils, tulips, and lilies of the valley. Overhead, lilac buds unfurled into white and purple clusters. Sparrows flitted around the salt marshes and both farm and city houses. In the forests robins made joyful caroling sounds. Black-headed gulls and arctic terns took up their sentry posts on granite peninsulas. Spotted sandpipers darted along the flat, sandy shores. High above, Canada geese arrowed their way north.

Spirits rose. House cleaning in fancy mansions and modest cabins began throughout the city. When not at the tannery, Will assisted Mrs. Haven with the heaviest of these tasks in the Clarkson home.

—※—

Interesting, Will thought. We could use something like that for hide washing. He'd taken a walk along the Piscataqua on Sunday afternoon and had stopped to view the turning of the waterwheel on the gristmill by a creek that emptied into the river.

That evening he made a drawing on his chalkboard of an enclosed waterwheel where hides could be placed and washed by the river water as the wheel turned. He showed it to James Sr., who, after some difficulty, finally understood what Will meant and became excited about the idea. Over the next two weeks the tannery crew constructed Will's waterwheel over the Piscataqua next to the tannery. They all cheered when the wheel started up and worked. They slapped Will on the back and shook his hand. James Sr. estimated that the wheel would do the work of two men over the course of a year.

Thanks to the waterwheel invention and his hard work every day, Will's stock was riding high with James Sr. and the other Clarksons. They usually granted his request to take one of the family horses to ride along the seashore on Sunday afternoons. One of his favorite routes was down past Odiorne's Point into Rye. The spot he headed for was a high rock ledge looking down on a long sandy beach. There he found a granite outcropping that leaned out over the sea in the form of a small porch complete with a stone railing. He often sat there for hours, enjoying the panoramic view extending for many miles north and south.

Straight off this spot the Isles of Shoals faded in and out, depending on the clarity of the day. The islands never looked the same. At times they seemed to float above the water in a kind of optical inversion. Some days they were just a pencil-thin black outline on the horizon. On others they were so clear that Will felt he could reach out and touch their trees and the three houses that stood stark in their bleach-white paint. Continually changing also were the hues of sea and sky in the background. On a bright day, the sky was laced with faint streaks of pink and oyster clouds above a smooth blue ocean. When overcast, rolls of clouds of varying shades of gray surged above a blackened sea.

The surf and tide most commanded Will's attention. At low tide he leaned forward from his perch as far as he could to see the dwindling ripples barely reach to the bottom of the forty-foot-high outcrop. When the tide was high, especially if there was a storm out to sea, he had to jump back to duck the spray as the rolling walls turned over and crashed against the top of his hiding place. His respect for the mighty North Atlantic grew quickly. Not a body of water he could hope to cross in a small boat by himself to return to Africa. No, it looked as though his road to freedom was going to be long and hard, not a quick journey.

The afternoon sun was sinking low, reddening the sky. For the third Sunday in a row, immediately after the winter weather eased, Will had spent a long day searching for bounty, to no avail, along the rocks of Odiorne's Point. Other searchers were also coming up empty-handed. He directed his horse past the coastal marshes where a group of men worked quickly even on the Sabbath to cut and bring in the fresh hay before it turned salty and useless. They were the grandsons of Rye legend John Locke, who'd been ambushed and killed by Indians as he labored in these same fields, and the great-great-grandsons of the Reverend Stephen Batchelder, the heretical preacher who in 1638 had founded the neighboring town of Hampton, New Hampshire, just to the south.

When he returned to the house, the family was abuzz with some good news—Mrs. Haven had announced that she was pregnant again, with her eleventh child. A smile broke across her face as Will shook her hand enthusiastically.

9

*T*he native American Indians who lived east of New Hampshire's White Mountains and along the Atlantic shores of New Hampshire and Maine were principally of the Abenaqui tribe. Prior to the invasion of the Europeans, this eastern division of the Abenaqui had numbered nearly twenty thousand people. The name Abenaqui means "people of the dawn" or "easterners." They spoke a version of the Algonquin tongue.

The Abenaqui were a strange lot. Rejecting tribal living arrangements, they preferred to live in small family groups. Their dwellings were dome-shaped wigwams covered with animal hides. Basically an agricultural people, they raised corn, beans, and squash and fished in summertime and hunted for birds, deer, fox, and bear in winter. They banded together only to fight the Iroquois and the English. Otherwise they were loners, the ghosts of the forests. This had been their way for thousands of years.

The Europeans brought with them various diseases, including smallpox, which decimated the Abenaqui. By the latter half of the eighteenth century, they numbered less than two thousand.

The Abenaqui never liked the white men and were mistrustful of the whites' Negro slaves.

The "injun" who worked at the Clarkson tannery was an Abenaqui. He was Simo, from York, in Maine, where he lived with a wife and two boy children. Simo was not a slave but a free man who was paid a wage, albeit a very small one, for his work at the tanyard. In Simo's eyes, Will was a threat to his job security.

When Will arrived at the tannery, he tried to make friends with Simo. He learned that the Indian had been raised as a man of the forest, intimately familiar with the woodlands extending west, north, and south from Portsmouth.

But the man rejected every overture and remained hostile to Will. Not only would Simo turn away and refuse to speak to him, he'd offer no assistance—or even refuse it—when a task required two men. Will resented the man's attitude, and it showed.

By the fall of 1756, a year after Will's arrival, the situation between the two had become nearly intolerable. There was much bumping and shoving as they went about their work. Invectives, often shouted and lengthy, flew back and forth in three languages. Andrew Clarkson spoke strongly to each of them, in separate sessions, ordering them to get on with their jobs.

Late one November afternoon, Will was finishing up, turning over some hides in the lime vats after the others had left for the day. As he leaned over the middle vat with the tongs, an object whistled over his head and stuck with a thud in the vertical oak beam behind him.

Will glimpsed the tomahawk shivering in the wood and whirled around to see Simo crouched and facing him about ten feet away, arms extended, with a large knife in his right hand.

The Indian lunged at Will. He missed with his knife hand but pushed Will toward the vat with his left. Will lost his balance and one leg slipped into the searing lime. He screamed but managed to swing the tong hard against Simo as the Indian lunged again to push him into the vat. Simo slid toward the next vat as Will pulled his leg out of the smelly, stinging lime.

In the next moment a gunshot rang out. Both men stopped where they stood and turned toward the front door to see Walter Clarkson walking toward them, a pistol in one hand and some lengths of rope in the other.

"Lucky for both of you I forgot my gloves," Walter said. He tossed two pieces of rope to the Indian. "Simo, tie this man by the hands twixt these two posts. I won't have our servant fighting with our other workers." Simo obeyed and then quickly followed Walter's second order to "Get out of here. Go home."

The youngest Clarkson then walked to the side of the building where a horsewhip hung on the wall. He grabbed it, came back to Will, and ripped off his shirt. He then proceeded to give Will ten vicious lashes across his back. Will clenched his teeth as he received each blow, refusing to cry out but seething with rage.

"Let that be a lesson to you, black boy. Remember who's boss around here and follow our rules."

Will understood some of the words but fought back the urge to respond.

Walter untied him and walked him back to the South School Street house at the point of his gun. Pushing Will into the front hallway, he was met immediately by James Sr.

He took one look at Will's bloodied back and said, "What the devil happened here?"

"Will started a fight with Simo," Walter said. "Had to break them up. I sent Simo home and whipped Will for attacking our employee. Can't tolerate that."

To Will's astonishment, James turned to him and said, "That right, Will?" He couldn't believe his master would want to hear his side. He didn't know the word for the weapon Simo had thrown at him. All he could do was point to himself, shake his head, and say "No."

"Did you see Will start the fight?" James asked Walter.

"Well, no, but I'm sure it was Will's doing."

James didn't seem convinced. He admonished Walter mildly, then told Mrs. Haven to clean up Will's back and provide him with another shirt.

For the next two days at the tannery, Friday and Saturday, Will didn't turn his back on Simo. On Sunday, after church, he went as usual to the public stable behind the North Meeting House, where he relayed the story in the Mandinka language to Caesar and Jack Odiorne.

"Walter lied. How am I supposed to work at the tannery with that Indian at my back, waiting to throw another tomahawk at me? You said you'd do something if this kind of thing happened."

The king frowned. "Nothing I can do. James Clarkson's business."

Will's friend Jack was outraged and repeated what had happened to several of his friends.

⹂

The real story began to circulate around town. James Clarkson heard it from a friend at the Pitt Tavern a week later. Five minutes later he was at Walter's house, demanding the truth.

Walter flushed and squirmed as he stood before his father. "I told you I didn't see the beginning of the fight. I may have jumped to a conclusion. I thought it was Will's fault because . . . Look, I apologize."

James sighed heavily.

"Walter, your attitude toward Negroes has got to change. Your prejudice made you wrong—and cruel."

"You're right, I don't like em. But at least I don't keep em as slaves."

James's mouth dropped open at his son's impertinence. But the barb hit its mark. He gave Walter a hard look. "I accept your apology this time, but in the future I will not abide such conduct." With that, the elder Clarkson turned and walked out the door.

He fired Simo the next morning. He decided not to press charges lest the Indian seek retribution against Will or himself after serving a jail term.

⹂

On the tanyard floor, Will noticed Simo's absence, realized what had happened, and felt profoundly grateful. From that time forward he kept a weather eye on Walter.

Apparently Simo could not find another position. Soon afterward, Will heard that he'd been killed in a knife fight with another Indian outside a Portsmouth tavern.

"Simo was mean, but it's really too bad," Will told Jack. "Coulda been a big help if my plan fails and we have to escape through the forest."

10

"*H*ow do the African elections work?" Will asked.

"What do you mean?" Jack said, also in Mandinka.

"Who decides who gets put up? How's the thing run?"

"Caesar makes a list. Others get put up if ten people support them. Majority vote rules."

"So I need to talk Caesar into putting me up."

"Right. Why so interested?"

Will tossed a stone into the river and watched the ripples. "Won't ever get anywhere here unless I can get on the court."

"Maybe so. But the list has been the same for a long time."

"Election in June?"

"Every year."

"Gives me six months. Think I'll talk to Caesar."

⁓

The king said, "You just got here. Still too young."

"That's the point. Couple of men on the court are old. You need young blood. I'm African born, and my owner's important in this city."

Caesar sighed. "I'll think about it."

⁓

"Don't you think it's a good idea?" Will was making a statement in Mandinka, not asking a question.

Cyrus Atkinson had long since forgotten his Mandinka and responded in English. "Gettin some younguh folks in make sense. Not sure I wanna step down yet."

"Think about it," Will said. "If you retire, I want a chance."

"You're it if I do."

"Tell Caesar." Will was whistling as he walked on down the Parade.

—⚔—

"Job take much time?" Will asked, exercising his improving English.

"More'n I realized," Pharaoh Shores said. "Gettin a mite tired of it."

"How bout moving down to deputy and letting someone else have the top job? Someone younger."

"Like you?"

"Why not?"

"I'll talk it ovah with Caesar."

"Thanks. 'Preciate your help."

Now to talk to Caesar's friends.

—⚔—

On a bright Friday morning late in June, Will leaped from his bunk early to complete his barn chores. There was to be no work at the tannery this day. This was the day of the elections. Tomorrow there would be a celebration with games and other festivities, and the coronation of the newly elected king was scheduled for Sunday noon. Usually this was all accomplished in a single day because the white owners did not want to give their slaves any more time off. But this year it was spread over the weekend because all the other Africans throughout the state—approximately five hundred and eighty, according to Caesar—were invited. Many were expected to attend, although those at the other ends of the state might not be able to travel this far. Will had attended last year and was looking forward to going again, now that he knew more people and could communicate better. He needed to know them well.

He broke into a broad smile—pretty girls were always there too. He'd been thinking for some time that even a slave needed female company.

For Portsmouth's African population this was the major political and social event of each year, an occasion for serious business as well as frolic. Although some whites worried about the potential danger of letting so many slaves gather together in one place at the same time, the majority of the population tolerated and even supported the election. The court and the shadow government it represented offered the members of the African community an opportunity to exercise their own sense of responsibility. By ceding some small governmental tasks to the Africans, particularly in the area of administering justice for minor legal infractions, the whites at least lessened somewhat the image of total white domination and African resentment.

It took Will almost half an hour to walk to the Plains, the field west of the main part of the city where the event was to be held. He arrived at about nine o'clock, but there were already more than two hundred people gathered around the camping area where those from out of town had staked out their tents to stay for the three days.

Along the opposite side of the field, groups were setting up makeshift tables and piling them with a variety of food and other items for sale or barter. Pies of dried apples, pumpkins, and squash, cornbread, and an African favorite—Indian pudding—were stacked high on big trays. On separate tables larger, communal bowls of brined ham, pickled mackerel, dried cod, and veal and lamb stews, laced with spices and herbs from the West Indies, were already being spooned up by the hungry crowd. All grown, caught and cooked by the participants, these were unusually sumptuous offerings for plain folks normally subsisting on the food provided by their owners. Will and his neighbors jostled to partake even though it was early in the day for such heavy fare.

In a separate table area, various items of new and second-hand clothing and all kinds of trinkets of both African and New World origin and style were displayed, examined, and discussed, and sales or trades were hotly negotiated. Will looked these over closely. A dark green sweater, apparently rejected by a slavemaster because of small holes in the elbows, caught his eye. Will would have loved to have it, but lacking anything to trade and wanting to save and increase the small amount of money he had, he passed on to the next table, where he and others laughed heartily as Jack Odiorne dickered at great length over the value of a small corncob pipe before purchasing it at half price.

Promptly at eleven, a gong announced the start of the opening parade, which would circle the Plains three times before settling in front of the rudimentary grandstand set up at the far end of the field. The first group in the parade was made up of the outgoing officers, led by King Caesar.

Caesar looked the part. He was astride Colonel William Bannister's chestnut gelding, loaned to his African servant for the day's festivities. Caesar had on Bannister's military uniform and brandished his master's sword. A scarlet sash emblematic of his official position was spread across his chest. His cocked hat was festooned with red, black, and blue feathers. Marching right behind him were his viceroy Cyrus Atkinson and Sheriff Pharaoh Shores. Both Cyrus and Pharaoh wore garlands of red rugosa roses around their necks and blue caps with black crow feathers on the side.

The musicians, about a dozen in number and under the direction of Cuffee Whipple, fell in behind the officers. Cuffee, dressed in white from head to toe, fiddled vigorously on his old violin as he danced along to his own beat. The flute, banjo, and tambourine players, as well as the buglers, were dressed in their best outfits, and each wore an orange cap. Their strains resounded across the plain and down over the city.

Next came the children from three to twelve years old, jumping and dancing to the music, each with some piece of bright-colored clothing. Two middle-aged women walked on either side of this group to keep the youngsters contained as they tripped along.

The women, about a hundred in number, marched behind the children. Some carried babies or led boys and girls beside them as they walked. Most of the women favored shiny jewelry and pink, yellow, or light blue ribbons to set off their otherwise drab clothing. They clapped and sang with the African tunes.

The rest of the men constituted the final group, walking three or four abreast in row after row. Will walked with these.

The total throng numbered more than three hundred people. Three times around the field they went, the cadence growing louder and stronger with each turn. Random gunshots rang out to great cheers. Finally they came to a stop in front of the grandstand of benches and stools facing a pulpit borrowed for the day from the South Meeting House.

Prince Whipple strode to the pulpit, gestured to quiet the crowd, and proceeded to read from the Christian Bible, the Book of Psalms:

> Blessed is the man that walketh not in the counsel of the ungodly, nor standeth in the way of sinners, nor sitteth in the seat of the scornful.
>
> But his delight is in the law of the Lord; and in his law doth he meditate day and night.
>
> And he shall be like a tree planted by the rivers of water, that bringeth forth his fruit in his season; his leaf also shall not wither; and whatsoever he doeth shall prosper.
>
> The ungodly are not so; but are like the chaff which the wind driveth away.
>
> Therefore the ungodly shall not stand in the judgment,nor sinners in the congregation of the righteous.
>
> For the Lord knoweth the way of the righteous; but the way of the ungodly shall perish.

and:

> My God, my God, why hast thou forsaken me? Why art thou so far from helping me, and from the words of my roaring?
>
> O my God, I cry in the daytime, but thou hearest not; and in the night season, and am not silent.
>
> But thou art holy, O thou that inhabitest the praises of Israel.
>
> Our fathers trusted in thee; they trusted, and thou didst deliver them.

They cried unto thee, and were delivered; they trusted in thee, and were not confounded.

But I am a worm, and no man; a reproach of men, and despised of the people.

All they that see me laugh me to scorn; they shoot out the lip, they shake the head. . .

Each verse was punctuated with hearty "Oh, yeah"s and "Amen"s from the audience, all of whom clearly perceived that it was the whites who were the ungodly and the African slaves who had been forsaken. Will noticed that everyone at the celebration was speaking, or at least trying to speak, in English. He was pleased that he could understand almost everything, even if he didn't always express himself correctly in English.

Will smiled as he realized that Prince was mimicking the gestures and intonations of the evangelist George Whitefield, who had visited Portsmouth and preached, making a lasting impression on everyone, both white and African, who witnessed him.

These readings were followed by the singing of two hymns popular at both the North and South Meeting Houses. Then several other men took turns at the pulpit, leading sections of the assembly in religious chants from separate African tribes that left Will depressed by memories of home.

"How come we pay 'tention to the white man's religion?" he asked Jack Odiorne and Caesar, who were standing next to him during the ceremony, in English. "Why don't we stick to our own?"

"Lot of us go to white church cause they force us," Caesar said. "Only one or two convert."

"None of us like being stuck in rear of the church or upstairs," Jack said. "Most of our people can't follow the white services anyway. Even if you understand em, they's dry and boring. Always goin on bout obedience. Make me sick."

"I see it different," Caesar said. "Christians are changing. 'Member that white preacher here awhile back? Got into the spirit of it, people screamin back, dancin around, even faintin'? Lot more like our religion. Some like it, most still keepin up tribal rituals. But not where our white owners can see it. Prince, he pick and choose what he like from white Christians—the rantin and ravin.

Half serious, half mockin em. Service ends up bein a mix of African and white."

Prince had returned to the podium to begin the election process. "All right, folks, pay 'tention. Been here before, you know how we do it. I'll tell you the nominees. Others can be made by any one of you. They'll be added if nominee has ten s'pporters. Nominees can take their case to our brothers this afternoon. Voice vote be at five o'clock. Tomorrow be games and socializin. Coronation of new king be on Sunday, after white church services.

"Couple of things bout this year's slate. Cyrus Atkinson is retirin from viceroy, and Pharaoh Shores don't want to be full-time sheriff. He willin to continue as a deputy. Caesar thinks some young blood needed. So slate be, for king, Caesar Bannister. For viceroy, Will Clarkson. For sheriff, Jack Odiorne. For deputy sheriff, Pharaoh Shores."

Will smiled. His hard campaigning with the other members of the court and Caesar's close associates during the previous few months had paid off. The viceroy was a deputy job—a perfect spot for him. He could use it as an apprenticeship. And he was surprised and excited about being joined by his friend Jack.

There followed several nominations from the crowd for each position, so Will figured he'd better make the rounds that afternoon to meet with as many people as possible.

"Hey there, Dinah, gonna support me?" he called over to Prince Whipple's sweetheart.

"Why should I?" she yelled back.

"'Cause I'm so good-lookin."

"Not enough, boy. What else you got to offer?"

"Hard work on the court. Take on the white folks. Get us educated. "

Dinah smiled a big smile. "Sounds right to me. I'm for you."

Several Africans questioned whether Will was too young to take a strong stand against white owners who persecuted them. Speaking in Mandinka, Will said, "I'm not afraid of those people. I've been learning their language. I'll be able to influence them." Both the women and the men nodded their satisfaction with his answer.

Will overheard several women urging their men to vote for him. His confidence mounted.

The vote at five o'clock confirmed his optimism: The entire official slate prevailed by more than a ninety percent majority.

When Will returned to the Clarkson household that evening, he was grinning as he told his owners: "I'm the new viceroy!"

Andrew and James Jr. slapped him on the back and shook his hand: "Congratulations, Will," Andrew said. "You've honored the family."

Lydia smiled at him. "Didn't realize you'd become a politician."

Mrs. Haven was smiling too. "I guess we better watch what we say to you, Will."

James Sr. said, "I'm not sure I like it. Bannister controls Caesar, and he and Caesar may now think they have some control over Will—my slave, my property."

"Maybe other way 'round," Will said. "Maybe I help you with Bannister."

James Sr. gave him a wry smile. "I guess this means I'll have to increase my annual contribution to the African election celebration."

For all Will's success and the family's pleasure in it, that night he ate alone in the kitchen as usual while Mrs. Haven served his white owners in the dining room.

After chores on Saturday, Will didn't arrive at the Plains until mid-morning. The games were already well under way. In one corner of the field young teenagers ran races, long-jumped, and wrestled, while the older ones held stick-fighting contests. Elsewhere, middle-aged and older men pitched pennies and played endless games of pawpaw, a game akin to craps. Will jumped into one of the games. He took his first turn throwing the cowrie shells and immediately went ahead with two throws that showed four (the significant even number) shell openings down. Thereafter he wasn't quite as lucky, alternating between even openings down and odd openings down. After about two hours he was breaking even for the day, so he packed it in.

He wandered down to the south corner of the plain, where the women had set up their food tables and produce market. He helped himself to some cider and two gingerbread cookies, then watched and listened for a while as buyers bartered for the best trades.

"C'mon over, mistuh new viceroy," a pretty young girl called out. "Don't yuh want some wahm apple pie?" Will smiled broadly, waved, and moved on.

In the middle of the field were the storytellers, a carryover from an ancient African tradition. These *griots* passed down the oral history of their tribes. Seated on stools in the midst of groups of twenty to thirty listeners, they spun all sorts of yarns.

Pharaoh Shores attracted the biggest cluster, which included many children and teenagers, for whom he spoke in English. He was telling of his capture into slavery: "I was a small boy workin in the fields with my mama and some other folks," he told them. "Suddenly, out of the woods on the side, a hundred warriors came screamin down on us, in bright battle dress and carryin long spears and shields. Pictures of their tribal gods painted on them. Some wore big, scary masks. They were all giants. Over seven feet tall. With glaring eyes."

Some of the children shrieked.

Shores paused and then continued in a lower tone, gesturing with his arms: "They grabbed us before we had a chance to run. Stuffed rags in our mouths and threw us into sacks. We were carried for a long time. Then we came to a village by the ocean, where we were sold to white sea captains in charge of big ships with many sails. They put as many of us as they could into the bottoms of the ships. The voyage across the ocean took three months. It was slimy and stinkin."

The teenagers held their noses and made faces at each other.

Shores shot a severe look at them. "Many got sick, some died and was thrown overboard," he continued.

The young listeners looked down at the ground.

"When we got to Portsmouth and were sold, we could hardly stand. Amazin any of us still alive. All of us expected to be chopped up and eaten by white savages. That never happened, but sometimes we wished it would."

Pharaoh's audience sat in open-mouthed awe. No one said a word when he finished.

Will walked nearby to the next group. There Primus Fowle entertained middle-aged listeners by throwing jibes at his owner, David Fowle, now publisher of the new *New Hampshire Gazette.* He was imitating the sanctimonious attitude of Portsmouth's fancy white masters. Ripples of laughter bubbled from this gathering. Will guffawed at Primus's peppery debunking of publisher Fowle's haughty treatment of his wife.

The third group consisted primarily of elderly people. The speaker was Cyrus Atkinson, well up in years himself, who was weaving an exotic tale of the soon-to-come heaven back in Africa:

"Everythin green and lush," he said. "Sun shine all the time. Africans do all the work while we lounge around and talk and fish. Watch out if you are mean and bad. Unless you change your ways, you be put in a dark hole filled with witches and hobgoblins. They scare you with piercin screams and put you in baths of boilin oil. Giant lions wander around the place. They pounce on anyone who disobeys the snake witches, who are the rulers. White masters who treat African slaves bad while they alive kept in sep'rit part of the hole."

His audience responded to Cyrus's last point with shouts and clapping. It was clearly a message these elders believed.

The final event of the afternoon was a military training display. Will sat and watched as King Caesar, again on Colonel Bannister's horse and in borrowed full military regalia, led about two dozen "troops" in coming to attention, marching, and carrying out various drills with their "muskets," which were plain sticks. Some had pieces of uniforms from their masters. In spite of Caesar's mock efforts to be serious and deliver a disciplined performance, his troops were bent on spoofing the white militia—sometimes marching off in different directions from the given commands, falling down, and becoming confused in handling their weapons—all to the great delight of the surrounding crowd. The field rang with gales of laughter. The drill ended with loud applause from all sides.

Will watched the spoofed military exercise with mixed emotions. While he laughed as hard as the others, it troubled him that they didn't seem to realize what a real fighting capability could mean to their future. These displaced Africans were losing their military heritage.

But how to get his views across? Will was realizing that this new land was a world of politics where sociability and popularity counted for a lot. And the best way to start politicking was to join in the social merriment of this election celebration.

The main social event of the weekend was the Saturday-night dinner and dancing, also held in the open air at the Plains, which was set up with long tables, benches, stools, and kerosene lamps. Fortunately it was a warm evening, with a full moon and stars shining down on the scene.

Kegs of hard cider and rum grog along with nuts and sunflower seeds came out first, and the men did not hold back, sloshing down one mug after another while Cuffee Whipple, wandering through the assembly, fiddled tune after tune. By the time the food came, many people were intoxicated and the noise level was high.

Joyous shouts greeted the food: great sides of mutton, well seasoned and cooked perfectly so that the meat was falling off the bones, and communal side bowls piled with potatoes, beets, leeks, onions, carrots, rye bread, sugared blackberry preserves, and brandied plums and cranberries.

Jack smiled through a mouthful of potatoes and lamb. "Best meal of the year," he said.

Most had not even finished their food when those eager to start the dancing began calling out to Cuffee to gather his group and begin the music. Amid much cheering, Cuffee rose and summoned his fiddlers, flutists, and banjo and tambourine players to the open area surrounded by the tables, where boards had been nailed together for a dance floor.

Several couples immediately jumped to the floor to step to the first jig of the evening. First to take their turn were Siras Bruce and Flora Stoodley. Siras was clearly the best-dressed man of the evening, resplendent in his official livery as the domestic servant of Captain John Langdon. His long, dark blue overcoat and white linen breeches were studded with metal buttons. Black silk stockings and silver-buckled shoes adorned his nimble legs and feet. A heavy gold chain and seals jangled from his neck as he and Flora, the servant of the tavern keeper James Stoodley, twirled about the floor. Flora was eye-catching in her own right: Her shining black hair was pulled back into a tight bun at her neck, just above a long red dress with a blue ribbon at the waist. The couple was generally acknowledged by both white and African observers to be the finest dancers in the city.

Soon many others, unable to resist Cuffee's beat, flocked around them. Prince Whipple and Dinah Chase danced vigorously, as did Peter Warner and Dinah Pearn. Boston and Violet Dearborn and Caesar and Jane Wheelbright, flashing bright clothes like the rest, were close behind as the couples moved through more jigs, hornpipes, double shuffles, and the most popular of all—the mazy dance.

Will was surprised when Jack Odiorne appeared on the floor dancing with Aiku. They were laughing and obviously having a grand time together. Will felt quite attracted by her smile and gracefulness.

For a while after Jack and Aiku had returned to their seats, he wondered how he could approach her. He had danced a little in Africa but was still unsure of himself. Finally, after balking twice, he pulled himself up and marched over to where she was sitting with some of her friends at the far end of the gathering.

"Show me how to jig?" She and her tablemates all giggled, but she smiled that wonderful smile.

"If you think you can."

The two trotted out on the floor to the clapping of their friends. Aiku danced as though born to the jig. Will was a bit stumble-footed at first, but after two dances he was making out quite respectably.

For a long time Will had been looking for an excuse to talk to Aiku, to find out what she was like. He wasn't disappointed. Aiku loved to chat. Mandinka made it easer and more casual for them.

"I'm not Aiku any more," she said as they danced. "My name's Abigail, Abigail Wentworth; John Wentworth's my owner. They call me Abi. He's a close friend of the king of England, you know."

"That important to you?"

"Not much. He's all right. But wife Frances is pretty hard on me and the two other servants, Tom and Semantha. They're both twelve years older than me, so I get all the drudge work. I hear you're working in a stinky old tannery."

"It's not so bad. Sometimes it's pretty interesting. What kind of drudge work?"

"Housecleaning, dishwashing."

"What so hard about Mrs. Wentworth?"

"Always criticizing. Watches everything we do. Always changing her mind. Put it there—no, there—no, over there—oh, put it back where it was." They both laughed.

"What about you and Jack Odiorne?" Will asked.

"Good friends. See each other."

"Any problem with seeing me too?"

"Jack doesn't own me."

Will let out the breath he'd been holding. "Like to visit the tannery sometime?" Abi grabbed her nose and made a face. They both laughed again. He whirled her around. "Then how about meeting at the women's market some Sunday?"

"Nice. When?"

"Next week. If it's a good day, we can ride down to the beach in Rye. Place I'd like to show you."

"Sounds like fun."

As the dances ended and the two returned to their respective tables, Will was full of smiles. He knew that Portsmouth's slave owners made it difficult for African captives of the opposite sex to see each other frequently or to get together for any extended periods. But at least he could see her occasionally on Sunday afternoons. As he and Abi parted, she'd called over her shoulder, "See you next week."

It was well after midnight before Cuffee and his music makers ran out of stamina and the multitude began to disperse. Will circulated among the tables and talked with nearly everyone, finding out what their lives were like and advocating an end to slavery. He was among the last to leave, a bit groggy from too much rum as he headed back to South School Street.

During church at the South Meeting House the next morning Will and the other African parishioners were restless, paying scant attention to Reverend Haven's exhortations as they thought ahead to the coronation of the new court, which was to take place as soon as they could rush back to the Plains.

It was nearly one o'clock before the crowd gathered. The closing parade then began, in the same format as the opener but this time only once around the field. King Caesar was now followed immediately by the new officers, including Will, who could hardly control his breathing as he basked in his elevated status. When the lead group came around to the grandstand, Caesar dismounted and strode briskly to the podium. He wanted to make a few final points after being crowned and before the election proceedings were officially ended.

When everyone had made the circle, Prince Whipple stepped forward, carrying the gold-colored crown for the newly reelected king. First he led the assembly in prayers, both to the Christian god and to the African tribal deities. He then placed the crown on Caesar's head, to a long ovation. The king turned to make his closing remarks:

"First a moment of silence in honor of our parents and ancestors."

As Will bowed his head, he heard many of the women sobbing quietly.

Caesar continued: "When our time comes, we join with them once again in our beloved Africa. Friends, thank you all for comin and participatin in this year's elections. Want you all to know that everyone on the court take our respons'bilities serious. We do everythin we can to keep order in this community ourselves, so the whites don't have to get involved. 'Member that as we suffer and try to go about our lives as comfortably as we can. Gods and the spirits bless you all. We meet again same time, same place next year."

The king's summation seemed to be just what many in the crowd wanted to hear. Loud applause and cheers rang out across the plain as everyone moved to sweep up their belongings and head home.

As he walked back to the South School Street house, Will pondered Caesar's words, wondering how many besides him thought they were too soft, that the Africans had to be more aggressive or they'd never change their lot.

⚓

From the back room in the Bell Tavern, Jack saw William Bannister and Walter Clarkson leave their booth by the front door, and wondered what they'd been talking about, their heads so close together. He put on his cap and went out through the kitchen.

The next day after church, as they walked back along Water Street, he told Will what he'd seen.

"Can't be anything good with those two," Will said. Then his eyes brightened. "Reminds me, Jack. We still don't know enough about what's going on in the white community—what they think and say to each other. If we're going to get free, we got to do better. Keep our eyes and ears open and be more organized about it. Separate out what's useful—the business, the politics, who's friends and who's not. From now on let's you and me keep a steady watch over them. Meet regularly and go over what we've seen, heard. Just two of us at first, then we bring in others we can trust to keep quiet."

⚓

"Makes sense for everyone who owns slaves, Mrs. Bickford," Walter said to the elderly woman and her husband the next day. "William Bannister and his Caesar can help us all keep the Negroes in this town under control. Caesar can make sure they don't get ideas about rising above the condition God intended for them or start claiming rights."

"But shouldn't Mr. Bannister be doing that anyway as part of his job as chairman of the selectmen?" asked Mrs. Bannister.

"Not really. This will take a lot of extra time and effort. That's what this new payment of ten pounds a year is for."

Mr. Bickford finally spoke up. "All right, Walter. I don't like it. But we'll go along if that's what everyone else wants to do."

"Everyone else is in. You're the last. Thanks, Charles. Caesar will be around to collect next week."

11

*F*or the bulk of Portsmouth's Africans, the weeks following Caesar's coronation were a letdown. Gone was the festivity as they returned to the bleak prospect of being told what to do minute after minute, hour after hour, day after day, week after week, month after month, year after year.

Will began immediately to focus even more on his education as an essential step toward being able to have an impact on his own life and that of the city's other Africans. Every night he and James Sr. spent an hour working on specific assignments in English and arithmetic. Then, alone, Will did up to two hours of "homework."

He convinced Andrew Clarkson to use him as a clerical and administrative assistant in his roles as selectman, surveyor, and fire warden. These tasks taught Will a whole new set of practical words and phrases. He used the opportunity to get to know a larger number of white citizens and their African servants. At the same time, he developed his natural flair for business, bartering small items and sometimes receiving money for them. His skills, combined with his pleasant disposition, had a welcome effect: Many Portsmouth townsfolk came to know and like him.

By 1760, he was not only reading and understanding English easily, he was conversing in well-spoken English with the most articulate men in the city.

He cultivated a special relationship with Reverend Haven.

"Can I come by your house later this afternoon?" he asked one Sunday after church.

"Sure," Haven said. "Make it about three."

This was the first of many visits to the big house on Pleasant Street. There, in the minister's study, Haven read aloud from the Bible, and Will read a few pages to him. The older man then talked with him about what they'd read, asked Will about his work at the tannery and his schooling, and told him stories of Jesus and his miraculous life and message.

He always concluded by reiterating, "Remember now, Will, Jesus loves all men, white and black, even those who've sinned or worshipped other gods."

"Why would I want to go to a heaven with all these white people who make life so hard for us Africans?" Will replied.

Will's concept of heaven, like that of many first-generation New England slaves, was a rebirth after death in Africa, rejoining his family in their village. And much more real to him, still, were the African spirits that populated various animals, plants, and buildings.

Haven tried to disabuse him of such notions, but Will continued to wear a string of rattlesnake buttons around his neck to ward off disease. One morning he appeared for work at the tannery with all his clothes turned inside out.

As the employees burst into laughter, Andrew asked, "Will, did you get dressed in the dark?"

"Master Andrew, I know it looks strange, but this is serious. Your horse Henry kicked me in the shin yesterday. Wearing my clothes this way will get rid of the evil spirit he spun onto me."

Will also never went inside or even near the tanyard after dark for fear of being set upon by the spirit of Simo, whom Will believed to be his eternal enemy.

The derisive laughter of the white men did give Will pause. *In their own way, with their black clothes and crosses, they're just as superstitious as us. But if they think I'm a fool, I'll never get anywhere with them. Better go easy on this.*

One day at the market, Will overheard Jack speaking to his owner, Chester Odiorne, in exaggerated beginner English, like a child. After Odiorne walked away, Will pulled Jack aside and accosted him in Mandinka.

"Why do you talk to your owner that way? You can speak English better than that."

"That's the way he wants me to talk. He thinks of me that way. Makes him feel better, bigger, not so likely to whip up on me. I'm fooling with him, but he doesn't know it."

"That sure isn't the way to gain his respect. Wish you'd stop that."

"Got to live with the man—least for a while."

Will frowned as he turned to move up the Parade. How can a man do that? A supplicating attitude will guarantee that we never get our freedom.

In addition to reading the Scriptures, with Reverend Haven's assistance Will soon obtained and pored over many other books, including a translation of Cicero's *Orations*, Addison's *Cato*, and the works of Milton, Voltaire, and Shakespeare. He particularly liked *Julius Caesar* and *Macbeth*.

Will's discussions with Reverend Haven were wide-ranging, at times touching on political, economic, or philosophical subjects. One day their conversation turned to the relationship between private property rights and freedom.

"Reverend," Will said, "how can a white Christian believe at the same time in both slavery and political liberty for all men?"

Haven pushed back his chair and took a long draw on his pipe.

"Setting the moral aspect aside for the moment," he said, "the first thing you must realize is that the founding of these English colonies in North America by white settlers is *all* about private property—primarily land, the quest for it, and the unrestricted use of it. It all started with John Locke, the seventeenth-century English philosopher. He believed that the protection of property is the main function of government. Those who received grants of land—property—in the New World became the recipients of privi-leges that were considered 'liberties' granted by the king to only a relative few."

"But doesn't 'liberty' mean more than that?"

"That's exactly right. 'Liberty' also refers to the common-law right to equality of treatment, including respect for their property, among members of the same class. Not only does this double mean-ing give rise to confusion, but when applied to the question of the legitimacy of slavery, its meaning becomes even more complex."

"I don't understand," Will said.

Haven sighed. "The right to own slaves as property in order to enhance the value of one's other property is at the heart of the economic independence and sense of personal worth the white colonist perceives to be the essence of his own freedom. Neither the state nor anyone else, therefore, should interfere with that right or 'liberty.' The white owners argue that the resulting incentives create value, which in turn benefits the common good, the whole community."

"But if one person, a slave, is forced to work for a master, he won't feel any pride, any worth. He thinks, why should I work hard? So his value to his master goes down."

"Precisely. Without even touching on the issue of the immoral-ity of slavery, the white slave owners in America are in fact caught in that analytical inconsistency. They never get to the moral issue because they're still wrestling with how to resolve that practical aspect within the confines of the economic structure they have in part fallen heir to and in part created themselves here in this new land. That of course is no excuse; it's simply a statement of the current reality. At the present time, simple inertia is what moves the slave owner down the same track."

"But how long can they close their eyes to the immorality of it?" Will asked.

"Not until the economics change—or they're forced to," the minister said. "We in the clergy keep reminding them of the incon-sistent moral answer, but we have few listeners."

"So why would a slave like me want to join a religion that closes its eyes to my biggest suffering in life?"

"I understand how you feel, Will, but as you continue to think this through, try to keep in mind the critical point that you're not just joining a group. Rather, as an individual, you're committing your soul to Jesus, who certainly doesn't condone slavery in any form."

Will was actually thinking along somewhat different lines. He began to consider how he could convince Haven to speak out against slavery from the pulpit. Or beyond that, even making a personal appeal to James Clarkson to grant Will his freedom.

Will liked to talk with Mrs. Haven as well. She was a willing listener, and he hoped to persuade her to help him in his efforts with her husband and the Clarksons. She in turn tactfully inquired about many aspects of his life.

"Do you miss your family much, Will?"

"I think about Africa and my family every day. My brothers and sisters are probably all married by now. Probably have children of their own I'll never know. I'll never be able to care for my parents in their old age. It makes me sad."

"How's the work at the tannery going? Pretty difficult is it?"

"Not so bad. Stinky. Hard physically. But not very challenging. The work I do for Andrew is much more satisfying. I really enjoy meeting the people he deals with."

"I'll bet lots of those pretty African girls are after you, Will. Got a sweetheart?"

"Kind of interested in one. She seems to like me, too. Abigail, the young woman who works for the Wentworths. Don't know anything will come of it. Them being English also complicates things. Think I'm destined to be single."

"Be careful, Will. I've heard you and Abi see a lot of each other. Don't go and make her pregnant without getting married. That's a sin. And as you know, slave owners don't allow even married Africans to live together. They call it 'singularity,' where the husband and wife are forced to live apart with their separate owners. It's awfully hard, but it's still better than trying to raise children at the wife's house without being married."

"I understand," Will said. "That's one reason why I really have to change my whole situation. Maybe someday you can help me do that."

12

Will wondered what this summons was all about. As he walked up the granite front steps of the Bannister mansion, James Clarkson's last words of advice were in the forefront of his mind: "Bannister's tricky. Listen courteously, but don't agree to anything until you come back and consult with me."

Caesar answered his knock and ushered Will into Colonel William Bannister's study. When Will sat down, at the colonel's direction, Caesar sat also, in a wooden chair in the back corner of the room.

"You're a smart boy, Will," Bannister began. "Caesar and I have supported you as viceroy on the Negro Court and we look forward to backing you in the future. But I'm sure you realize politics is a two-way street. We support you, you support us."

"Sure. I understand that, generally. What do you have in mind?"

"Oh, nothing specific right now. We just want to make sure you appreciate how the system works. What I want is what's best for the people of this city. And Caesar wants what I want."

"Caesar and I work well together, Mr. Bannister. I'm sure we'll be able to smooth out any differences we might have."

"I'm not talking about smoothing out, Will. I'm talking about going along with us. Otherwise you're out as viceroy. Do you understand?"

"I get the message."

"Good. Now I don't want to hear any more talk of ending slavery or grousing about the way we treat our slaves. Hear me?"

"I hear."

"Oh, one more thing, Will. We don't approve of men sleeping with women when they aren't married."

"Of course."

"That will be all, then. Please give my regards to James Clarkson."

As he walked out with Caesar, the king said, "Colonel Bannister means business, Will. Better mind yourself or there be trouble."

Will looked at Caesar, measuring. He said nothing.

"And learn to talk like a slave to white men," Caesar said. "Understand?"

Will turned and and headed down Water Street to the Clarkson house.

—⚓—

"So?" James Sr. said.

"Nothing much," Will said. "He just wanted to make sure Caesar and I are working well together on the court. I told him we were."

Clarkson looked skeptical, but he let it pass.

—⚓—

Will met Abi at the market the following Sunday, and they took a ride down to the beach at Rye. As they strolled along the shore, he told her what had happened.

"Caesar and Bannister don't mess around," he said. "I've got to figure a way to outfox them."

"Caesar's right about one thing," she said. "You got to watch how you talk to the whites."

"I speak just fine."

"That's it. Soon they'll think you too smart and uppity for your own good."

Will stopped for a moment to think about that, then, with a big smile, continued in a shuffling gait. "Sorry, sorry, Miz Abi. Di'n mean no hahm."

Abi laughed and elbowed him in the ribs.

—※—

"Wonder how much Bannister knows about what we're up to," Will said to Jack a day later. "I haven't done anything lately to catch his attention. Something's going on. Better add a couple more men to our watch group."

13

Will left the door of his hut open so he could read the document. He'd written it two years before but had never put it to use because the opportunity had evaporated. Whenever the timing again appeared right—or when he was on the verge of losing hope about his situation and plans—he pulled it out from its hiding place under his bunk and thought about whether to act on it. The document read:

> To Whom It May Concern:
>   This letter is to certify that I, James Clarkson of Portsmouth, New Hampshire, do hereby as of the undersigned date free my slave Will Clarkson in recognition of his good conduct and service to me since I purchased him from John Martin in 1755. Henceforth no man shall be entitled to claim said Will Clarkson as a slave.
>   Signed: James Clarkson
>   Witness: Andrew Clarkson
>   Dated: August 30, 1760
> Examined, stamped and filed August 31, 1760: Samuel Penhallow, Justice of the Peace, Rockingham County.

The signatures were forgeries. Will had based the body of the document on a real "Freedom Certificate" owned by Silas Ream, an elderly Portsmouth African who had been freed some years earlier when his owner became ill and subsequently died. Will had then copied James's and Andrew's signatures from the business documents he maintained for them.

He sat staring at the false certificate, depressed. Neither he nor Jack had been able to uncover any more information about Bannister's suspicious activities. On the Negro Court, Caesar continued to dismiss out of hand whatever Will proposed. Will was running out of ideas as to how to motivate and activate his fellow Africans. Perhaps the time had come to make a run for it—south to Boston, or even New York or Philadelphia. Then use the certificate to establish his freedom there and start a new life. Find work as some kind of apprentice and then maybe even start a small business of his own.

But the sunlight that broke through the early-morning fog on this August Saturday began to lift his spirits. The certificate ruse might even work, but what would it prove? It would be selfish, with no compensating sense of personal accomplishment or satisfaction. He'd be alone in a different city where he knew no one and no one knew him. He'd already invested a lot of effort here in Portsmouth, not just for himself but for the other Africans as well, and for their relations with the whites.

He was at the point when he could and should be starting a family here, with Abi if she'd have him. That would be better than being single in another place, even with the shackle of singularity. No, he had to stick it out here and see what he could do for Portsmouth's Africans and for his future wife and children. Somehow he had to do that and break the Bannister/Caesar connection and prevail.

14

*T*he African populace continued to reelect Caesar, Will, and the rest of the official slate to be the officers on the Negro Court. Will's duties as viceroy weren't demanding or time-consuming. Other than helping preside at the annual elections, his main task was, with Caesar on Saturday evenings, to resolve routine squabbles among members of the African community and determine the guilt or innocence of people charged with misdemeanors of various sorts, including petty thefts and minor assaults.

When an African was convicted of such a crime, the penalty was often a public whipping at the town pump across from the North Church on the Parade. Either Caesar, Will, or both presided at the levying of these sentences, while Sheriff Jack Odiorne or his deputy Pharaoh Shores performed the actual whipping. But on one occasion, when a man named Prince Jackson was found guilty of stealing an ax and sentenced to twenty lashes, Odiorne and Shores were both absent. Caesar walked over to Will.

"Will, you gotta do the whippin. Jack and Pharaoh aint here."

Will froze. "I really don't want to," he said. "It's not my job, and I'm not good at that kind of thing."

"Got to, Will. Court will lose respect if you don't. You refuse, I won't put you up as viceroy at the elections next year. Now get out there and do it." The king then called out: "Gentlemen, here's how we support our government. Will, pay on!"

71

Will stepped forward. Jackson's hands were tied around a post near the pump as he knelt. He shrieked at every one of the blows, and after the first few lashes, blood oozed from the wounds and began to flow freely down his back to the ground. Will squinted with each blow, trying not to look at the effects of his swings. His stomach was knotted and sweat poured from his brow as he delivered the final stroke.

When it was over, Will went straight to Reverend Haven's house. He burst into Haven's library as soon as Mrs. Haven answered the door and poured out what had happened.

"It was awful, Reverend. There I was, doing one of the same terrible things whites do to us Africans. I felt like Walter Clarkson. How can I ever be forgiven?"

The minister laid a hand on Will's shoulder. "My son, you've done this under duress. You can't be held fully responsible. Your agony is proof of your innocence and your penance."

Will felt better—some. He later told Caesar that he'd never perform that duty again. The king glared at him a few moments. When Will didn't back down, he shrugged his shoulders.

"Maybe I'll find someone with a stronger stomach."

⁓

In October 1762, Clarkson's son James Jr. married a Boston widow named Sarah Holland. The new Mrs. Clarkson was described by her contemporaries as "a lady of spirit"—meaning, it seemed, that she was often aggressive and caustic in otherwise polite conversation both within and without the family. Will was happy to see her and her husband off to Boston aboard the recently established stagecoach service for an extended wedding trip.

Andrew Clarkson passed away in the summer of 1765. Will felt this loss deeply, for Andrew was a kind man who had been as much a companion as a master. The loss also put significant strain on operations at the tanyard, which was already undermanned. James Sr. finally purchased a second slave from Captain John Langdon to spread the workload, an eighteen-year-old named Glasce, but the untrained youngster was no replacement for the experienced and savvy Andrew.

Will was at a significant crossroads. With Andrew's death, he had lost not only an ally he'd been counting on to help pull himself out of slavery but also the most interesting and challenging part of his daily duties, the clerical work. He faced the issue promptly. He spoke to James Sr. and convinced his owner that he could both assume a major portion of the administrative and clerical chores at the tannery and be assigned as Glasce's supervisor. Perhaps the new Clarkson slave could be an unexpected gift—an impressionable full-time partner in Will's cause.

In November came the British Parliament's Stamp Act, the first direct tax laid on the colonies. The colonists would need a special stamp supplied by the crown in order to execute certain legal documents. The English would not supply the stamp until the parties had paid a heavy tax—thirty-three percent of the value of the underlying transaction. Resentment and rejection erupted instantly throughout the colonies, the resistance being focused in groups who called themselves the Sons of Liberty.

When James Sr. was told that the stamp tax applied to sales invoices for his tanned products, he was furious and immediately joined the Portsmouth Sons of Liberty. At the tannery, he complained loudly to James Jr.

"I used to feel free here in New Hampshire," he said. "But no more. This Stamp Act is pure extortion. If King George doesn't watch it, he's going to have an insurrection on his hands."

"Better watch your words, Father. There are a lot of English sympathizers here in Portsmouth."

That night Reverend Haven was a guest at the Clarkson dinner table. "Samuel, this stamp thing is killing my business," James said. "I've just about had it. You've got to help me make our friends realize we have to do something."

"Whoa, James," the minister said. "We don't want to get ourselves thrown in jail. Let me ask around and see how the others feel."

Two days later, on January 6, 1766, a man named George Meserve arrived in Portsmouth. He was the agent appointed by the

British king to distribute the stamps in New Hampshire. Meserve found the opposition to his task so belligerent that he immediately resigned his commission. James Clarkson and the other Sons of Liberty appeared on his doorstep and demanded that he turn over the commission document to them, which he did. The rebels raised the document on the point of a sword and marched it through the city amid shouting and cheering down to the Swing Bridge on Water Street, where they raised a flag on a pole, proclaiming "Liberty, Property and No Stamp." Thereafter the bridge was known as Liberty Bridge.

The reaction in the other colonies was similar, and in March, Parliament repealed the Stamp Act, recognizing the futility of trying to enforce it against such firm and united opposition. The colonists had won round one, but as James Sr. said to Will on the way home after work one day, "There'll be plenty more to come."

He was right. In June 1767, Parliament came back with the Townshend duties on English products sold in the colonies, including pipe, glass, paint, and tea. The American response was a boycott on the purchase of all such goods.

Then, in the fall, the news came to Portsmouth that George III had appointed John Wentworth, Abi's master, as governor of the royal province of New Hampshire. Wentworth was known in the community as a pleasant and good man, but the tension between the crown and the American colonies soon engulfed him and divided the seaport into two militant factions—the loyalists, or "Tories," who remained true to England, and the radicals, later "patriots," who resisted England's attempts to convert the colonies into a source of revenue and became increasingly convinced that independence was the only and inevitable option.

Will figured something had to break open before long. That's when he'd make a move.

"What do you think of the English?" Will asked in Mandinka.

Glasce shrugged. "No different from the other white men. They're all my enemies. They work me, beat up on me, same as the rest of these white pigs."

"We might be better off if the colonists get free," Will said.

"Don't see how."

Will looked at Glasce and shook his head. "Well, back to your lessons. Here are the English words for you to learn by tomorrow. Let's go over them once again."

He'd been working with Glasce on his English for several months, with limited success. The boy was only now starting to show some progress.

15

"Governor Wentworth's new job doesn't make it easier for either of us," Jack said.

"Maybe it will," Will said. "Every development means a good opportunity sooner or later."

"See Abi much?" Jack asked.

"Every so often. Too busy."

"Think she'd marry either of us?"

"Who knows?"

Jack looked hard at him. "Going to meet her now. I might ask her."

"I won't say good luck."

Will watched closely as his friend walked off. He and Jack had remained rivals for Abi's affection ever since that first dance at the African election celebration several years ago. She seemed to enjoy playing them off against each other. But then last week she and Will had been together and she'd brought up the subject of her feelings, even mentioning marriage. Will had felt he had to talk realistically. He hadn't exactly encouraged her. Now he was afraid Jack might be able to take advantage of the situation.

He resumed chopping logs for the four fireplaces in the big house. He gritted his teeth, swinging the ax faster and harder with each stroke.

Abigail sat in her attic room in the stately brick Wentworth house, on the corner of Pleasant and Washington Streets not far from the Clarkson residence, sewing buttons on one of her mistress's dresses. She was humming a tune Cuffee Whipple had played at the African coronation feast some months before, and she was thinking of the way the sunshine had fallen on Will's face as he turned to glance at her while he was parading with Cuffee and the other African officers. At twenty-five, she was used to receiving rapt glances from men in the slave community, including Jack Odiorne, who delighted in making her laugh.

Only last week, she'd accidentally overheard a discussion between her mistress Frances Wentworth and Frances's sister-in-law Hannah. "That slave of yours has grown into a handsome woman," Hannah had said. "So tall and well developed. A pretty face and a very pleasing figure."

"She has," Frances said. "And the Negro men are all but panting after her. I'm just scared to death one of them is going to get her pregnant."

"That would be a bother," Hannah said. "Not to mention the extra expense. But Abi minds well, doesn't she? I mean, you've had her since she was, how old?"

"Twelve. Yes, she's docile enough, but you know the Negro men here outnumber the women by almost three to one. They're bound to tempt her, and I just can't have it. It's too complicated."

As Abi glided back into the kitchen and closed the door, she felt the same pain in her heart she'd felt when she and Will talked about the barriers to relationships between slaves. He'd said, "The situation isn't normal. Slaves can't live together, even if we have a public church wedding. And it gets worse—sometimes one or the other gets sold to a different owner, even in another town far from here. And then, who do the children belong to? They usually stay with the wife's owners, but you never know."

Will was in fact racking his brain trying to think of a way around the dilemma. He understood the wisdom of Mrs. Haven's advice that he remain patient and control himself so as not to burden Abi with pregnancy and perhaps the pain of separation forever from her child or from him. He tried hard to hide the frustration he experienced every time he saw her. Apparently he hadn't succeeded, for James Clarkson had spoken sternly to him—something he rarely did—on the walk home the previous night.

"I had a visit from Wentworth," James had said. "It seems his wife has noticed that you're attracted to her maidservant. She wants you to stay away. He asked me to forbid you to see her."

Will had struggled to remain calm.

"As you know," James continued, "there's friction developing between the American colonists and the British, including Tories like Wentworth. Perhaps it's better if you do stay away from the girl."

"That's a tough order, Master James. We're pretty close."

"I know, Will. But it's best for all of us. See what you can do to break it off."

"I'll talk with her, Master James. But I'm not so sure about it."

He could see James hesitate. Then James said, "Well, let me know. We've got to be very careful these days."

Will was upset. Although he'd tried to hold back the depth of his feelings, he knew that he loved Abi fiercely. He'd known that the political situation, along with the white folks' refusal to let their African male and female servants live together to create families, would prove to be huge obstacles. He'd hoped against hope that they could somehow be overcome, but now things looked bad. If he couldn't see Abi, there was a chance that Jack Odiorne would step in and win her hand. *Damn, I've got to do something.*

Will saw Abi next at the African women's market on the following Sunday afternoon. She was in tears again as she told him of her mistress's position and said she had put off Jack Odiorne's proposal. Will told her what James Sr. had said, which moved her to fresh tears.

"Shhhh," Will said. "I'm not going to accept this. I'll talk to Reverend Haven about it—I will find some way to see him this week. You sit tight and meet me here same time next Sunday."

On Wednesday evening, Will sat in the minister's study explaining his dilemma.

"Well, one thing's for sure," the pastor said. "Your master's feelings cut off the option of my marrying you, even if the two of you were to be christened first."

"How about if I ask Cyrus Atkinson to perform an African ceremony? Then we'll just have to see each other whenever we can."

"That helps morally, although it's legally questionable."

"Legally? What's legal about my being a slave? The white man's law is killing me. Legal? Hogwash."

Haven flushed. "I know, I know. But any society has to have some sort of framework. Anyway, the real problem comes if you have children. Then what will you do? Also, if you decide to go that route, don't tell me about it—so I won't be caught between you and James."

When Will left, he'd made up his mind. On Saturday he sought out Cyrus Atkinson in the stable.

"All right, I'll marry you," Cyrus said. "Jest the usual simple ceremony. But you ought to know, the whites don't recognize the legality of African marriages that don't have the blessing of the Christian church or aint performed by a white justice of peace. Could lead to nasty situation down the road."

"Understood, Cyrus. Reverend Haven went through it with me. We want to go ahead with it anyway. And soon. Can you do it two weeks from tomorrow?"

"Sure. Let's say two o'clock here by the horse stable."

On Sunday Will and Abi sat on their rocky perch at the seashore in Rye, overlooking the Isles of Shoals floating on the glimmering ocean in the afternoon sun. They held each other and looked into each other's eyes.

"Will you have me, Abi?" he whispered.

She kissed him lightly on the cheek. "Thought you'd never ask."

"It's quite a comedown, when you think about it," he said, "and it's going to be tricky. In Africa this moment would be a joyous occasion. Here we have to plot with Cyrus to be married in secret. And whether we'll ever be able to have children and raise them properly is still doubtful."

Abi sighed. "I know, but we can't let the whites make us bitter. We got to be positive." She smiled up at him. "Don't think I told you, I want just two children. One boy and one girl."

Will grinned and poked her in the ribs. "Planning already, are you? Might have guessed. Two sounds just right to me, too."

They dozed off until a cool sea breeze awakened them at dusk.

Will and Abigail were married a week later, on July 6, 1768. The bride and groom met Atkinson in the back of the public stable next to the North Church. Will presented Abi with a brass ring, which she accepted. He then tied the traditional cotton string around her waist. Atkinson said a blessing and declared, "You're now man and wife." Will and Abi kissed, and the three participants departed. The entire ceremony lasted less than five minutes.

On the way back to the Wentworth house, Will said, "Sorry about the ceremony. No long talks between our families about what my parents would pay to make sure I treat you properly. No celebration, no waterfall of blessings, no feasting and dancing for a whole week. It—"

"Doesn't matter, Will. Now we can be man and wife without feeling guilty, maybe someday have a family. It will be wonderful—just you wait and see."

That evening Will sought out Jack Odiorne in the kitchen at the Pitt Tavern and told him the news. Jack took a second to control his face, then smiled and wished his friend well.

Their lifestyle turned out to be even more challenging than they had foreseen. They rarely saw each other—usually just at Sunday market—and they could never spend a night together. Only on an occasional Sunday afternoon by the beach at Rye did they make love freely.

Abi managed to disguise her pregnancy until the fifth month, but the watchful eye of Frances Wentworth picked up on it in early January of the following year.

"So, let's have it, Abi. Who's the father? Is it that Clarkson boy? I want the whole story. You know you're in big trouble for directly disobeying my order."

"Mrs. Wentworth, Will's a good man, and he's my husband. We were married in an African service. He works hard, he'll be a good father and won't cause any trouble. He'll stay away—I'll take care of the child."

"Nonsense, Abi. The financial and social burden will be on the governor and me. That's unacceptable. I'm going to talk to the governor this evening, and we'll decide how we're going to dispose of this problem." Mrs. Wentworth stalked out of the room, shutting the door louder than necessary behind her.

Abi sat choking in sobs as the afternoon darkened, and she listened for the governor's footsteps indicating he'd returned home from his meeting in Exeter. At last she went to the kitchen to begin preparing the family's evening meal.

———

When John Wentworth did arrive, a bit later than usual, the atmosphere at the dinner table was silent and tense as Abi served. Frances had indicated to her husband that she had to speak to him about a serious matter afterward and that the subject was Abi.

As Abi cleared the table and began washing the dishes, the discussion began. She crept to the door and listened, appalled, to her mistress's opening salvo.

"Abi is pregnant, Mr. Wentworth. I told her not to see the Clarkson boy. Not only did she disobey me, she's gone and married him in some heathen service. The child has got to go. It may be too late for an abortion, but as soon as it's born it's got to be out of here. I expect you to take care of that."

John Wentworth winced at his wife's mention of an abortion. Under both English and New Hampshire law, the procedure was a misdemeanor prior to the quickening of the fetus and a felony beyond that point. He was silent for a few moments; then he spoke:

"We've got to be cautious here, Mrs. Wentworth. What you're suggesting is hardly the Christian thing to do. And there's a practical aspect—I already have enough problems with the troublemakers in this place, including the Clarkson bunch. They'll be inclined to rake me over the coals publicly if I'm cruel to a child. And if word got back to King George, he could be embarrassed and very upset with both of us."

His wife paled at the mention of George III, but pressed on. "There's no reason to look at this as cruel. It's just practical in light of our position. Think about placing the child with another family or an orphanage. Perhaps in Boston."

"I don't like it. Let me think about it."

⁂

Abi breathed a sigh of temporary relief as she washed and rinsed the dishes. But once upstairs in bed, she scarcely slept. She decided not to tell Will that the Wentworths knew she was pregnant until there was a resolution.

But Will wanted this child desperately, particularly a son, so important to African tribal nobility. And he knew her very well. So the next time they sat alone by the Piscataqua and he talked about the baby, he noticed the look on her face and in seconds had the truth out of her about what was happening in the Wentworth household.

He held her and said, "We'll work it out somehow."

After leaving Abi off at the Wentworth back door late that afternoon, he went around to the front of the mansion and knocked on the door. The governor answered.

Will said, "Governor Wentworth, Abi is my wife. Her child couldn't be more important to me. I pray as one man to another that you'll do the Christian thing and let Abi raise him." He bowed, turned, and walked up the street.

For several evenings, after dinner the Wentworths went back and forth on the issue, often shouting at each other. Abi cowered out of sight, listening as closely as she could, but shaking in fear.

Finally, more than a week later, just after returning home from the Queen's Chapel service, Governor Wentworth appeared at the door of Abi's room. Her hands flew to her mouth and she began quaking.

"It's all right, Abi, don't be afraid. Mrs. Wentworth has agreed that you can keep the child here. But you have full responsibility for it, and I don't want to see Will Clarkson around here, ever."

Abi knelt at the governor's feet. "Thank you, Master John. Thank you. Thank you."

Wentworth patted her softly on her shoulder and left the room, closing the door quietly.

16

*T*he baby was born late one Sunday evening in April 1769 in Abi's attic room in the Wentworth house. Abi was attended by Shelia, Dr. Hall Jackson's African midwife servant, while Will paced outside on Pleasant Street until summoned.

"His name's William, William Clarkson Jr.," Abi announced as she cuddled the baby in a warm blanket in her arms. Speechless, Will beamed and hugged his wife.

Shortly thereafter, Abi appeared with the boy at the Sunday market, all smiles as she showed off her plump baby to her friends. When his father showed up, she handed William Jr. to him. Bursting with pride, Will cradled him, lifted him, rocked him, and displayed him to all as he strolled up and down the Parade.

But it wasn't easy for either parent thereafter: for Will, who got to see the boy at best only once a week, or for Abi, who like all her fellow slaves bore the full burden of caring for the baby with no lessening of the work for her owners.

Not that the care was a burden to her. She delighted in her son. And as young Willie began to walk, talk, and develop his own personality, Will's joy knew no bounds

During the sixteen years since arriving on the *Exeter*, Abi had regularly attended the Sunday services at Queen's Chapel, the

Wentworths' church. The pastor there, Reverend Arthur Brown, had schooled her and several other Africans on the Anglican liturgy and Bible reading. In 1772, at Brown's urging and with Will's agreement, she decided to convert, and was christened on October 19. She occasionally raised with Will the prospect of his converting as well, but he resisted.

"I'm glad you're happy in your new faith," he told her. "Really, I am. But I'll be darned if I'm going to join a church with people who keep me a slave. Besides, I just don't want to give up the beliefs of my parents and ancestors."

"Please keep an open mind. It makes me feel less at the mercy of other people."

In 1772 Abi became pregnant again and in October gave birth to a daughter they named Naby. Frances Wentworth raised no ruckus this time, though Abi could sense she wasn't pleased. But Abi had done a good job of keeping young Willie out of sight of the white populace, and there'd been no adverse reaction among Frances's social peers. Abi's conversion to Christianity had also helped her image in Frances's eyes.

Will called Glasce over to the door of the tannery. "Here's a list of new tools we need from the store. Then stop by the lumberyard and pick up the two-by-fours and boards we need to patch that rotted-out spot in the corner. The people in the store can read it." He repeated everything in Mandinka. "Stay away from that back room at the tavern," he added. "I expect you here by four o'clock."

Glasce took the piece of paper listlessly and walked out the door.

Will shook his head and turned back to preparing his weekly accounting.

Tensions in the colonies were mounting. The entire Portsmouth community, black and white, was jolted when a young African named Crispus Attucks and four others were killed by a redcoat guard force in Boston in March 1770 in what quickly became known as the Boston Massacre. Ironically, on the same day, the British Parliament, reacting to the colonists' boycott, repealed the Townshend Acts with the single exception of the duty on tea. But news of the repeal did not quell the outrage of the Americans, who saw the confrontation as the murder of peaceful citizens by brutal, out-of-control soldiers. Attucks came to be a hero as the first American killed in the Revolution.

Back in Portsmouth, Will and his African comrades felt a mixture of horror and pride when news of the incident reached the city.

"Fool," Jack said. "Gave his life for people who kept him a slave."

"But look at the whites' reaction. They're praising him to the skies. Thing for us may be to fight on the side of the American rebels."

The Clarkson family began to disperse. In 1771 Andrew's widow, Lydia, married the Reverend Jonathan Parsons, of Newburyport, Massachusetts, and moved there with her young children, including James III. Now twenty, James was already embarking on a maritime career, having signed on as first mate on a coastal merchant ship trading between Boston and Philadelphia.

17

"*H*ow they treat you?" Jack asked. He was lying in the long yellow grass with Sarah, a slave belonging to Charles and Emily Bickford, on the north bank of the Piscataqua River in Kittery, Maine. They were looking southeast toward Portsmouth and the Great Island and on out to sea.

"Been decent till now," Sarah said. "But since last Monday they been snappin at me. Don't like it. Make me nervous."

"What happen Monday?"

"Caesar come by and talk to them for a while. They got excited. Shoutin back at him."

"Bout what?"

"Could only hear part of it. Couldn't really figure it out. Seem Caesar wanted more money from them to give to William Bannister. Said ten pounds wasn't enough. Needed fifteen. They wouldn't give it to him, so Caesar said they wouldn't get protection any more. Could mean trouble for them. They said they could take care of their own slaves without Bannister's or Caesar's help. They stood up to him, but I think they scared. Seems whatever it is has been goin on for a long time, but no one's found out about it."

"Interesting. . . Be best you don't mention it to anyone. Now come closer, sugar."

Will smiled and stroked his chin. "So that's what they've been up to. A protection scheme. And now Caesar's decided he needs an extra cut for himself."

"Man's rotten," Jack said. "Should get a gun and shoot him. Tell everybody what he and Bannister been doing. We—"

"Not so fast, Jack. He's a bum, all right, but that's not the smart way to handle this. If we spread it all over town, everybody's up in arms. I'll bet most if not all the white owners are in on the thing. They'll be angry and embarrassed that they've been discovered, and they'll take it out on us Africans."

"Can't let this sit."

"We're not going to. What we're going to do is keep this quiet for now and give Caesar lots of rope to hang himself. We can turn this into a benefit for all of us slaves and show that Caesar needs to be replaced as king. We can beat him in the elections. Throw him out of office. Then get some things done. More education for Africans. More respect. Better conditions. Freedom sooner. This can't just end as a story about one bad man and then nothing happens, more of same."

"Bannister?" Jack asked.

"If Caesar falls, Bannister's power base comes apart. He's the one who controls slavery in this town, keeps it going. If he loses support of the white population, he'll fall too. It'll break the back of slavery in Portsmouth."

"Maybe, but some of our folks are going be upset about taking on Caesar—the sheep who don't want to make waves and believe his 'patience and time' junk."

"A risk we'll have to run." Will picked up a flat stone and skipped it across the top of the Piscataqua from where they stood outside the tannery. "Seven hops. Pretty good." He grinned at Jack. The two men turned and walked back up the riverbank, past the tannery, and down to South School Street, where they separated to go on to their respective owner's houses.

—⚓—

Will spied Romeo Rindge at the far end of the women's Sunday market and hailed him over.

"Romeo, I need you to do some sniffing around for me. I want financial information on William Bannister—what accounts he keeps in your owner's bank and what deposits and withdrawals he's made in the last six months. Think you can do it?"

"Won't be easy. . . May have a way. Be back to you in a couple of weeks."

"Good. Very secret. Don't even tell your wife."

—※—

Will got up from his bunk to answer the knock. It was Romeo.

"What'd you find out? Anything good?"

"Interesting. Here's my notes. Man keeps two accounts in the bank, WB Personal and Owners Account. Couldn't figure out what money was going where."

"I'll sort it out. Great job, Romeo. Remember, no word to anybody."

—※—

The following Sunday, Will stopped Caesar on the Parade and looked the king firmly in the eyes. "Caesar, I just want you to know that I know what's going on, what you're up to. Some day it will all come out." Caesar's black eyes stared right back at Will. Without a word he turned and moved up the street. Will smiled and continued in the other direction.

His undercover watch group now included a dozen of his close African friends. It was paying off.

18

Will was at the tannery examining a hide Glasce had just scraped. He frowned and shook his head. The younger man still did sloppy work.

Will had been optimistic at first. He not only spent a lot of time at the tannery with Glasce, trying to teach him the trade, he'd tried to be a friend to the man. Will worked for hours teaching him English and discussing slavery in Portsmouth. But Glasce remained indifferent and only partially responsive. He said he hated the smelly tannery. He hated being a slave, but he seemed to think about slavery only in terms of his own situation.

Will walked across the big room to where Glasce was piling hides to be taken to the next station.

"You've almost got it finished," he said in English. "Now go over these three places where the flesh still hangs on."

Glasce looked up at Will. "Why you care bout this white man's business?"

"Mr. Clarkson's been good to me. I've been able to work my way up in the business and the town. I expect to be a free man soon. I'll have some education and skills to count on."

Glasce glanced up from the dock to make sure they were alone. "You different from me," he said. "You speak English better, got wife and children. I got no chance for either. No young girls round here no more. Gonna spend my whole life scrapin animal guts and mindin master. No way to live. You ever think bout runnin?"

"At first," Will said. "But it didn't make a lot of sense to run off and get killed in the woods by slave hunters or Indians or winter. So I made a better plan. You need a better plan."

"Think these white folks goin to war for liberty?"

"Looks like it. I heard Mr. Clarkson tell Reverend Haven just yesterday he'd talked to most of the men in town and many of them will fight before they'll give in on the taxes."

"Man's got to fight when other men put him down," Glasce said. "You think if they win they'll do anythin for us?"

"They've got to. Caesar's not sure, but I am. How can they fight for liberty and then keep slaves?"

"Caesar gonna die an old slave man," Glasce said. "Not me. I got to do somethin. You don't help yourself in this life, you a fool."

Will at least liked that attitude. But given such conversations, he was not entirely surprised when one Monday morning in the winter Glasce failed to show up for the walk to the tannery. James Jr. went to the hut and found it empty. Glasce's few belongings were also gone.

James went immediately to the office of the *New Hampshire Gazette* to advertise for the runaway. On December 11, 1772, a notice appeared in the newspaper:

Ran Away from James Clarkson of Portsmouth, Lord's Day Evening, the 6th Instant, a Negro Man named Glasce, aged about 25 Years, about five Feet and a half high; a flat Nose, a little upon the yellow Complexion; had on when he went away, a green Coat & Jacket, snuff colored breeches, made of Serge; a Hat and a Wig; speaks good English, and reads well. Whoever shall take up the said Negro, and return him to his Master shall have Four Dollars Reward, and all necessary Charges paid by James Clarkson.

All Masters of Vessels are forbid carrying him off.

Days and then weeks passed with no response to the notice. Then one afternoon William Bannister came to the tanyard and spoke to James Sr. outside the building. James then came back inside and called everyone together.

"I'm saddened to report that Glasce is dead. He was caught by local authorities in western Massachusetts, but on the way to the jail he grabbed the pistol of a deputy sheriff and killed himself with a shot to the head. God bless his soul."

Will went outside and sat on a rock by the river where he could be alone and think. Glasce had shot himself. He'd been willing to die rather than live as a slave. James Clarkson, by virtue of luck in being born white and marrying a wealthy woman, owned Will's body, his labor, and even, Will sometimes felt, his mind. He and Abi had brought children into this world. What was their status, their future? Did they belong forever to the Wentworths, to be taken wherever the Wentworths chose to go?

Suicide! Glasce had been either courageous or crazy, Will couldn't say for certain which. But as he thought more about it, he brightened. This event, terrible as it was, presented an opportunity to further his strategy.

"We win either way, Jack," Will said. "By pushing Caesar to do something, we get him farther out on his limb. If he does something, that'll help us by showing that being more active works. If he does nothing, we point to it later as another instance of his failure. It even supports the fact that he's been scheming with Bannister."

Will asked Caesar to call a meeting of the Negro Court for the following Sunday at the stables. "Caesar, this is much more important than just the death of one man. It goes to your 'patience and time' strategy. I think we need to talk about that, reexamine it."

The four officers met and proceeded to go back and forth on the issue in a heated argument. Caesar and Pharaoh Shores upheld the current strategy. Will and Jack pushed for change.

"Glasce's suicide is an example of how frustrated the African community is here in Portsmouth," Will said. "This can't continue. We've *got* to do something about it. If we—"

"Will, calm down," Pharaoh said. "We all know Glasce was a hothead. You can't generalize based on what he did."

"Maybe not," Jack said. "But everyone's looking at us on this one. They expect us *do something.* If we just sit back like we always do, they be disgusted. Should be."

Caesar stared back at Will. "Just what is it you expect us to do that would make one lick of difference?"

"At least send a public letter. Submit it to the editor of the *Gazette,* demanding better treatment for all the Africans in the city."

"You gonna stand up and say to James Clarkson that he mistreated Glasce?"

"That's not the issue."

"Certainly *will* be the issue for the whites. This aint the right case to make a hullabaloo about. Won't work." He looked around at the others. "We're getting nowhere here. Tell you what, Will. Make an agreement with you. We wait and see how these disputes between the English and our white owners work out. Then look at it again. We'll do something different if it's still a problem."

"That won't do," Will said. "We are *not* going to drop this issue. 'Patience and time' is what doesn't work."

Caesar glared at him. "Remember your conversation with Mr. Bannister, young fellah."

"It worked, Jack," Will said as they made their way back down Water Street. "Mark up another time he's taking no action. Either he's too soft or he doesn't want to do anything to mess up his crooked business."

"Or both."

19

James Sr. died in the fall of 1773. The South Meeting House was packed to standing room only at the funeral service, including the "Negro pews" on the upper level. William Bannister and John Langdon led a series of eulogies to the popular tanner. From his high seat looking down on his dead teacher in the open pine casket, Will wiped his eyes with the back of his hand.

James Jr. inherited the bulk of his father's estate. He and his wife, Sarah, moved into the big house on South School Street, and he took command at the tannery. Will's working relationship with Junior was reasonably good, but he steered a wide berth around the volcanic Sarah, dealing solely with Mrs. Haven at the house.

Within two months, everyone's attention was again riveted on the British. The issue was the tax remaining on imports of tea. In the preceding five years the colonies had imported and paid the duty on nearly two million pounds of tea, while smuggling in large amounts from other sources.

The citizens of Portsmouth met on December 16 to consider what they should do to resist. They passed resolutions that read:

> *Resolved,* That every virtuous and public-spirited *free-man* ought steadily to oppose to the utmost of his ability, every artful attack of the Ministry to *enslave* the Americans.

Resolved, That the power given by Parliament to the East India Company, to send out their teas to the colonies, subjected to the payment of duties on being landed here, is a plain attempt to enforce the Ministerial plan, and a direct attack upon the liberties of America, and that it is an indispensable duty of all true-hearted Americans to render this effort abortive.

Resolved, That in case any of the Company's tea shall be brought into this Port, in order for sale, we will use every method necessary to prevent its being landed or sold here.

This action, considered to be bold by the New Hampshire men, heartened Will and his African colleagues. But it was Boston that acted more dramatically and grabbed King George's attention. There, on the same night of December 16, the Sons of Liberty were ready when three tea ships sailed into the harbor. Disguised as Mohawk Indians and Africans, three companies of fifty men each stormed the ships and emptied three hundred and forty-two chests of tea into the water.

In early December of that year Will wrote an anonymous letter to the editor of the *New Hampshire Gazette* advocating the abolition of slavery. The letter was published, and two weeks later, on December 31, a response was printed in the newspaper:

In looking over the latter part of the first chapter of Genesis, I find an account of God's having granted to Adam and his posterity, not only a dominion over 'the fish of the sea, the fowl of the air, cattle, and everything that <u>creepeth</u> upon the earth,' but likewise in a particular manner, over the Negroes of Africa.*—I beg therefore you would mention this in your paper, to silence those writers who insist upon the Africans belonging to the same species of men with the white people, and who will not allow that God formed them in common with horses, oxen, dogs, etc. for the white people alone, to be used by them either for pleasure or to labour with their other beasts in the culture of Tobacco, Indigo, Rice, and Sugar.

A CUSTOMER.

* "And the beasts of Ethiopia shall bow down to thee, even they whose figure and speech are like unto thine own, and whose heads are covered with a covering like unto fine wool,—They who dwell on the sea coast shall serve thee, and thy seed after thee, even they who shall sojourn in the Islands afar, even where the sun hath his going down."

Will and Jack were enraged at the ugly comparison, particularly when Will checked the Bible Reverend Haven had given him and found that the footnote did not even exist. They couldn't show the letter to Caesar fast enough, arguing for a response. As the king read the page, his face hardened into a cold, dark stare. He looked away, shaking his head. But he would only say, slowly, that it merely showed that the time was not yet ripe.

Will said, "Damn it, Caesar. How long do we have to wait? No time's ever ripe with you." The older man kept his cool manner and said nothing further.

"Mark up another one," Will said to Jack. "This is getting to be an impressive list of donothings."

It didn't take Parliament long to react to the Boston Tea Party. In March through June 1774 it passed a series of laws that became known in the colonies as the Coercive Acts, the most punishing of which were the Boston Port Act, blockading the entire port, and the Quartering Act, which gave royal governors the right to commandeer private homes in any of the thirteen colonies in order to quarter soldiers. Protestant New Hampshire also reacted vociferously against the Quebec Act, which established French civil law and the Catholic religion in the province of Quebec.

The colonies were in a quandary. Most people were far from ready to strike for independence, but something had to be done about the Coercive Acts, which were too oppressive for almost everyone's blood.

The slave communities, including Portsmouth's, were also watching these events unfold with great interest, wondering what would happen to them when and if the white colonists managed to gain their own liberty. Will was one of those keeping an intense eye on these developments. His attention became even more focused in August, when Primus Fowle rushed up to him one Sunday waving a small booklet titled *Poems on Various Subjects, Religious and Moral,* by Phillis Wheatley, identified as "Negro Servant to Mr. John Wheatley of Boston."

"Gotta read this, Will. Very interesting. Specially for you."

"What's so good about this? Who's Phillis Wheatley?"

"Take a look inside the cover."

Will opened the book and read:

AS it has been repeatedly suggested to the Publisher, by Persons, who have seen the Manuscript, that Numbers would be ready to suspect they were not really the Writings of PHILLIS, he has procured the following Attestation, from the most respectable Characters in Boston, that none might have the least Ground for disputing their Original.

"WE whose Names are underwritten, do assure the World, that the POEMS specified in the following Page, were (as we verily believe) written by Phillis, a young Negro Girl, who was but a few years since [1761, between 7-8 years old], brought an uncultivated Barbarian from Africa, and has ever since been, and now is, under the Disadvantage of serving as a Slave in a Family in this Town. She has been examined by some of the best Judges, and is thought qualified to write them.

His Excellency THOMAS HUTCHINSON, Governor (and seventeen other signatures including John Hancock)

Will looked up at Primus. "Can I keep this copy?"

"Sure."

Later that afternoon, back in his room, Will was wide-eyed as he read:

Twas mercy brought me from my
    <u>Pagan</u> land,
Taught my benighted soul to
    understand
That there's a God, that there's a
    <u>Saviour</u> too:
Once I redemption neither sought nor
    knew.
Some view our sable race with scornful
    eye,
'Their colour is a diabolic die.'
Remember, <u>Christians, negros,</u> black
    as <u>Cain,</u>
May be refin'd, and join th' angelic
    train.

He loved the poetic beauty of the piece, though he was a little uncomfortable about the extent, apparently, to which Wheatley had accepted the Christian life. He was reassured and felt a renewal of energy when he opened a page from *The Connecticut Gazette*, dated March 11, 1774, which had been stuck inside the back cover of the book. The Wheatley letter published there read:

> In every human Breast, God has implanted a Principle, which we call Love of Freedom; it is impatient to Oppression, and pants for Deliverance; and by the Leave of our Modern Egyptians I will assert, that the same Principle lives in us.

Will was greatly moved. He was not ready to accept the Christian aspect of Wheatley's words, but here in his hands was a clearly written articulation, by a fellow African, of feelings he recognized, beliefs he held deeply. His hopes for a happy outcome to his own beleaguered existence soared.

The hopes of Will and his black brethren were not without support from some corners of New Hampshire's white community. In July of 1774, Dr. Jeremy Belknap delivered a sermon in Dover in which he posed some direct questions to his congregation:

Would it not be astonishing to hear that the people who are contending so earnestly for liberty are not willing to allow liberty to others? Is it not astonishing to think that, at this day, there are in the several colonies of this continent some thousands of men, women, and children in bondage and slavery for no other reason than that their skin is of a darker color than our own? Such is the inconsistency of our conduct.

Will and other Africans in Portsmouth heard of Belknap's sermon and discussed it among themselves.

"Change is in the air," Will said to the king the week after the sermon.

"Don't hold your breath," Caesar said.

20

As 1774 progressed, the pace of popular rebellion quickened in Portsmouth as well as throughout the colonies. Despite the resistance of Governor Wentworth, a Committee of Correspondence was established and met at Exeter on July 21 to elect delegates to a Continental Congress on September 5. Neither James Clarkson Jr. nor Reverend Haven was a delegate, but both were active in the growing opposition.

After much debate, the Continental Congress promulgated a Declaration of Rights declaring that Americans were entitled to all English liberties and also adopted a nonimportation, nonexportation, and nonconsumption agreement, cutting off all imports from Britain after December 1, 1774, and exports to Britain after September 10, 1775, if by those dates the Coercive Acts had not been repealed. With that action the congress ended on October 22, 1774, setting May 10, 1775, as the date for a follow-up meeting if England did not grant redress.

But redress was not to be. Indeed, three days earlier, on October 19, a royal order had prohibited the export of powder and arms to America. This measure had a particularly negative impact on the New Hampshire populace, who still felt the need for firearms to protect their frontier from the Indians and the French.

A month and a half later, the Boston Committee of Correspondence learned that the royal governors were taking steps to secure existing stores of arms and ammunition. They immediately dispatched Paul Revere to warn their Portsmouth counterparts.

Will was in the kitchen at the Pitt Tavern talking with his friend the cook at the end of the day on December 13 when Revere galloped up. He was looking for Samuel Cutts, a prominent merchant and chairman of the local Committee on Ways and Means, to deliver the news that British troops were on the way to guard the arsenal at Fort William and Mary in Portsmouth Harbor.

The committee met that evening, and by noon the next day the sea captains Thomas Pickering and John Langdon collected the Sons of Liberty and a large crowd, James Jr. among them, at the Parade by the North Church, summoned by a drum beaten up and down the city streets. Governor Wentworth sent Chief Justice Theodore Atkinson to direct the group to disperse. They did not.

Reinforced by men from Rye and Newcastle, the mob of four hundred marched to the fort, which was guarded by only six men. At the riverbank, the rebels secured two gondolas to ferry part of the force out to the fort. They easily mounted the sloped turf ramparts on the western side and surprised and confined the garrison. Although shots were fired, no one was injured. It was recorded that "the mob triumphantly gave three huzzas as they hauled down the King's colors." The successful foray was described "in the British Annals as the first action of the rebels against British soldiery, preparatory to the war of the Revolution."

Ninety-seven barrels of gunpowder were then hauled off to Durham for safekeeping, and on the following day a second group, led by General John Sullivan, returned and took away sixteen cannons, about sixty muskets, and other military stores.

Governor Wentworth was embarrassed and furious, but lacking troops, he was virtually powerless. He wrote to Admiral Graves in Boston asking that a man-of-war be stationed in Portsmouth Harbor, and on December 19 the *H.M.S. Scarborough* entered the Piscataqua and moored there. On December 26 the governor issued a proclamation of rebellion, ordering the magistrates to imprison the offenders. The order was ignored.

Will and Jack Odiorne followed these events intently, pondering whether full-scale American rebellion and independence could aid the cause of freedom for themselves and the colonies' other African captives.

"Colonists could lose," Jack pointed out. "Bad for us."

"If we—they—fight," Will said, "I think they'll win."

On March 30, 1775, George III signed into law the New England Restraining Act, which stated that New Englanders could not trade with any country of the world except Great Britain and Ireland and denied them access to the fishing banks off Newfoundland and Nova Scotia.

On the night of April 18, Gage, the British general in command in Boston, sent a detail to neighboring Concord to destroy the colonists' munitions there. Paul Revere and others warned the towns in the area, and by break of day on the nineteenth, when the redcoats reached Lexington, they were met on the green by militia from as far away as New Hampshire. A black slave by the name of Prince Estabrook was among those minutemen. Firing broke out and continued as the British marched to the Concord Bridge, where they were repulsed by "the embattled farmers" and forced to retreat back to Boston.

News of this dramatic clash spread like wildfire throughout the colonies, back to London and, indeed, to the whole world. American radicals were eager to push on, but when the Second Continental Congress met as scheduled in May, its actions were ambivalent. On the one hand it appointed George Washington as commander in chief of the "Army of the United Colonies," that being the militia fighting in Massachusetts; on the other, it concocted an "Olive Branch Petition" to King George, begging him to stop the war.

When the Congress finally ended its session in July, Will said, "Offering an olive branch to a scoundrel is like handing a gun to a criminal. The whites have got to stop this appeasement."

In Portsmouth, Captain Barclay of the *Scarborough* established a blockade of the harbor, seizing provision ships and sending them to Boston for the use of General Gates and his troops. He also began impressing colonial seamen. At the town meeting that was called immediately, Captain John Martin declared that he had lost two ships and nineteen sailors.

He pounded on the rostrum. "You Tories are killing trade and destroying this town," he shouted.

The outcry was heightened when Barclay seized the colonial sloop *King Fisher* for attempting to violate the New England Restraining Act. That act was imposing great hardships on the city's mercantile and shipping families, many of whom had not engaged in revolutionary activity of any sort up to that point. Further, many of the city's less fortunate were losing their jobs. Slave labor became even more important to the city's businessmen.

Governor Wentworth himself was becoming submersed in hotter and hotter water. On June 13 he was visited by a friend, Colonel John Fenton. Fenton had told his Exeter neighbors that "Conciliation with the crown is our only hope. We don't have the resources to challenge the mightiest country in the world!" But Fenton's efforts to placate them infuriated his fellow townsmen, and the provincial congress at Exeter determined to capture the Tory and bring him to trial. While Fenton was at the governor's house, a large mob armed with a cannon appeared outside the residence.

"Fenton, we know you're in thayuh," a man called out. "Tell your friend the Gov'nuh that we'll blow his house to the ground 'less you come out—now!"

Fenton wisely opened the door and surrendered. The crowd, bearing torches in the darkness, carted him off to Exeter.

Wentworth saw the handwriting on the wall.

Later that same evening he called Abi into his study. His voice was shaking as he explained that he needed her assistance so he and his wife could escape to safety at Fort William and Mary, under the protective guns of the *Scarborough*.

As he pulled papers from his desk and packed them into leather satchels, he told her, "You must come with us in the rowboat out to the fort, then return the boat to the dock so no one will realize we're gone."

Still grateful to the governor for his support in letting her keep William Jr., Abi readily agreed. "But what do I say when people find out?"

"If anyone comes to the door, tell him we're upstairs asleep."

After darkness fell, the three stole down to the dock on the mill-pond at the back of the property and climbed into the rowboat, carrying the papers and one small bag of their belongings. The governor rowed silently across the river inlet to the fort. He and his wife stepped onto the island.

As Abi was about to row back to the dock by the house, Wentworth said, "As soon as our absence is discovered, Mr. Theodore Atkinson, the chief justice, will come by the house to pick you up. He's your owner. I sold you to him."

Sold! *Re*sold. Abi had friends who'd been resold. You could never be sure about the temperament of the new owner, how you were going to be treated.

"Governor Wentworth," she said, "please, set me free. I worked hard for you. I deserve freedom. Please think of my children. Won't you—"

"I'm sorry, Abigail. I've already spoken to Mr. Atkinson. The matter is closed."

Abi felt numb. She tried to take some solace in the fact that Atkinson had a reputation as an affable and fair man. But he was a Tory, and as she rowed back across the inlet she became very nervous about what lay ahead for her as well as for the children.

In August, Captain Barclay, facing a refusal of the townsmen to provision his ship, told Governor Wentworth that he was returning to Boston. Realizing that his protection would be gone, the governor and his wife boarded the *Scarborough* on the August 23. Back to Boston they went, and from there, later, to England.

After the departure, the townsmen demolished the fort. Wentworth was never replaced. By default, the government of New Hampshire was assumed by the revolutionary Committee of Safety sitting in Exeter.

Abi quietly moved with her two children to the Atkinson house on Jefferson Street three days after the Wentworth escape. She was hoping her life would settle down, not become more complicated or endangered. But she worried more and more that the American patriots would take reprisals against her Tory owner, threatening both her and the children.

⚜

Will's hopes had been buoyed by the news from Boston in June that the raw colonial militia had inflicted a thousand casualties on the British regulars under General Howe, incurring just over four hundred casualties themselves at the battle of Bunker Hill, in Charlestown. Will and all other New Hampshire men took pride in the reports that their own Colonel John Stark and more than seven hundred men from their province had figured prominently in the battle. The African community in Portsmouth was also pleased to hear that two black soldiers, Peter Salem and Salem Poor, had been with the American minutemen. Will told Abi that he was seriously considering asking James Jr. for permission to enlist in the army General Washington was putting together in Cambridge, Massachusetts. Abi was horrified.

"Will!" she cried. "You might be hurt or even killed. Why do you want to fight for these people?"

"I've done a lot of thinking lately, Abi. Lot of things have come together in my mind. They all point in the same direction. First of all, it's better than going on like we are. I believe it's our only chance. I don't think there's any way the whites can deny us freedom if we go to war for them. And if we're going to get fair treatment and participation in the new government when the Americans win the fight, we're going to have to be *in* the fight. I've got to be part of it. Not just for myself, but for you, the children, all of us here. Fighting alongside the white soldiers, I'll get to know them better, and they can get to know me. I can build their confidence in me by showing what I can do."

Abi wiped away a tear, then looked closely at Will. "That's all very high and mighty. What are you *not* saying?"

Will stood up and paced. "All right ... I'm excited by the thought of going to war. My father, his father, all our ancestors were warriors. They used to tell me stories of their battles. It's a family tradition—"

"Men and their fighting."

"Someday Africans here in America are going to have to fight. Somebody's got to be experienced enough to be a leader."

Abi sighed deeply. "I hear the governor of Virginia has offered freedom to all Africans who'll desert their masters and fight against the American rebels," Abi said. "Hundreds of men have already joined him. Wouldn't it be better to do that?"

"Virginia's a long way away," Will said. "Besides, how can you trust him? God knows where we'd end up even if the British turn back the rebellion, but you know what? I don't think they can. Besides, that's the wrong way to go, philosophically. The English are against freedom for anyone on this continent. The Americans are for it. And I don't like what the English are doing any more than the whites do. I don't like them. I think the colonists are right and that they—*we*—should fight for the freedom we believe in."

"But why fight for either white side?"

"Fighting is the only way left for me to gain enough respect in Portsmouth to take on Bannister and Caesar. If our own leaders are helping keep us enslaved. . . . I'm making progress on my plans to push them aside, but right now they've still got me boxed in. And—"

She put two fingers on his lips. "I give up. You probably got six more reasons." She kissed him. "Guess when I married you, I got your principles *and* your stubbornness."

21

*T*he afternoon of Thursday, September 14, 1775, was a warm one with only a slight breeze off the harbor. As James Jr. and Will approached the South School Street house on the way home from the tanyard, they were surprised to see a horse and wagon pulled up by the front walk. James III had driven up from Newburyport for a visit with his uncle. The two hugged each other tightly.

"Good to see you too, Will," the younger James said. "How've you been?"

"Fine, thanks, Master James. Missed you around here."

The two white men turned into the parlor to talk. Will headed back to the kitchen, which was within earshot of the conversation through an open door. He listened while he helped Mrs. Haven prepare for supper.

"I'm living in Newbury now, Uncle James, just below Newbury-port. Would you believe it? I'm owner and captain of my own topsail schooner, the *Broad Bay*. That's the reason for my visit—I'd really like your take on the current political situation. How heavily should we get involved, particularly with the radicals?"

"I don't think we have any choice," James said. "King George and Parliament have taken away all other options. We'll have to support those who're working to preserve our freedom—even if it means fighting. I'm personally getting too old, and I have no one who could run the tannery in my absence. But I belong to the Sons of Liberty here and support the cause. Reverend Haven, by the way, is solidly behind us."

"I'm glad to hear you say that, because I'm on the verge of signing up. I've been approached by a man named Tracy, Nathaniel Tracy, who's one of the richest men in Newburyport. At the request of General Washington, he's put up seven hundred pounds of his own money to fit out a fleet of eleven ships to transport a thousand troops to a certain destination. That's all in confidence, and I can't tell you any more than that. I've got to go back tomorrow. I'll agree then to head up the flotilla with the *Broad Bay*."

"Anybody from New Hampshire involved?"

"Yes, that young doctor from Epping, next door, Henry Dearborn. He's a captain in charge of a company of New Hampshire men he trained up here last spring. He's in Cambridge with General Washington right now."

At that moment Will came into the parlor under the pretext of serving coffee. "I remember Dr. Dearborn—trained under Dr. Hall Jackson here in Portsmouth. Good man. I'd like to serve in the army under him."

James Jr. laughed. "Come on, Will. You aren't serious!"

"I think he is, Uncle Jim. Why not let him come back with me tomorrow and we'll see what can be arranged? Other Negroes serve in the militias, even though General Washington at first opposed it. He faced reality and changed his mind after so many slaves accepted Governor Dunmore's offer in Virginia and went to fight for the British. At the very least, Will could help ready my ship for the voyage and then come back."

"How long an expedition are we talking about?" James asked.

"The voyage itself, up and back, will probably be over and done with in a week. The campaign by the troops could take several months."

"Well, it's an interesting proposition. I've been concerned about no one from the family being in the fight. And work at the tannery has fallen way off, so the timing is good. Will, if you really mean it, you've got yourself a deal. Just so long as you are back here by next spring when the tannery gets busy again."

Will was so excited that he could hardly gobble down his supper fast enough. He had three important stops to make right away.

The first was to see Caesar, over at the Bannister residence. There he simply told the king that he would be away for several months with the Clarkson nephew in Massachusetts. Both agreed that Jack Odiorne could do double duty as viceroy while Will was away.

The second stop was at the house of Elijah Hall, the white owner of the ships supplies business. His slave Seneca had been on the *Exeter* with Will.

"Seneca, I've got to be away for a few months. While I'm gone, I'd like you to try and find something out for me. We know the whites are still bringing in slaves to Portsmouth. They try to hide it—only one at a time with no public auction. The captive is quietly placed with one of the slave trader's good customers. What I want to know is how this trade is financed and who's doing it."

"Wondered the same thing myself. If you say I got a couple of months, maybe I can come up with something."

"Good man. Careful, now. Don't want anyone to know."

"No problem. Take care of yourself."

The third stop was a difficult visit to the Atkinson mansion to tell Abi. He swore her to secrecy, then filled her in.

"I've got to go, Abi. I've explained why."

"Don't explain again—I understand. But I'm so scared." Tears welled up in her eyes.

Will pulled her to him and hugged her as hard as he dared, rocking her back and forth, assuring her over and over that everything would be all right.

"But you'll be gone for so long. You could be killed. How will the children manage without a father?

"You're a strong woman and a strong mother. You'll be able to handle them just fine. And you won't have to raise them without me—I'll be back safe and sound by spring."

They slipped up to Abi's room, where they gazed at the sleeping boy and girl for several minutes. Finally Will leaned forward and kissed each of them. He then kissed Abi, turned around, and slipped out the door, pulling on his cap as he stepped into the chilly night air.

The next morning Will was up well before daybreak to complete his barn chores before leaving. James III arose shortly thereafter, and by the time the sun was rising over the Atlantic, the two men were on the wagon rolling south to Massachusetts.

During the ride the young sea captain disclosed a few additional facts about the expedition. "The leader is going to be Colonel Benedict Arnold. He's already distinguished himself as a fighter. The destination is Quebec, Canada. My job will be to ferry the troops from Newburyport to the mouth of the Kennebec River in Maine. From that point, the soldiers will proceed by river and land up the Kennebec, cross westerly on the Dead River, and then travel down the Chaudière River to the St. Lawrence and Quebec City. This week the troops have been marching from Cambridge up to Newbury and Newburyport. By tonight everyone should be assembled."

Will said, "I can't wait to start."

He slept in a back room at Clarkson's house in Newbury that night. James woke him early on Saturday morning, and they went immediately to the Newbury Trayneing Green to seek out the New Hampshire company, commanded by Henry Dearborn. Dearborn was nowhere to be found. Finally, James and Will learned that the captain had marched his men to Newburyport that morning and they were assembling on the common there. Will and James promptly hitched up the wagon and made haste to the port city, where they spied Dearborn directing his men in pitching their tents for encampment next to the Presbyterian meetinghouse where Jonathan Parsons, James's stepfather, was the minister.

The captain remembered them both and was happy to see them. James explained his objective—to have Will join as a soldier with one of Arnold's units, preferably Dearborn's. Dearborn was skeptical at first, not only because of potential racial difficulties but also because Will had missed the training at Cambridge.

"Can Will be trusted with weapons?" he asked.

"Not a problem," James said. "His sole objective is to fight for the colonists."

"Well . . . I need every man I can get. All right, James, Will is sensible and smart, so I should be able to handle any race reaction, but he's got to start at full clip today—fitted up by my supply officer, then into the drills we're continuing right here on the common. What experience have you had with weapons, Will?"

"None with firearms, sir."

"We'll have to fix that. I'll assign you to one of my men to take you through the basics."

James Clarkson at this point took his leave of the other two to look for Colonel Arnold and receive further instructions for the voyage to the Kennebec. Dearborn directed Will to a large tent, where supply officer Lieutenant Ammi Andrews issued him a musket, a tomahawk, a long all-purpose knife, and a uniform consisting of an ash-colored hunting shirt, leggings, and moccasins—garb fashioned after that of the New England Indians.

He was then taken to the tent of Lieutenant Nathaniel Hutchins, second in command of the company. Dearborn asked him to have one of his men brief Will on the training that was taking place and run him through the basics of weapon handling and cleaning.

"Have him ready by Sunday morning at ten forty-five," the captain called as he left to return to his own tent. "Colonel Arnold will be here at eleven o'clock sharp to review the company. I want every man standing tall on the common by ten-fifty."

Hutchins chose a sergeant, Jonathan Perkins, to give Will intensive training during that day and the following morning in preparation for the review by Arnold.

Perkins immediately set Will up in a tent with three other men, then took the four of them aside and ran them through various formations and marching exercises. After that, alone with Will, he demonstrated how to break down and clean the musket. Will next joined the other soldiers, who were busy making cartridges for their muskets. He learned how to open a keg of powder, roll pieces of cartridge paper into cylinders, fill the cylinders with powder, twist the ends, and pack the cylinders into cartridge boxes. Perkins then took Will to a makeshift shooting range and showed him how to load the weapon with a cartridge by biting the paper from an end, pouring the powder into the barrel of the musket, and using the cartridge paper as a wad, which then was rammed down the barrel, pushing the powder and ball compactly into the butt end. Will practiced this maneuver and actual shooting—which he seemed to be good at—for several hours before darkness halted his training.

After an evening meal of pork, bread, and water, he returned to his tent. His three tent mates told stories about their experiences with Dearborn at Bunker Hill. Finally, tired, the men rolled over for some much-needed sleep.

On Sunday morning, a bugle awakened everyone before dawn. All turned out for morning formation, then breakfasted on hard rolls and coffee. Lieutenant Hutchins took Will aside again and walked him through basic battle formations and tactics. Will soaked up the information instantly with no need for repetition.

He liked the army.

PART TWO

War: 1775–1777

22

*A*t ten fifty in the morning of September 17, 1775, Will and the other New Hampshire musketmen were ready and lined up at parade rest on Newburyport Common. Will seemed to be the only African in the expedition. He received strange looks from some soldiers who must have wondered about or feared the sight of an African in uniform with a gun.

At precisely eleven o'clock, a drum roll announced the arrival of Colonel Arnold on horseback, and on command the men snapped to attention. Arnold dismounted, chatted briefly with the battalion and company commanders, then began his review.

Will was the next to last man in the first row of Dearborn's company. From that vantage he had a clear view of the colonel as he passed by. About thirty-five years old, he was a good-looking man, though short and stocky. He walked and spoke with the confidence of a born leader, but with a touch of affability that appealed to the men who served under him. When he reached Will, he paused and looked the African deep in the eyes. Will felt as though the colonel was peering right into his mind and soul. He appeared to be satisfied. He said nothing and moved to a central point in front of the battalion to address the troops.

"Men, at the personal request of General Washington, we've been asked to embark upon a secret and important expedition. As you know, the Canadians, who are mainly French, have not seen fit to join the colonies in our campaign against the British. That leaves the American colonies in a vulnerable position. If the English garrison at Quebec was significantly strengthened, it could be used as a base for them to strike through Lake Champlain and down the Hudson River to New York City, splitting New England from the rest of the colonies to the south, destroying our unity and probably ruining our chances for success.

"Our orders are to proceed by sea to the Kennebec River and then by land and river up to Quebec. We'll be joined there by a force under General Philip Schuyler and General Richard Montgomery, who'll move up from New York, take Montreal, and then come to help us in overcoming the British fortifications at Quebec City.

"I want to emphasize that a secondary, peaceful objective of our mission is to win over the hearts and minds of the French Canadians. So putting aside our cultural and religious differences with them, it's essential that we treat them fairly and pleasantly and make it clear that we have no quarrel with them, only with their British masters. Godspeed."

Will felt proud to be going to war under such a strong leader.

After the colonel's speech, the men were dismissed and given the opportunity to attend a church service led by Reverend Samuel Spring, the army's chaplain. Will tagged along. Spring spoke clearly, but he lacked Reverence Haven's intensity and passion.

The weather was heavy and windy that afternoon, so Arnold and his staff elected to delay boarding the transport vessels. But on Monday, when Arnold's scouts reported no signs of British ships or troop movements, the colonel ordered his officers to begin loading even though it looked as though the weather wouldn't clear until Tuesday. By four in the afternoon more than a thousand troops were embarked on eleven sloops and schooners. Colonel Arnold was aboard the lead ship, *Broad Bay*, with Captain Clarkson.

Dearborn's company, on *Eagle*, was second in line for the eighty-five-mile voyage to the mouth of the Kennebec River. Buoyed by a favorable wind, the fleet moved out swiftly along the coast. Standing on deck, Will breathed deeply the clean, cold ocean air. As the cawing of the gulls at the dock stilled in the distance, he felt an exuberance he had never known. Here he was, on a ship, and not belowdecks. Part of a significant military action, with a chance to gain his freedom.

A fair number of men became seasick, but the trip was uneventful until they reached the Kennebec, at approximately ten o'clock the following morning. A fifty-mile passage remained, up the river to the town of Gardinerston, where they were all to rendezvous. But the sight they now faced was terrifying. The Maine coast at this point was little more than an endless series of jagged rocky islands and peninsulas. Will looked up and saw a black storm gathering in the eastern sky that promised to make the passage even more treacherous.

Carefully, one by one, the ships entered the channel, aided by a local pilot on the *Broad Bay*. Will's heart was racing as the *Eagle* slowly followed. The ships separated at this juncture in order not to impede each other's course through the narrow, twisting channels.

On Wednesday, the twentieth, Dearborn elected to proceed very cautiously, traversing only nine miles before weighing anchor. The next day he made about the same distance up to Swan Island. Arnold had pressed ahead. Each ship was virtually on its own, and each found itself in one difficulty or another. The rains from the storm that blew in blurred the helmsmen's sight lines, and the winds kicked the boats about like wooden toys.

Will was on the foredeck when suddenly he was pitched forward. He barely managed to grab a gunwale to keep from slipping overboard. The ship had struck an underground shoal, fortunately of sand rather than rock, at a place called Lovejoy's Narrows. Dearborn immediately ordered Will and several others to jump into the water, both to lighten the load and to begin pushing the ship off the underground sandbar. Half an hour later they worked it free and climbed aboard, tired and soaked. Shortly thereafter *Eagle* came to anchor at the upper end of Swan Island. Dearborn and some of his officers went ashore to meet the local inhabitants and spend the night.

Will stayed on the ship with the rest of the men. After a cold meal, some of them started playing checkers on deck. Will watched for a while and quickly grasped how the game was played.

"Mind if I get in the game?" he asked when one of the men decided to stop. The man's opponent looked up at Will, then looked down at the board.

"Don't think so. Had enough for today."

Will smiled. "Sure. Been a long day." So he was going to have an uphill battle here. Not exactly a surprise. One reason he'd signed on was to meet this kind of reaction and overcome it.

He wandered over to two men who were discussing the tough passage up the river they'd experienced that day.

Will said, "At least none of the ships that ran aground was damaged. Soft riverbed." The men stared at him for a few seconds, then turned and walked away down the deck.

All right, men. If that's the way you want it. But he wasn't going away. It was going to be a long expedition.

The next day the ship proceeded to a place called Agry's Point, where a Major Colborn had hurriedly built more than two hundred big wooden canoes, called bateaux. Each bateau, capable of carrying six or seven men with their provisions (one barrel of pork, one bag of meal, and two hundred weight of biscuit per man), was propelled by four oars, two paddles, and two "setting poles" to help keep them off the rocks on the shore as well as push them forward. The bateaux were high and steep at each end, with flared sides and flat bottoms. It took four men to carry one upside down above their heads on a portage.

Will liked the feel of the oar in his hands as he helped pull the bow of the first heavy bateau through the water. September 23, 1775, was a shiny day showcasing thick red, orange, and yellow foliage nearly to the edge of the river on both sides. Will and another soldier in the stern, on orders from Arnold and Dearborn, were rowing the boat from Colborn's yard up to Fort Western, seven miles above Gardinerston. The rest of the two hundred bateaux were filed out behind them for some two miles. As Will's boat made its way upstream against a strong current, he could catch glimpses of the main force of the army on the march as it threaded in and out between the trees along the western bank.

Suddenly, at his feet, the caulking between the boards of the boat's wall gave way and water spewed in, quickly filling the boat with four inches beneath the seats. Will pointed the bateau toward the riverbank, and the men hauled it up on dry land. Cursing their luck, they bent to the task of recaulking. They had to wait for the caulk to set; then they proceeded back into the channel and renewed their voyage. The sun had set before they got to their destination, the last to arrive even though many other boats had similar problems thanks to having been built hastily and with green wood.

At Fort Western, the men were directed to a private home, where several other soldiers had been drinking and eating for an hour or so. Will sat with his boat mate in a corner as they ate their red beans and pork with water, watching and listening to the dozen men gathered in the main living room of the house. Most of them had consumed a fair amount of rum, and the noise level in the room grew louder and louder.

A quarrel broke out between two men over the ownership of a warm red plaid jacket. It was apparently resolved when the others turned one of the two out of the house, a man named James McCormick. But within minutes McCormick reappeared outside a window near where Will sat. He was pointing a gun toward his adversary, a Sergeant Reuben Bishop. Will yelled a warning, but it was too late. McCormick fired a shot into the room, narrowly missing Will's forehead. Bishop fell, the red jacket shredded by the musket ball and splattered with blood. Will ran to him to help, but he was dead. Others ran outside and seized McCormick.

Will returned to his chair and finished his meal. *Stupid. There'll be plenty of fighting for all of us soon enough—crazy to be shooting each other. Our officers are going to have to tighten up on discipline or we'll be in big trouble when the battle starts.*

By the evening of the twenty-fourth, everyone, including those from the late arriving *Swallow*, was ensconced at Fort Western. The troops were about one hundred and seventy-five miles from Quebec City in a straight line, but no one, including Colonel Arnold, knew how much farther it would be on a winding course through the mountainous forest.

Over the next three days, they loaded their provisions into the boats and began to embark, two thirds of them in the bateaux and some birch barks, the rest on foot along the riverbank. They were headed first toward the head of the Kennebec to a point called the Great Carrying Place, where they would portage west about fifteen miles to the Dead River. A scouting party assigned to ascertain and mark the paths led the way in light barks on the twenty-fifth.

The next day, McCormick was tried and found guilty of murder in a court martial at which Will and several others testified. He was then turned over to Captain Clarkson, who was directed to return the man to General Washington for sentencing. Clarkson also took a number of sick troops back with him. Before leaving, James came to visit.

"Take care of yourself, Will. See you in the spring."

That evening, as Will sat alone on the front steps of the house he was assigned to, he overheard two men talking as they passed by.

"What's that nigger doin heah?" one of them said. "Should be back on the fahm."

"Guess we're hahd up for anyone who can fight," said the other.

"Sad state of affairs. Looks strong enough."

Will was now in a totally new situation, away from friends and people who knew him. Who trusted him. That must be what the army was like for everyone. Completely cut off from the outside world. And being black was sure no help. This was like starting all over again to establish himself. He'd better watch his back.

Later, as he drifted toward sleep, he longed for Abi, the children, his friends, even his white acquaintances back in Portsmouth.

———

Captain Dearborn's company was moved out of Colonel Enos's battalion and put under Major Meigs with three other companies. They were in the middle group to embark into the wilderness, on the twenty-seventh, with provisions for forty-five days.

Will was the front oar in the lead bateau with Lieutenant Hutchins, Sergeant Perkins, and four other soldiers—Privates Eliphas Reed, Caleb Edes, Edward Fox, and Joseph Boynton. The men found the fully loaded bateau clumsy and difficult to maneuver. They were rowing against a rapid current on a river full of rocks and increasingly shallow. Soon they came to a half-mile stretch of roaring rapids, and the entire contingent was forced to land portage around them.

Dearborn and Hutchins jumped from their boats and took charge, shouting commands and encouragement as their men stumbled along the bank, each carrying two hundred pounds on his back. The leaders pitched in themselves to carry loads, sweating profusely along with the rest. Although aided by oxen and wagons borrowed from local inhabitants, the portage took almost five hours to complete. Will and his boat mates threw themselves on the ground for a ten-minute rest before they could proceed. Then they were up and off again, pulling hard against the rattling current.

That evening, in recognition of the troops' strenuous work, Major Meigs bought four oxen from the locals and had one dressed for Dearborn's company. Will ate all he could of his portion and packed the remainder in the bow of the bateau before returning to his blanket, padded with leaves on the ground.

In the middle of the night he was awakened by a scraping noise near the bateau where he was sleeping. In the dim moonlight he could see the figure of another soldier rummaging through the sack where Will had stowed his ox meat.

He jumped up and called out, "What are you doing there?" He barely had the words out when he was jumped from behind by two other men and thrown to the ground. He recognized them as Brubaker and Eshelman, from one of the Pennsylvania companies. They both landed on Will and began to pummel him with heavy sticks.

Brubaker said, "This is just a taste of what you're going to get if you stick around, nigger. We don't want you here."

The third man, Kroll, called out from the bateau: "I've got his extra meat and his other stuff. Let's go."

But at that moment Will broke free from the first two men. He grabbed a log and swung hard at Brubaker, connecting across the neck. As Brubaker slid to the ground, unconscious, Eshelman ran at Will, plunging a knife toward his chest. Will sidestepped and tripped his attacker in one quick, graceful movement. He was on the man before he hit the dirt, pounding Eshelman's face with his fists. The third man, Kroll, saw them, dropped Will's food and belongings, and ran.

Will stood up, pulled Eshelman over to Brubaker, and threw him at his cohort, who was beginning to regain consciousness.

"Pick up your friend and get out of here," Will said. "Try that again and I won't stop till you're dead."

Eshelman pulled Brubaker up. Without a word the two brushed themselves off and headed back to the Pennsylvania regiment.

Will picked up his property, stowed it, and went back to his blanket. It was now clear that living with white men who had that kind of hatred was going to be more complicated than he'd envisioned. But as he curled up on the ground and tried to get some sleep before dawn broke and his regiment moved out again, he felt more determined than ever to achieve his goals.

Hitting those white bastards sure felt good.

The portage process was repeated several times during the next five days. As each impassible point was reached, the men leapt into the water and took the lading ashore. Then they passed two hand spikes under the bottom of the boat, and four of them raised and carried it up the bank. The toughest carry was at Norridgewock Falls. Thirty feet straight up. Will finally found a break in the granite precipice about five hundred yards to the east where they could get up and through. Through this period they were making only three miles per day.

After the falls, civilization ended.

Then the rain began, a soft, soothing wash at the start, then hard and biting. The river level rose nearly six feet, and soon the temperature dropped at least twenty degrees. At the end of the day, Will's clothes were soaked through. By the middle of the night they were frozen stiff. He couldn't stop shivering. Several of the men in the company got sick and were sent back or left aside to recover.

On October 10 the contingent arrived at the "Great Carrying Place," where the bulk of the Arnold expedition was already encamped. The weather turned milder, and they took the following day off to catch their breath. Colonel Arnold ordered a few men to build a blockhouse to shelter the sick. While many of the men took the occasion to repair their bateaux and add to their stores of cartridges, Eliphas Reed and Will decided to try and catch some salmon and perch in the river. They discovered that the fish were plentiful and laughed as they raced to see who could land more. In just two hours they caught one hundred and fifty between them. They were cheered by their comrades that evening at the company's fireside meal.

Later that night, for the third day in a row, a sour-faced sergeant assigned Will to latrine duty, which meant covering the full hole and digging a new one. Will carried out the dirty task cheerfully and returned to his blanket without a word.

At dawn the men took stock of their provisions, much of which had been damaged by river- and rainwater. Bread and dried peas were spoiled. Dried fish and beef had lost most of their salt and had to be thrown away.

By the afternoon they were on the move again, staggering toward the Dead River under heavy loads of boats, baggage, and provisions. Three large ponds broke up the effort through the tangled growth of dead and moss-laden trees. Often they sank into the mud up to their waists, their loads falling to the ground.

They arrived at the Dead River on October 16 but couldn't begin its ascent because the weather changed again. Snow flurries swirled around them as they huddled under skeleton trees. Their provisions were running even lower than they'd thought, not only due to spoilage but also because many of the men had failed to follow their daily allowances and had eaten too heartily in the first weeks. Colonel Arnold ordered Major Bigelow to go back with men and boats to Enos with orders to give him all the provisions he could spare. Four days later the bateaux returned with only two barrels of flour.

Despair set in among many of the men, for the only remaining prospect for supplies was at the French settlements on the Chaudière River, still a long way to the north. All they could do was push on.

That evening Will was called with several others to the command tent. Arnold, Dearborn, and a Captain Archibald Steele, from Pennsylvania, told them they were to be part of a scouting party under Steele with orders to move ahead of the main army and to capture or kill a Penobscot Indian named Natanis, who was suspected of being a spy for Carleton, the British commander at Quebec.

"We'll likely find him at a place he supposedly lives in just ahead along the river," Steele said.

The party of a dozen men ate hurriedly and set off into the woods. At about four o'clock in the morning they spotted a clearing some one hundred yards ahead. In the center of it a small cabin stood out in the moonlight. Steele ordered them to encircle the clearing and on a bobwhite whistle from him to close in quickly.

At the signal, Will darted out from behind his spruce-tree hiding place and ran toward the cabin as fast as he could, musket at the ready. His footsteps sounded like drums in his ears, but no one appeared from the building. The others arrived just behind him. Steele rushed the door. The rest ran in right behind him. The room was warm; embers of a wood fire in a corner fireplace were still burning. A pair of Indian moccasins lay by a wooden bunk against the far wall. The cabin was empty. The bird had flown.

Steele charged outside and ordered the men to search the surrounding woods. After several minutes they all returned. No one had been found. The party went back to the campsite and Steele reported to Arnold.

Will walked to his tent, his eyes straining to pierce the darkness of the forest for the red man watching from the trees.

The fates continued to be unkind to their mission. The snow stopped but was replaced with rain, even heavier this time. The river and adjoining ponds rose at least another eight feet, and trees crashed down around them in the face of a roaring wind.

Then came the flood. In the early-morning darkness they awakened to the deafening rush of water. Before they could react, the campsite was engulfed by four feet of water. Several bateaux were capsized and a considerable quantities of guns, clothing, and provisions were lost.

They pulled together what they could of their gear and pushed on. But somehow, confused by the absence of a distinct river channel due to the flooding, Will's group and several others in Dearborn's company took a wrong course up a side river. Will led a search party the next morning that found the way back, but a precious day of forward progress had been lost.

Over the next two days the rain turned to snow, and a vicious wind cut right through Will's shirt, again making him shiver uncontrollably as he pushed through the drifts. He fought off the torment by envisioning warm days at the shore with Abi and the children. He gritted his teeth in desperate resolve to make it to the destination where he could participate in the victory.

Finally the lead companies reached the head of the Dead River, and then began a ten-mile march that crossed ponds, tributaries, and even waterfalls to a high mountain ridge known as the Height of Land. During the stretches over water, Will's view from the bateau was virtually cut off by blinding snow squalls, and several times the men had to row ashore to bail out the boat.

The Height of Land rose before them at an average angle of thirty-five degrees, but in certain sections it was almost straight up. This carrying place over a gap in the ridge and another twenty miles to Lake Megantic, the head of the Chaudière River, was called the Boundary Portage, being the crossing point over the boundary between Maine and Canada.

The territory that lay before them up the ridge was not only trackless but nearly impassable as well. As Will plowed forward with the bateau held above his back and the backs of three others, he soon came to an area where acres of trees had been laid flat by storms, forcing the company to go far to the west around it and recover their bearings as best they could. Slipping into mire holes and bogs, and with twigs snapping in their eyes, they could make no more than two miles per day. Then it was up, up, and up around craggy outcroppings. Will's feet were cut through his moccasins, which were falling apart, leaving blood spots in his footprints on the snow. Many of the men had frostbite. Finally they reached the top. The men fell to the ground, exhausted.

After a short rest, they pushed on to a large, flat meadow where Arnold's advance company had established camp. By the afternoon of October 28, the entire expeditionary force had arrived from over the mountains.

Except Colonel Enos and his men.

The news raced through the camp: Colonel Enos, citing dwindling provisions but without permission from Arnold, had turned back to the Kennebec with the three hundred men under his command and the bulk of the remaining provisions. In a single stroke, the army had lost nearly a third of its number.

"God damn it!" Will said, glad Reverend Haven wasn't there to hear him.

"Hope they burn in hell," said Edward Fox.

Eliphas Reed said, "I hope they all drown on the way back."

"They won't," Will said. "They were in the rear—we cleared their way, made it easier for them."

"You got that right," Reed said.

Apart from the men, many guns and much ammunition had been lost. The lack of food was now so severe that starvation became their main enemy.

Eliphas Reed said to Will and Joe Boynton, "My God, we'll never make it."

"Stop that kind of talk," Will said. "We've got to. So we will."

Arnold immediately cut the food ration still further and dispatched Captain Hanchet with fifty-five men to proceed to the French settlements and send back provisions. Then he walked throughout the camp, encouraging his men and assuring them that relief was not far away.

At dawn the march to Lake Megantic started. The going was somewhat easier for most of the route, but difficulties remained. To reach the lake, they discovered that it was necessary to cross a small river.

"It's got to be fordable at some point," Dearborn said. With Will rowing, he set off in a canoe to find the right place. Eventually they came across Captain Goodrich, who had waded up and down the river, sometimes up to his armpits in water and ice, looking for a ford. He looked half frozen.

"Too deep in both directions," he said.

Dearborn and Will pulled Goodrich into the canoe and returned to the other men. They began the crossing in the bateaux and several quickly constructed rafts.

Once across, they came upon another stream, which they followed, thinking it flowed into the Megantic. Unfortunately, it did not, and both companies lost their bearings and ended up about fifteen miles off course into the forest, away from the lake. It was only with the help of a young Indian they met who had some knowledge of the country that they made their way to the lake a day later. The Indian reminded Will of his old enemy Simo—in appearance, but fortunately not in disposition.

During their trek, little semblance of military order remained as they walked slowly through the falling snow in scattered groups of threes, fours, and fives.

Lake Megantic lies almost eleven hundred feet above the St. Lawrence, and the straight distance to Quebec is some seventy-five miles. The lake and the river are connected by the Chaudière, which means "cauldron" in English, a word that well describes the boiling, foaming stream.

Weak from lack of food, Dearborn's men prepared to run the gauntlet.

That day Will and several others boiled cartridge boxes, tattered shoes, and pieces of clothing into a soup, to put something, anything, into their stomachs. Two men in the company begged Dearborn to give them his dog to eat, and he finally relented.

Meanwhile, Hanchet's advance party and Arnold's own company had canoed rapidly down the Chaudière, interrupted only by several portages around stretches of rapids, reaching the first French inhabitants on October 30. Stopping at several small villages, Arnold purchased, largely with his own money, every item of food the inhabitants would sell, including flour, horses and cattle for slaughter, potatoes, oatmeal, and mutton, and immediately sent the bulk of it back to the men in the rear.

Dearborn's company followed down the Chaudière with difficulty but no major pitfalls and caught up with Arnold on November 6. Dearborn himself had developed pneumonia during the
week and at this point was so ill that he put Lieutenant Hutchins in
charge of the company and hired lodging with a local family, just
below the town of St. Mary, until he could recover and rejoin the
army.

Hutchins then set off down the river. After a three-day march
through deep snow, on November 9, more than seven weeks after
setting sail from Newburyport, they stood on the south bank of the
St. Lawrence at Point Levi, opposite the city of Quebec.

Miraculously, some six hundred and fifty men had made it.
They were thin. Their ripped clothes hung off their shoulders like
rags. Some men had moccasins made of fresh hides, the shoes of
others were falling apart, some had no shoes at all. Only a few had
hats.

All of them stood in awe at what they saw across the broad
river. Quebec, Britain's Canadian stronghold, rose on the north
bank of the St. Lawrence.

"The Gibraltar of America," Arnold said.

The upper part of the city was a natural fortification, a rocky
promontory rising over three hundred feet above the river and the
lower town, which lay to the west. The city had a spacious and
deep harbor. A small river, the St. Charles, flowed to the northwest
from the eastern tip of the upper city. The British had held Quebec
since 1759, when General James Wolfe gave his life in seizing it
from the French. Ed Fox's reaction was that the stronghold looked
impenetrable and that it would be foolish even to try to attack it
with their weakened force.

Will nodded, but said, "Looks like they might be vulnerable
from the west."

23

Colonel Arnold surveyed the situation and quickly devised a strategy. His first objective was to transport all of the men to the north side of the river to a point west of the lower town, which lay to the left of the fortified bluffs as he viewed the scene from the south. This was not an easy task because the British frigate *Lizard*, of twenty-six guns, and the sloop-of-war *Hunter* lay before them in the river, easily a mile and a half across at this point.

Will noticed guard boats from the two ships passing back and forth in front of the troops. The American army's presence had been discovered.

The challenge was compounded by the fact that all canoes belonging to the French inhabitants on the south side of the river had been destroyed or taken by the British to foil an American crossing. Arnold calculated that he would need forty canoes for the purpose, but he presently had only fifteen in safe condition. Will and a dozen others immediately set about repairing the damaged ones. Arnold sent two officers in each direction along the river to try and procure more.

The men had food now, but their provisions were still severely low. Arnold instructed his officers to canvass the local residents and buy clothing and food. Some men with money of their own spent it for shoes or warmer garb.

The French were quite willing to deal cordially with Arnold's troops when it came to taking their money. And a number of local families took in and cared for many of the men who were sick. But in other respects the reception was far short of what General Washington and Arnold had hoped for. The colonel circulated throughout the area a letter from Washington to the people of Canada urging them to join with the southern colonies in casting off the tyranny of the British and assuring them that Arnold's army came as friends and liberators. Arnold and the rest of the men followed Washington's instructions to be courteous and friendly to these townspeople in the hope that many would rally to the fight against King George's garrison on the hill.

But the French were cautious. They preferred to see how the battle played out first. About forty Indians and only a few Canadians cast their lot with the Americans. The rest stood aside and watched or even sided with the British. In a letter to General Montgomery in Montreal, Arnold made the excuse that the Canadians would have assisted if the Americans had arrived with a sufficient force. He also noted that a large number of English reinforcements had recently showed up—had he only gotten there ten days earlier, he'd no doubt have taken the city with ease.

Nor was the weather cooperating. For three days the winds were so strong that many canoes would surely capsize if an attempt was made to cross the river. The Americans put the time to good use by building new boats and making preparations for scaling the walls of the fortress.

On the thirteenth, the weather relaxed, and Arnold decided to make the move across the St. Lawrence that evening. Between ten and eleven o'clock, the army assembled as quietly as possible on the beach and embarked in shifts aboard thirty-five birch barks. Will was in the third wave, riding in a heavy-laden canoe with Captain Steele and two others, proceeding slowly and silently between the two British vessels, which were moored about a half mile apart. Fortunately, surveillance by the guard boats had stopped at dusk.

Suddenly one of the men in Will's boat shifted too quickly, and the canoe tipped under the weight and scuttled. The icy water was such a shock that Will almost passed out. Three canoes nearby pulled him up along with the two other privates, but the boat that maneuvered over to help Steele was so full that there was no room for him. He was forced to throw his arms around the stern while a man in the boat held tightly to his arms. He was hauled through the freezing water for the remainder of the crossing to Wolfe's Cove, about a mile and a half above the city.

By four a.m., some five hundred men had been ferried across. While the canoes went back again for yet another load, some of the men already on the north side found some driftwood on the beach and lit a fire to fend off the cold. The British caught sight of it, and the Americans heard bells in the city sounding an alarm and drums beating to arms.

Arnold decided to halt the crossing and bring the rest across the following night. He marshaled those who had made it across and headed west over the Plains of Abraham to a mill and farmhouse owned by Quebec's former lieutenant governor Major Caldwell, who was absent in the city. Arnold and his officers took over the house as their headquarters. Will and many of the other men moved into the several outlying buildings. This place marked the left, westernmost end of the American line. Guards were posted for four miles to the east, down to a point opposite the city.

Will threw his gear down in a corner of one of the Caldwell sheds and sat down on a bare bunk, thinking back over the long march and ahead to the fighting yet to come. He hoped the people back home in Portsmouth would hear about that march and appreciate what they were going through up here. So far it had been mainly a matter of survival. Now he had to show what he could do in battle. He couldn't wait to hear Arnold's plan.

Exhausted, he wrapped himself in a blanket Hutchins had given him and lay back on the bunk. Within seconds he was asleep, and he didn't awaken until ten hours later, in mid-afternoon of the following day, most appreciative of the extra rest.

⸻

Arnold and his staff were busy that morning analyzing their best course of action. When a courier reported that General Montgomery had taken Montreal, Arnold requested in a dispatch that the general proceed with his 2000 men down the St. Lawrence to Quebec, a distance of just over one hundred and fifty miles, yielding a combined American force of more than 2600—a number Arnold believed would be sufficient to overpower the British total of 1900, even though the defenders of the city were well entrenched. Arnold also asked Montgomery for food, clothing, and provisions for his own men.

While he waited for Montgomery, Arnold sent Will and two others with another dispatch—a demand, in the name of the United American Colonies, for immediate surrender—to the Honorable Hector T. Cramache, the reigning lieutenant governor of Quebec, threatening to storm the city if the demand was rejected. The British responded with a rain of fire upon the three Americans as they quickly ran back to cover.

Arnold ordered an evaluation of their stock of arms and ammunition. Will and many others found that most of their cartridges were unfit for use—there were only between five and ten serviceable rounds for each man. Arnold pulled the force back to Point-Aux-Trembles, about twenty miles north of Quebec. The British sloop *Hunter* and two schooners followed them up the river and moored opposite their campsite, but took no aggressive action. In the meantime, Arnold's spies reported that the British continued to collect provisions and buttress the defense of the city's walls and that they had burned Major Caldwell's farm buildings to prevent further use of them by the Americans.

Finally, on December 1, General Montgomery arrived with some artillery—and not 2000 men but only three hundred, putting the total American force at nine hundred and seventy-five soldiers, many of whom were barely fit for duty. Montgomery also brought a group of Canadians, numbering somewhere between two hundred and four hundred, but their willingness to enter the fray was not at all clear.

The next order Will received was two days later, when Hutchins informed the company that they were to march back down to the Plains of Abraham. Will drew down new clothing and moccasins from the stores Montgomery had brought with him and joined the others in the march to the east.

On arriving at Quebec, Montgomery moved to the village of St. Johns, Arnold to the village of St. Roche. Montgomery's troops began to set up their artillery on the Plains. As this work continued, on the ninth, Will looked up from where he was digging a breastwork around a cannon and noticed a tall, frail man emerge from a carryall carriage about a hundred yards to the rear and begin to walk, with the aid of a cane, toward the company. It was Dearborn! Returning to the fight. Cheers rose from his men as they rushed to surround and greet their leader. They were overjoyed—they'd heard rumors that he had died from his illness.

Dearborn grasped Will's hand and several others' and called out to all: "Thanks, boys. It's good to be with you again. But I can see there's lots of work being done, so get to it. I've got to see Colonel Arnold now. I'll be back to you shortly."

An hour later he returned and brought them up to date on the plans. "Here it is, men. As soon as the artillery units are deployed, we'll begin a siege of the city, blocking the peninsula from here, and hit them with cannon and mortar. We'll look for a night with heavy weather to enter the city at two points. Montgomery will hit the upper town. With Arnold, we'll attack the lower. We're outnumbered, but we can prevail if we concentrate on just two narrow points. We expect the French inhabitants to come over to our side at that time."

Will raised his hand. "Sir, what if they don't join us?"

Dearborn just looked at him for a few seconds. Then he said, "Good question, Will. In that case, we'll adjust as necessary to the situation. I'll raise your point with Colonel Arnold."

Several soldiers seemed to look at Will in a new way. As they all returned to their respective bivouac areas, he heard one say, "That nigger's got a head on his shoulders."

<hr/>

The next morning the enemy began a heavy cannonade on their emplacement, and the Americans responded in kind. The fusillades continued intermittently for seven days. Only a handful of Americans were killed or wounded, but several came down with smallpox. Will was astonished at how quickly the disease took its toll. A man in his company named Joshua Wiggins, who'd been very pleasant to Will, came down with the plague one afternoon, consumed by a high fever. Two days later he was dead. Ed Fox and Will managed to dig a shallow grave for him in the frozen ground near the camp. Ed made a wooden cross and stood it in the soil on top.

The clear weather held. The busy activity and better food helped to restore Dearborn's health, and he discarded the cane.

Arnold and his staff became concerned about further delay because the enlistments of many of the men expired on the first of January. Many were grousing, and some had even deserted.

That night Will was sitting with Joseph Boynton in their room in one of the three houses where Dearborn's company was quartered, talking about when they expected the order to move forward into battle.

"Will, I've been meaning to ask you," Boynton said suddenly. "What in the world are you doing here?"

"Same thing you are."

"I had to come, I was drafted. But you're a slave, you didn't have to join up."

"I'm hoping that if I fight well, the Clarksons will grant me my freedom."

"I sure wish you good luck on that, but if I were you, I wouldn't count on it."

"What do you mean?"

"Nobody's going to give up a slave for that reason. Only if they need the money and sell him, or they don't have the work for him anymore, or he's no good and giving them trouble."

"Then what do *you* think I can do to improve my chances of being freed?"

"Nothing. It's a matter of economics and what kind of man your owner is. It's circular. The harder you work for him, the better job you do, the more he figures you're worth to him and the less likely he'll be to let you go. Think about it. You—"

A British cannonball crashed through the wall of the room and rolled across the floor between them. They dove for cover under their bunks, but nothing else happened. They nailed a tarp across the hole and turned in for the night.

The weather turned foul the morning of the January 31, 1776—cold, windy, and the beginnings of snow flurries, ideal for a surprise attack. Their leaders made one last-minute adjustment: Attacking the upper and lower towns at the same time was deemed too difficult, so they'd all go after the lower at the same time, Arnold on the side of St. Roque, Montgomery by way of Cape Diamond, on the edge of the St. Lawrence. A false attack was to be made east of St. John's Gate. When the two battalions met in the middle of the lower town, they'd mingle priests, women, and children with the troops and attack the upper town.

At their officers' direction, Will and the others affixed hemlock sprigs in their hats to distinguish themselves from the enemy during the fighting. They joked about whether it would really help in the flurry of battle. Ed Fox said, "I'll probably get shot while I'm trying to see whether the other fellow has one of these things on."

At five o'clock, the appointed hour, the attack began.

Arnold and his men led off, followed by Captain Lamb's artillery company with a six-pounder mounted on a sled, and then Captain Daniel Morgan's riflemen. Moving through St. Roque, they came upon a two-gun British picketed battery, which they rushed, their field piece having bogged down in the snow and been left behind. A battle raged for nearly an hour, with several killed on both sides, before the Americans overran the battery and took thirty prisoners. In the process, Colonel Arnold was wounded in the leg but shouted: "Rush on, brave boys, rush on!"

At Cape Diamond, disaster immediately struck General Montgomery and his men. They quickly surmounted the first picketed barrier and started to move into the town, Montgomery shouting at them to step faster—"Come on my good soldiers, your general calls upon you to come on." As he spoke, he was unknowingly close to a British battery of several cannon loaded with grapeshot, which fired and cut down the general, his aide-de-camp, Captain McPhearson, Captains Cheeseman and Hendricks, and four privates. A Colonel Campbell took command. Missing a good opportunity to rush in, he ordered a retreat.

This development left the British free to turn to Arnold's sector and focus their forces there. The main body was late in coming up to support Arnold's lead detachment, having become confused in the storm and temporarily lost its way. Dearborn's company brought up the rear.

Will was in the middle rank as the company proceeded single file through the streets of St. Roque. The snow was already two feet deep, and it continued to fall heavily. Several wounded men passed him going the other way. He saw the wounded Colonel Arnold returning, being helped along by Parson Spring and Major Ogden, who was also wounded, in the shoulder. Will's alertness intensified as the reality of battle unfolded before him.

They soon came under fire from the English pickets hidden in both lower and upper stories of the houses along the sides of the streets, which were no more than twenty feet wide. At first Will did not realize that the quiet *flit-flit-flit*s by his ears were the sounds of enemy musket balls just missing him through the driving snow.

The company fell in behind Captain Morgan's riflemen, who were getting stiff resistance from a second British battery armed with four cannons firing grapeshot. Will and the two men on either side of him found they could not fire their guns because the powder had become wet. This problem was so widespread that Dearborn ordered everyone into the lower room of a nearby house to prime their guns and prick dry powder into the touchholes. He then ordered them to split into two groups. The first stayed with him. The second, including Will, was put under the command of a Lieutenant Pierce and directed to swing back one block of streets, loop around, and flank the battery from a side street.

Pierce's detachment moved out at double time and quickly circled in from the side against the redcoats. But as they started firing, British soldiers in the houses and behind the wooden barricade returned a heavy fusillade that felled two men on either side of Will. Lieutenant Pierce kept moving toward the barricade with the intent to overrun it, calling to his men to follow. As he walked forward, a British soldier stood and took aim at him. Will had just reloaded and saw the danger. He swung his musket around quickly and shot. The redcoat lurched back from a direct hit in the chest, blood spurting forth as he fell behind the barricade.

Pierce once again spurred on the men, but at that moment the main force of Dearborn's company around the corner was surrounded, and the captain was forced to surrender to save his men from annihilation. He called out to Pierce—and as many of the men as could hear—to escape. Pierce immediately ordered his men to retreat and to rendezvous back at the hospital where Arnold had been carried.

At that point it was up to every man to save himself and avoid capture. Will turned and began running back down the side street as musket balls flew by him. He made it to the corner safely but kept on running at full clip for nearly a mile, until he cleared the walls of St. Roque. He slowed to a fast walk for the final mile to the hospital, and was gradually joined by twenty others from the detachment, including the lieutenant.

"Thanks, Will," he said. "You saved my life."

"Just doing my job, sir."

They reached the hospital at about eleven o'clock in the morning of January 1 and reported immediately to Colonel Arnold, who was lying on a low bunk in the large main room of the dark hospital with his left upper leg heavily bandaged. Apparently in great pain and only partly able to focus, he became distraught at the news of the defeat. He put Colonel Campbell in command until he could get some rest and evaluate the situation with a clear head. With that and a grimace, he rolled over and tried to sleep. As Will walked away with the others, down the long crowded row of bunks filled with wounded, moaning soldiers, he had to cover his face to shut out the stench of blood and festering wounds.

Colonel Campbell ordered guards posted on the road down to Quebec and directed the rest of the troops to retire to their assigned houses to rest until mid-morning the next day.

When they mustered the following morning, Campbell outlined the sad details of the defeat: Six officers had been killed during the battle and five wounded; forty sergeants, corporals, and privates killed and sixty wounded. The British had taken thirty-three officers and some two hundred sergeants, corporals, and privates as prisoners. Counting reinforcements under colonels Livingston and Clinton and possibly some Canadians, the American force now numbered fewer than eight hundred men, most of whom were in no condition to resume the attack. The British outmanned them by at least two to one and were well dug in and provisioned. Colonel Arnold's orders were to continue the siege while he sent dispatches to Colonel Wooster in Montreal, General Washington, and the Continental Congress requesting another 5000 men with artillery.

Until the Americans received substantial reinforcements, they were in a highly vulnerable situation. The siege was a siege in name only, for if the British came out from behind the city walls, they would in all likelihood defeat the colonists soundly.

Colonel Arnold placed Lieutenant Pierce and his detachment into Major Ogden's company. They were told that the reassignment was necessary because Captain Dearborn, Lieutenants Hutchins and Andrews, and twenty-nine other soldiers from Dearborn's company had been captured and were now in the British jail.

Will was deep in thought as he sat on the porch of his designated house one evening the following week while everyone awaited word on reinforcements.

Overwhelmed by the enemy and having to run for my life. And our good officers captured. At least they're still alive. This whole thing is blowing up in my face. No one, not even James Clarkson, is going to be proud of us unless we start winning battles. Why did I ever get involved in this mess? Boynton thinks my fighting is useless—might be true as to me getting my own freedom, but it has to help the whites' view of Africans as a group if I continue to do well here. Saved an officer's life. That counts for something. And what I do here will increase my standing in the African community—I've got more than one horse in this race. And I want to help the Americans win. Whatever the outcome, slinking back to Portsmouth now with my tail between my legs would make my situation worse.

His concerns only deepened the following day upon learning that more than a hundred officers and men whose enlistments had expired had left the camp that morning, heading for Montreal before starting the long march home.

He and Joe Boynton, Ed Fox, and several others from Dearborn's old company, including Lieutenant Pierce, spent most of the next few days rehashing the failed battle for the city.

"Colonel Campbell should never have backed off," Boynton said. "That was the problem."

"Wrong and unfair," Pierce said. "You can't blame anyone for the fact that Montgomery and McPhearson got themselves killed. After that, Campbell had no choice but to try and save his unit."

"Even after that happened," Will said, "the situation could still have been saved if Dearborn hadn't gone out so far ahead that he was surrounded."

Eliphas Reed shook his head, staring back at the city walls. "If only the French had helped out. Will's question to Dearborn was right on the mark."

Ed Fox said, "No, you're all wrong. The problem was our wet powder. We just couldn't get off enough shots."

Their arguments went round and round. They knew they couldn't reverse the outcome, but they tried to at least salve their wounded egos. Interesting. The battle and their talk about it produced a strong bond among those who survived. Will realized he cared deeply for these men, and it was apparent that they now cared for him. Simply because they'd fought and endured a life-threatening challenge together. And they were ready, together, to try again when their superiors gave the order. Now it was about protecting each other. Their experience had developed a life of its own, bearing no relationship to their lives before this war. Here Will felt he was not a slave. Here he was a man among men.

He was proud of the way he conducted himself. He wondered how his warrior ancestors in Africa would have fared in the same circumstances and whether they would have approved of his performance. He thought so.

On January 14 came word that the Continental Congress, in recognition of Arnold's courage and the difficult march, and notwithstanding the unsuccessful attack, had elevated the colonel to the rank of brigadier general. Buoyed by this news, Arnold became more determined than ever to continue the siege until a new effort could be made to conquer the city. To better train and keep his men sharp, he ordered weeks of repetitive, boring drills and guard duty.

One morning, looking across the frozen river, Will spied small figures moving slowly across the ice toward them. The reinforcements! Nearly 1500 men joined them, mainly from New Hampshire, Vermont, and New York, under the command of General John Sullivan. But by the end of March, smallpox had taken such a toll that out of a total of 2500 troops, Arnold had only fifteen hundred men fit for duty. By this time he was up and about with the help of a cane, even riding a horse, and he was eager to make another try at Quebec.

He was trumped by his senior officer, General Wooster, who moved down from Montreal in mid-April to take charge. Sorely disappointed, Arnold asked to be sent back to Montreal to assume command there. His request was promptly granted, and a day later Benedict Arnold left camp with a small contingent, the city he'd hoped to enter in triumph receding in the mist at his back.

Will stayed behind with Major Ogden's company, but not for long. Many of the enlistments under Sullivan ran out on April 15, and those men wasted no time in heading home. Then, on May 6, Will awoke and looked out on the river to a startling sight:Thirty-two British transport vessels with 6000 fresh troops under the command of General John Burgoyne were now moored in the bay.

Within minutes, Wooster and Sullivan ordered everyone to break camp. They fled up the St. Lawrence toward Montreal. The "siege" of Quebec had ended. Will's hopes for a victory were dashed. He now feared for his life.

24

*A*s he grabbed his gear and fell into line, Will looked back at the city walls. Just at that moment the gates were flung open and redcoats began streaming out. Lieutenant Pierce saw it in the same instant and ordered the troops up the road at double-quick. They could soon see that the enemy was about a thousand strong, in two columns and closing fast. Sullivan told the men to abandon the cannon; many also jettisoned their muskets so they could run faster. Will held on to his in fear that he would soon have to use it. But all military discipline disappeared from their ranks. The British soon caught up with the weak and the stragglers, killing or capturing nearly two hundred men.

After about nine miles, the redcoats relaxed their pursuit. Will, Edward Fox, and Joseph Boynton kept pace with the company for another ten miles until darkness, when General Sullivan called a halt for the night. Each man brushed back enough snow for a bed, and they were asleep seconds after hitting the ground.

The next morning they were off again, and by mid-afternoon were nearing Montreal, arriving at a small post known as the Cedars. There, just as their forward garrison of about four hundred men under General Wooster threw down their packs for a rest, a large force of Indians and Canadians under the command of British officers suddenly encircled them and attacked. Wooster immediately saw the futility of his position and surrendered.

"Be careful, Will," Joe Boynton whispered. "Those aren't Aben-aqui. They're Iroquois. They'll cut your throat in a blink if you give them an excuse." The two men were in a long line of American prisoners being herded forward toward the river's edge and loaded into thirty-six-foot-long bateaux to be transported downriver. The ambush was one of the most harrowing experiences of Will's life, bringing back the awful moments when he was captured as a youth and hauled off to the slave ship in Africa and when Simo had attacked him from behind with a tomahawk in the tannery.

It seemed like only seconds before they were surrounded by red-and-black-painted Indians, screaming and firing their rifles into the American ranks. Behind them the French Canadians in their heavy fur coats moved within musket range and began pelting the force. White flags of surrender flew up over the entire battalion. A British colonel on horseback appeared at the edge of the woods with his redcoat staff. Wooster approached him and received the terms of surrender, which were simple and direct: Immediately lay down all arms and ammunition, proceed under guard to the river, and get into the bateaux. Anyone making a false move would be shot. Wooster agreed, and the embarkation began right away.

As they were moved toward the river, Will became an object of curiosity and derision by his captors. "*Vite, vite*, neegair!" called out a French sergeant as he prodded Will along with the barrel of his rifle. A large Indian with a multi-feathered headdress approached him and rubbed him with his hand to see if his black color was real or some kind of war paint. Other Indians gawked and giggled as they poked at him with their spears. Will kept quiet and didn't react.

After boarding, they were carried about a mile downriver and then encamped under heavy guard on the north bank. Later in the day, Will could see an American detachment approaching in bateaux, but they were quickly driven off by British cannon from the shore. After that, the campsite became very still as darkness fell and the prisoners nervously awaited signs of their fate.

After a nearly sleepless night, Boynton and Will gathered together several others at dawn to talk in low tones about various escape strategies. Then, late in the morning, with no explanation, the British officers circulated among them and told them they were free to go—to walk this time, back to Montreal. Confused and afraid this was a trick that would justify the enemy's shooting them, they nevertheless began walking slowly west, up the river. After about an hour's march, they were met by an officer and sergeant from General Sullivan's battalion, who assured them they'd indeed been freed by an exchange agreement with the British. With the news, their pace quickened, and the men soon came to an outpost at the mouth of the Sorel River, where they bedded down and awaited further orders.

Sullivan and Thomas, at the head of the rest of the troops about a half mile behind, had beheld the tragic ambush and quickly directed their men to the south, close to the river, moving as rapidly as possible to skirt the attackers. Sullivan sent a courier ahead to General Arnold in Montreal, pleading for instant reinforcement.

Montreal sits on an island in the middle of the St. Lawrence River. Since arriving there in mid-April, Arnold had made a thorough evaluation of the strength of the garrison and taken a number of steps to buttress its defensive capabilities. Then he learned that he was to face a major political issue: The Continental Congress had appointed Benjamin Franklin and four others as a commission to visit Montreal, evaluate the military situation and make a final attempt to win over the Canadians to the American side. When the five commissioners arrived, on April 29, Arnold was ready. He arranged an opulent welcome dinner.

But the next morning and throughout the following week, Arnold pulled no punches as he brought the commissioners back to the dismal reality. He ushered into their meeting room a number of irate French creditors who demanded to be paid gold in place of the worthless continental paper they'd been forced at bayonet point to accept for provisions they supplied to the American soldiers. General Arnold then explained in detail why it would be impossible to withstand an attack by the British Commanding General Carleton when the river ice broke up and he was able to reach Montreal with Burgoyne's fresh troops.

It was at this point that General Sullivan's courier arrived at Arnold's doorstep with the terrifying news that the siege of Quebec had been abandoned and the retreating army was being pulverized by the combination of English, Indians, and Canadians. Arnold immediately deployed a detachment under his command to attempt a rescue of Wooster's captured troops, but when he approached the site of the ambush, he realized he was too late. He threatened fearful retribution if the Indians harmed the prisoners. The response was that if Arnold followed them, the Indians would massacre all of the captives. After holding a council with his staff, Arnold determined to risk the consequences and set out after the enemy in canoes and bateaux. But when the British answered with heavy cannon fire that threatened to sink Arnold's flotilla, he ordered a retreat.

The following morning the British commander sent a message to Arnold that the captives would be killed if Arnold attacked, but they'd be released if Arnold allowed the enemy force to retreat unmolested and promised that the congress would release in exchange an equal number of British prisoners. Arnold agreed.

Upon returning to his headquarters in Montreal, Arnold convened the commissioners, reported what had transpired, and then proceeded to rail against the French Canadians, whom he had come to believe were the Americans' "bitter enemies." Hearing that, Benjamin Franklin concluded that the American effort to convince the Canadians to become the fourteenth rebelling colony had failed and that the American force would soon be driven out of Canada. Accordingly, he decided to return to Philadelphia, which he did on May 11.

As these events unfolded, General Sullivan prepared to make a stand against the British where most of his men were encamped—at the confluence of the St. Lawrence and the Sorel Rivers. Arnold dissuaded him from this strategy by pointing out that the British could simply bypass that point, proceed to St. Johns at the northern tip of Lake Champlain, and cut off the line of retreat. Better for Sullivan to head directly to St. Johns himself.

The next day Arnold received word that a number of English warships were on the way. Within hours he had crossed the St. Lawrence with his detachment and was also en route to meet Sullivan.

———

At the end of the first week in June, Will found himself on the move again, marching south along the Sorel to St. Johns.

The remains of the army that gathered at St. Johns were a pitiful sight. They looked more like a mob than an army. They were decimated by fatigue, sickness, and desertion.

They seized three English gondolas stationed at St. Johns, loaded them with as many of the sick and wounded as possible, and sent them out first toward the south.

Will was one of the lucky half of the troops who did not have smallpox, but he was thoroughly emaciated as he managed to lift himself into the large bateau that would carry him south to the American end of Lake Champlain. As the boat pulled away, he looked back at St. Johns engulfed in flames and smoke above the ice blue lake. Arnold had ordered anything that could be of help to the enemy to be set on fire. The general was the last man to board a bateau, after first destroying his fine horse. As their boats moved out onto the lake, British troops under General John Burgoyne appeared at double-quick over the low hills behind the town. Will was aghast.

On the run again.

25

*L*ake Champlain is more than a hundred miles long at the shoreline and covers about five hundred square miles. Its waters are below forty degrees in early summer and are churning almost constantly from late-spring storms. About ten miles of shallow water below St. Johns made it impossible for the British simply to sail their ships on the St. Lawrence south on the Sorel River and into the big lake. The lake is at its widest, about thirteen miles across, near the town of Plattsburg, opposite the southern tip of Valcour Island, fifty miles below St. Johns. Its current flows north, up the Sorel River and into the St. Lawrence.

Arnold led the remnants of his army past Valcour Island and then another forty-five miles farther south to the old fort at Crown Point, on the western side of the lake. There in mid-June they encamped amid the ruins of the fort. Five thousand and two hundred men had made it. Of those, it was estimated that 2800 needed hospitalization.

During the next three weeks, Will, Joe Boynton, and Edward Fox spent most of their time trying to mend their tired and sore bodies. From local farmers they each obtained better if worn sets of clothing and some hot food in return for performing various chores for the families.

On July 7 General Philip Schuyler, overall commander of the northern department of Washington's Continental Army, met at Crown Point with Arnold, Sullivan, and Major General Horatio Gates. Gates had recently been appointed to head up the American army in Canada, which no longer existed. They agreed on four points. First, Lake Champlain must be held at all costs or the British generals in Canada, Carleton and Burgoyne, might join up with English forces in New York City and New Jersey under Sir William Howe and effectively split the American colonies and their army in two, spelling certain defeat for the Americans. Second, in order to hold Champlain, they'd have to build a fleet of ships to fend off a British fleet already being built at St. Johns. Third, Benedict Arnold, who'd been successful in maritime businesses before the war, was the right man with the necessary experience to build such a fleet. And fourth, the American forces now encamped at Crown Point should be withdrawn and moved south, to the more defensible position at Fort Ticonderoga.

―※―

Three days later, Will found himself once again climbing into a bateau for the thirteen-mile voyage south to "Fort Ti," also on the western side of the lake, which had gained new notoriety in May 1775 when Arnold, Ethan Allen, and the "Green Mountain Boys" had captured it from the British "in the name of the Great Jehovah and the Continental Congress" and established it as the principal American bastion in the north woods.

Given all he'd heard about Ticonderoga, Will was surprised as the flotilla approached the site of the old fort. Situated on a high hill with a commanding view up and down Lake Champlain as well as southwest toward the portage from Lake George, it was in a sad state of disrepair.

As Will and Joe Boynton walked through the old fort, Boynton described its history. Constructed by the French in 1755–57 to protect the French settlements in the Champlain valley against British advancements from the south, it was a large, star-shaped structure mounting thirty-six large cannons. Its wooden walls were filled with dried mud and faced with stones. The buildings inside the fort included a powder magazine and barracks big enough to bed up to four hundred men. In 1758, fifteen thousand British troops under General Jeffery Amherst had marched on Ticonderoga, then called Fort Carillon. Anticipating defeat, the French commander blew up the magazine and fled the fort. The British took over, rebuilt the magazine, added many cannons, and renamed it Fort Ticonderoga, Mohawk for "between two great waters"—Lake George and Lake Champlain.

The effectiveness of the fort had been weakened just four months before Arnold's arrival, when forty-three of its English- and French-made cannons and sixteen mortars were removed by the American general Henry Knox, a former Boston bookseller, and hauled by sled over the snow-covered mountains to Boston. There the weapons were set up on Dorchester Heights, putting the Americans under George Washington in a commanding position over the British fleet in the harbor and the city. The British army there, under General William Howe, along with many Massachusetts loyalists, was forced to leave and sail up to Halifax. Washington's men took over Boston on March 17, but they would soon meet Howe again in New York with a reverse result.

Lieutenant Pierce came out of the meeting of General Arnold's staff and walked over to where Will, Ed Fox, and Joe Boynton were up on a barracks roof repairing a gaping hole just above their bunks.

"Good work, men. When you finish there, go over to the main gate where those other fellows are putting up new doors and give them a hand." Pierce then ordered a second group, of a dozen soldiers, to fill in two large openings in the wall of the fort with dirt and to pile stones in front of the filled-in areas. He next examined the entire perimeter of the fort. When he finished, he gathered up a hundred troops who were physically able and directed them to move all the remaining cannons to the wall of the fort that fronted the north of the lake—where the British fleet would be coming.

The work of repairing and preparing the old fort continued for the next two weeks. The days were long and hard. Will was exhausted every evening as dusk came, but he was thankful that at least he was being fed and recovering his strength.

One night he sat on the edge of his bunk and wrote a letter:

Dear Master James,

I am writing this letter to you from Fort Ticonderoga in New York. As you may be aware, our expedition was repulsed at Quebec, and during the winter we were forced to retreat back to Montreal and then south on Lake Champlain.

Fortunately, I have escaped a capture, although our transit has been difficult and we are in rather poor condition.

General Arnold expects that the British will soon follow us down the lake to this fort, and we are preparing to defend it. At this time we do not how long this process will take.

Having told you that I expected to return to you and the tannery this Spring, I feel obliged to ask your permission to stay here with the troops and finish the mission. I do not know what hardship this may cause you at home or in the tannery, but I'm confident that you appreciate the importance of our objective here.

I respectfully await your answer to this request.

I trust that this letter finds you, Mrs. Clarkson, and the rest of the family all well.

Sincerely,
Will

When Will finished, he put down the paper and sat back to ponder whether he should have asked Clarkson for his freedom. No. Needed to be face to face when he did that. But the way this fight was going, he might have to amend his plan.

Ed Fox watched Will seal the letter in an envelope to give to an army courier, who would take it to Boston for forwarding to Portsmouth.

"Where'd you learn to read and write, Will?"

"My first owner had been a schoolteacher. I asked him to teach me. He figured I'd be more useful to him in his business if I had those skills."

"You're mighty lucky. Not many white folks speak as well as you. Or write either, probably."

"Only problem is, it doesn't make me free."

"That ability plus your record here might do it. I think you'll get your freedom when you return."

Will walked over to give the letter to the courier. *At least Ed is one white man who thinks my plan will pay off. Be good not to have to come up with a new one. Wish I could write to Abi, too. But she can't read without help. And her new owner's a loyalist, so I'd have to be mighty careful what I wrote. Oh, my, seems forever since I saw her or the children.*

On the morning of July 18, Will was awakened early by loud chattering among the troops gathered across the inner courtyard in front of General Arnold's office. He got into his clothes and hurried over to find out the cause of the commotion. As he approached, he saw Ed Fox and other men clustered around the expedition's notice board, reading a document posted there. Ed motioned him over.

"They've done it, Will. They've done it! The thirteen colonies have declared their independence from England!" Will looked over Ed's shoulder and read the second paragraph of the document:

> We hold these truths to be self-evident, that all men are created equal, that they are endowed by their Creator with certain unalienable Rights, that among these are Life, Liberty, and the Pursuit of Happiness. . .

He could read no further. His vision was blurred by the tears that welled up in his eyes. *This has to do it; they'll have to free us now.* He wiped his wet cheeks and joined in the celebration as the men all cheered and slapped each other on the back. The phrase sounded over and over in his head: All men are created equal, all men are created equal. *All* men. All.

They were the most beautiful five words he'd ever heard.

The task of building America's first naval fleet was approved by General Washington, who also agreed that Benedict Arnold was the best man to oversee the construction. The job was to take place at a shipyard at Skenesborough, New York, twenty miles south of Ticonderoga. At the start, Arnold had no materials to work with. One man said, "A declaration of independence is a fine thing to hang on a wall, but unless oakum and a few spikes arrive soon, the British will blow hell out of us.'"

Arnold officially took charge of the effort on August 7 and immediately addressed an even bigger issue: They had very few workmen, let alone many who had any experience building ships. The general, now acting admiral, had to draw the plans for the ships himself. George Washington ordered military battalions to serve as builders to supplement Skenesborough's house carpenters, and the Continental Congress passed a resolution to obtain fifty ship carpenters from Rhode Island. Soon additional experienced shipbuilders followed from other parts of New England, New York, New Jersey, and Philadelphia. Blacksmiths came from Crown Point, and Ticonderoga sent iron and axes. Arnold impressed three hundred conscripts from two New Hampshire regiments, including Will, thereby rendering moot his letter to James Jr. back in Portsmouth.

Thus, during August and September, Will became a shipbuilder, a shipwright raising beams, pegging them together, and hammering boards in place with heavy spikes to finish the hulls. Heavy work, but he found it to be the most satisfying job he'd ever had, mainly because of the feeling of accomplishment he had when he looked at the finished product. Joe Boynton and he agreed that being able to work outside in sunny, moderate weather also had something to do with their sense of satisfaction. As he hammered away at the next hull, he thought how wonderful it would be to choose his own occupation, one like this in the clean outdoors. To have time with Abi and the children when he wanted it. To set an example of hard work and success for Will Jr.

While they worked, General Arnold came by to watch them. He walked over to Will and shook his hand.

"Will, I heard about your fierce fighting at Quebec. Congratulations for that. And your work on these ships is excellent. Keep it up."

Stunned and flattered, all Will could think to say was, "Thank you, General. I do my best. Good luck to you, for the rest of us, in this naval campaign." As Arnold moved away, Will was wondering how to make use of his goodwill.

Arnold had posted three captured vessels at Crown Point to be on lookout for the British. These were the two schooners, *Royal Savage* and *Liberty*, and the sloop *Enterprise*. The men on the ships sent word that the British were also working feverishly, at St. Johns, to construct their own fleet.

The race was on.

Unlike Arnold, the British had plenty of experienced ship-builders, sailors, and supplies. They'd stripped down two schooners, *Maria* and *Carleton*, and carried them overland from the St. Lawrence to St. Johns. They'd knocked down a third ship, *Inflexible*, at one hundred and eighty tons and armed with eighteen 12-pounders, and reassembled it at St. Johns. Twelve prefabricated gunboats were brought in from England and assembled. They had also constructed a large radeau from scratch and armed it with six 24-pounders, six 12-pounders, and two howitzers, far outgunning any ship Arnold was building. All told, the fleet General Carleton finally amassed to sail south on Lake Champlain against the Americans comprised twenty-nine armed ships and twenty-four others carrying provisions and equipment.

The most ships the Americans could assemble, including the three that had been captured, was sixteen. The *Royal Savage* carried four 6-pounders and eight 4-pounders, and the schooners *Revenge* and *Liberty* were equipped with four 4-pounders and four 2-pounders each (before the battle *Liberty* was converted into a hospital and supply ship). Arnold also had four galleys, the *Lee*, *Trumbull*, *Washington*, and Arnold's flagship *Congress*, each armed with one 18-pounder, one 12-pounder, two 9-pounders and six 6-pounders. The sloop *Enterprise* was a small fast one-masted vessel, full rigged with bowsprit and armed with twelve 4-pounders. The final eight ships in the fleet were gondolas—small, flat-bottomed, single-masted gunboats propelled by sail or oars. The gondolas were *Connecticu,,*

New York, Boston, Jersey, Philadelphia, Spitfire, Providence, and *New Haven.*

In addition to the disparity in the number of ships, the American fleet could throw only six hundred pounds of shot compared to the British capability of 1,100 pounds.

"I think we're ready," Will said.

Joe Boynton fidgeted. "Not so sure. They've got a lot more ships, more firepower. Comes down to Arnold's strategy."

Ed Fox continued carving a pin whistle from a piece of maple. "Better be good. This is our last shot to stop 'em."

"Getting late in the year," Will said. "Maybe all we have to do is slow them down. In any event, I've got to do a good job this time."

"Not just you," Boynton said.

26

When General Gates put Arnold in charge of the fleet on August 7, he emphasized to his "admiral" that he should stay near the southern, American end of Lake Champlain.

But Arnold was fully appreciative of the superior strength of General Carleton's force. He well knew that if he attacked the British in the open lake, he'd be destroyed. His only chance was to set up in a protected, hopefully surprising defensive position and let the British attempt to attack him. As soon as some of his vessels were launched, he sailed off with them, on September 7, north toward St. Johns, training his green crews as he went.

Will considered himself fortunate to be on the *Congress* with Arnold. Suddenly a sailor, Will's mind was racing as he concentrated on learning his role in yet another incarnation. Ed Fox and he practiced aiming the cannon assigned to them, but they'd been told not to fire it because of the low supply of balls and powder.

"Doesn't make sense," Will said. "We need at least a couple of practice shots or we won't know what we're doing when the fight starts."

"That's so," Fox said. "But the lieutenant said no. What can we do?"

Will looked around, still fuming. He spotted Colonel Arnold talking to two of his officers on the far side of the ship and headed toward him.

"Colonel Arnold," he said, "may I have a word with you?"

"What is it? Can't you see I'm busy?"

"Colonel, none of us has ever fired a cannon. We need some practice shots or we'll probably put the first five balls into the water. Give us three shots now and it'll save more than that in misfired balls—and precious time and momentum later in battle."

Arnold gave him a long, measuring look. "I see your point, Clarkson. But just three shots."

A cheer went up from the other gunners when Will returned to his weapon. Ed Fox grinned. "Gutsy move for a private."

"Sailor," Will said. "Please, Ed. Sailor."

―⚓―

Arnold had two immediate objectives besides retraining his men: First, he paraded his fleet offshore from St. Johns so Carleton would spend more time building additional ships; second, he scouted the lake for a strategic place to lie in wait for the British when they came out.

Soon he found just the spot. Valcour Island lies roughly one third of the distance from St. Johns to Fort Ticonderoga, toward the western (New York) side of Lake Champlain. As the rest of his vessels joined him from Skenesborough, he outlined a plan to arrange all of them in a straight line across the narrow channel, three quarters of a mile wide, between the island and the New York shore. The spot was toward the southern tip of the island and hidden from the British if they chose the logical course of sailing south through the wider channel to the east of Valcour. They would then have to tack back upwind in single file toward Arnold's line.

American lookouts sighted Carleton's fleet at ten o'clock in the morning on October 11. When one of Arnold's commanders on board a gondola beheld the size of the British armada, he rushed to the *Congress* and tried to convince his superior to fight in a retreat down the lake to Crown Point. Instead, Arnold ordered the *Royal Savage* to move down to the southern tip of the western channel, where it would be in full view of Carleton aboard the *Maria* after the British leaders took their flotilla to the southern end of the island via the eastern channel.

Will's heart was beating fast as he stood on the deck of *Congress*—which, with the other three galleys, was following *Royal Savage* but staying hidden behind the island's bluffs. Every American ship flew high the rattlesnake "Don't Tread on Me" banner. The combined anxiety and excitement was greater than anything he had felt during the land battles in Canada.

When the British spotted *Royal Savage*, they immediately came about to the northwest, but as Arnold had calculated, they had to fight their way into a stiff breeze and consequently proceeded very slowly. Unfortunately, the *Royal Savage* was also caught by the wind, fell to leeward, and was hit by three 12-pound balls from the *Inflexible*. She ran aground on the island and had to be abandoned.

Will was awestruck as this panorama unfolded before his eyes. Because of the narrow channel, the British vessels couldn't attack and were soon just bobbing about in the mouth of Valcour Bay, making no progress. Canoes full of Indians in bright red war paint paddled in and out among the ships of their British allies. More Indians could be seen in the woods along the shore, making Will and his shipmates more frightened than they already were.

Suddenly the British schooner *Carleton* was caught up in a countertwist of wind and thrown headlong toward the American ships, arranged in a half moon line. Immediately the guns of the American boats opened up on her and inflicted heavy damage. By then, however, seventeen of the British gunboats, which could be moved by oars as well as sails, rowed within range of Arnold's line. Guns boomed forth from both sides. At shortly after noon, the battle was on in earnest.

Will and Ed Fox began firing their cannon as fast as humanly possible. Arnold ran up and down the deck, personally aimed each weapon, then rushed to aim the first again as the last one fired and was reloaded. The confrontation went on and on through the afternoon, for nearly five hours. Many of the cannonballs were poorly aimed and splashed into the water, throwing great fountains into the sky. Soon Will was soaked from head to foot. *Congress* took more than a dozen hits, including one on her mainmast. Will barely leapt out of the way of falling rigging several times, and a musket ball creased his arm. The wound, though only superficial, bled profusely.

Ed Fox was hit directly in the neck and fell dead instantly. Will ripped a sleeve off Ed's shirt to bandage his own wound and kept firing with the aid of another seaman, who stepped in to take Fox's place. Dying and wounded men were strewn across the deck.

By the middle of the afternoon, only three British gunboats had actually been sunk, but all ships on both sides had suffered hits and were riding lower in the water. Cheers rang out from each crew as their broadsides struck home. A British officer led a crew to the *Royal Savage* and leveled her guns at her American mates. Soon driven off, he set fire to the ship as he left. The British finally towed away the *Carleton*, giving rise to more cheers from the colonial sailors. But as night fell, the *Inflexible* had moved within range and was raking the American line by the time the carnage stopped for the day.

On the foredeck of the *Congress,* as the breeze swept away the last vestiges of smoke and the smell of powder, Will leaned his head against the warm barrel of his cannon and wept at the loss of his friend Ed Fox.

That evening Arnold took stock. Technically the fight had ended in a draw, but the prospects for the Americans on a second day were bleak. As he made the rounds, *Philadelphia* swamped and went under. *Washington* could barely float. *New York* had lost almost all of her officers. Over seventy-five percent of the colonists' ammunition had been used up. About sixty men had been killed or wounded. Although many British ships had suffered damage, less than a third had actually been called into action. Carleton was now cordoning off the southern entrance of the eastern channel by forming a line across it.

The northwest wind that had held off the British was now too feeble to help the Americans. But in the early-evening darkness, a dense fog was settling over the bay.

Arnold called a council of his staff and outlined a bold plan to avoid certain annihilation in the morning. He ordered a lantern set in the stern of each ship, covered on three sides so that it was visible only to the vessel immediately in its rear. Oars and oarlocks were covered with shirts or other cloth to muffle any sound. Then, led by the galley *Trumbull* and followed by the remaining ships in single file a hundred yards apart, the entire fleet quietly slipped through the English line. *Congress* went last. Will rowed as cautiously as he could through the dim glow of lights marking the British vessels. He could hear occasional voices through the mist, but no alarm was sounded. It appeared as though Carleton had failed to post a sufficient number of sentries.

Once he felt that they were safely clear, Arnold gave the word to his sailors to row for their lives as fast as they could. By dawn the pus from Will's broken blisters was dried and caked on the handle of his oar as fourteen ships pulled slowly into the harbor at Schuyler's Island, ten miles to the south.

Back at Valcour Island, the British breakfasted and waited for the fog to lift so they could move in for the kill. When the sun broke through, they were astonished to see the bay still . . . and empty. A Hessian soldier aboard the *Maria* wrote: "General Carleton was in a rage. He at once had anchors weighed and sailed off in pursuit. But in his haste and excitement, he forgot to leave instructions for the army on the land, from whom, as a consequence, he became more and more separated. The wind, however, being averse, and nothing having been seen of the enemy, he returned and cast anchor in the bay in which he had passed the previous night."

Some of Carleton's ships continued to press southward against the wind in an effort to catch the Americans.

At Schuyler, while his men rested, Arnold examined the condition of his vessels. Three gondolas, *Providence, New York,* and *Jersey,* were so badly damaged that he had them stripped of their guns and scuttled.

On October 13 the race to Crown Point resumed. Arnold's ships continued to fight a headwind while the English soon took advantage of a northeast breeze and bore down on the galleys *Washington* and *Congress. Washington's* captain was forced to strike her colors as *Congress* and four remaining gondolas were subjected to murderous broadsides from *Inflexible, Maria,* and *Carleton.* Arnold took his only option. He ordered his men to row to windward into Buttonmould Bay and up a shallow creek where the deep-draft British ships couldn't follow. He ran all five ships aground, stripped them of everything of value, and set them afire with their flags still flying: funeral pyres for many dead comrades left aboard.

They then set off through the woods for Crown Point, where they burned the remaining buildings and stores. When that was accomplished, they disappeared into the forest again, barely escaping ambush by Carleton's Indian allies. Those who were able carried the wounded in slings. They arrived at Fort Ticonderoga at four o'clock the following morning, many sick and all exhausted. The total cost of the battle of Valcour Island: eighty men dead, one hundred and twenty captured, and the fleet destroyed.

But not for nothing. A week later Carleton's flotilla appeared in the lake opposite Ticonderoga as he evaluated the prospects for taking the fort. Factoring in the damage the Americans had inflicted at Valcour Island, he concluded that taking Ticonderoga would require a lengthy siege extending into the winter, which was now bearing down on them. He ordered his fleet back to Canada until spring. Inside the fort, cheers rose into the cold air as the British ships slowly turned and headed north. The all important delay had been achieved.

Once the British ships were out of sight, General Arnold circulated among the men in the fort, thanking them for their bravery and effort. When he came to Will, he motioned for the two of them to sit on a log bench.

"Will, I've been very impressed with your conduct and fighting ability during this expedition and at Valcour Island. I want you to know how much I appreciate it."

"Thank you, General," Will said. "That means a lot to me."

"What's your future now?" Arnold asked.

"Not sure. I'm still a slave. I belong to James Clarkson, a tanner back in Portsmouth. Got to see if he's willing to set me free based on my military service."

Arnold slapped Will on the knee and stood up. "Well, good luck to you."

Will quickly spoke again. "If you wouldn't mind, sir, a letter of commendation could be a big help."

"Of course. Have it to you this afternoon." The general turned and went on to the next group of soldiers.

Ten days later Arnold was on his way to Albany, awaiting his next assignment from General Washington, and Will was trudging through the woods on his way back to Portsmouth, the letter tucked securely in his pocket.

27

On the first day of November 1776, Abi was standing at a window of Colonel Theodore Atkinson's house at 41 Court Street in Portsmouth. As she was cleaning a gravy dish from the household's large silver collection, she kept a watchful eye on her two children playing in the family's garden early in the sunny afternoon. Willie was six years old, and Naby was four. If only Will could see how much they enjoyed themselves and each other, how healthy they were. He'd been away so much longer than he had said he would be. Was he badly wounded? Or even still alive?

Several months ago she'd run into Jack Odiorne at the women's market. They talked about Will and old times, and he'd taken to dropping by.

One day in the kitchen, he said, "Abi, don't want to upset you, but I heard something last night at the tavern you need to know about. One of the soldiers at Quebec who just returned said he personally saw Will hit in the battle there. Soldier didn't think he survived." Abi fell into his arms, crying. Quietly Jack said, "Don't worry. If he doesn't come back, I'll care for you and the children."

Abi had found working for her new owner to be reasonably pleasant and satisfying. Colonel Atkinson was rich. He owned more than a fourth of the land in the province. He was now seventy-nine, having served as councilor, judge, and secretary of New Hampshire. He was a jovial, popular man on good terms with his fellow townspeople, even though he was a vocal loyalist who advocated reconciliation with England. His wife had died several years earlier, and he was quite content to delegate authority to Abi in managing the affairs of the household. He was always kind to her and provided nicely furnished rooms on the attic floor for her and the children.

Abi decided to take a little break from polishing silver and walked out to join the children in the garden. As she closed the door behind her, she glanced west down Court Street toward Pleasant. Her mouth dropped open. Walking slowly up the street was a barely familiar figure in worn brown clothes carrying a small cloth bag over his shoulder.

"Will!" she cried out as she broke into a run toward him. Will dropped his satchel as they burst into each other's arms and kissed. Within seconds they were joined by Will Jr. and Naby, who'd heard their mother cry out and seen their daddy. They squeezed each other, everybody talking at once except for Will, who was too happy to speak for several minutes.

They walked back into the house together. Then Will described his journey and what he'd seen along the way. He stayed away from the details of the battles. Finally they settled the children into the room next to Abi's and went into her room to whisper and have some privacy until the afternoon waned.

By the time Colonel Atkinson returned home for dinner, Will had already left for the Clarkson house on South School Street.

Mrs. Haven answered his knock. Her big hug and Lydia's were followed by a strong handshake and slap on the back from James Jr. Mrs. Haven immediately gave him a supper of baked beans and brown bread. He ate two helpings. Afterwards, James Jr. came into the kitchen, and the two men talked for nearly two hours. Will gave him the disappointing details of Arnold's expedition, and James confirmed Will's expectation that he and the general populace viewed the Canadian episode as a mistake and a failure—though some appreciated the strategic significance of the American fleet's causing Carleton to return to Canada at least until the following year. Will told James that his superiors, including Arnold, had told him he'd done a good job, but the tanner did not seem impressed.

Finally James stood up, stretched, and said, "All right, Will, you contributed our part. But you've been away too long, much longer than I agreed. Tomorrow it's back to reality at the tannery. Business here has been slow, but we're so shorthanded I really need to lean on you, starting first thing in the morning."

On the next Sunday afternoon, after the family had returned from church, Will followed James Jr. into his office. He stood back as James sat in his chair, arranging his paperwork for the next day.

"Master James, I need to talk to you about something that's important to me."

"Yes, Will, what is it?"

"I'd like to know if you and the family will grant me my freedom in recognition of my military record. I have here a letter of commendation from General Benedict Arnold testifying to my exemplary service."

James looked at him for a moment as though he'd never before laid eyes on him. Then he seemed to collect himself and reached for the letter Will was holding out. He barely glanced at it, then handed it back.

"Will, I'm sure you were a fine soldier, but I don't see how we can possibly do what you're asking. The family needs your services both at the tannery and at the house."

Will had been expecting something along those lines and was ready with his respone. "If that's the problem, I can still work for you even after you free me. The only difference will be that you'll be paying me wages."

"But I'd have expenses for you, so you'd have to pay me for rent and food in return—more than your wages. No, it just won't work. I'm sorry, Will. As you know, we had no such understanding when you went away. But I have no problem with you keeping your army pay for yourself."

He turned back to his papers. Although dismissed, Will didn't leave. He spoke again, softly but intensely. "Master James, I fought for your liberty. What about mine?"

Clarkson looked at Will, then down at his desk. "Two different situations," he said. Raising his head again, he said, "That's all, Will. No further discussion. I'll see you in the morning."

Upon returning to his hut, Will lifted the heavy chair and smashed it first against the wall and then the floor, shouting curses at the top of his voice.

Son of a bitch didn't even read the letter!

Damn chair didn't even break.

He sat down heavily on the edge of the bunk with his face in his hands, seething.

James Jr., back in the house, heard the noise, but neither he nor anyone else said anything about it or went out to see what was going on.

"So, Will, you was off to war and didn't even tell me," Seneca Hall said when Will went to see him on Saturday. "Welcome back. Been busy while you was off having fun. Found out what you asked for."

"What's it look like?"

"Money for the slave trade comes from Bannister. Goes to shipmasters to pay for voyages. Captains split the profits with him. He's doing the same thing in a bunch of towns up and down the coast."

"I thought so! Nice work, Seneca. That completes the picture. Now the only question is when and how to go public with the scandal."

Being home with Abi and the children, at least on the weekends and occasionally on a weekday evening, made this period in one sense the happiest time of Will's life. Colonel Atkinson's willingness to abide conjugal visits made family life a lot easier.

But the return to slavery bothered him much more than he could have imagined. His military service didn't make a bit of difference—

neither the white community nor the African recognized in any way his significant service on the Canadian expedition.

"You did a wonderful thing, Will," Mrs. Haven said. "It's a shame no one appreciates it. Take comfort in your own knowledge of your accomplishment. The important thing is, you're back safe and sound for Abi and the children."

The work at the tannery was hard, but that had never been the issue. Nor were his masters harsh. The problem was the constant awareness that the white people he interacted with daily regarded him as chattel. He was more conscious of the slights and diminishments of his everyday life. Whites' attitudes were sometimes overt, as with outright derogatory comments, but more often the slights were subtle, reflected in a condescending tone of voice or a demeaning look. Such attitudes were particularly galling after he had risked his life for these people's freedom.

On the first Sunday after his return, Will saw Jack at the women's market and talked about his feelings. Jack's were the same.

"Way they think about us make my skin crawl."

"I promise you, Jack, when this war is over, we'll get back to this."

In the army it had been different. To be sure, a few of the soldiers hadn't liked him or had resented his presence. But overall, and particularly in times of battle, racial differences melted away. That pure taste of equality lingered on Will's lips, giving rise to a thirst that could not be quenched.

His frustration was compounded by the fact that the expedition's failures meant his stature in Portsmouth hadn't been enhanced. That and his continuing slave status left him still subservient to William Bannister and Caesar in reputation and position.

But then Jack approached him after church one Sunday: "Will, you didn't tell me you was a damn hero up there in Canada. Joe Boynton just told me about it over at Pitt Tavern last night."

Will brightened. "I didn't want to blow my own horn. But here's an idea—you could blow it for me around town, give us more ammunition when we're ready to go up against Caesar."

"Be a big boost, especially to our watch team," Jack said. "I'll get em to spread the word, too."

In the evenings Will often went over to Reverend Haven's house, at the corner of Pleasant and Gates Streets. There he usually found the minister laboring in his saltpeter works on the vacant lot just north of his residence. The manufacture of this gunpowder substance and the actual making of bullets, along with his strong Sabbath oratory, were the good reverend's principal contributions to the cause of the American insurgency, to which he was firmly committed. Haven was frustrated by the army's failures in Canada, but he remained optimistic about ultimate victory. He was profoundly influenced in this regard by a pamphlet published just six months before the Declaration of Independence, called *Common Sense,* written by a Philadelphia journalist named Thomas Paine. Haven gave a copy to Will, who read it quickly and was also persuaded by its logic:

> Small islands not capable of protecting themselves are the proper objects for kingdoms to take under their care; but there is something very absurd in supposing a continent to be perpetually governed by an island. In no instance hath nature made the satellite larger than its primary planet, and as England and America with respect to each other reverses the common order of nature, it is evident they belong to different systems; England to Europe, America to itself.

Paine scorned the concept of a hereditary monarchy and put forward the premise that all rights emanate from the people. Reconciliation with England was therefore impossible and independence the only conceivable outcome. Paine's brilliant pamphlet became an instant best-seller throughout the colonies, inciting Americans to blame the British king George III for their problems and press forward toward revolution.

Will summed up the major points of Paine's philosophy for Caesar, Bannister, and Prince Whipple. Caesar was skeptical of the colonists' chances of victory, primarily because loyalists continued to comprise nearly half of the population. And he remained opposed to African activism or intervention on either side.

Will said, "Damn it, Caesar, there comes a point when you have to choose, to pick a side. We can't walk the fence forever."

Prince agreed, but said Will was a fool for not getting agreement in advance from James Clarkson that he'd be granted his freedom if he served in the army. Will walked home, angry at both of them.

News from the war fronts drifted into Portsmouth during the winter and spring of 1776–77. New Hampshire regiments under General John Sullivan and Colonel John Stark crossed the Delaware with General Washington on December 26, 1776, led the bayonet charge against the Hessians at Trenton, then returned home when their troops' enlistments expired.

The following March, the state's three Continental Army regiments were reorganized, and General Washington ordered them to Fort Ticonderoga in anticipation of the return of the British, under Burgoyne, from Canada.

In April, in Connecticut, Benedict Arnold dashed back into the picture, raising troops to thwart a British landing at Norwalk and barely escaping capture. His heroism led the congress finally to commission him as a major general, but it declined to restore his seniority over other officers they'd earlier promoted over his head. That slap, together with the congress's failure to pay him money he declared he was owed, led Arnold on July 11 to submit his resignation.

Burgoyne had by this time sailed south on Lake Champlain and by the clever tactic of fortifying a high hill overlooking Ticonderoga had forced the abandonment of the fort. Units of Burgoyne's army set off into Vermont in hot pursuit of the fleeing Americans, including the New Hampshire regiments that had been just approaching the fort. Facing a crisis, General Washington prevailed upon Arnold to table his resignation and gallop north to Albany to help General Schuyler.

The fall of Ticonderoga sent chills throughout New Hampshire. The residents could easily perceive that if Vermont came under Burgoyne's control, they would certainly be next. Immediately they turned to Stark, their hero of Bunker Hill and Trenton and their most experienced and popular leader. In response to a request from the state of Vermont for assistance, on July 18 the New Hampshire legislature convened and appointed Stark brigadier general of the state's militia. Between July 19 and 24, in just six days, 1492 officers and men signed up under Stark.

Will was one of them. Now chafing under the dirty work at the tanyard and the memory of defeat in the Canadian expedition, he wanted desperately to participate in a successful military campaign. But he would take no chances this time. He had to have an express written agreement *in advance* that he'd be freed. First he sought the advice of Reverend Haven.

"The colonists are doing the Lord's work, Will. It's essential that you go with Stark to achieve victory. Just as the defeat at Quebec was God's will, so it is that the colonies will ultimately prevail. This isn't just about obtaining your freedom from James Clarkson; it has to do with freedom for all of us, without which your own freedom will be meaningless. The failure in Canada has strengthened your character and purpose. It's time to fulfill that purpose as God has decreed. In return, you certainly deserve your freedom. Go to James and tell him what I've said."

Will was skeptical of Haven's reasoning, based as it was on belief in the Christian god, but it was the support and approach most likely to persuade his owner. He offered his thanks and returned to the Clarkson house, where he immediately reported what the minister had told him, virtually word for word. As he spoke, he watched his owner's face. James didn't seem to be paying much attention.

"He said I certainly deserve my freedom."

James picked up a pen and began to write. "You must join Stark. It's essential."

Will hadn't put much stock in Reverend Haven's arguments, nor, he surmised, had he needed to. James Clarkson was probably more than willing for Will to rejoin the troops. The prospect of General Burgoyne's storming into Portsmouth must terrify him. The letter he wrote guaranteed Will his freedom if he joined Stark and completed the campaign against the British.

James's fear was well founded. The British force under Burgoyne was over 7,000 strong. In addition, they had incited the Mohawk Indians to join them, hoping their skills in forest fighting would buttress the redcoat army in the wooded frontier. Along with several other tribes, the Mohawks, whose name in Algonquin means "man eaters," had been scalping and hacking to pieces the frontier's settlers for months.

The Indians' tactics, well publicized, had frightened the colonial residents and soldiers. The *New Hampshire Gazette* recounted the gruesome tale of the latest Indian atrocity—the murder of one of their prisoners, named Jane McCrea, a beautiful young woman with long red hair who'd fallen in love with and become engaged to a loyalist fighting with the British. The two Indians who captured her got into an argument over her. One became so angry that he killed Jane, scalped her, stripped off her clothes, and mutilated her. He took the scalp to the British camp where her fiancé just happened to be. The fiancé recognized Jane's hair as the Indian danced about with it. Burgoyne and the other British were mortified, but the melodramatic story quickly became known to all New Englanders, who became more determined than ever to stop Burgoyne.

Will shivered as he finished reading the *Gazette* article and handed the newspaper back to Jack Odiorne. He stood up and leaned over to kiss Abi, Will Jr., and Naby. Then he put on his cap and headed up School Street. He was off to join Stark.

28

On July 25, in Portsmouth, General Stark sent seven hundred men ahead to join Colonel Seth Warner in Manchester, Vermont. Warner had only one hundred and fifty men at his disposal to defend his state. Stark followed with the rest of his brigade to Charlestown on the Vermont border, then moved on to Manchester.

To Stark's dismay, on his arrival in Manchester on August 6 he found General Benjamin Lincoln, of Massachusetts, ordering Stark's advance New Hampshire brigade to move out, ostensibly under directions from a New Yorker, General Philip Schuyler, in charge of Washington's northern department of the Continental Army, which had just been run out of Ticonderoga and was retreating toward Albany and Saratoga. In a stiff confrontation, Stark told Lincoln that the New Hampshire militia was *not* part of the Continental Army and *not* under the congress's control and that he was *not* taking orders from Schuyler. Upon hearing that Stark's own plan was to attack Burgoyne's flank and rear, most probably in Bennington, a strategy consistent with Schuyler's in any event, Lincoln diplomatically sidestepped the issue of control and withdrew.

Several miles to the west, in New York, John Burgoyne was drawing up orders to give to the Hessian Lieutenant Colonel Frederick Baum to march to Bennington, Vermont, and take control of a rebel supply store and a herd of horses there that were reportedly under thin guard.

The opposing brigades converged toward Bennington.

—⚔—

Will's spirits were high as he marched from Manchester toward Bennington on the morning of August 14. The journey from Portsmouth was difficult, but everyone was buoyed by Stark's presence and the impressive outpouring of volunteers. As the troops marched along the road four abreast, families sometimes came out from their houses to cheer them on. There were occasional Africans among them. At one point a little African girl who could not have been more than five years old ran out from her mother to present Will with a yellow flower. He felt tears well in his eyes.

General Stark led the way on a coal-black horse at the head of the column, occasionally turning back to ride alongside the men as they marched, alternately joking with them and urging them to keep up the pace. He was an engaging officer whom Will found most impressive. A large, strongly built man, he projected unmistakable authority the men responded to very positively. Everyone knew of his earlier exploits in the French and Indian War and at Bunker Hill. He was hard as nails but a true friend of the foot soldier. The respect was mutual.

Will was deployed in the New Hampshire militia's Twelfth Regiment, commanded by Colonel David Hobart, of Plymouth. At midday, covered with dust, they arrived at the campsite selected by General Stark. It was located on the north side of the Walloomasac River, five miles northwest of Bennington on the easterly side of the road leading to Sancoick, New York. The camp was only a mile from the New York border. The men pitched camp as the colonel walked off to find Stark and receive his orders. Rumors were rampant.

A small reconnaissance force posted at Sancoick to warn of the advance of any British troops had just sent a message to Stark. An Englishman named Baum, with more than eight hundred infantry comprised of redcoats, Tories, Hessian dragoons, and Indians, was advancing south through Sancoick. The Americans had briefly skirmished with them but were withdrawing. Stark sent a call for help to Seth Warner and his Vermonters and began moving the men toward Sancoick. They soon spotted the British, and both sides stopped to look each other over. At that point Baum's men were spread across a hill just on the New York side of the border in a strong defensive posture, so Stark pulled his back about a mile to his camp. He spent the rest of the afternoon gathering more information about the strength and precise positions of the enemy and formulating a plan of attack.

The next day brought heavy rain that never stopped, preventing serious attack by either side. Baum ordered his men to construct a redoubt on the top of the hill, set up his two three-pound cannons overlooking a river bridge, and had the Tories build a breastwork to the south, his right flank. Stark settled for sending out patrols to snipe at Baum's Hessians.

Will was in one of those patrols. Hobart, his commander, taught the men an effective fighting technique: Hide behind a large tree to load and shoot, then run for another tree and duplicate the process. Do the same thing over and over again, creating the impression that the patrol was much larger than it actually was and confusing the Hessians as to where to shoot. Will thought at the end of the day that he'd picked off at least five of the enemy.

Baum became worried and sent a message to Burgoyne for help. The British general reacted immediately, dispatching a relief column of five hundred and fifty men. Unfortunately for Baum, the column's cannon and ammunition wagons bogged down on the muddy road, and by nighttime he was forced to encamp, still twenty miles north of Bennington.

By noon on August 16 the weather had cleared, and Stark called his officers together to outline his plan of attack. He decided to divide his forces into four elements and attack Baum's army on all sides simultaneously after encircling the Hessian placements. One regiment would go north around Baum's left flank. A second would make a pincer movement by proceeding to the south, then veer north to squeeze the enemy against the fire of the first. Will's company would storm the Tory breastwork just south of the river. Stark's own force of reserves would then follow through the center directly at the hill.

Will and the other soldiers immediately set about preparing themselves: checking their weapons, making cartridges, counting all their gear to ensure that nothing was missing, and talking nervously and excitedly with each other.

Joe Boynton said, "Here we go again, Will. Jus like the old days at Quebec."

"Yeah," Will said. "At least it's not snowing."

Just before giving the command to move out, Stark gestured toward the hill and said, "There's the enemy, boys, the redcoats and the Tories. We'll flog them, or Molly Stark sleeps a widow tonight." Will smiled at his leader's grit.

He and the other men in his company held back while the flanking units headed out through the thick woods to get into position. Will took a long slug from the dram of rum that circulated among the men as they all secured cornhusks in their hatbands so they could distinguish friend from foe when the fighting got close.

The delay in receiving the order to go forward was agonizing. Finally, at three o'clock they heard musket fire from the flanking regiment on the north, and within seconds the British responded with cannon and musket fire of their own. The southern regiment opened up, and Will's unit burst forward toward the breastwork amid a deafening din of explosions around the entire battleground.

Will was firing and reloading as fast as he could as the company ran through a ravine toward the Tory breastwork with bayonets fixed. They soon reached it and leapt over. No time to load and fire anymore. A heavy Vermont farmer without a cornhusk ran at Will with a bayonet. Will sidestepped, clubbed the man with the butt of his weapon, and stabbed him to the ground with his own bayonet. As blood gushed from the man's stomach, Will turned to thwart a charge by another screaming loyalist. The Tories knew they could expect no mercy, so they fought fiercely. As some of his comrades fell dead or wounded around him, Will felt like a whirling madman with the club and bayonet of his musket in the hand-to-hand combat, propelled as much by fear as by courage.

Within half an hour it was over. The New Hampshire flankers overran Baum's hilltop redoubt and sent the Hessians streaming downhill from their prepared positions into the relentless fire of Stark's men, who had at first suffered numerous casualties from the grapeshot of the Hessian cannons. The Tories in the breastwork fought until the last man went down, none wanting to be taken prisoner by his rebel neighbors. Will and his companions stepped over scores of dead bodies as they left the breastwork, reaching to assist their own wounded.

An hour later Will sat on the ground with the survivors of his company, still panting for breath, totally spent. Up on the hill he could see Stark's men rounding up prisoners and marching them back toward the American camp. Many of the militia soldiers were wandering about in a daze, but happy about what appeared to have been a rout. Will shouted over to Joe Boynton, "I saw you take out at least five Tories, Boynton. Not a bad job for a white man."

Boynton grinned at him. "You were doing pretty well yourself, for an African."

Will returned the grin. "My ancestors were pretty good at this sort of thing."

The men's high spirits were premature. Suddenly word flew to Stark that the British relief column, comprising mostly Hessians, was marching down the road from Sancoick and was just twenty minutes away. Stark knew instantly that he was in serious trouble. His men were drained, scattered, and out of formation from their units. Many were drinking, some heavily.

Stark called to his officers to reconsolidate their units as he led his own company up the road to meet the new threat. Within minutes the two sides were again engaged with the Hessian force, which was advancing in orderly fashion behind their two cannons, throwing never-ending rounds of grapeshot into the rebel ranks. Stark responded with the cannon captured from Baum as the American musketmen struggled to form up into effective fighting positions.

Will ran into the fray, shooting from tree to tree so furiously that his gun barrel again became too hot to hold. Cursing, he threw it aside, grabbed a musket lying beside a dead Hessian, and resumed firing.

The Hessians returned the American fire shot for shot and stood firm. The danger of a reversal in the outcome of the battle loomed.

Suddenly Will and his comrades were startled by wild shouting to their right. It was Seth Warner's Vermonters, driving into the Hessians' left flank at Warner's command:

"Fix bayonets! *Charge!*"

Rejuvenated, the Americans whooped and ran forward. Soon the Hessians were racing back up the road to Sancoick with Stark at their heels. Many of the Germans were killed or captured. Only darkness enabled them to escape annihilation. The German general survived and ordered a retreat during the night, thus salvaging the lives of the rest of his men.

The New Englanders all dropped to the ground right where they stood after firing their last shots at the retreating enemy. Asleep on the spot.

The Americans had a resounding victory at last. Stark had lost only seventy men killed or wounded, while he claimed two hundred and seven enemy dead and seven hundred prisoners. A relatively small encounter had sent Burgoyne a message he would not forget. When Will awoke as the sun came up the next morning, he stretched and smiled. *Winning sure beats losing.* The feeling became even sweeter when Colonel Hobart approached him.

"Well done, Will. You're some fighter!"

General Burgoyne wrote to his superiors in England: "The Hampshire grants in particular . . . now abound with the most active and rebellious race upon the continent, and hang like a gathering storm upon my left." Gentleman Johnny's bravado was substantially diminished as his main force moved slowly but inexorably south—toward Saratoga.

29

On the evening of September 18, 1777, Will stood before Benedict Arnold in the general's tent at Saratoga, New York.

"Did your owner free you?" Arnold asked.

"Not yet, sir. The losses at Quebec and Valcour Island didn't help."

"Too bad. This time I think you'll have a better justification. I believe we're going to give Johnny Burgoyne a dusting he won't soon forget. Tell me, did you get an advance understanding this time that you'll have your freedom in return for this military service?"

"I did, sir."

"In writing?"

"Yes."

"Excellent. That should hold up. I'm glad you've learned that tough issues have to be met head on. Now, the reason I called you in here is that when I noticed you in Henry Dearborn's regiment today, I told him you're to be assigned primarily to me for administrative assistance. But you'll be at his beck and call if he needs you for significant fighting. I understand you write English well?"

"Yes, sir."

"Then your duties for me will mainly be to write dispatches and act as a courier. Also, I want you to be another set of eyes and ears for me among the troops. Other than that, it'll be whatever comes into my mind at the moment. Be here at daybreak tomorrow to begin your duties. Dismissed." He turned back to his desk to complete some paperwork.

As he walked to his regiment, Will was stunned and elated: *That man really understands the Africans' situation and how to approach it. What an opportunity!*

At Saratoga, Stark's and Arnold's exploits were the talk of the camp, including among Will's African friends and new acquaintances. Several of these men were from New Hampshire. A few were gathered around a fire next to the Dearborn regiment food wagons when Will returned from Arnold's tent.

Prince Whipple was there. His owner, William Whipple, had been promoted to the rank of brigadier general. Prince had also obtained his owner's prior commitment to free him if he went along. Prince Light and London Daily from Exeter were also there, as was Oxford Tash, who was about Will's age, from Newmarket.

Prince Whipple had brought two others to meet Will. The first man was Sampson Moore, a volunteer under Captain Benjamin Sias in General Whipple's brigade. He was a very big man, a slave of Colonel Archelaus Moore of Canterbury, New Hampshire, who had also promised his slave freedom in return for fighting in the Revolution.

The second was Jude Hall, from Exeter, attached under Enoch Poor in Scammell's Third Regiment. Hall had served in the army since Bunker Hill and had gained a reputation as a great soldier. He was affectionately called Old Rock.

Two other Africans had introduced themselves to Will. The first was George Knox, from Enfield, near Hanover. Knox, of deep black complexion, was an enlistee attached to Captain John Wheelock's company in Colonel Jonathan Chase's regiment. A slave of the family of Eleazar Wheelock, the founder of Dartmouth College, he was an experienced fighter. The Saratoga campaign was his third enlistment. He had just arrived from his home in northern New Hampshire.

The second man was Wentworth Cheswell, from Newmarket. At thirty-one, he was seven years younger than Will, and a private in John Langdon's independent company. Cheswell was a quadroon, the light tan son of a white mother and a well-known Negro housewright, also by a white mother. Cheswell had been formally educated at Dummer Academy in Byfield, Massachusetts, then returned to Newmarket as a teacher. At twenty-one he married a white woman, Mary Davis of Durham. By 1770 he owned one hundred and fourteen acres of land, held a pew in the Newmarket Meeting House, referred to himself as a yeoman, and listed his occupation as husbandry. In March 1776 he signed New Hampshire's Association Test, by which the citizens of the state, including James Clarkson, endorsed and sent to the Continental Congress their votes in favor of declaring independence from King George. He was accepted as white by the white citizenry, yet he also moved freely in the African community as one of them. By the time of the Revolution, he already held administrative positions in the Newmarket town government. He was chafing to be part of the fight, but Langdon's company had yet to see any action.

"Congratulations, Will," Prince Whipple said when Will told his friends about his assignment to Arnold. "Now you rank with me." They were both aides to generals.

"Whipple's done nothing compared to Arnold," George Knox said. "In fact, Arnold's a much better fighter than Granny Gates. Gates is too cautious, only thinks about defenses. Arnold attacks."

"Arnold's smart, too," Sampson Moore said. "Way he tricked the English last month at Fort Stanwix was amazing. Convinced the Indians he was coming against the British with thousands of men when he only had a couple of hundred. Indians deserted the redcoats, and they had to abandon the fort."

Jude Hall said, "Stark's good as Arnold. Saved the day at Bunker Hill. And look what he just did at Bennington. Our first real victory."

Will said, "Stark's strong, for sure—saw it myself. But Arnold was tremendous at Quebec and Valcour. Outside of maybe Stark and Dan Morgan, I'd rather fight with him. He knows what he's doing."

"Will, I'd still be careful if I were you," Wentworth Cheswell said. "I'm not so sure about Arnold."

"Why not?" Will said.

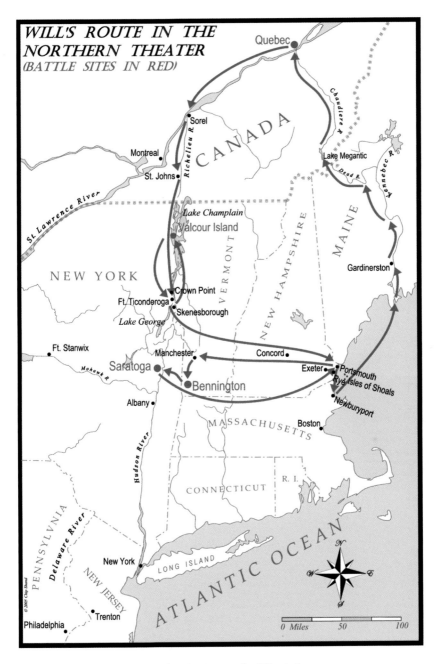

Map by Charles Shand, of Lake Barcroft, Virginia

"For one thing, he can't seem to get along with anybody, particularly his superiors."

"What else have you heard?"

"He's ambitious. All he cares about is his own fame, money, and social rank. His pride gets hurt whenever someone else is praised. Thinks he should be number one all the time, can't take orders."

"Not good, if it's true," Will said. "All I can tell you is he's fearless in battle and he cares about his men, including Africans. Been good to me."

"You oughta be glad someone's concerned bout you," Prince said.

"Meaning what?"

"Jack Odiorne's been sniffing around Abi again. Over at Atkinson's house every weekend. Sometimes in the evenings."

"He's a long time friend of the family," Will said. "There's nothing to it."

"If you say so," Prince said.

The others looked the other way, and nothing more was said.

But as Will lay alone in his bedroll later that night, he had to rein in his imagination.

30

*U*nfortunately for Philip Schuyler, the American general in command of Washington's northern department, news of the favorable developments at Bennington and Fort Stanwix had reached the congress in Philadelphia too late to save Schuyler's job. The loss of Ticonderoga and the enmity of the New England delegates did him in, and on August 19 General Horatio Gates arrived in Albany to assume command at Van Schaick's Island.

"Granny" Gates inherited an army saved from destruction by Schuyler's decision to abandon Fort Ticonderoga and retreat to the south, burning bridges and crops and appropriating horses, cattle, and other livestock. The Americans had thus become well provisioned, while Burgoyne's supply lines were stretched longer and longer by the day.

Burgoyne's objective was Albany, even if that meant a confrontation with the colonial insurgents. In early September he directed his army to cross from the east bank to the west bank of the Hudson River at Batten Kill, New York. Once across, they encamped at a large house in Saratoga, twenty-nine miles north of Albany.

At that point Gates's growing force was stationed just five miles south of Burgoyne. The American general had grown confident; with reinforcements flowing in daily, he now had over 10,000 men in his command. He had halted Schuyler's retreat and ordered his men north to Bemis Heights, a high plateau also on the Hudson's west bank, just south of Saratoga. There his Polish chief engineer, Tadeusz Kościuszko, began felling trees and fortifying the site. Soon a three-sided earthwork nearly a quarter-mile long emerged on the bluff.

New Hampshire was well represented in Gates's army. Enoch Poor's brigade had been with Schuyler since Ticonderoga. General Whipple's brigade had arrived, as had the First New Hampshire Regiment under Colonel Joseph Cilley, the Second now commanded by Colonel George Reid, and the Third under Colonel Alexander Scammell. An independent company under Colonel John Langdon, of Portsmouth, had also marched to Saratoga and joined Gates. Several smaller units from towns throughout the state arrived and were variously attached.

Second in command of the New Hampshire Third was none other than the irrepressible Henry Dearborn, now a major. After his capture during the Battle of Quebec on New Year's Day 1776, Dearborn had spent four and a half months as a prisoner before being released on parole on May 16. Traveling by boat and through the forest once again, he didn't arrive at Portsmouth and his home in Nottingham until July 16 of that year. Responding to his state's call for troops in April 1777, he signed on with Scammell's regiment and went immediately to Ticonderoga, arriving only in time for the retreat south toward Albany.

John Stark was not yet at Saratoga. After the battle at Bennington, he remained in that area, although many soldiers had already opted to return home when their short enlistments expired. Finally, on September 11, six hundred of Stark's New Hampshire men, including Will, arrived at Gates's camp, followed four days later by the general himself.

On September 18 Will's enlistment, like those of the rest of Stark's men, was due to expire. General Gates was offering a ten-dollar bonus to those who extended and stayed with him, but most of the troops were planning to pack it in and go home.

Will, facing a big decision, headed for General Whipple's brigade to discuss the situation with Prince. After they caught up with each other, Will said, "Prince, it looks like this is going to be a major battle. I want to be in it. Question is what officer that I know will have me and treat me fairly."

"You're in luck. Your old leader Henry Dearborn is here—go talk to him. From what I hear about your fighting at Bennington, bet he'll be glad to have you."

Will smiled. "Great idea. Where do I find him?"

"He's with Scammell over to west of us. Dan Morgan's riflemen there too. I hear Dearborn's light infantry's been attached to Morgan."

"Good. Morgan was at Quebec too. He's a good man, and nobody's a tougher fighter, especially in the woods."

"Bet you'll like that extra ten dollars they give you for re-upping," Prince said.

"Damn right. That plus the six dollars and sixty-six cents a month regular army pay beats the zero dollars I get working for the Clarksons." Both men knew these sums were pretty good money when a journeyman carpenter got only fifteen dollars a month and an apprentice would receive only ten dollars for a whole year. Will was a happy man at the end of each month as he pocketed his pay from the quartermaster. He'd need it for the carpentry business he planned to start when he got his freedom.

Major Dearborn remembered Will and was very pleased to see him again, shaking his hand vigorously. When Will outlined his situation, he said, "Sure thing, Will. If Stark and his troops aren't going to be here, we'll be delighted to have you."

He assigned Will to Company Four. Will was particularly happy when he learned that his old friend Joe Boynton had been moved up and was commissioned as the ensign in that company. Joe gave Will a quick rundown of the unit, reviewed its tactics, and supplied him with some equipment he was missing, including a tomahawk, fifteen rounds of cartridges, six flints, a pound of powder, forty lead balls, and a canteen.

"That should fix you up. I sure feel better that we're back under Dearborn. When the thing starts, let's stay tight. I heard about your fighting at Bennington—you're getting quite a reputation. Maybe

I was wrong. Clarkson may be willing to give you your freedom when he hears about it."

"I got him to agree to free me if I came this time."

"Good man. When we meet the lobsterbacks this time, give em hell again."

"Count on it."

Stark and the bulk of his troops marched off at midday on September 18. Only a few remained other than Will.

31

Will awoke at four o'clock to a cold and damp morning on September 19. He had breakfast with the other men in Dearborn's companies and then headed for Arnold's tent to report for his first day of duty for the general. As he left, Dearborn's other men were falling into formation in preparation for finishing a bridge across the Hudson.

Just as Will entered Arnold's tent, a courier pushed past him to deliver a dramatic report: The British had begun to march toward them along the river and inland.

Arnold immediately directed Will to follow him as he flew out of the tent and toward Gates's headquarters. They arrived just ahead of the rest of Gates's staff and some of their aides. The commander outlined his plan.

"Gentlemen, here's the way I want it. We'll all deploy behind Kościuszko's new fortifications. We'll let the enemy come to us and try to break the barricade. I believe they'll destroy themselves in the process.

"I'll take the east end down to the river. Langdon's troops and the continentals under Glover, Nixon, and Patterson will be with me. Arnold, you take the west end on the left. You'll have Morgan's riflemen and Dearborn's light infantry. Learned and Poor, you'll be in the center. Poor, you'll have overall command over the three

New Hampshire regiments—Cilley's, Reid's, and Scammell's. Any questions?"

Arnold immediately spoke up.

"General, I'm concerned about that height of land to the northwest. If the British seize it and attack our left flank with cannon and bayonets, we'll be in trouble. As you know, they're at their best in frontal assaults in the open. We have the advantage in the woods, particularly since a lot of Burgoyne's Indian allies have deserted him. I think we've got to seize the initiative and attack through the woods and get control of those heights."

Gates gave Arnold a penetrating look, then said, "We'll have plenty of time to react if Burgoyne tries that, General Arnold."

"Not if we don't know about it early enough. Even if the attack is unsuccessful, we can fall back on these prepared positions and fight defensively."

Gates looked unconvinced. He finally agreed that Arnold could send Morgan and Dearborn out to the northwest to reconnoiter and counter any British moves at the American left.

Will was impressed with the way his boss had challenged Gates and angry at the way the commander had treated him.

As they left Gates's headquarters, Arnold said, "Will, you go with Dearborn and make sure I'm kept up to date on everything that happens out there on the hill."

Just before noon, the three hundred men of Dearborn's and Morgan's units moved into the forest. As they cautiously pressed north from tree to tree, Will stayed right on Joe Boynton's heels, keeping a sharp eye open for any unusual movement that could be the British. By one o'clock they reached the Freeman Farm clearing and took up positions, to wait and watch—some in the deserted log cabin in the center of the field, some behind a rail fence, most behind or up in the trees along the perimeter.

Burgoyne had indeed perceived the point that worried Arnold: Control of the heights to the northwest of the American left flank could be critical. The British light infantry was to reach the heights to the west, encircle the Americans' left flank, and push the rebels toward the Hudson River, where Burgoyne would riddle them with devastating firepower.

Shortly after one o'clock, Will peered out from behind the rail fence at the clearing where he was lying and looked toward the far end of the field to the north, about three hundred and fifty yards away. At that moment a column of British redcoats, perhaps a hundred in number, emerged from the woods and slowly approached the log cabin and the other farm buildings in the center, bayonets fixed.

Joe Boynton, lying next to Will, saw them at the same time and put his hand on Will's arm, indicating to delay shooting.

Two minutes later, as the British reached within a hundred feet of the cabin, the American troops inside opened up, with devastating effect. Will and the rest of Dearborn's men instantly rose as one and began running, yelling, and shooting toward the British, as did Morgan's riflemen from the trees. The redcoats, already hit hard, turned and ran back toward the woods with Will's company in hot pursuit.

But at that moment, to the Americans' left, the British light infantry hit their flank, opening up with deadly cannon fire. As many in the regiment fell, the rest scattered into the woods in disarray. Chaos prevailed amid the thunder of musket and cannon fire. Morgan's renowned turkey call in the trees brought the Americans back to order, and they began to collect themselves and their wounded on the south side of the clearing.

Fortunately, the British were equally confused as they continued to shoot in the crossfire, sometimes hitting their own men as they also attempted to pull their wounded to safety in the woods. Both sides soon broke off the engagement to consolidate their troops. The battle had lasted just forty minutes.

Joe Boynton and Will sat against two oak trees twenty feet from the southeast corner of the clearing, panting.

Back at the American headquarters, Gates concluded from the gunfire and reports that the British had begun a full-scale assault. He ordered General Poor to send two New Hampshire regiments, Cilley's First and Scammell's Third, to reinforce Morgan and Dearborn.

Two hours later, after Cilley and Scammell had arrived and taken up positions, the former on the far left flank and the latter in the center, the battlefield suddenly exploded again, with the loudest and most incessant roar of cannon and musket fire Will had ever heard. The opposing armies pushed against each other like two giant prehistoric mammals.

The men in Dearborn's regiment fought side by side with Scammell's. Will could hardly believe the intensity of the fight as his unit overran the clearing three times, on each occasion taking the British field pieces and turning them on their owners. But every time they were forced to run back to the woods as a British countercharge retook the cannons and once again turned grapeshot on their backs. Will's ammunition had long run out, and again he had to scoop up a musket and cartridge case of a fallen redcoat. Soon that also ran out, and with the others he found himself in hand-to-hand combat, wrestling with his bayonet against one British soldier after another.

During a respite, he spotted Arnold, as he later told Joe Boynton, "riding in front of the lines, his eyes flashing, pointing with his sword to the advancing foe, with a voice that rang clear as a trumpet and electrified the line."

Will also caught sight of General Burgoyne some distance away in the thick of the fighting at the head of his men. By contrast, General Gates never left his headquarters, miles to the rear, although he ordered Poor and Learned to send men forward to support the fray.

Twice Will's Third New Hampshire Regiment was in danger of being destroyed, only to be rescued by their brethren, first by a Connecticut regiment and then by Cilley.

Toward the end of the day, Burgoyne directed his regimental commander, still posted with little fighting on the British left flank at the river, to bring as many men as he could to assist the forces in the center and on the right. Those relatively fresh troops drove into the right flank of Will's company.

As darkness fell, the Americans turned the redcoat regiment back, but neither side could move the other. Technically, the British had prevailed in that they retained possession of the ground, but their losses were massive: one hundred sixty dead, three hundred and sixty-four wounded, and forty-two missing. The American losses were less than half that.

But Will was down. Just as he jumped a fence after three British soldiers, one wheeled and fired at him on the run. The awkward shot was lucky: The musket ball hit Will in the left leg just above the knee. A hot, searing sensation immobilized the leg and sent him rolling onto the wheat field, where he crawled to retrieve his gun, in and out of consciousness, trying desperately to stay alert to parry any enemy soldier who approached him.

Bullets were still flying, so he stayed as flat to the ground as possible. Blood poured down his leg, and he was afraid he would bleed to death. He managed to reach down, pull off his belt, and secure it tightly about his upper leg as a rudimentary tourniquet. It seemed to lessen the flow, but he knew he could pass out and release the pressure.

He had never felt such pain. Faced with death, he prayed fervently to the African spirits and the Christian god. He couldn't be particular under the circumstances—he'd accept help from any source.

The colonial soldiers had retreated into the blessed cover of the trees, but the wounded and the dying remained out in the clearing. Joe Boynton and the other men in Dearborn's unit dared not venture into that open area to assist Will and the other wounded for fear of being shot.

Will's own pain was made much worse by the groans and calls for help from the other wounded and the dying. Knowing there was nothing he could do for himself or to help the others became a real-life nightmare that would haunt him for years. And there would be a follow-up British attack in the morning.

Mercifully, at about three o'clock in the morning, he fell asleep.

The follow-up attack the next day never materialized. Burgoyne had flinched and pulled back. His generals urged him to keep up the pressure from the previous day and attack immediately, but the British commander was concerned about the extent to which his men had been cut up, and he had a message from Sir Henry Clinton in New York that he *might* send 2000 reinforcements in about ten days. Notwithstanding the vagueness of the promise, Burgoyne decided to wait.

⊰⊱

As the sun rose in the clear sky, Will was nudged awake by Joe Boynton, who gave him water to quench his severe thirst and summoned a field surgeon to evaluate his condition. The doctor determined that the leg was broken just above the knee. Fortunately, the musket ball was partially visible against the knee and accessible. He gave Will a strong slug of rum and a piece of wood to bite on, then cut out the ball. He bandaged the wound and set the leg in a makeshift splint of tree limbs. Two privates put Will on a stretcher and carried him forward to where Dearborn's unit had been bedded down. One of the other men in the company made a pair of crutches out of two tree branches.

The pain was still excruciating, but Will knew he was lucky to be alive. The thought crossed his mind once again that he must have been destined to survive, that a greater force was protecting him. He remembered that Reverend Haven had once mentioned a Christian doctrine called predestination. Will decided he'd ask Haven to tell him more about that when he got back to Portsmouth.

⊰⊱

Will, on crutches, watched again in Gates's tent as Arnold requested permission to attack immediately. Gates ignored him and even failed to give him credit, in reports to General Washington, for his contributions at Freeman's Farm on September 19. Over the course of the next two and a half weeks, clashes between the two reached the point where Gates effectively took over all of Arnold's troops himself, though he did not explicitly remove Arnold from command.

"Sometimes I feel like I'm put upon as much as you slaves, Will," Arnold said one day. "I can't stand the way that man treats me."

"I can't either, sir." But the man had no idea, didn't know a fraction of what it was like. If Will could get to Arnold's rank, he could do something about it. But the whites would never understand. Which was all the more reason to succeed.

By October 4 Burgoyne had tired of awaiting further word from Clinton. He called his generals together to set the strategy. By this time, his officers were of a mind to fall back to Batten Kill and wait for Clinton—or, lacking such reinforcement, to move up to Ticonderoga or even back to Canada for the winter. But Burgoyne wanted no part of anything that smacked of retreat or defeat and was willing to risk all in a final confrontation. He compromised somewhat, settling for a reconnaissance in force, with 2000 men under General Fraser, to explore the enemy's left wing. The force would advance on October 7. If the situation looked promising, they'd attack on the eighth. If not, they would fall back to Batten Kill on October 11.

Shortly before two o'clock in the afternoon on the 7, Burgoyne and his officers and soldiers pulled up on a wheat field. They saw nothing that looked ominous, but one of the officers expressed concern as the troops settled there: The right and left flanks both touched the woods, vulnerable to potential enemy fire.

The Americans were indeed in the woods, and they had already sent word to General Gates, who this time reacted immediately: "Well then, order on Morgan to begin the game."

Will received a message from the field that there was some enemy activity in the northwest and reported it to Arnold. Arnold requested permission to investigate, which Gates granted. When those two returned and reported that a substantial enemy force was moving on the Americans' left flank, Gates proposed to order just Morgan and Dearborn to move quickly to the far left and outflank Fraser.

Arnold blew up in Gates's face.

"That's nowhere near enough men! Send Learned and Poor as well."

Gates ignored Arnold and appeared to dismiss him altogether from the battle, but Lincoln convinced his superior to send Poor's brigade to meet the enemy's left flank while Morgan and Dearborn hit from the right. Learned's brigade was held in reserve to attack the center once Morgan, Dearborn, and Poor were in position. Now backed by nearly twelve thousand men, Gates exuded confidence.

Morgan, Dearborn, and Poor's men, comprising the three New Hampshire continental regiments, proceeded to attack strongly on the British right and left flanks, but the redcoat center held firm.

Learned's American brigade was moving slowly against the British center when Arnold appeared on horseback, and without orders effectively took command of Learned's three regiments, urging the men to follow him.

He drove an attack, swinging behind the two British redoubts. He had them surrounded, and the Americans were squeezing the enemy into submission. Suddenly Arnold's horse was killed from under him. He tumbled off, and the horse fell on him, breaking Arnold's leg. Several of his men pulled him out from under the horse and carried him back to a field hospital, where, before passing out, he overruled the unanimous opinion of a group of doctors and refused to let them amputate his leg. It would be months before he recuperated.

In the next few minutes, two of Burgoyne's key generals, one of them Fraser, were killed.

The fight was effectively finished as darkness fell. Morgan, Dearborn, the New Hampshire regiments—and Arnold—had carried the day.

The British and German losses were two hundred seventy-eight dead, three hundred thirty-one wounded, and two hundred eighty-five captured. The Americans reported thirty killed and one hundred wounded.

Aware that his remaining elements could be overrun in the morning, Burgoyne ordered his troops to retreat to the safety of the large redoubt in the rear. The escape route he had in his sights was slightly to the northeast, up the Hudson River toward Batten Kill.

—⚔—

The next day Will visited Arnold, who was in the same field hospital. The general was obviously in great pain, but he managed a smile when he saw his African aide.

"A fine pair of soldiers we turned out to be, Will," he said. "Not much help to our comrades in this condition."

"Right about that, sir. But the situation is looking good, thanks to your quick move in seizing command of Learned's men. Looks like it should be over soon. They won't even need us anymore."

"Appears that way." Arnold looked sad at the thought of no more fighting. "We may be going different ways now, Will. But I want you to promise me you'll never give up your fight for freedom and dignity. Life's not worth living without it."

"I won't, General. You have my word on it." Will looked straight into Arnold's eyes and saluted. He then turned to leave quickly, so the general wouldn't see his eyes glistening.

Arnold called after him: "If there's ever anything I can do for you, Will, don't hesitate to call upon me. I'll even come to Portsmouth on your behalf."

During the next week, as the Americans pursued the British up the Hudson, Will followed in the back of a wagon.

On the morning of October 13, John Burgoyne awoke to discover that his escape route had been cut off by John Stark, who suddenly showed up out of the woods with over a thousand newly enlisted New Hampshire militiamen and crossed the river at Batten Kill to the west side.

That afternoon Burgoyne called his staff into a council of war. They concluded that the situation was hopeless and that surrender was the only viable option. Word was sent to Gates. Over the next three days, the terms of the convention were negotiated, then signed on the sixteenth. The ceremony was set for the next day.

Between two o'clock and dusk on October 17, Burgoyne's remaining 5895 troops stacked their arms and began filing between two lines of American soldiers. The victors were a motley, bedraggled lot, but they stood tall in the clear afternoon sun.

On his crutches, Will was proud to be in that line. He had done what he came to do. Now back to Portsmouth, to check on his family and capitalize on his accomplishments.

PART THREE

Consequences: 1777–1789

32

News of the great victory reached Portsmouth and the rest of the eastern seaboard six days later, on October 23, 1777. The rejoicing was punctuated by the firing of cannons over the harbor and celebrated by dancing and parading in the streets.

Abi and the children's exuberance was cut short by the news from Jack Odiorne that Gates's army, including Poor's New Hampshire regiments, wasn't returning home. They were now on their way south to join George Washington's troops facing Lord William Howe and Sir Henry Clinton at a place called Valley Forge, outside of Philadelphia, which had fallen to the British on September 26. Will's life could still be in danger. Who knew when she would see him. Worst of all, she didn't even know whether he'd been wounded—or killed—during the fighting.

As she was cleaning the dishes on Thursday evening, she heard a loud knock on the door. She'd been in the back of the house—how long had whoever it was been knocking? She opened the door to find Will, on crutches with his leg in a splint, a wagon full of soldiers pulling away from the house. She cried out and threw her arms around him, almost knocking him down.

They hugged until they were both breathless, then went inside and Abi called the children. More hugs. After several minutes, Will and Abi followed Willie and Naby as the children skipped back to the kitchen.

But just as Will walked in, through the side window of the kitchen he caught sight of Jack Odiorne closing the back gate and proceeding down the street. Will wheeled on Abi.

"What in hell was he doing here?"

"We was just talking. He brought me some vegetables."

"Damn it, Abi. You're making me look like a fool in this town—I heard about you two all the way up in Saratoga. I—"

"How can you say that? How can you *think* it?" Nobody had ever looked at him with so much hurt and anger. "Stop talking that nonsense. Who told you—"

"Prince. The other men seem to know about it too."

"Did all that fighting beat the sense out of you? You listen to me, Will Clarkson, and listen good. Jack's been kind and helpful to me while you been gone—who'd you think I was going to talk to? He's a good friend of mine, and he's the best friend you got in this world. And I wouldn't cheat on you with him or anyone else—even if it got me my freedom and all the money there is. Don't you know Jack? Don't you know *me*?"

Will looked into her eyes and knew that every word she said was the truth. He pulled her to him and hugged her tight. She cried and her body shook as he said over and over, "I believe you, honey. I'm so sorry . . . so sorry."

After a while Abi calmed down and asked him what had happened at Bennington and Saratoga. But she didn't press when it became obvious that he didn't want to talk about it. He was much more interested in hearing how Abi was and what Willie and Naby had been up to.

As it was getting dark, Will set off for the difficult walk on his crutches down Water Street to the Clarkson house.

Mrs. Haven hugged him warmly when she answered the door. "Thank God you're alive and home, Will." She stared at his leg. "How bad is it?"

"Should be completely healed in six months, but I may end up with a limp because the leg was set wrong on the battlefield."

She sighed and said, "I'm afraid we've got bad news here. Mr. Clarkson has had a severe stroke. Walter's moved into the house and taken charge at the tannery. He's not home yet."

"Where's Master James now?"

"In the chair in the living room. Come in and see him, but . . . be prepared."

Nothing could have prepared Will for what he saw when he entered the living room. James sat slouched in the chair, staring straight ahead. His hair was disheveled and much whiter than Will remembered it.

"He can't speak," Mrs. Haven said. "Doesn't recognize anyone or respond in any way to other people. We have no idea how long he'll be like this. It's very sad."

Will shook his head. James Jr. had been a decent owner most of the time, except when he'd refused to free Will after the Canadian expedition. Wasn't the man his father had been, but better than most owners in the city. *Now what do I do? Looks like I have to deal with Walter. Doesn't bode well.*

He went to the kitchen for his supper and then to his hut for the night.

Will spent Friday at the Atkinson house with his family. Then, early Saturday morning, along with the Clarksons and many other Portsmouth residents, Will and his family repaired to the southern water's edge of the Piscataqua River. There they watched the brand new Portsmouth-built sloop-of-war *Ranger,* three hundred and nineteen tons and mounted with 18 nine-pound guns, set sail for France from Rising Castle Island under Captain John Paul Jones. A cheer rose from the city's inhabitants on the shore as the ship caught a fresh breeze and headed out toward the Isles of Shoals and the open Atlantic. Captain Jones stood on the quarterdeck in full uniform as one hundred and fifty officers and men snapped to his orders. From her stern, a bright new red-and-white-striped flag with thirteen stars on a blue background, designed by Betsy Ross in Philadelphia, flew for the first time on an American warship.

Will looked on with special interest and pride. Abi had heard that two of the *Ranger'* s crew were free Africans from Newburyport, Massachusetts—Scipio Africanus and Cato Carlile.

And Will had been told that Captain Jones had developed a friendship with Phillis Wheatley while in Boston and had recently sent her some verses of his own.

⎯⎯

On the way back from the *Ranger* ceremony, Will saw Walter Clarkson returning to the house. He moved over on the road to walk alongside him.

"Mr. Clarkson, I'll be gathering up my things later this week as soon as I arrange for other lodging. If it's all right with you, I'll stay at the house until then. I assume you have another man at the tannery by now. But if not, and you'd like to hire me, I'd be interested in discussing an appropriate wage."

Walter stared at him for a long moment. "What are you talking about, Will?"

"My freedom, as Master James agreed."

"I know nothing of such an agreement."

Will handed him the letter James had signed. "I have it in writing."

Walter only glanced at the piece of paper. "The war's not over— we don't know yet how it will play out. I'm sure James was talking about the end of it all, when we've won and we're safe. More than that, Colonel Bannister has been talking to me about these agreements. He doesn't think they're a good idea. Certainly not enforceable. I'll expect you to be at the tannery on Monday."

Clarkson walked on without looking at Will, who came to a full stop. Reneging. Breaking the agreement as though it never happened. Bannister! Will walked over to a bench by the side of the road and sat down, holding his head in his hands. Abi and the children caught up with him.

"What happened? What's the matter?" Abi put her arm around his shoulders.

'He broke his word, Abi. He won't honor James's agreement."

"Oh, Will! What'll you do?"

"Got to be careful. Can't just shoot the bastard or run away. The courts won't help. Trying to go public and embarrass him into complying would be sure to backfire with Bannister still in charge here. I have to think this through. Find an answer that doesn't throw everything out the window. . ."

After a few moments, he stood up with Abi's help and resumed the walk back to the Atkinson house. While the children played outside, they went up to her room and talked about his predicament. In the end he concluded that for the moment he had no alternative but to accept Walter's unfair position. But he would write immediately to Benedict Arnold and ask him to come and try to reason with his owner. His prestige might change Walter's mind.

In the meantime, he'd stick to the other aspects of his plan. Continue to press forward in spite of this setback. And see a lawyer about enforcing his contract.

"Will, please sit down and tell me about Saratoga," Reverend Haven said a week later when Will showed up in his library. "What was it like?"

Will hadn't discussed the campaign with anyone, but he couldn't hold out on the minister. For the next hour he described the battles at Freeman's Farm and in the wheat field at Bemis Heights, including how he'd been shot and wounded. When he finished, he posed his own question to the minister.

"Reverend, there's something I want to ask you about. Before I went away you mentioned a Christian doctrine called predestination. What exactly is that?"

The minister smiled. "I'm intrigued. Why the sudden interest in that subject?"

"Several times in the war—the march to Quebec, the battles at Valcour Island, Bennington, and Saratoga—it was practically a miracle I wasn't killed. I kept asking myself,

Why? Was it for some reason? Was some . . . higher intelligence watching out for me?"

"That may well be, but first, the doctrine. Predestination emanated from the teachings of Martin Luther and John Calvin, the Protestant reformers, in the sixteenth century. The biblical basis is found principally in the Romans and Ephesians scriptures. The simplest way to define predestination is that God has 'elected' certain people for eternal salvation."

"Isn't that unfair to the ones who haven't been elected?" Will asked.

"Think about it. No one *deserves* to be saved. We've all sinned. God's decision, through Christ, to save some of us and not others isn't unfair to the others—first because they're getting what they deserve and second because they fail, within the earthly confines of their free will, to make their own decision to follow Jesus. To the extent that this reflects an inconsistency, we simply accept it as a mystery. A human being's freedom to take responsibility for his own life is merely a gift from God, which isn't diminished by God's *divine* will, power, and responsibility."

"But what if someone wants to be saved but can't be because he's not one of the elect?"

"That can't happen, because no one can desire God unless God has first moved in his heart."

"Can an African, a slave, be one of the elect?"

"Certainly. Although I can assure you that many white slave owners in Portsmouth would probably be surprised by my answer— particularly in that they're rightfully afraid they themselves might not be so fortunate."

Will laughed. "Reverend Haven, do you think it's possible that I am one of the elect?"

"I do. Certainly the signs you've noticed—your survival in extremely difficult circumstances and your close calls with death— raise the prospect. Also, you've lived a good life and done things that suggest you may be qualified in an earthly sense if not at the divine level. But that alone isn't enough. None of us earns salva- tion. A person has to take positive steps to demonstrate that he accepts God's grace in electing him. Your calling out to God when you were injured on the battlefield at Saratoga, although somewhat ambiguous because you also invoked pagan deities, is an indica- tion that you're moving toward that acceptance. Only by accept- ing Jesus Christ as your savior and becoming a Christian can you possibly become atoned as an elect human being."

Will stood up. "Thank you, Reverend. I still need to think about this some more, but I'm tending toward becoming a Christian. I'll let you know."

"Excellent, Will. I'll do everything I can to help you, including the necessary preparation."

The two shook hands, and Will left. He was pleased with the way the discussion had gone. *This should also help make my enslavement seem even worse to the whites. Make Reverend Haven even more eager to help me.* Another step in the plan.

Will's interest in Christianity was genuine, but the practical aspects clinched it.

Two weeks later, after the Sunday service at South Church, Will spoke to the minister.

"I talked it over with Abi, Reverend. She believes that my becoming a Christian would be a blessing, a final consecration of our marriage."

Three months later, in November, after teaching sessions during the autumn with Reverend Haven, Will was baptized a Christian at the South Church. Abi, Will Jr., Naby, and Mrs. Haven were the only witnesses to the simple ceremony. Will felt a distinct glow as they walked to the Clarkson house.

⎯⎯⎯

For the first four months back at the tannery, while he was still on crutches, Will worked on the final finishing of the leather products. He then worked at inside jobs, handling the hides in the vats, until the following May, when the freezing winter relaxed its grip. When 1778's warm weather arrived he was outdoors again, scraping the fresh hides on a beam over the river.

He did see a lawyer about his contract with James Clarkson. The lawyer filed a suit, but it was dismissed on the grounds that James's incapacity prevented him from defending the case and that as a slave Will had no standing to sue.

In July Will and Abi stood up for Jack Odiorne and Matilda, another slave of the Odiorne family over in Rye, at their wedding. Matilda was a friend of Abi's, so Abi was pleased. The friendship between Will and Jack grew even stronger.

Events in the war moved slowly. Spurred by the American success at Saratoga, France on February 6, 1778, had signed two treaties with the United States, one of amity and commerce and the second of alliance. By midyear, France, Spain, the Netherlands, and the United States were all aligned against Great Britain, but little progress was made by either side on the battlefield. In June the first shots were fired between France and England, off the Brittany coast. Thereafter, neither side made a significant move.

Only John Paul Jones delivered any good news that year, harassing the British off their own shores, to their great embarrassment. Aboard *Ranger* he made raids at Whitehaven and St. Mary's Isle, two British towns on the Irish Sea, and captured *H.M.S. Drake*, terrifying the English populace and beginning the undermining of support for the war in Parliament.

There was a happy occasion on the family front: In July, everyone climbed aboard wagons and traveled down to Newbury for the wedding of James III and Elizabeth Kimball. Will was pleased to see that his favorite white Clarkson had chosen such a pretty and pleasant young lady as his bride.

The British returned John Paul Jones's favor early in 1779, conducting hit-and-run raids on the middle Atlantic and New England coasts, burning and looting several seaside towns, including Portsmouth, Virginia, and Fairfield, Connecticut.

In France, Benjamin Franklin convinced the French admiralty to supply a task force of five ships under the command of Jones, who'd turned *Ranger* over to Lieutenant Thomas Simpson for the return to Portsmouth, New Hampshire. The flagship of the new Jones task force was an old East Indiaman renamed *Bonhomme Richard*. Jones led the force clockwise around the British Isles, taking a number of prizes. Then, on September 23, 1779, he faced off against the newer, faster, and more heavily armed *H.M.S. Serapis* off Flamborough Head in the North Sea. In a dramatic battle lasting more than four hours, Jones outmaneuvered and outlasted his British adversary, who finally struck his colors first. *Bonhomme Richard* was so badly damaged that she soon sank. Jones transferred his flag to *Serapis* and sailed with his prizes to a neutral Dutch port.

—✦—

Concerned that he hadn't received a reply from Benedict Arnold, Will wrote a second letter seeking his assistance.

—✦—

Two traumatic developments hit Will and Abi in the late spring 1779. First, in May, Theodore Atkinson died, leaving Abi and the children with little sustenance or direction until Atkinson's executor sold her and the children to John Meechum, a storekeeper who'd recently moved to Portsmouth and wasn't yet well known in town. Both Will and Abi were fearful of what the change would bring. Then in June, James Clarkson Jr. died. James III was named executor of the estate, but his absence in Massachusetts left Walter Clarkson still in charge at the tannery. Walter now took every opportunity to give Will assignments that were difficult to carry out with his limited mobility and to make disparaging comments to Will, most often in front of others.

Otherwise, elsewhere in Portsmouth word of Will's military exploits had significantly enhanced his reputation with both whites and Africans. The recognition built his confidence as he pursued his plan to achieve a leadership role to improve his situation as well as that of the entire slave community in New Hampshire.

On the last day of June a letter from Benedict Arnold finally arrived.

Dear Will:

Please accept my deepest apologies for the delay in getting back to you. My only excuse is that unexpectedly it took nearly a year for me to recover from my injury and I remain crippled. Since then, in addition to fulfilling my duties as commandant of the city here in Philadelphia, I have been completely occupied with defending unfounded claims against me and seeking recovery for expenditures I made on the government's behalf. I foresee that these exertions, which are very difficult for me, will continue until next summer.

Do not despair. I shall be there then. I am confidant that in the meantime your own considerable abilities may resolve your dilemma.

> Sincerely yours,
> Major General Benedict Arnold

Will put the letter in his pocket and looked out across the river. *I'm on my own. I've got to get to it.*

33

On the Fourth of July 1779, Will suggested to Caesar Bannister that several Portsmouth Africans issue a "declaration" of their own to the New Hampshire Legislature, proclaiming unilaterally their right to freedom. Caesar was resistant, but he finally agreed to call a meeting of the Negro Court the next Sunday afternoon in the back of the public stables near the North Church. He also invited several other prominent Portsmouth Africans, including Samuel Wentworth, Windsor Martin, and Prince Whipple. And at Will's suggestion, Wentworth Cheswell was asked to come down from Newmarket as an outside adviser.

The meeting, attended by twenty-one men sitting on hard wooden benches, lasted some four hours. Everyone spoke in English. Somewhat to Will's surprise, with the exception of Jack Odiorne there was strong opposition to his proposal. Most favored taking some type of action, but it was thought that a declaration was too drastic, would have little chance of bringing about actual freedom, and would leave no options as a follow-up other than armed attack and full rebellion—which again would have little chance of success. There was also a question as to whether the twenty Portsmouth Africans at the meeting would be speaking only for themselves or could purport to represent the other Africans in the city, much less throughout the state.

Will and Jack were of a mind to minimize such arguments, which went back and forth at great length. Finally Will went over to Wentworth Cheswell and had a whispered conversation with him. Cheswell then rose.

"Gentlemen, Will and I believe that by some careful craftsmanship we may be able to have it both ways. If you were to call the document a petition rather than a declaration, there'd be much less emotional opposition to what you're trying to achieve. I appreciate that you probably don't like the word 'petition' because it has a subservient ring, smacks of supplication. But it should be possible to include in the body of the document statements of a declaratory nature that should satisfy your desire to be assertive. For example, some sentences could evoke the same sentiments and philosophy that are set forth in the preamble to the white men's own Declaration of Independence."

Will's compromise broke the deadlock, and it was agreed that Will, Samuel Wentworth, and Windsor Martin would try their hands at a draft document and report back to a second meeting on the first Sunday in August. Outnumbered by his own people, Caesar Bannister also agreed to be on the committee.

It turned out to be the middle of September before the draft could be completed and everyone was available. Cast in terms of moral principles and evoking subliminally the approach of the Declaration of Independence, it was well received by the group. But the draft mentioned redress only for those who signed, not the entire Portsmouth or New Hampshire African population. The feeling was that the twenty who were to sign had all come from Africa and, having once been free, could speak most forcefully to the issue. Nevertheless, in order to garner broader support in the African community, it was decided to request that the legislature enact "laws and regulations," presumably of general scope, that would free all New Hampshire slaves.

Will spoke up about a second aspect of the draft.

"I know I agreed with the draft in committee," he said. "But on thinking about it, the petition needs to state much more clearly that it's justified by the white slave owners' Christian religion. Even though most of us aren't Christians, we need this emphasis. That's their weak point, logically and morally." The others concurred that the strategy made sense.

With the final changes made, all twenty Portsmouth men agreed to sign, although Will noted that Bannister was frowning as he affixed his mark. Will volunteered to transcribe enough copies for submission to every member of the council and the House of Representatives. This was done, and everyone finally signed on November 12th. That evening Will borrowed the Clarkson horse, Henry, and delivered the copies to the legislature in Exeter.

The Petition read:

Petition to the New Hampshire Government
1779

To the honorable Council and House of Representatives of said State now sitting at Exeter in and for said State:

The petition of Caesar Bannister, Pharaoh Rogers, Romeo Rindge, Cato Newmarch, Cesar Gerrish, Zebulon Gardner, Quam Sherburne, Samuel Wentworth, Will Clarkson, Jack Odiorne, Cipio Hubbard, Seneca Hall, Peter Warner, Cato Warner, Pharaoh Shores, Windsor Moffatt, Garrett Colton, Kittindge Tuckerman, Peter Frost, and Prince Whipple, natives of Africa, now forcibly detained in slavery in said State most humbly sheweth that the God of Nature gave them Life and Freedom upon the terms of the most perfect Equality with other men;

that Freedom is an inherent right of the human species not to be surrendered, but by consent, for the sake of social life;

that private or public tyranny and slavery are alike detestable to minds conscious of the equal dignity of human nature;

that in power and authority of individuals derived solely from a principle of coercion against the will of individuals and to dispose of their persons and properties consists the completest idea of private and political slavery;

that all men being amenable to the Deity, for the ill improvement of the Blessings of his Providence they hold themselves in duty bound, strenuously to exert every faculty of their minds to obtain that blessing of freedom which they are justly entitled to from the donation of the beneficent Creator;

that through ignorance and brutish violence of their countrymen, and by the sinister designs of others (who ought, to have taught them better) and by the avarice of both, they, while but children and incapable of self defense, whose infancy might have prompted protection, were seized, imprisoned and transported from their native country where (though ignorance and un-Christianity prevailed) they were born free, to a country where (though knowledge, Christianity and freedom, are their boast) they are compelled and their unhappy posterity to drag on their lives in miserable servitude!

Thus, often is the parent's cheek wet for the loss of a child torn by the cruel hand of violence from her aching bosom! Thus, often, and in vain, is the infant's sigh for the nurturing care of its bereaved parent. And thus do the ties of nature and blood become victims, to cherish the vanity and luxury of a fellow mortal! Can this be right? Forbid it gracious Heaven!

Permit again your humble slaves to lay before this honorable assembly some of those grievances which they daily experience and feel. Though fortune hath dealt out our portions with rugged hand, yet hath she smiled in the disposal of our persons to those who claim us as their property; of them, as masters, we do not complain, but from what authority they assume the power to dispose of our lives, freedom and property we would wish to know.

Is it from the sacred volumes of Christianity? There we believe it is not to be found but here hath the cruel hand of slavery made us incompetent judges, hence knowledge is hid from our minds!

Is it from the volumes of the law? Of these also, slaves cannot be judges but those, we are told, are founded in reason and justice. It cannot be found there!

Is it from the volumes of nature? No! Here we can read with others, of this knowledge slavery cannot wholly deprive us. Here we know that we ought to be free agents! Here we feel the dignity of human nature. Here we feel the passions and desires of men, though checked by the rod of slavery. Here we feel a just equality. Here, we know that the God of Nature made us free!

Is their authority assumed from custom? If so, let that custom be abolished which is not founded in nature, reason nor religion.

Should the humanity and benevolence of the honorable assembly restore us to that state of liberty of which we have been so long deprived, we conceive that those who are our present masters will not be sufferers by our liberation, as we have most of us spent our whole strength and the prime of our lives in their service. And as freedom inspires a noble confidence and gives the mind an emulation to view in the noblest efforts of enterprise, and as justice and humanity are the result of your deliberations, we fondly hope that the eye of pity and heart of justice may commiserate our situation and put us upon the equality of freemen and give us an opportunity of evincing to the world our love of freedom, by exerting ourselves in her cause, in opposing the efforts of tyranny and oppression over the country in which we ourselves have been so long enslaved.

Therefore, your humble slaves most devoutly pray for the sake of injured liberty; for the sake of justice, humanity, and the rights of mankind; for the honor of religion; and by all that is dear, that your honors would graciously interpose in our behalf and enact such laws and regulations as you in your wisdom think proper, whereby we may regain our liberty and be ranked in the class of free agents and that the name of slave may not more be heard in a land gloriously contending for the sweets of freedom; and your humble slaves as in duty bound will ever pray.

Portsmouth November 12th, 1779

Seneca Hall	Pharaoh Rogers
Peter Frost	Will Clarkson

Zebulon Gardner   Windsor Moffatt
Peter Warner   Romeo Rindge
Prince Whipple   Jack Odiorne
Quam Sherburne   Garrett Colton
Cato Warner   Cato Newmarch
Caesar Bannister   Cipio Hubbard
Samuel Wentworth   Kittindge Tuckerman
Pharaoh Shores   Cesar Gerrish

The petitioners were at first optimistic. When the House next convened, on April 25 1780, the document appeared to be moving through the legislative process in the usual manner, steered by the speaker, John Langdon, and the council and set for a hearing.

34

Will was silhouetted against the bright morning sun, standing at the end of the black granite peninsula at Odiorne's Point in Rye. He was gazing out across the waves pounding the rock ledges below, past the islands six miles offshore, all the way to the thin line where the deep blue of the sea met the pale azure of the sky. His left arm was folded across his chest, his right hand holding his chin. Then he sat down on a large flat rock and drew some folded paper sheets from inside his dusky red shirt. It was that day's edition of the state newspaper—the *New Hampshire Gazette,* Saturday, July 15, 1780. Four pages, each ten inches wide and fifteen inches high. He read again the editorial introduction to the lead item on the front page:

> The following is a copy of a petition of a number of the Negroes now detained in slavery at Portsmouth, N.H., lately presented to the General Assembly of this State, who accordingly granted them a hearing; but, we hear, the further consideration thereof is postponed to a future day. By particular desire we now insert it for the amusement of our readers.

Will stared at the word "amusement" for a few seconds. Then he flung the paper to the ground, raised his face to the sky, and sent a howl into the unattended air. He reached to pick up the newspaper, which he folded and put back into his shirt. Then leaned forward and held his head in his hands as he looked down at his bare feet on the stone. His whole body was shaking.

He sat on the rock for nearly an hour. Finally, he pushed himself up and walked with his slight limp back to the stand of birch trees where he'd tethered a heavy plow horse. He headed the old horse west, back into the town of Portsmouth. He talked to the animal as they went.

"I'll speak to Caesar, Henry. We'll have to get the court together and talk this thing over, figure out what to do now."

"This can't stand, Caesar. We've come too far to let it go."

"Just what do you suggest we do? Grab rifles and storm the legislative chamber in Exeter?"

"I'm mad enough to do that if I thought it would solve anything. But at least we should get all the signers together and talk this thing through."

On Sunday, August 20, everyone met once again in the North Church.

Will got to the point as soon as Caesar brought the meeting to order. "As you know, the legislature isn't going to do a thing about our petition. They don't even have the guts to reject it, they just tabled it indefinitely. It's dead. This is bad news for us, not just because we didn't get what we asked for but also because of the way the *Gazette* treated the petition—it's a real slap in the face to us as leaders of the African community here in Portsmouth. The question now is whether there's anything we can do to salvage the situation. As I see it, we have six options.

"First, we could simply do nothing, just go on about our daily work as slaves as though nothing happened.

"Second, at the opposite extreme we could stage some sort of uprising—a rebellion.

"Third, as a middle approach, we could organize a series of demonstrations protesting our enslavement.

"Fourth, we could start a runaway of most of our folks here in Portsmouth.

"Fifth, we could resubmit our petition and demand to know when it will be addressed, or request reconsideration of the decision to table it.

"Sixth, we can leave it up to each of us in the community to attempt to persuade his or her owner, or negotiate with the owner, for freedom on some basis. In other words, switch from a group strategy to an individual approach.

"Now I suggest we discuss each of the options. First, who's for doing nothing, letting it go?"

A burst of no's came from the group. Unanimously rejected.

"Well, are you ready for an uprising, a rebellion?"

A chorus of no's almost as loud followed.

"Can't put our families at risk by opening up all-out war," Caesar said.

Will stared him down. "Maybe not. But we can't go on like this either. The truth is that the 'patience and time' strategy has been a failure. The whites will never pay attention to us as a group until we do something dramatic."

Jack said, "If we're not going to rebel, we should at least have some demonstrations to let em know how we feel."

Seneca Hall and Zebulon Gardner chimed in, arguing that demonstrations were bound to have at least a gradual effect over a period of time. But most others felt they'd just set up the demonstrators for reprisals against them by the white owners. This option was rejected as well.

Kittindge Tuckerman spoke up in favor of the fourth option, running away. "The other options are unrealistic," he said. "I just want to get out of Portsmouth, away from this miserable life." The rest were skeptical—both because of the difficulties of taking along families and because of the questions of where to go and how to get there.

"How about some kind of resubmission or follow-up with the legislature?"

Pharaoh Shores said, "Think we gotta deal with the legislature. Our problem's with them. Should keep at em, if only to embarrass em into doing something."

Only Cato Warner backed him up. The others were put off by the probable futility of pursuing this option and were persuaded by Prince Whipple's argument: "You still don't understand the strength of what we're up against. Not just the legislature. Their whole damn way of thinking and doing things."

The final choice—switching from a group to an individual approach—precipitated the longest discussion. "Problem with just doing that," Shores said, "is it'll look like we're doing nothing."

Samuel Wentworth said, "I want to know how a deal for freedom with my owner would work. Would it mean I stay with him and work for him but get paid for it? Do I have to then pay him back for rent and food? Would that work out about even? Might be my choice, but not a big improvement in my situation. I might not even feel free."

From the beginning, Will had realized that this approach was the only one that could win the approval of the group at this time. He himself was in the particularly ticklish situation of not knowing whether he'd end up with Walter as his owner, which would be bad, or be sold in an estate sale to someone even worse. Others were also concerned that their owners wouldn't be receptive to granting their freedom on any basis.

To ensure that at least this option would prevail, Will had arranged that Prince, who was highly regarded by every man there, was the last to speak. "When all is said and done, last option is only one likely to work. Each of us got to look himself in the mirror and figure out if he's got the gumption to talk to his owner and how he'll do it. You might not like doing it, but for now this approach is all we got."

As Prince spoke, many in the group sighed but nodded their heads. When he finished, Caesar stood up. "Gentlemen, that's it unless anybody can think of something else. How many in favor of the last option?" The decision was unanimous.

As they filed out of the church, Will said to Jack, "I doubt whether I'll get anywhere with Walter. We'll have to push forward with other parts of the plan."

Will said, "Sure would like to know how the petition got tabled." It was a hazy August day. He and Wentworth Cheswell were sitting on Cheswell's porch in Newmarket, smoking their pipes and discussing the political landscape. "How'd you like to nose around with your white friends and see what you can find out?"

"Consider it done. I'll get back to you."

⸺⸱⸺

A week later Cheswell rode over to Portsmouth in his wagon and found Will at the market.

"William Bannister," he said to Will. "Killed it dead. Called in some markers from his political friends."

"Might have known," Will said. "Well, I'm not giving up. One way or another, he and Caesar have to go."

Where's Arnold? Said he'd be here by now.

35

A month later, at the end of September, Will learned from the *Gazette* why Benedict Arnold had not come to Portsmouth.

On June 29, General Washington had put West Point and the surrounding area under Arnold's command. Two weeks later Arnold wrote a letter to John André, an intermediary with the British, offering to surrender West Point for 20,000 pounds, a fortune at the time. The offer was accepted on August 24 by Sir Henry Clinton, who, as it turned out, had been receiving intelligence from Arnold for more than a year. But as Clinton and Arnold readied themselves for the handover, the Americans on September 23 captured André, who had in his possession a pass from Arnold and papers outlining the garrisons and defenses at the Point. Arnold's treason was uncovered; his plan was never implemented. Two days later he joined the British army as a brigadier general.

The news sent shock waves throughout the colonies. Arnold was widely vilified as a traitor.

Will was devastated. How could a man who had accomplished so much for the American cause switch his allegiance for any amount of money to the side he had fought against so fiercely and so well? *I'll never know. Makes me mad in any event. Let the country down, let me down. But I never knew a white leader so supportive of Africans. Doesn't make sense. One thing for sure—traitor or not, I'm going to keep my promise to him.*

There goes one of my main strategies, though. Damn! Now I have to be careful that my connection with him doesn't become a liability.

36

On November 10, 1780, James Clarkson III filed his final inventory as executor of James Jr.'s estate. James Jr. left all his property to Walter. Along with the house, Will was on that "property" list at a "value" of only fifteen pounds because of his age and limp. Will was desolate, but he felt a little better when Jack told him Walter was rumored to be in financial difficulty and would have to sell everything.

Will immediately went to Walter and offered to buy his freedom for the fifteen-pound value.

"I can get more for you on the open market," Walter said. "Besides, William Bannister doesn't like freeing slaves, and I agree with him. Answer's no."

So who would his new owner be? Will knew there were worse owners than Walter.

Then he heard at the market, from Romeo Rindge, that Colonel Pierse Long was interested in buying the Clarkson house. Long had known Will for years and seemed to like him. He was aware of Will's literacy and his service as an administrative assistant to Andrew.

He was a lifelong Portsmouth citizen of some prominence, a well-educated merchant. In 1775, he'd been a delegate to the first provincial congress at Exeter and a member of Portsmouth's Committee of Safety. In August 1776 he was made colonel of an independent regiment sent to reinforce Fort Ticonderoga. He participated in the orderly retreat from that post and fought in the battle at Saratoga. He came back to Portsmouth, suffered a yearlong illness, then returned to his business and political activities.

A slave trader early in his business career, Long later concluded that the practice was immoral and stopped. But he made a distinction between trading and merely owning slaves.

Will decided he needed to have a talk with Mr. Long. He walked to his house and knocked on the door.

"Walter Clarkson needs the money and has decided to sell me rather than free me," he said. The two men sat across from each other in Long's living room. "I don't have enough. Would you be interested in buying me along with the house?"

"I could use your administrative assistance, since I'm going to be involved in politics for some years to come. And your help at the house and with the animals. I'll talk to Walter."

Walter sold both the Clarkson house on South School Street and Will to Long. The Bill of Sale for Slave provided:

> Know all men by these presents that I, Walter Clarkson of Portsmouth, in the county of Rockingham, New Hampshire, for the consideration of the sum of 30 pounds lawful money to me in hand paid before the delivery hereof by Pierse Long of said Portsmouth, the receipt hereof I do hereby acknowledge, have given, granted bargain and sold and by these presents do give, grant, bargain, sell, release and quitclaim to him, the said Pierse Long, all right, title, interest, property, claim, and demand to a certain Negro man named Will Clarkson, 40 years of age, and also all the right to his services and labors, and all my Power and Authority which I heretofore have had a right to exercise over the said Will Clarkson, to have and hold the said Negro named Will Clarkson and the privileges, profits, and services that may be derived from the said Will Clarkson to said Pierse Long and his heirs and his assigns to him proper benefit, forever thereby engaging to warrant and defend the said Negro named Will Clarkson, granted as aforesaid against all claim or demands of any sort.
>
> /s/ Walter Clarkson
> December 8, 1780

Long moved into the Clarkson house on January 1, 1781, and Will took up his duties for the colonel on that same day, quite happy to leave Walter and the tannery work behind forever.

His new owner suffered frequently from attacks of gout and needed crutches to move about. Will therefore was of great help in running the household, and was most thankful that Mrs. Haven had agreed to cook all the meals for the colonel. But it was his work as an assistant to Long in his business and political activities that benefited Long the most and gave Will the most stimulation and gratification.

Long had continued his father's business in Portsmouth, maintaining a store with a full range of retail goods including perishable foods and items such as cloth and furniture. He was also a wholesale trader, shipping lumber abroad and importing sugar and cotton. The colonel learned that Will was a precise bookkeeper; he trusted him entirely with his business records.

In Long's political activities, Will functioned as a legislative assistant, keeping track of all the bills and administrative items Long had to follow as a delegate to the congress. Will expected that this training in the affairs of government would soon be of great benefit to him in elevating the Africans' position as the new country came into being.

Will Jr. and Naby were also a source of great joy during this period. Will Jr., still skinny at age fifteen, was developing into an alert young man who helped his mother with her duties at the Meechum house, although he was starting to assert his independence in various teenage ways. It was becoming apparent that ten-year-old Naby was very slow—probably a little retarded—but she had a lovely disposition that made her a pleasure to be around. Will spent as much time as he could with them at the Meechum house in the evenings and often took the children fishing at a tidal creek in Rye on weekends during the warm months.

He was teaching his son how to read and write, employing the same methods James Clarkson had used with him years earlier. And he spent hours telling the children about their ancestors and his own experiences when he was a young man in Portsmouth and during the war.

Although his work for Colonel Long was satisfying, Will did not forget his objective. Remembering his failure with James Clarkson and without much hope of success with Long, he approached him nonetheless in the spring of 1781.

"Colonel, as you may know, in spite of my service during the war, Walter reneged on James Clarkson's promise to free me. I've been hoping you'd see fit to grant me my freedom."

Long looked at Will for several moments, then gazed out the window for a while longer. At last he turned back and faced his slave. "I can't do it, Will. I'm getting old and I need you. You know I spent a lot of money to buy you from Walter. You're not in a position to compensate me for that."

"What if I were freed but continued to work for you?"

"It would leave me vulnerable to your leaving at any time. And I'm not prepared to pay you wages on top of what I paid to buy you." Long's expression softened. "I'm not a hard taskmaster, Will. The work here is just right for you. The best I can do is promise to provide in my will that you're to be free upon my death." Long's eyes were downcast when he finished.

Will rose. "Well, I thank you for that, anyway."

Later that day Will asked his son to accompany him for a walk. As they strolled along the bank of the river, he told Willie what had happened with Colonel Long.

"This is a great disappointment to me, son, but I want you to know that I'm not giving up. And I don't want you to. Never give up! General Arnold was right on that point. We'll find a way."

On the war front the action shifted to the South.

The American general Benjamin Lincoln surrendered 5500 troops to Sir Henry Clinton at Charleston, South Carolina, in May 1780, and Horatio Gates's loss to Cornwallis at Camden, New Jersey, in August of the same year finished Gates's military career. Then Gates's replacement, Nathaniel Greene, and General Dan Morgan, perhaps the Americans' best fighter, restored American morale with a strong victory at the Battle of Cowpens in North Carolina as 1781 began.

On March 1, 1781, the new Articles of Confederation went into effect. The provisions authenticated the Continental Congress, which was renamed the Congress of the Confederation. Every state had just one vote, and the emphasis was on preserving the independence of each. Congress could appoint executive departments but it had no power to levy taxes or regulate commerce. There was no federal judiciary.

In the same month, Louis XVI of France dispatched Rear Admiral the count de Grasse with a fleet of twenty fighting ships across the Atlantic to help his American ally. After skirmishing with the British in the West Indies, de Grasse entered Chesapeake Bay on August 21.

Ten days later, back in Portsmouth, Captain John Paul Jones returned to the city, armed with orders from Congress to get *America*, the new ship-of-the-line under construction there, launched and put to sea. The ship was impressive—the biggest vessel ever built at Portsmouth, over one hundred and eighty-two feet long, and she could accommodate at least seventy-four guns.

After spending a month at the Rockingham Tavern, Jones moved next door to a house, where he was to spend the next twelve months working at his task. During that time the townspeople were amused by stories of Jones's romancing Portsmouth's most attractive eligible ladies. Will enjoyed seeing the famous hero about town on several occasions, although he wasn't happy that all the heroes were white.

On the same day that Captain Jones reached Portsmouth, George Washington, after setting a number of ruses to dupe Sir Henry Clinton into thinking the Americans were going to attack New York, began moving his army south, toward Chesapeake Bay. Upon arriving at the upper Chesapeake, he met and coordinated with General Rochambeau and Admiral de Grasse in the Bay. Then he waited.

Victory's key came from the sea. Late in the afternoon of September 5, de Grasse struck the British fleet under Admiral Graves and defeated it soundly. As Graves then steered his wounded ships to New York for repairs, Washington and Rochambeau moved in on Cornwallis, now cornered on the peninsula at Yorktown. After a series of American attacks, Cornwallis surrendered his entire army of 8000 men on October 19, 1781.

In April 1782, peace treaty negotiations led by Benjamin Franklin began in Paris.. It took until November 30 to sign a preliminary document, and the definitive treaty, officially called the Peace of Paris, was not inked until February 3, 1783, coordinated with British treaties with France, Spain, and the Netherlands. The treaty confirmed United States control from the Atlantic to the Mississippi River and from Canada to the Florida border.

Back in Portsmouth, more than a few citizens commented on the fact that it had taken a force of French Catholic seamen to bring the Protestant colonists their freedom.

The British general Sir Guy Carleton, in command in New York City, evacuated on November 25, 1783, and on December 4 General Washington and his officers met for dinner at Fraunces Tavern on Wall Street to celebrate the American victory. The tavern was owned and operated by a black man, Samuel Fraunces, who was of French West Indian extraction. "Black Sam" had been a staunch patriot throughout the battles for independence.

On Christmas Eve, Colonel Pierse Long went into his kitchen, where Will, Abi, and the children were eating, to wish them Merry Christmas and thank God for the country's success.

That evening, for the first time, Will told Abi he thought freedom for all of the new nation's Africans was a realistic possibility. *At last I'll be able to confront the Bannister/Caesar conspiracy.*

37

*T*he end of the war had a devastating effect on the New Hampshire economy and on the lives of both its white citizens and their enslaved African servants. Trade dropped to nearly zero as demand for farm products collapsed along with land prices. Depression set in as the state government retired the inflated currency issued during the war.

Even the likes of John Martin, the prosperous sea captain who had brought Will to America, were not immune from the financial ravages. Martin's son Peter had fled to the West Indies to avoid the consequences of a bankruptcy proceeding, at which the family's two slaves were sold and carted off to a new owner somewhere in Massachusetts. The father moved into the mansion on Market Street, but his resources were stretched to maintain his lifestyle. His various businesses had dried up, and he had to rely on the funds he had earlier acquired from his mix of honest and questionable activities.

The stress from the flagging economy helped fuel an ironic and unbecoming phenomenon of the Revolution's aftermath: the new patriots' pernicious crusade against the loyalists, who had supported England. As early as 1775, General John Sullivan wrote to George Washington from Portsmouth:

> That infernal crew of Tories, who have laughed at the Congress . . . walk the streets here with impunity; and will,

with a sneer, tell the people in the streets that all our liberty-polls will soon be converted into gallows.

During the war, concern about loyalist activities was justified: They spied for the British, spread false rumors, and discouraged enlistments in the American army, and many fought in the British army. Accused individuals were tried before both the state house of representatives and the local and state Committees of Safety. Most loyalists fled to Canada to escape being tarred and feathered, beaten, drawn through mud and water, indefinitely imprisoned, and having their property confiscated. In 1777, the legislature gave people opposed to the Revolution ninety days to sell their property and leave the state without molestation, and made aiding and conspiracy with the British punishable by death. Lesser, vaguely defined crimes such as spreading false rumors were made misdemeanors punishable by fines or imprisonment.

More than a hundred loyalists and their families left the state; very few returned after the conflict. Former provincial governor John Wentworth's personal secretary and his friend John Fenton, who had caused the incident leading to Wentworth's departure, were among them.

As late as 1782, the state legislature passed an act confiscating the property of all loyalists who had left. Although the law was not enforced after the Peace of Paris treaty prohibited such actions and provided for restitution of properties already seized, such restitution was made in almost no cases, and the Committees of Safety and New Hampshire residents continued to persecute suspected Tories in various ways. Gossip and hearsay ruled the day, and fair trials were the rarest of exceptions. Basic rights the English afforded their own people were forfeited.

On the evening of Friday, January 6, 1784, Abi answered a knock at the front door of the Meechum house and was suddenly surrounded by four men, grabbed, and carried off in a waiting wagon. She was gagged before she could even call out for help.

Will was back in the kitchen with the children. Meechum was eating supper in his dining room. Both men rushed to the front door when they heard the scuffle, only to realize they were too late as the wagon disappeared around a distant corner. Will thought he recognized the blue hat and red plaid shirt of one of the men in the back of the wagon as belonging to the city sheriff, well known in Portsmouth as a man who detested both Tories and Negroes.

Will asked Meechum to stay with and calm the children as he broke into an ungainly trot, heading back to the Pierse Long house on South School Street.

Long had completed a term as a member of the state Committee of Safety in '76–'77 and had been appointed a delegate to the Congress of the Confederation in Philadelphia. When he heard Will's story he immediately suspected that Abi's capture was the work of the three new members of the local committee, who were known zealots when it came to loyalists. He told Will the problem could be related to the period when Abi had been a slave to former governor Wentworth. He promised Will he would try to find out where she was and why she was being detained. Will reassured Willie and Naby as best he could but spent a desperate weekend with them, for Long was unable to find anyone with knowledge of the situation until Monday.

When he returned on Monday evening, his news could hardly have been worse. Abi was being held in the Portsmouth city jail, charged with fornication and treason, punishable respectively by commitment to the stocks or the pillory and death. Her trial would be held in one month at the Exeter Courthouse before the local Committee of Safety.

Will was shaking with rage and bewilderment. *"Treason?"* he said.

"The allegation is based on Abi's having assisted Governor Wentworth to escape to Fort William and Mary, then covering it up, Will. The fornication charge is that she had a sexual relationship with you without being legally married to you under the laws of the state of New Hampshire."

⚖

The local Committee of Safety was an institution that belied its name. It had arrogated to itself the role of pursuing and punishing all loyalists, as well as anyone who supported or aided them, in the New Hampshire seacoast area. In that capacity it functioned simultaneously as grand jury, de facto prosecutor, and trial court. The committee first decided whom to indict, then handed a file to a puppet prosecutor who was told what to do, and finally heard all the evidence and itself ruled on all questions of both fact and law.

Nor were any of the three current members of the committee of a nature or background calculated to ensure fairness or due process to the accused.

Samuel Morris was an unmarried farmer, twenty-eight years old, who lived in North Hampton, just below Rye. He had fought at Saratoga and lost both legs. His injuries had severely limited his ability to work his farm's cattle and bean and corn crops, leaving him deeply embittered at a young age.

Jonathan Blake was a carpenter from Exeter. Twenty-three years old, he'd been jailed in 1773 by Governor Wentworth for distributing anti-British pamphlets. His wife had left him in 1780, complaining loudly to anyone who would listen of Blake's brutality.

The chairman of the committee was thirty-nine-year-old Reginald Woods. His favorite of four sons had been killed at the Battle of Bennington. He owned and operated a mill in Newington and a textiles store on Court Street in Portsmouth. Hard hit financially by the war, he had almost lost both businesses. His vocal hatred of the English thereafter was unrelenting.

None of the committee members made an effort to attend any of the area's several churches or purported to be Christians.

John Richards was the designated prosecutor. Richards was a clerk in Ladd's clothing store. He had no legal training.

Abi's situation was made worse by several additional factors: Defendants before the committee were not usually afforded the benefit of counsel; there was no discovery process to verify the specifics of the allegations; and she would have no advance idea as to the identity of her accusers, the "witnesses" who would testify against her at the trial.

Within days, Abi's incarceration gave rise to a growing controversy in Portsmouth and throughout the state. With virtually no knowledge of the facts, everyone nonetheless seemed to have something to say about the propriety of the indictment and Abi's guilt or innocence.

Will called together his friends to gather information about the public's reaction and to calculate ways of making use of that sentiment in devising his strategy.

Within the white community the range of opinions seemed endless.

All John Meechum cared about was getting back his slave. He complained vociferously in that regard and even wrote a letter to committee chairman Woods demanding her immediate release — without stating a reason. Meechum was not given the courtesy of an answer.

Loyalists James Stoodley and William Atkinson talked quietly between themselves about the development. "It's ironic," Stoodley said. "The rebels complained about the English persecuting them, but they have no compunctions about victimizing others."

"She's only a slave," Atkinson said, "but I'll be glad when this retribution mania comes to an end."

William Bannister and his political friends took a careful middle path, waiting to see how their constituents reacted.

Ardent patriots like Joshua Pierce and Ebenezer Trefethen backed the committee. Addressing a meeting of war veterans in the North Church on a Saturday afternoon, Pierce pontificated, "We've got to make an example of all these loyalists. I don't care whether she did anything on her own or was directed by Wentworth. This is a matter of self-preservation for us now." Trefethen and the others nodded in agreement.

John Langdon and James Hackett, patriotic leaders who were more moderate, also supported the committee's action, but expressed concerns about adverse reactions in the Negro community, particularly if the evidence of Abi's involvement was weak.

White women were more inclined to speak in Abi's defense.

When Trefethen relayed the discussion at the veterans meeting to his wife, she blew up at him. "Ben! How could you? That woman is being hung out to dry on false charges!" Trefethen slunk into his living room to avoid further disagreement.

As Catherine Cutts and Susan Ladd shopped with their baskets in and out of the stores along Congress Street on a freezing winter day, the Negro woman's plight was their main topic of conversation. "That poor girl," Mrs. Cutts said. "I just don't see how they can blame her for doing what her owner told her to do. And if we prosecuted every unmarried Negro woman who had a family, half our servants would be in jail."

"We force them to live apart from each other to suit our own purposes," Susan Ladd said. "We can't have it both ways. I never did like Frances Wentworth. I blame her for all this."

Mrs. Cutts and Mrs. Ladd were pillars of the North Church aristocracy. There was quite a different mind-set among non-churchgoers such as Melinda Morrison, who overheard the two ladies and yelled at them, "They oughta hang that Negro whore!"

The clergy were in Abi's camp. On the Friday after the news broke, Reverend Haven, Reverend Buckminister, of the North Church, and the new minister at Queen's Chapel, John Cosens Ogden, were having their monthly ecumenical lunch at Richard Waldron's tavern on Bow Street. Haven raised the subject.

"Gentlemen, I can't tell you how distressed I am by the jailing of Meechum's servant, Abi Clarkson. She's a fine woman who has served several Portsmouth families well. She's a Christian—a member of your parish, John. Each of us should take a stand in one of our next sermons, objecting to her treatment."

Buckminister said, "I'm certainly willing to do that, but I'll have to be rather soft about it. More than half my congregation are strident patriots, with no love lost for the loyalists."

Reverend Ogden said, "I'll speak up about it, very strongly. As her pastor, I feel obligated to." All three ministers did in fact follow up on the next Sunday, calling for Abi's release pending trial and questioning the fairness of her indictment.

—✕—

Word of Abi's story spread up and down the New England coast. In Boston, Abigail Adams, wife of John Adams, had come into the city from the family farm in Braintree to see some friends and visit her seamstress in preparation for traveling to London and

France to join her husband, who was there to negotiate a treaty of commerce with Great Britain.

As she sat for tea Alice Cabot's home that afternoon, she asked, "Have you heard what's going on up in New Hampshire? The jailing of that Negro woman Abi, for supposedly helping the English?"

"Yes, I heard," said Mrs. Cabot, whose husband, Sebastian, was the city's leading private citizen. "I think it's outlandish, but what are the facts?"

"It sounds as though she's innocent. At worst she just did what her owner, the English governor, told her to do," Mrs. Adams said.

"Well, I have no sympathy for those people who helped the English. But it looks like the Committee of Safety up there is overreaching."

Mrs. Adams said, "I'm going to write my cousin Cathy Cutts, who lives in Portsmouth, and urge her to advocate Abi's release."

Back in Portsmouth, Violet Dearborn and Matilda Odiorne, two of Abi's closest friends, were particularly incensed. "What in the world they want from us?" Violet said. "Bad enough that we work like animals for them, care for them when they're sick, bring up their children, do whatever they ask. Then they throw us in jail?"

"You're right," Matilda said. "Who knows how Abi's holding up."

Will and some of the other African men were thinking about how they could storm the jail to release Abi forcibly. At the women's Sunday market, Prince Whipple cornered two of his friends and exhorted them to action.

"Abi won't get no justice. We gotta do something now to get her out."

"Say when, just let us know," one of them said. The other nodded his agreement.

"Need to talk to Will first. I'll let you know." Prince turned and left.

King Caesar remained calm. He told his owner, William Bannister, "Aint helping things between whites and Africans in this city one bit. Can't be sure about African reaction if it aint cleared up fast."

"All right, Caesar. I'll check with the Committee of Safety, see if I can influence them. In the meantime, you do everything you can to silence and stop any uppity Negroes who might take the law into their own hands."

As in the white community, African churchgoers tended to be much more sympathetic to Abi than those who didn't attend church. Flora Stoodley, a regular at Queen's Chapel with the tavern owner's family, cried when she heard of Abi's predicament and tried to visit her at the jail. "Get outta here, lady," the jailer said. "That Clarkson woman is charged with serious crimes. She's going to get what she deserves."

⚓

At the women's market on the second Sunday after Abi was taken to jail, however, a free African woman was overheard to say, "I don't feel sorry for her. For a slave, that one's a mighty snobby woman." Several similar comments reached the ears of Jack and Matilda Odiorne, but they never mentioned them to Will.

But Will heard it anyway, from his own surveillance sources. The stories were gut-wrenching, but they did not deter Will from taking action. The next step was to find the right lawyer willing to take Abi's case. The first three he approached turned him down.

⚓

At the jail on Islington Road, the object of all the discussion lay curled up in a fetal posture on a rotting wooden bunk in a tiny cell. Her eyes, now dry but still red from crying, surveyed the cell and looked out through the bars of the bolted door, across a hall to another cell, where a drunk and disheveled white man sat leering at her.

A fat black rat, almost a foot long, broke the silence as it screeched and ran out from under her bunk, jumping through the bars of the door and zigzagging down the hall toward the jailer's office in the front of the building.

White paint blackened by an ancient fire was peeling off the stone walls. A bucket half full of the excrement of prior occupants stood on the floor in the back corner of the room. The floor was littered with the remains of old newspapers, some dated five years earlier.

The stench was unbearable, causing Abi every few minutes to choke and gasp for breath.

Once the man in the other cell shouted across at her, "They're goin to hang yuh, yuh know. I heard the jailer talkin bout yuh. Says yer a slut and a traitor. They hang traitors. Wha d' yuh think of that?"

Abi curled up tighter and remained silent as the man prattled on.

An iron door opened down the hallway, then clanged shut. Abi heard footsteps—it sounded like two men approaching. Then joy flowed through her body as she looked up and saw Will standing before her cell, accompanied by the jailer.

The jailer unlocked the cell door, and Will rushed in to help her stand and to hug her.

Abi sobbed on his shoulder. "Oh, Will, thank God you're here. It's been so—"

"Thirty minutes. That's all you've got." The jailer locked the cell door and headed back down the hallway.

"How'd you get em to let you in here?" Abi asked.

"Paid him. But he said this'll be the only time."

Abi told him she had no idea why she'd been seized or what the charges were, so Will explained what was happening. He carefully omitted what the sentences could be.

"We're doing everything we can to get you out of here or at least prepare for the trial," he told her. "Reverend Haven and Colonel Long are helping out."

"Oh, Will. I'm so sorry for all the trouble I'm causing you."

"You're never trouble to me, honey." Will pulled her closer and kissed her very gently. "I love you and I always will."

For the precious time they had remaining, they held each other's hands and talked about Willie and Naby and how to protect them from the terrible effects of what was happening. Will said he'd brought them to Colonel Long's house and that Mrs. Haven was taking care of them. Abi said she'd been praying for all of them, and this had made her feel better. She and Will prayed together for her safety and release.

Too soon the jailer reappeared and said, "Time's up." As he left, Will assured Abi he'd try to get word to her somehow about his efforts to help her out of her situation.

⁓

Jack was waiting for Will when he came out the front door of the jail, looking exhausted. "How's she doin?" he asked.

"Not good. But I think she'll hold up. Bastards shouldn't put a woman in a hellhole like that."

"Prince and some of the others are ready to go, take some action now."

"Good," Will said. "But rein them in until I figure out the right moment." He sighed. "You know, this whole thing is strange. It doesn't make sense. I've never heard of the white patriots going after an African for being a loyalist. That's another battle, a fight between two groups of whites. It's got nothing to do with us. Something else is going on here, and I need to find out what it is. Could be the property thing. They don't want to let go of us."

"Well, even if you're right, how we going to get at it?"

"Right now I don't know. But I'd like you to quietly ask some questions around Portsmouth and the surrounding towns to see what we can come up with. Don't limit yourself to our usual surveillance group. But you'll have to be careful. We don't want to alert the white authorities that we're nosing around. I have an idea we were surprised by this because it originated from outside Portsmouth."

⁓

Thomas Simes was a respected Portsmouth barrister who had been born and educated in London. He had practiced law there for several years and was active in the English abolitionist movement, led by Thomas Clarkson and Granville Sharp. He emigrated to America before the Revolution, largely in search of religious freedom because he didn't agree with the dictates of the Church of England. In Portsmouth, he became a fast friend of Reverend Haven and an ardent patriot. Simes was no friend of the loyalists, but he was a staunch advocate of the rule of law, particularly its procedural protections, and he was sympathetic to the plight of the African people enslaved in the New World. When Reverend Haven told Simes about Abi's imprisonment, he came to Colonel Long's house that evening to determine the facts and discuss the legal aspects of the case.

After Will told Simes everything that had happened, Simes outlined how he thought the case should be defended. "I'm assuming, of course, that Abi will be given an opportunity to present a defense of some sort," he said. "The defense to fornication, a misdemeanor, is very straightforward. Abi and Will have been married properly in a civil ceremony in accordance with African law and tradition, which should be recognized as legal because the white community has recognized and encouraged the Negro Court.

"As to the treason charge, there are four defenses. First, as a slave, Abi cannot be held responsible for obeying the orders of her rightful owners. Second, neither the United States government nor the state of New Hampshire was established at the time of the governor's escape in 1775. Therefore, there can be no treason against governments that did not even exist at the time. Third, related to the second defense, the charges are ex post facto—retroactive—and therefore prohibited. Finally, the prosecution of this charge fails because the events on which it is based all occurred prior to the applicable seven-year statute of limitations."

Simes encouraged Will's effort to uncover any facts about possible undisclosed reasons for the committee's actions against Abi. "But be careful," he warned. "Keep your investigation secret."

<hr />

During the next two weeks, Will and Jack were unable to discover anything that seemed unusual or otherwise significant about Abi's case or any of the members of the Committee of Safety. Then one day Jack asked his wife, Matilda, "Wasn't there another

African servant working for Frances Wentworth before Abi arrived on the *Exeter*?"

Matilda's face lit up. "Yes. Woman wasn't a good worker, so Mrs. Wentworth decided to buy another slave. Some time after Abi was bought at auction, Mrs. Wentworth sold the woman to a man in Newmarket named Shackford. Heard some time later she blamed Abi for being sold and still had a grudge against her. I think she's still around."

Will asked Jack to talk to some of his friends in Newmarket and find out what he could about the woman's current status and reputation. On Sunday afternoon, Will saddled Henry and rode to Newmarket. Cheswell was delighted to see him again and the two men spent a few minutes talking about the prospects for New Hampshire and the new country. Will then explained the reason for his visit and asked Cheswell if he knew anything about the woman or her owner.

Cheswell puffed on his pipe and smiled. "Matter of fact, I do. Shackford runs a potato farm right down the road from here. He's been a bit slick in his business dealings, so he doesn't enjoy a good reputation. The woman's name is Semantha. No last name that I know of. Rather ordinary. Don't know much about her except she lives farther out of town with an African named Ned Sherwood."

Years ago Ned Sherwood had lived in Portsmouth. He had made a couple of passes at Abi, who'd rejected him in no uncertain terms. The last time he'd been furious, and Abi had said she thought he was still angry with her. Will told Cheswell that part of the story and then asked, "What's Sherwood doing now? Is he free?"

"He's owned by a man named William Woods, another farmer just outside town."

"This is starting to look a little too coincidental. We're going to have to do some more research. Thanks a lot for your help."

As Will arrived back at Colonel Long's house that evening, Reverend Haven was just reporting that he and Reverend Ogden had visited Abi at the jail that day. They'd talked and prayed with her for an hour and felt when they left that she was in better spirits. Will was silently miffed that the ministers could spend as much time as they wanted with Abi when he couldn't, even though he was her husband.

Simes came to the house and told Will and Haven he'd filed a brief with the committee that morning requesting that he be permitted to be Abi's counsel at the trial. He'd also given a copy of the brief to the *New Hampshire Gazette* and posted additional copies on the bulletin boards of the North and South Churches and Queen's Chapel in order to put public pressure on the committee to grant his motion.

"The trial's getting close, Will," he said. "Have you got anything for me about ulterior motives or other improprieties behind the indictment?"

Will relayed the information he'd gotten from Wentworth Cheswell that afternoon. "And Ned Sherwood's owner is William Woods, another farmer—"

"That's *it*, Will. You've done it!" Haven cried.

"Done what?"

"William Woods is the *brother* of Reginald Woods, the chairman of the Committee of Safety."

"Very interesting indeed," Simes said. "But proving that Sherwood or his woman Semantha poisoned William Woods' mind and that William in turn influenced his brother Reginald to bring the indictment would be mighty hard to prove. Particularly since we have only five days before trial."

"You'd be surprised what Jack and I can accomplish in a few days," Will said.

⸺⸻⸺

Two days before the date set for the trial to begin, Simes was in his office early in the morning preparing Abi's case. He was scheduled to meet at ten o'clock with Will, Colonel Long, Jack Odiorne, Reverend Haven, and Caesar to receive the reports of their further investigations, to determine who would be the witnesses on Abi's behalf, and to go over their testimony.

Just after nine o'clock there was a knock on his office door, and a messenger entered from the Committee of Safety with a ruling on Simes's motion to act as Abi's counsel. He was happy to learn that the motion had been granted. But the order contained a second ruling by the committee, replacing John Richards as prosecutor with an experienced Portsmouth trial lawyer named David Thacher. Simes smiled at this development. "Well, I've always said I'd rather have my opposing counsel be somebody who knows what he's doing."

The others on his defense team arrived soon thereafter, with some interesting news.

Jack Odiorne reported first that a friend of his who lived in Newmarket had told him Semantha and Ned Sherwood were telling everybody in town who would listen that they knew Abi, that the charges were true, that she was a terrible person who deserved to die.

Will had some information that was much more compelling. Another friend of his in Newmarket, Peter Walker, a freed slave whose help he'd enlisted, had been having dinner in the back room of Bell's Tavern there two days earlier. William Woods happened to be sitting at the bar out front with two of his friends. After several drinks, Woods began to talk openly and loudly about Abi's case. Specifically, he said he'd learned of Abi's "crimes" from his slave Ned Sherwood and Ned's girlfriend, Semantha. Sherwood and Semantha had also convinced him that a significant number of Negroes in New Hampshire still favored the British, and they needed to be taught a lesson. Woods said he'd talked to his brother about it, and they'd both concluded that Abi was guilty and that convicting her would force the Negro community to support the efforts of the patriots and the new country.

"So that's how this all happened," Simes said. "Somewhat as we surmised, I must say. I'll have to subpoena Woods, see what I can get out of him. At least this gives us a hook to throw some doubt on the prosecution's allegations."

Will and the rest of the group then turned to the task of preparing themselves for the trial presentations. Their work continued throughout that day and all of the next.

After a final night when Will and many others in the town got scant sleep, the day of the trial arrived. Will, Reverend Haven, and Colonel Long, all of whom planned to testify on Abi's behalf both as to the facts and her good character, drove early with Simes in Colonel Long's wagon to Exeter. The ride took about an hour, and the trial was scheduled to start promptly at eight o'clock. They parked the wagon behind the Exeter courthouse, which was located on the top of a hill just above the river flowing through the center of the town. They walked around to the front door, pushing themselves through a crowd of about a hundred people who had already assembled on the courthouse steps, even though no members of the public were to be permitted inside to view the trial.

The courtroom, about fifty feet square, was cold and austere. There was nothing hanging on the white walls and no curtains on the two windows on each of the side walls. The wide pine-board floor creaked as they walked on it, and their voices echoed in the bare room. At the far end and to the right was a long table with three chairs behind it for the committee. In front of that were two other smaller tables, one on each side with two chairs behind them, for the lawyers and their clients. Two unpainted wooden benches for witnesses flanked the aisle leading up to the committee table.

When they entered the courtroom, the prosecuting attorney, David Thacher, was already at the lawyers' table on the right, with his files and what appeared to be three witnesses. These were Edward Jones and his wife, Hannah, a white couple who had also worked, albeit intermittently, for both Governor Wentworth and Theodore Atkinson, and Ned Sherwood. There was no sign of William Woods. Apparently he had simply ignored Simes's subpoena, perhaps even at his brother's direction.

At eight o'clock the clerk called the hearing to order, and the three members of the Committee of Safety entered and took their seats behind the bench. The case was called, and Abi, walking slowly in chains and without shoes, was led into the courtroom by two guards. Will was aghast at how she looked. Her face was drawn and haggard. Her gray dress hung soiled and limp from four weeks of day and night wear. Her hair was unkempt. She sat as instructed in the defendant's chair to the left of the bench.

Thacher made a brief opening statement of the prosecution's case.

"Members of the Committee," he began, "this is a very simple and straightforward matter. The defendant, Abigail . . ." He proceeded to outline the charges essentially as they had been described to Colonel Long three weeks earlier, making a particular point of denigrating Governor and Mrs. Wentworth.

Thacher then called his first witness, Hannah Jones. After the usual introductory questions, he said, "Mrs. Jones, would you please describe for the committee what happened on the night of June 13, 1775, the day Governor Wentworth left his home?"

Simes stood up. "Mr. Chairman, we will stipulate that the defendant, at the direction of her then owner, Governor Wentworth, on June 13, 1775, assisted the governor and his family to relocate from their home in Portsmouth to Fort William and Mary on the Piscataqua River. This testimony is unnecessary."

"Rejected and overruled, Mr. Simes," said Woods. "We will hear this. The witness may answer."

Mrs. Jones said, "Mr. Jones and I were passing the governor's house on Pleasant Street when a neighbor came up and told us—"

Simes jumped up. "Objection, Mr. Chairman. That testimony is redundant to our stipulation, and what a neighbor told Mrs. Jones is hearsay in any event. I ask that it be stricken and disregarded."

"Denied," Reginald Woods ruled.

Mrs. Jones said, "The neighbor told us the governor and his family had gone out on the British ship *Scarborough* the night before and that their slave woman Abi had helped them escape."

Thacher said, "Do you recognize Abi, the woman you mentioned, in this courtroom? If so, will you please point her out?"

"That's her over there in the chair on the other side of the room."

"Did you ever ask Abi whether the story was true?"

"No, because I heard from another neighbor that Abi wouldn't talk about it."

"Objection, hearsay," Simes called out. "Where is the neighbor?"

"Denied."

Thacher asked the witness to step down and called Mr. Jones to the stand.

Simes rose immediately. "Mr. Chairman, am I not to be permitted to cross-examine these witnesses? Is that not a basic right afforded to all defendants in this country?"

"I'm sorry, Mr. Simes. Cross-examination is not allowed before this committee. You may proceed, Mr. Thacher."

"Mr. Jones, is what your wife said true?"

"Objection," came from Simes. "Vague and incompetent. No foundation laid for the witness to testify on the subject."

"Denied," Woods said.

"Yes, it is," the witness said.

"How do you know it's true?"

"It was widely talked about in the neighborhood at the time."

"Objection, hearsay, no foundation," Simes said.

"Denied."

"What do you know about Abi's reputation?"

"Objection, what he thinks is irrelevant, no foundation, hearsay."

"Denied."

"She's haughty and doesn't speak to anybody. She's borne two children by Will Clarkson, she isn't married to. She's not well liked by either Negroes or whites because she isn't truthful."

"Thank you, Mr. Jones. You may step down. The prosecution now calls Mr. Ned Sherwood to the stand."

"Mr. Sherwood, do you know the defendant, Abi?"

"Yes, I do. Very well."

"Is it true that she is unmarried and has had two children by a man named Will Clarkson who does not even live with her?"

"Objection. Leading the witness."

"Denied."

"Yes. That's all true."

"Isn't it also true that Will Clarkson was an aide to the infamous traitor Benedict Arnold?"

"Objection. Irrevelent. Leading the witness. It is well known that Will Clarkson's service to his country was heroic."

"Objection denied."

"Yes. Clarkson was an aide to Arnold."

"Move to strike the question and answer."

"Denied."

"Do you know what her sympathies were during the war with the English?"

"Yes. Many people said that she was very fond of Governor Wentworth and often defended the actions of King George."

"Objection, hearsay, move to strike and disregard."

"Denied."

With that the prosecutor dismissed Sherwood, looked over at Abi, paused, and said, "No further witnesses." He rested his case and asked the committee to find Abi guilty of both charges.

Simes rose and said that he wished to call witnesses on the defendant's behalf.

"The request is out of order and therefore denied," Woods said.

Simes said he wished to make a statement for the record in lieu of evidence. He then proceeded to delineate all the defenses he had outlined to Will, Pierse Long, and the others, and stated what each of the witnesses would have said had they had been permitted to testify. He added that the defense was prepared to offer evidence and proof that the indictment had been improvidently and improperly issued by reason of false and fraudulent information received from third parties and tainted by a blatant conflict of interest on the part of the chairman.

The committee chairman attempted to stifle Simes by twice more ruling him out of order, but Simes continued until he had made all his points. When he finished, he made an oral motion that the chairman recuse himself.

"Motion denied," Woods said for the last time.

The chairman thereupon declared the case closed and banged down his gavel to indicate the end of the trial. The Committee would begin its deliberations immediately, he said, and the court would reconvene when they were finished. They retired, and Abi was returned to her holding room in the rear of the courthouse.

"These fellows appear to have already made up their minds, Will," Simes said. "The trial was a travesty. The only reason I made my statement was to preserve the points for appeal to the state committee. I hope we get a chance to speak to Abi to explain the strategy and boost her spirits. She looks terribly distraught."

They didn't have to wait long for the verdict. Within twenty minutes the clerk called the room to order once again and the three committee members filed back to the bench. Abi was brought in and placed in her chair.

"The committee, having heard all the evidence, has fully considered this case and unanimously finds the defendant guilty of both charges. She is hereby sentenced to one week in the stocks on the Parade in Portsmouth and thereafter to prison for an indefinite period. Case closed."

Abi fell from her chair. She writhed on the floor and cried out, "No, No! Will? Where's my Will?"

Will rushed to her but was restrained by Abi's guards. He yelled over their heads, "Don't worry, Abi! We'll take care of it, this isn't over! Everything's going to be all right." Abi stared back at him in anguish as the guards pushed her through the rear door.

Colonel Long ran up to console Will. Simes shook his head and stared at the floor. Haven was slumped forward, covering his face with his hands. From the other side, Ned Sherwood swept past them in the aisle, rushing to relay the verdict to the crowd outside.

Within seconds the crowd, which had tripled in size, erupted, bellowing its reactions to the ruling, both approval and dismay.

Simes stood up. He drew Will and Haven aside and said, "We'll immediately file an appeal with the state Committee of Safety, which will sit for this purpose in Concord, and request a stay of the sentence until the appeal is decided. Colonel Long and I know the men on that committee. We'll talk to them about a reasonable settlement."

Will glared at him. "Mr. Simes, I'm not interested in a half-baked compromise. This kind of justice isn't what I risked my life for in the war. Not what so many died for. I know you tried hard, but I will hold you responsible for fixing this."

Simes gulped, then looked Will in the eye. "I'll do my best."

⟨⟨⟩⟩

"Outrageous!" Simes said to Haven as they exited the building via the rear door to avoid the crowd in front. "Allowing pure hearsay. No cross-examination. And no chance even to take the stand and deny. I'm obliged to say that this sort of thing could not have happened, even to an African, in England, from whose dominion we have just fought so hard to free ourselves. Absolutely outrageous!"

That afternoon Long and Simes filed the appeal and request for a stay of the verdict, and the next day both men boarded Long's wagon to travel to Concord to speak to the state committee. They did not return for three days.

The news of the committee's decision swept through the seacoast towns. Seventy percent of the population, both white and African, were shocked and outraged. The thirty percent that applauded the outcome comprised almost exclusively strident anti-loyalists, many of whom also disliked or even feared the presence of Negroes in their midst.

Arguments raged privately and in the stores and streets.

King Caesar, fearing an outbreak of violence, called for a meeting of the city's entire African population the following evening at the Plains. He had to bang a hammer on a frying pan to control the noise level enough to be heard. "Folks, we gotta keep calm while the appeal goes forward. Stay in your houses and workplaces. Don't argue with your owners. We don't want bloodshed and retalia—"

Caesar's words were drowned out by catcalls and boos. They fell off when Will stood up and signaled for quiet. "Caesar's wrong," he said. "I say we all march to the jail and free Abi."

Cheers and cries of "Yes, let's go now, let's go now!" rang out.

Will raised his arms to ask for quiet again. "But we have to be smart about how we do it. Let Prince and me scout the jail and come up with a plan. Go back to your houses. We'll send word to you later this evening."

When the gathering had dispersed, Caesar returned to the William Bannister house.

⸻

Half an hour later, Will, Jack, and Prince Whipple stood in the darkness of the woods behind the Islington Street jail. "That back door with the window is the weak point," Will said. "But we'll need a disturbance out front to distract the jailer."

"How many people you think we got with us, Prince?" Jack said.

"I'd say easy fifty. Caesar didn't convince many."

"The jailer has two more deputies since the whites got scared of some sort of confrontation," Will said. "All of them will be armed. We can sneak a few guns from our masters, and a couple of free Africans have guns. But we need to avoid bloodshed if at all possible. I'll be out front and try first to negotiate Abi's release. Any questions?"

The other two shook their heads.

"That's it, then. Probably Caesar has spilled the beans to Bannister, but I think I can deal with that. Let's get the word out. Have everyone here first thing in the morning."

⸻

They were all there at daybreak. Men and women, eighty strong. When they spied the jailer moving around inside, they began shouting at him. None of them saw one of the deputies slip out the back door and into the woods. By the time Prince and Jack took up their positions in the trees, the deputy had already reached William Bannister's house in downtown Portsmouth.

After an hour, as the chanting continued and grew louder, the jailer, Paul Saunders, opened the front door and stepped outside, holding a musket aimed at the crowd.

"All right, folks. This ruckus aint going to work. I'm not authorized to release the prisoner. I direct you all to disperse. Return to your homes or to work. If you want to pursue this thing, you'll have to take it up with William Bannister. Now go on."

Will stepped forward, holding out his arms to show that he was unarmed. "Mr. Saunders, we're not going to disperse. We're staying here until Abi is released. I'd like to come inside and talk to you about how this can be resolved without gunfire and bloodshed."

Saunders hesitated, probably suspecting a trick. No one in the crowd moved a muscle. They were leaning forward intently, their eyes burning in on the jailer. "All right, Will, come on in. But my deputy will be covering the rest of you with his musket while we talk."

Will turned to Pharaoh Shores and whispered to him to rush the building if he was still inside after an hour. "I'll try to neutralize Saunders and the deputy as you men charge. Tell Prince and Jack to hold off until then too." Will then entered the building alone. Shores turned and told the crowd what he'd said. Everybody calmed down and waited.

One hour later they were still waiting. And growing restless. Suddenly a shot rang out, and the right front window of the jail shattered. One of the Africans had shot and wounded Saunders' deputy.

In an instant the crowd rushed forward and surged into the building, overcoming and tying up Saunders and his wounded deputy before they could react. Will pulled the keys from Saunders's belt and hurried back to Abi's cell.

Almost simultaneously, the Africans heard running feet and new shouting outside the jail. A hundred and fifty white men, led by William Bannister, quickly surrounded the jail as Jack Odiorne and Prince Whipple watched helplessly from their hiding place in the woods. Outside the front door, Bannister shouted to the Africans inside to throw down their arms and surrender.

Will released Abi from her cell, rushed to the jailer's office at the front of the building, and called to Bannister through the broken window. "We won't throw down our arms or release the jailer and his deputy or come out until you agree that Abi will be released permanently and that there'll be no charges pressed against any of the men who've taken over the jail!"

"I'll make no such agreement," Bannister said. He then turned to his fellow townsmen and instructed them to dig in around the building. They would wait until the Negroes capitulated. "If necessary, we'll starve em out."

Prince and Jack left their hiding place and quietly made their way through the woods toward the city. At the Whipple stable, Prince brought Jack a fast-looking horse and an army canteen of water. The two men talked briefly, then Jack mounted and galloped out of town to the northwest—toward Concord.

Simes' and Long's trip to Concord had taken five hours. Upon their arrival, they checked into the inn at the edge of the Merrimack River and went to lunch in the small tavern next door. As they ate, they discussed the approach they would take with the state Committee of Safety, which comprised five men, one from Concord, two from Portsmouth, one from Exeter, and one from Hampton. David Thacher would also be present, defending the ruling of the local committee in Exeter.

The hearing on the appeal began the next morning at nine o'clock. Simes opened with a detailed description of Abi's excellent character and hard work, explained what had happened when Governor Wentworth escaped from his house with his family, and outlined once again the legal basis of Abi's defense and the testimony he would have introduced if permitted by the local committee. Finally he described Ned Sherwood's, Semantha's, and William Woods's role in causing the indictment to be issued in the first place. He requested that the conviction be set aside and that Abi be released from jail immediately.

Thacher's presentation was short and succinct: Simes' legal points were not applicable, and his factual arguments were irrelevant and speculative. There was more than adequate evidence for the conviction, which should be allowed to stand.

Charles Treadwell, the chairman of the committee, was clearly looking for a way out of the politically charged situation.

"Gentlemen," he said, "the committee is impressed by the arguments both of you have made. This is a very difficult case to decide. We wonder whether you have discussed a settlement of the matter."

"No, we have not, Mr. Chairman," both attorneys said, almost in unison.

"Well, we suggest—indeed, we direct—that the two of you get together and try to work this out. If you wish, you may use the room next to this one to conduct your discussions. Report back to this committee promptly at ten o'clock tomorrow morning."

Throughout the rest of the day and into the evening, Thacher and Simes shuttled back and forth to each other within the courthouse and then at the hotel, offering alternative solutions. In the end they remained far apart. Simes was rigid, remembering Will's admonition not to enter into a half-baked compromise. They went to bed that night exhausted, physically and mentally.

When they reported their lack of success to the committee the next morning, Treadwell said, "Gentlemen, if you cannot reach an accord by two o'clock this afternoon, this committee is prepared to hand down a ruling that will leave both of you quite unhappy. Try again! Be here at two."

As they left the courtroom, Simes turned to Thacher. "David, it's obvious they mean business. I have an idea about resolving this that has worked in other cases. Meet me at noon in my room at the hotel and we'll talk about it."

Thacher agreed. The two men convened at twelve o'clock and began to hammer out a resolution. At two o'clock they reported their results to the committee, all of whom seemed greatly relieved to escape the necessity of making their own decision.

At the request of both attorneys, the terms of the settlement were to be kept secret until approved by their respective clients. But just as the attorneys and the Committee were ready to affix their signatures to the document setting forth the tentative agreement, the door of the courtroom burst open and Jack stumbled down the aisle to the table where the others were gathered.

"Mr. Simes, I need to talk to you right now."

The attorney excused himself and walked out into the hallway with Jack, who spilled out the details of the drama unfolding back in Portsmouth. Simes then drew a blank sheet of paper from his case and for the next few minutes filled it with words the African couldn't read. Simes signed his name at the end and beckoned Jack to follow him back into the courtroom. There he told the committee and Thacher what Jack had told him and offered up to Chairman Treadwell the document he'd just written in the hallway.

"Gentlemen, I believe there's no question but that this committee has original jurisdiction to rule on this petition. It summarizes what I've just told you and requests a judgment that all the Africans involved in the insurrection at the Portsmouth jail be released unharmed, that no charges be pressed against any of them, and that there be no recriminations of any kind against any of the participants.

"This matter is now an integral part of the issue—Abi's release— we've been discussing. I hereby request that the two proceedings be consolidated. Under no circumstances can I now enter into the agreement we've been contemplating unless this petition is granted and made a part of it.

"I appreciate that this request is extraordinary," Simes continued. "But the present circumstances clearly warrant it. Without such a comprehensive resolution, we're facing the likelihood of a massacre in Portsmouth. This explosive situation could spread to a rebellion in every slave community in New England. I don't want that on my conscience, and I'm sure you don't either. Wouldn't you agree, David?"

Thacher gulped at being put in a corner, but he pulled himself up, faced the committee, and responded in a steady voice. "We must resolve this, Thomas, but we can't let these Portsmouth rebels off scot-free. They can be released, but they should still be subject to later prosecution for their illegal actions."

With that Treadwell banged down his gavel and said, "Gentlemen, we shall withdraw to consider this further and be back here shortly."

Within fifteen minutes the committee returned. "Counselors," Treadwell said, "this situation is indeed dangerous. Our order will be entered immediately. It will require your signatures and then the signatures of William Bannister, Abi, and Will Clarkson on behalf of the African insurgents."

All signed, and with a "Good luck" from Treadwell, the four Portsmouth men—Simes, Long, Thacher, and Odiorne—climbed onto their waiting wagon for a frantic nighttime ride back down to the port city. Although a full moon lit the way, the trip through the darkness still took much longer than the ride up to Concord.

At dawn the wagon, the Whipple horse tethered and trailing, pulled up in front of the jail on Islington Street. The four very dusty and tired men climbed down and walked stiffly toward William Bannister.

The situation appeared to be much the same as when Jack Odiorne had left the day before. A large group of white men still surrounded the building and the Africans were still crowded inside the jail.

As Thacher began telling the white leaders what had transpired in Concord, Simes, Long, and Odiorne went inside to speak to Will and the other Africans.

Will was satisfied with the resolution Simes had achieved. A tragedy was avoided. Simes's petition absolving the Africans was granted in full, and he and Long had negotiated an agreement with Thacher and the state committee that Abi's two sentences would be commuted if she agreed to sign a public recantation that read:

> Whereas I, Abigail Clarkson, have, for a period of nearly ten years both done and said many things that I understand have proved disadvantageous to the city of Portsmouth, the State of New Hampshire, and the Confederation, I am now determined by my future conduct to convince the public that I will risk my life and interest in defense of the city, state, the Confederation, and the constitutional privileges of the Confederation, and humbly ask the forgiveness of my friends and the Country for my past conduct.

The actual charges were to be withdrawn and the recantation was so general that Abi never really admitted to anything.

Will said, "We've still got to explain this fully to Abi."

Standing in her filthy cell, they told her the pros and cons of signing the recantation. In the end she sighed and looked up at Will for the answer.

Will glanced at Simes and Long and then said quietly, "Yes, I think you should sign." With that reassurance, Abi took up the pen and signed her name as Will had taught her.

Colonel Long took the papers outside to Bannister, who was telling Thacher the Africans should still be held responsible for shooting a deputy jailer, although he had only a minor flesh wound. But upon Thacher's insistence that the agreement was essential to avoid a massacre, Bannister signed Simes's petition.

When Long returned, he put his hand on Abi's shoulder. "It's over, Abi, you're free to go home." Abi arose with difficulty from the decrepit wooden bunk. She was crying. Will took her hand and together they walked out the front door of the jail into the sunlight on Islington Road, passing through two long lines of white men who looked down at the ground and spoke not a word. The other Africans then emerged from the building and headed back to their homes in the town.

Word of what had happened flashed around the city. In spite of some grumbling by people on both sides of the issue, everyone realized that a serious tragedy had been averted. The great majority of citizens and slaves alike accepted the outcome and prepared to move on with their lives.

That afternoon, Will and Abi had a long discussion about of the trial, the storming of the jail, and their current situation in Portsmouth and their new country. At the end, Will sighed and said, "Well, that's where we are, like it or not, Abi. The reality is, all we've really got is each other." His jaw tightened. He still had to deal with Caesar and Bannister. No more reasoning with their sort. It didn't work. Now he appreciated the power of force in these civilian matters as much as in the military. And he realized he wouldn't make any more headway unless the majority of the Africans were with him.

—※—

Early that evening, as she lay with Will in her room in the Meechum house, Abi felt a sense of relief, despite her exhaustion, that she had not known for a long time. But in that same moment she knew she would soon have to tell her husband the terrible dilemma she'd never disclosed to him.

38

*L*ate that same night, long after Will had left, Abi heard the door to her room close quietly and sensed the shadow looming over her bed in the silvery moonlight coming through her window. She cringed and stiffened as she prepared herself for what was about to happen, again.

It had started four years earlier, soon after John Meechum purchased her from the Theodore Atkinson estate. Meechum, a forty-year-old bachelor, had returned to his Middle Road home from his hardware store on Sheafe Street earlier than usual on a particularly cold November afternoon. It was nearly two hours before his normal suppertime, and Abi had not yet begun to prepare his evening meal.

Meechum went into his study, started a fire in the fireplace, and for an hour sat at his desk working on his account books. After a while, he moved over to the couch in front of the fireplace and began to review his general ledger.

Abi came into the study to confirm that he'd be satisfied with haddock for dinner. Meechum replied that fish would be fine and then said, "Abi, come over and sit down with me for a minute. I want to talk to you."

She sat down at the opposite end of the couch.

"Abi, we should get to know each other better. I really appreciate your help and would like to talk with you more often. You're a bright and attractive woman, you know."

Abi felt uncomfortable but didn't know what to say other than "Thank you, sir."

Her discomfort increased when Meechum slid next to her. Seeing the expression on her face, he said, "Don't be concerned, Abi. I just think we should be closer friends. Don't you agree?"

"Our relationship is different, Mr. Meechum. As my owner, you have control over my work. But I'm a married woman with two children."

"Now, Abi," said Meechum, reaching out and putting his hand on her knee, "I want you to come up to bed with me. Is that clear? I wouldn't want to have to harm you or the children. I know you don't want that. Come along now."

Terrified, Abi tried quickly to sort out her thoughts and devise a way to extricate herself from this predicament. But she saw no escape. She couldn't risk the retaliation he threatened. And who knew what he would try to do to her physically if she resisted. In a moment of utter confusion, she stood up and followed him upstairs.

For a while after that first time, Meechum's demands were fairly frequent. Once a week, usually. Abi was thankful that he had the courtesy not to make the children aware. And that Dr. Hall had told her after Naby was born that she could have no more children.

But by the time a year had elapsed, Meechum abandoned any pretense of care or subtlety. He would just appear in her room late at night, unclothed, and climb into her bed and have his way with her.

Once, at about the two-year point, she attempted to reason with him, begged him to stop.

He said, "Now, Abi, this is the way it's going to be. If it stops, you know the consequences."

She never tried again. But the predicament was wearing her down. Sometimes she felt she could not look Will in the eye because of her unfaithfulness, even though it was not her fault.

That night of her return from jail was worse than usual. Meechum, who smelled of whiskey, stayed in her room for a long time, and his aggressiveness bruised and hurt her.

After he left, Abi cried for an hour and resolved to tell Will about the gruesome situation when she saw him on Sunday afternoon. She prayed that he would react tenderly and rationally and figure out a way to solve her dilemma. He was her only chance, her only confidant.

That Sunday at the women's market, when Abi, in a shaky voice, said she wanted to walk down by the river to talk, Will knew immediately that something was seriously wrong. They sat on the riverbank by one of the wharves, and Abi tried to get out the story. Sobbing uncontrollably, at first she couldn't say anything. When she finally did, Will exploded. For the first time in his life outside of combat, he wanted to kill another man. Pacing along the bank, he cursed Meechum more and more creatively.

Abi sat on the grass, crying quietly as he stormed about.

Finally he sat down, holding and soothing Abi. But his mind was racing as he tried to determine what to do. He walked Abi back to the market and asked her to stay there while he went to talk to Pierse Long.

He returned an hour later and the couple headed for Meechum's house.

When they arrived, Meechum was in his study. Will went into the room alone, and Abi went upstairs to her room.

"Mr. Meechum, do you have a minute? I have something I need to talk to you about, a proposal."

Meechum looked surprised but motioned him in.

Every sinew in Will's body strained to leap over Meechum's desk and strangle the man. But he kept himself calm.

"Mr. Meechum, I would like to buy Abi's freedom from you. I'm prepared to offer you fifteen pounds."

Meechum froze. "I don't know about that, Will. I rely heavily on Abi's help here at the house. I'm afraid I have to reject your offer."

Will was prepared for that response, and he quickly came back at Meechum in a more confrontational tone. "You may want to reconsider. Abi has told me about you imposing yourself on her for a long time. I've discussed this situation with Colonel Long, who's prepared to let Abi and the children live at his house. If you accept my offer, no one will ever hear about what you've done to Abi. Colonel Long, Abi, and I will keep silent. On the other hand, if you persist in rejecting my offer, Colonel Long and I will pursue the matter with public rape charges."

As he spoke, Will watched Meechum's face. The little man was doing his best to control his emotions but his jaw muscles were twitching, his teeth were clenched, and his lips pursed.

"How do I know you've got fifteen pounds? Where did you get it?"

Will drew the coins from his pocket and slammed them down on the desk. "There it is. From my army pay."

"Maybe you're lying about talking to Colonel Long. How do I know you're not bluffing?"

"If you don't believe me, go talk to him."

Will continued to stare intently at his adversary. *He knows I'm telling the truth. Wondering how he can get out of this box. May have a pistol in that drawer by his right hand. Won't try it. Long and Abi could dispute any story he could come up with that I attacked him and he acted in self-defense. He'll take the offer and cut his loss.*

"All right. I want her and the children out of here today."

"First, sign this bill of sale."

He glared at Will, grabbed the paper, and read it. Then he reached for pen and ink and signed.

Will took the paper. As he turned his back to leave, he heard the sound of a drawer opening, then an ominous metallic click. He dove to the floor just as a shot rang out and a bullet whistled over his head. He then leapt back and threw himself over the desk at Meechum, pinning him against the wall and floor. Will yanked the gun from his hand and threw it out the door. He proceeded to pummel Meechum until the white man could barely move.

Will then stood up, wheeled around, and went for Abi and the children, who were cowering at the top of the stairs.

"He pulled a gun on me, Abi. He won't try that again." He gathered them up and left, slamming the door behind him.

Half an hour later they arrived at South School Street. The children went into the hut, and Will and Abi went to the rear room in the ell. Mrs. Haven came in to greet them.

Will told no one what had happened. He and Abi heard nothing about the incident from anyone else, and Meechum never said anything further to them or attempted any retaliation.

39

Will thought he had a reasonable chance of winning.

Examining his personal list of the people at the 1785 African elections celebration, he estimated that he could get nearly half the vote, which was to take place that afternoon.

Jack was looking over Will's shoulder at the notations on the page. "Still close. Caesar's holding on to the old-timers who've been with him for years. Young ones are all for us."

The two men had been campaigning hard for several weeks leading up to this balmy June day. Yesterday Jack had officially submitted the requisite paper with ten names nominating Will and his slate to challenge Caesar Bannister for king of the Negro Court.

"We can't take anything for granted," Will said. "We'll work the crowd right up to the last minute. You take the south side of the field, I'll take the north."

Throughout the afternoon the two men made the rounds, shaking hands and making their case:

"Will's a war hero. Caesar never even served."

"Where was Caesar when we confronted the white folks at the jail? He's not our leader anymore."

"Caesar's too old. We need fresh blood."

"Caesar's a lackey for his owner."

"Caesar stands for living with slavery. Will will fight hard to abolish it."

There had never been a serious election challenge to Caesar, and emotions ran hot on both sides. On several occasions shouting matches broke out between supporters of the two nominees. A fist-fight near the food tables was barely averted as calmer bystanders pulled apart the men. By five o'clock the noise from the throng was a near roar. Everyone wanted to get on with the vote.

Prince walked to the podium and waved his arms to quiet the crowd.

"All right, folks. As you know, this year we got a contest for leadership of our court. King Caesar's being challenged by Will Clarkson. You've heard what they have to say for themselves. Time for the vote.

"First, those in favor of Caesar Bannister."

A loud chorus of ayes rose in the air.

Jack frowned. Will said nothing.

"All those in favor of Will Clarkson."

A second loud roar.

"Too close to call," Prince said. "Need a show of hands. Primus Fowle, you and Romeo Rindge are on opposite sides. You two do the counting and check with each other. Now, let's see the hands for Bannister."

Will and Jack stood still as Primus and Romeo did their slow count, confirmed the numbers with each other, and gave the answer to Prince.

"Seventy-six for Caesar," Prince said. "Now all those for Clarkson."

Primus and Romeo repeated the laborious process, then walked up and spoke to Prince, who looked startled by their report. Will licked his lips.

"Seventy-six for Clarkson," Prince said. "But I can vote to break the tie. I vote for Will. Clarkson's the winner by a final vote of seventy-seven to seventy-six."

Cheers rang out for Will. There were a few isolated boos from Caesar's supporters, but most were happy to fall in behind Will as their new leader.

The crowd gradually dispersed for the evening, everyone looking forward to the next day's games, dinner, and dancing.

Jack put his arm around Will's shoulders. "Sure took awhile,
my friend, but worth the wait."

At the far end of the Plains they could see Caesar, slumped,
slowly riding off on his master's horse.

———

Later that year, in November, William Bannister was also up
for reelection, as chairman of the selectmen in the city of Portsmouth. It appeared at first that no one would come forward to
run against him, but in September Will heard that Samuel Cutts,
a strong supporter of the Revolution, was considering a challenge.
That evening Will went to the man's house. He described in detail
to Cutts, who owned no slaves, the elaborate extortion scheme
Bannister and Caesar had engaged in for years to maintain their
influence in the city, including the ten-pound protection fee, and
the additional information Romeo Rindge and Seneca Hall had
uncovered. He meticulously took Cutts through Seneca's notes of
individual transactions revealing how Bannister had turned the
owners' funds to his personal benefit.

Will then took Cutts to visit the Bickfords, who agreed to tell
the story during the election campaign. Cutts decided to run for the
office under the slogan "End the Corruption." After a bitter election
battle marked by public outrage, the Bannister domino fell when
the larger, non-slave-owning portion of the populace voted to end
the chairman's reign of nearly forty years.

40

*I*n addition to Will's new duties as king, his work for Colonel Long continued. Abi assisted Mrs. Haven in the house and took particular interest in helping Long's two beautiful daughters until they were married. Both weddings were major social events in the port city.

Life was difficult for Will's and Abi's own children. Naby did in fact turn out to be somewhat retarded. Consequently there were no suitors for her; her life consisted of helping her mother with simple tasks. Will Jr. began to assume a number of Will's duties, but the boy became more and more restless as his teenage years progressed.

In the fall of 1788, Will Jr. broke some news as he and his father took an evening walk along the river.

"Pa, I'm going to ask Colonel Long to free me, so I can go down to New York City. They hire free African workers there. A whole bunch of us are there already, and they're a lot better off than us here in Portsmouth. I'm nineteen. I got to be free, live my own life. Can you talk to him with me?"

"You sure you want to do that?" The two reached a favorite log and sat to watch the river tide come in. "Being freed by Colonel Long won't guarantee you financial security or peace of mind. Escape from slavery is the first step, but true freedom means a lot more than that. It has to do with your ability to rise above your troubles, to stick to your own views and your own character. That's when a man becomes free. Do you understand me?"

"I know that, Pa, but right now the first thing for me is to get out. I can't stand being pushed around like an ox and told what to do like a child."

"All right then. I'll back you."

Father and son went together the next day to talk with Long.

"Colonel, my son is now old enough to make his own way in the world. You said you couldn't afford to free me, but can you at least give him a freedom certificate and let him go?"

This time Long didn't even pause. "Can't do that, Will. He's now doing a lot of your work, and my own workload has been increasing in the last couple of years. I need him, too."

"But it's not fair to visit the same burden on my son. He—"

"Sorry, Will. I'll give him the same understanding I gave you. He goes free when I pass away. That's it."

Two days later the colonel stopped Will in the front hallway. "Where is he? Come clean with me!"

"Don't know," Will said. "When I got up this morning, he was gone. Took only what he had on his back."

Long sat down on the bench outside his study and held his head in his hands. Finally, he looked up at Will. "It would be too expensive and probably futile for me to try and pursue him. You realize you'll have to do all his work as well as your own." Then he stood up and shook his head. "God knows, if I were that young man, I'd probably have done the same thing." He walked into his study.

As the colonel closed the door, Will thought about the freedom certificate with Pierse Long's forged signature on it he'd made for his son the day before. Looked authentic. He hoped it would work.

"Why doesn't he ever come back or write to us, at least let us know he's safe?" Abi said one day weeks later.

"He can't," Will said. "He never will. He doesn't know what the colonel might do to force him back into slavery. But even if that danger wasn't there, it's too difficult here. I couldn't come back if it was me, even if I was freed. Leaving forever was his only choice. As a boy here, he was always treated as inferior to the whites. The curse of being considered nothing more than a piece of furniture is everywhere in this town, even for the Africans who've been granted their so-called freedom."

She squeezed his hand. "I know. Like me." Will had freed Abi in writing days after he bought her. In lighter moments the document was a joke between them.

"Freedom doesn't mean a damn thing unless the whites treat us as equal," Will said. "Willie knew he had to cut off all contact with Portsmouth…forever. Settle some place where he won't be reminded, day after day, of his life as a child. So he escaped, including from us. It's eating my heart out. All we can do is pray that the separation does it for him."

Abi sighed. "Think I understand. Guess Naby's the only one who can be happy here. She don't know bout all the injustice."

Abi started to cook their supper. Will stoked his pipe. *Now they're telling us, "Here's the door to your freedom," but there's no door. Who do they think they're kidding?* Some days he got so fed up with their stupidity that he just wanted to leave, like Willie. *But for Abi and me it's too late. We're too old. We're stuck.*

There must be something I can still do.

41

*A*fter the cruel winter of 1789, in which storms dropped an accumulated sixteen feet of snow on open flat ground and twice that in drifts, first Walter Clarkson, Will's old nemesis, and then Pierse Long died in the early spring. Long kept his promise and in his final testament made Will a free man.

Clarkson and Long were buried in the Auburn Street cemetery on the northeast side of South Road toward Rye. Walter's funeral, on March 20, 1789, was attended by just Reverend Haven and James III, who came up from Newburyport more out of family fealty than affection for his uncle. Will felt no guilt in absenting himself. By contrast, more than three hundred people squeezed into South Meeting House for Pierse Long's service a month later. Colonel Long's patriotic military and civil service were extolled in long eulogies. Will left the church buoyed by the celebration of the colonel's life and thankful for what Long had finally done for him.

His reaction to freedom was complicated. Euphoria was followed quickly by the dulling realization that not much had changed. In some ways, in fact, his situation had worsened. Pierse Long had provided that from his estate a small lump sum of money would go to Will, and the executor was also to supply a tiny stipend. But he still had to find lodging and fend for himself for daily sustenance. Without a patron such as Andrew Clarkson or Pierse Long who knew his administrative skills and had use for them, he was

262

forced to take odd jobs as a general fix-it man around the city. Abi managed to arrange for several housekeeping jobs. The meager income from these sources enabled them to rent half of a house in Sheafe's Pasture west of the city toward Newington and Dover.

Will discovered that his office as king took much more time than he'd anticipated. Apart from listening to requests and complaints from his constituency, he gave speeches and met with white merchants and politicians in an effort to abolish slavery completely in the Granite State. He urged his African neighbors to obtain help to teach their children to read and write, but the scarcity of people who could and would teach them made that difficult. Despite the slow progress, he kept up the effort.

More important, he began to organize the Africans. He formed a military company of the young men and drilled them two weekends every month. On the odd weekends he held meetings of the women and older men, lecturing them on the importance of banding together to speak with one voice and act as a single strong arm to see that their needs and views were recognized. He preached the gospel of the strength of unity and the importance of using that strength.

The white population respected that strength. They were fearful of Will's activities, but they did nothing to impede him so long as the Africans took no overt steps toward open rebellion.

———

From the political and governmental standpoints, 1789 was momentous. On June 21, 1788, the state of New Hampshire had had the honor, as the ninth state to ratify, of putting the new United States Constitution into force in accordance with the terms of the federal convention in 1787. The old Congress Federation named New York the first capital and arranged for the first elections. On April 30, 1789, George Washington took the oath of office before massive crowds on the balcony of Federal Hall on Wall Street. The Judiciary and Organic Acts of 1789 fleshed out the framework of the government. The major weakness from the 1781 Articles of Confederation—the absence of a strong national government—was fixed. At President Washington's urging and with the brilliant political maneuvering of James Madison, the Bill of Rights was added in September and ratified by the states two years later. But the issue of slavery remained unresolved. Many in the North believed it would simply die out over time.

Abroad, the capture of the Bastille on July 14, 1789, triggered the French Revolution, which was followed with great interest throughout the United States. "Freedom's contagious," Will said to Jack.

In Portsmouth, townspeople read the exciting news in the October 20 issue of *Osborne's New Hampshire Spy* that the new country's first president would visit New England, including Portsmouth, after the close of the initial session of the first congress, which had convened in New York in September. Preparations began immediately.

Will planned to go to the Massachusetts state line to see the great man as the president was greeted by New Hampshire's leading politicians and gentry. As king of the Negro Court, he was part of the official state entourage. And as a veteran, he was to be among the troops commanded by Major General Cilley to pass in review before Washington on the Parade on October 31.

The day after the news broke, Reverend Haven mentioned to Will that the president's schedule included a meeting with him at the president's suite in the Bannister boardinghouse on Hanover Street. The meeting wasn't related to religious matters but instead arose from one of the minister's many other interests—he was to show Washington the process of making dyes from local corn and exhibit samples of cloth dyed in several colors.

Upon hearing this, Will had an idea he hoped would result in the major accomplishment of his tenure as king. The next day he asked the pastor if it would be possible for him to join the meeting long enough to deliver a brief message from Portsmouth's African community.

Reverend Haven seemed startled, but didn't say no. He just looked Will in the eye for a few seconds, harrumphed, and turned back to the draft sermon on his desk. "Let me think about it," he said.

It was a week before Will saw him again, passing on Pleasant Street by the North Church.

"All right, you can do it," the minister said, "but when you said 'brief,' I trust you meant it. I know you'll be respectful. And don't mention this to anyone."

42

On the big day, the thirty-first, President Washington arrived at the state line in a carriage with his secretary, Colonel Tobias Lear, a Portsmouth native, who had helped arrange the visit. General John Sullivan, the president of the state, was there to meet him, along with Senator John Langdon and other notables. A hundred or so of the local populace were also there.

Will arrived well ahead of time. He rode down on Cicero, the horse Pierse Long had given him.

Upon alighting from the carriage and shaking hands with members of the greeting party, including Will, Washington mounted a large white stallion, seventeen hands high, for the rest of the trip to Portsmouth Plains to meet Major General Cilley, his troops, and other officers.

No sooner was Washington astride the horse than for some reason it whinnied and reared back on its hind legs. Most riders would have been thrown, but Washington easily rose to his feet in the stirrups with a tight rein along the animal's neck and quickly settled the horse down. Will had heard of the president's superb horsemanship, but this display of expertise made him gasp. *The Father of his Country indeed!*

As the rest of the official entourage began its way north to the port city, Will broke off and headed quickly up the shore road by himself. He had to be in uniform and with the troops before the president arrived in Portsmouth. He happily breathed in the pungent, salty air of the Hampton marshes as he cantered home.

Arriving at the house at Sheafe's Pasture, Will jumped off Cicero and ran into the bedroom, where he'd carefully laid out his new dress uniform made especially for the occasion. Within minutes he was fully changed. He marched into the living room, where Abi sat in her soft chair. They beamed at each other. It was impossible to say which of them was more proud. They stood and hugged for a long moment, then Will stepped back, turned around, and posed.

"My, aren't you fine," Abi said.

He certainly looked the perfect picture of a continental soldier. His shiny black boots were topped by white stockings that reached to just below the knees. Tight white trousers and a white vest with brown leather buttons lay beneath a bright red waistcoat-type open jacket with white trim, also with buttons, slightly larger. A dark blue shirt could be seen underneath the open vest collar. A white bandolier across the left shoulder held a brown leather pouch for cartridges and powder, and a small black cloth knapsack was on his back, bound by a strap over each shoulder and one across his chest. A hard felt three-cornered black hat with white trim perched on his forehead. Best of all, on his left chest were two pins, one above the other. The top one read "Third New Hampshire Regiment" and the bottom said "Private Will Clarkson."

Will went to the wall above the fireplace and took down the musket he'd used at Saratoga. Then he affixed the black iron bayonet that had been resting on the mantel. He, Abigail, and Naby then went outside, locked the front door, and hitched up Cicero to a small wagon. They climbed into it and began the drive to the assembly spot near the center of town.

The troops rubbed their hands together and blew into them as they mustered in the chilly air shortly after noon for the march to the city center. There were three companies of thirty men each, all under the command of General Cilley and Colonel James Hackett. They lined up and sounded off in the square where hay from local farms was weighed, valued, and sold on Saturdays, about a quarter of a mile from the reviewing stand and only half a mile from the pier where Will had been sold into slavery thirty-four years earlier.

From all parts of the state, the men had been with various regiments during the war; they were now formed together as a single artillery battery.

Twenty additional troops were already stationed by the reviewing stand to welcome the president with a salute from ten prepositioned five-pound cannons. At precisely three o'clock, they fired a twenty-one-gun salute to the commander in chief to announce his arrival. At this signal Hackett's troops, marching three abreast and carrying muskets with fixed bayonets, began the march up Middle Road and onto the Parade, down to the stand where Washington stood with the city and state leaders. Will was lucky to be in the right column for a clear view as they passed. At twenty paces short of the stand, upon command, all the men snapped their heads "eyes right" to face the president. Thunderous applause arose from the crowd, gathered ten deep and in doorways and at windows. Will had trouble keeping his eyes dry as the troops came to a halt just past the stand, where they stood at attention for the duration of the ceremony.

The big bell in the North Church, immediately behind the stand, and the five other church bells in the city rang for three minutes over continued cheering. Then the judge of the district court assumed the podium and delivered a stirring tribute to the president, "who with a magnanimity peculiar to himself under the smiles of heaven, defended the rights and gave birth to the empire of America." In closing, the judge made reference to the damage done to the city's commerce by the war. Washington stepped forward and answered with a brief, modest reply. Immediately, across the Parade on a second stage, a band struck up rousing music and a choir sang three odes to the president.

General Cilley led the troops in review before the grandstand, the officers saluting the president as they passed, and proceeded down Pitt Street to the Stavers Hotel. The men were then dismissed. Washington was conducted to his lodging at William Bannister's boardinghouse.

Will rejoined Abi and headed back to Sheafe's Pasture, where he stayed, with the exception of attending Sunday service at North Church, until his scheduled meeting with Reverend Haven and the president Monday at noon. For several hours on Sunday he sat alone on the porch smoking his pipe, thinking about what he was going to say.

A grand dinner was held in the evening, attended by the state's political leaders and local gentry. Brewster later recorded that "the State House on the Parade was beautifully illuminated, and rockets were let off from the balcony."

On Sunday the president attended two church services—in the morning at Queen's Chapel and later in the day at North Church, where the Reverend Dr. Buckminister made a powerful address praising the country's new leader. Will and Abi sat in the balcony with the other Africans.

At five o'clock on Monday afternoon, Will was at Reverend Haven's doorstep, again outfitted in his dress uniform, which Abigail had ironed carefully. Haven was also ready. He answered the knock immediately and pulled on his heavy gray overcoat as he came out the door.

⸺⸻

The brisk walk to the Bannister boardinghouse took just fifteen minutes. Haven introduced Will to the guard at the entrance as "my aide" and the two climbed the stairs to President Washington's second-floor suite, where they were met in an entry room by Tobias Lear, the president's secretary, who greeted them warmly. After a short wait, Haven entered the president's sitting room while Will waited his turn. An hour later the door opened and Haven beckoned Will to enter. He walked in and saluted the commander in chief, who invited Will to sit in the straight-back wooden chair directly across from his desk. The president sat erect in his large Chippendale armchair. Haven and Lear were on a brown leather couch to the president's left.

"Welcome, Private Clarkson," Washington said. "Your friend Reverend Haven has shared your story with me. I thank you and congratulate you for your military service during the war with

England and on your election as king of the Negro Court. Negro troops made a significant contribution. I understand you have something important you want to talk to me about."

Will sat up as straight as he could. He cleared his throat and said, "Mr. President, one in every seven soldiers in the war was an African. Given the clear impact of our service, we'd like to know: What are you going to do to abolish slavery?"

Washington looked surprised—perhaps at Will's question, perhaps at the directness with which he'd asked it—but he responded calmly. "That's up to Congress. They pass legislation and amendments to the Constitution. As president, I just administer the laws and the Constitution as they exist. I can't do anything about slavery unless or until Congress passes and sends such a change to me."

"But you can surely propose amendments for them to pass or issue executive orders," Will said.

"I could do that, but it would be very dangerous. It could even precipitate an ideological split that would tear the country apart."

"But isn't the alternative dangerous? Slavery is so oppressive that it's going to have disastrous consequences unless you address it now."

"Private Clarkson, before the Constitutional Convention in Philadelphia two years ago, unity among the states was on the verge of collapse because there was no strong central government. During the debates about what to do, everyone, North and South, acknowledged the iniquity of slavery. Blame was directed all around—at the English, at the southern plantation owners, at the northern shipowning slave traders. But in reality the problem was and still is one of economic interests and political control."

Washington held up a hand as if to forestall a rebuttal. "We could never have agreed on the new constitution with a strong national government if we'd tried to solve the slavery issue as well. All I can say is that at Philadelphia, I was stuck in the middle. I did the best I could on the one hand to save the Union and on the other to establish a framework that will permit future congresses and presidents to see to it that slavery is abolished over time. At the political level right now, I can do no more."

Will did not take his eyes off Washington. "Mr. President, what you're telling me is that I'm the one stuck in the middle. I and my fellow Africans. We're the sacrificial lambs upon which the United States Constitution is resting. All of us have worked our backs off to build this country. Some of us have gone to war for it, risking our lives, even died. What we got in return is either unmitigated slavery or a purgatory of poverty and discrimination with little hope for significant change in our lifetime."

This time Will held up the silencing hand. "Ten years ago—right here in New Hampshire, Mr. President—twenty of us, all born in Africa, petitioned the state legislature for an end to our enslavement. Not only did they decline to act on it, our petition was mocked in the press as well. Just how long is this going to last? For how many decades are we being asked to submit to captivity and ownership? Either all men are created equal or they're not."

Washington adjusted himself in his chair, leaning forward, elbows and forearms on the desk. "I didn't know about your petition," he said, "but I'm afraid the answers to your questions aren't consoling. The changes you want will come, but in my view the transformation is going to take several generations."

Neither man spoke for a long moment. Then Will said, "Mr. President, you have to do something. What about yourself? Are you willing to set an example now by freeing your own slaves?"

The president smiled. "I control only half the slaves at Mount Vernon. The other half belongs to my wife, Martha. And she's limited by the provisions of her Custis family estate, where they originated. I'm exploring the feasibility of renting my entire plantation except the mansion to tenant farmers from England on the condition that they hire the Negroes, whom I'll free as each parcel rents. If that plan doesn't work, I'll provide in my will that all the slaves be freed when Martha dies. I promise you, one way or the other it will be done."

Will felt that the discussion had gone as far as it could productively. He rose to his feet. "I appreciate that, Mr. President. I thank you for your time. And I share your hopes for a strong nation dedicated to freedom."

Will and Reverend Haven made their way to the door, down the stairs, and out into the bracing November air. As Haven pulled his coat collar closely around his neck, Will broke the silence. He whirled on the minister. "That's what we get in return? He talks a good line, but all he really said was that he's powerless. I don't buy it. It's just more excuses."

"I don't think so, Will. What we saw is that our new government isn't a monarchy but rather a republic, a constitutional representative democracy. Mr. Washington isn't a king who can snap his fingers and his wishes will be implemented. His heart's in the right place, but deep down he's a very practical politician. He's not going to take a position that doesn't stand a chance of succeeding at this time—or, worse, endanger this young, fragile country."

"Then some things are clear," Will said. "Democracy doesn't mean justice. Democracy doesn't mean liberty. Democracy crawls along like . . . like a sick drunk, getting nowhere. It can even get in the way of freedom, give slavery an excuse, try to justify it. This new country is just like your old one. Political expediency and money always prevail. Christian? A moral wasteland." Will spat in the street. "Don't expect us to forget this."

"All I can say, Will, is keep the faith, take solace in your family and work, and pursue every opportunity to push forward without alienating the white community."

The two men walked on in the moonlight. Finally Will said, "That's not good enough, Reverend. Whites will just take advantage of us. We'd probably be better off back in Africa, but we are here. This is our country. We've fought for it. Our children speak only English. Now there's just . . . no other place to go. We can't lie back and take this. Whatever morsels you throw at us. Now it's another war. A tougher, different kind of war. . . . Thanks for your help, Reverend. Good night."

Reverend Haven stepped into his warm home. Will limped down the street and into the backyard of the old Clarkson/Long mansion to retrieve some old breeches he'd left in his dark hut.

Overhead, a lone sparrow, songless, flicked between black limbs of bare oak and maple rooted deep in granite rock.

EPILOGUE

Within two months, in January 1790, Will had to step down as king of the Negro Court because of ill health—the joints around his old wound became severely arthritic, limiting his movements so that he was greatly incapacitated. Will had groomed Jack Odiorne to be his successor, but Jack developed heart trouble and died in the fall of 1790. Thereafter, the court and the annual elections were discontinued for lack of a sufficiently strong leader. There was no longer a formal vehicle to focus attention on the Africans' progress or lack thereof. Portsmouth's Negro population was dwindling, due primarily to the aging of the remaining slaves.

Informally, Will did attempt to keep a dialogue going by getting together on Sunday afternoons with Prince Whipple, Romeo Rindge, and some of the younger black men in town who were eager to hear their elders recount their exploits and urge the next generation to fight on aggressively. The young ones never forgot. Will came to believe that these conversations were his most important legacy.

The United States census of 1790 indicated that six of the twenty signers of the 1779 petition had become free and independent family heads. Because Pierse Long's estate was not finalized until the end of the year, Will was not listed among them; by December, though, he had become the seventh.

For the next three years, despite their impoverished situation, Will and Abigail lived a tranquil existence in the house in Sheafe's Pasture. Friends and the people at the Court Street Almshouse helped with food and clothing. The couple tilled a small garden at the side of the house and managed to coax a few vegetables from the rocky New England soil. They foraged enough pieces of dry wood on the outskirts of town to keep themselves warm by the fireplace during the subsequent winters, which were relatively mild for New England. Their deep love for each other sustained them.

They never saw or heard from Willie again.

In the early 1790s, Abi's health began to deteriorate. Dr. Hall Jackson's diagnosis was consumption. Her hacking coughs grew more frequent and convulsive, allowing her little sleep. Her weight loss was dramatic to the point of emaciation. Will stayed awake through many a night, holding her tightly in his arms as though to suppress the coughing. In April 1794, Abi slipped away as sunlight flooded through the window on an early dawn.

Will's grief was at first numbing—for days he felt nothing, not even sorrow—and then overwhelming. Only the companionship of his many friends made life bearable. Matilda Odiorne, who had lost Jack, was one person Will could talk to. Naby's presence in the house both helped and hurt. Her lovely temperament soothed him, but her limited communicative ability at times seemed to underscore the great void in his life.

After a while, Matilda Odiorne moved in with Will and Naby. They attended Matilda's church regularly—St. John's, the former Queen's Chapel. The name had been changed on January 15, 1791, when the parishioners voted to divest themselves of any semblance of a relationship with the English crown.

As the eighteenth century came to a close, it became apparent that Protestant Christianity's message was evolving at least slightly toward greater generosity. While most ministers still stressed obedience, thereby continuing to alienate many first-generation Africans, some pastors emphasized the ultimate redemption and hope for the downtrodden that Jesus promised. Some African-Americans responded positively.

In December 1799, shortly before Christmas, Will was just rounding the North Church onto the Parade when he saw a young man on the church steps sounding a bell. He was shouting "George Washington dead at Mount Vernon, the president has died in his sleep at home in Virginia. George Washington dead at Mount Vernon, the president has died in his sleep at home in Virginia. . . ."

Will recognized the impact this death would have. *He let me down. But he was the strongest leader the white men had. Who'll lead the country now? Will the visions of freedom and democracy survive? Even for the whites?*

The young nation mourned through February 22, 1800, Washington's birthday. The government called for citizens to wear black bands on their left arms for thirty days. Mock funerals were held in many cities and towns. Black crepe and cloth banners hung from the street lanterns in Portsmouth. On consecutive Sundays, church ministers eulogized the fallen president in sermons lasting up to three hours. In whispered conversations on the streets and in their homes, white citizens, freed Africans, and those still enslaved worriedly discussed the same questions that had crossed Will's mind.

George Washington did keep his promise to Will. He freed a number of slaves during his lifetime and provided in his estate that the rest be freed upon Martha's death. Martha in fact accelerated that schedule and set them all free in December 1800. Sadly, many were unprepared to live as free people and did very poorly. They were subsequently given pension payments or taken back on the plantation staff by the Washington heirs. The president had also provided that the children of his former slaves be taught to read and write, but Virginia law, forbidding the education of Negroes, thwarted that goal.

Somehow, of course, life continued on under President John Adams. Political infighting grew more intense at all levels, but the Republic stood.

Benedict Arnold died on June 14, 1801 in London of "dropsy brought on by the gout" and a "perturbed mind." He was buried in a "jumbled, unmarked grave" with no military honors.

Portsmouth records reveal that Will and Matilda were formally married there on September 14, 1802, and include the interesting note that it was "after a courtship of 30 days." Their life together was pleasant, but time had taken its toll on Will. His hair was long and gray now, and the creases in his face were deeply etched. His shoulders bowed forward as he limped through Portsmouth's narrow streets in search of whatever odd jobs the city's white citizens were willing to give him.

In Portsmouth as well as throughout the country, the torch was passing to a new generation of leaders who would have to wrestle with the great issues of economic survival, foreign opposition, and internal division over slavery and states' rights. In 1807 a young Dartmouth graduate from "upstate" opened a Portsmouth office for the practice of law on the west side of Market Street, three doors from the square on the second story. An imposing man with large, piercing eyes and a massive brow, Daniel Webster quickly gained a reputation as one of the best lawyers in the area and then served in the U.S. House of Representatives from the Granite State before moving to Boston and into the U.S. Senate.

Webster's positions on slavery-related issues were inconsistent. By his oratory on the Senate floor, he was personally responsible for the rejection of the doctrine of nullification, in which each state reserved the right to interpret the federal Constitution within its own boundaries. Webster declared then that slavery was "one of the greatest evils, both moral and political" but nevertheless maintained that there had never been "a disposition in the North to interfere with these interests in the South."

In a speech in Massachusetts in 1840 he said that he believed it to be "the duty of every man to do all in his power by the exercise of moral influences, to ameliorate slavery's condition and to terminate its existence." Yet later he was the principal architect of the Compromise of 1850 (deciding which new states would be free states and which would be slave states) because he felt it was essential to preserve the Union—even though a key piece of the compromise was a Fugitive Slave Act, which provided for the restitution of runaway slaves. Although Webster also made it clear that he opposed the expansion of slavery into the territories or any new states, he was denounced strongly by antislavery advocates.

Webster was a link to three generations of Americans before the Civil War. His compromise did not hold, and the Union was nearly severed by a clear moral issue beclouded by rigid economic, political, and social forces that have yet to be swept away eight generations later.

Notwithstanding passage of the 1784 state constitution, including a bill of rights, the subsequent abolitionist movement, and other well-meaning efforts, slavery was not completely abolished by the legislature in New Hampshire until 1857. It simply died out in the first decades of the nineteenth century as more slaves were freed by their owners and those remaining died and were not replaced. Instances of discrimination and racism continued.

Henry Dearborn served in several campaigns after Saratoga, including Yorktown, and ultimately attained the rank of major general in the militia. He was appointed Secretary of War by President Thomas Jefferson, a post he held for eight years. President Monroe sent him as minister to Portugal from 1822 to 1824. He then retired to Roxbury, Massachusetts, and died there in 1829.

John Stark was elevated to the rank of major general by brevet in 1783 and given the personal thanks of George Washington. After the Revolution, he settled down on his farm in Dunbarton, New Hampshire, with his wife, Molly, and their ten children. He rarely made public appearances, but in 1809 he offered a toast—"Live free or die"—to the citizens of Bennington for a ceremony commemorating the battle. In 1945 the toast was adopted as New Hampshire's official state motto, and later it was inscribed on all the state's automobile license plates. Stark died in 1822 at ninety-four, the last surviving continental general of the Revolution.

Reverend Haven died in 1806.

James Clarkson III died in 1808 in Newburyport, Massachusetts. His son James IV was a sea captain during the War of 1812.

City records show that Will died on April 17, 1809, but no burial marker has been found.

Matilda hung on, living with Romeo Rindge's widow, Patience, at the house in Sheafe's Pasture, until November 10, 1820, when at eighty-eight she died, according to city accounts, "of old age."

In 1782 General Washington had created by General Order the Badge of Military Merit—the "Purple Heart"—to be awarded to any soldier who performs "any singularly meritorious action" (today, to any soldier wounded) and directed that the names of recipients be enrolled in a "Book of Merit." The original Book of Merit from the Revolutionary War was lost and has never been found. Whether Will's name was listed is therefore not known. There is no evidence that anyone ever saw fit even to propose him for that award, either while he was alive or posthumously.

Throughout the United States today there are a number of African-American families that bear the surname Clarkson. Whether any of these are the progeny of Will is not known. No further information or written records of any of his descendants have been uncovered.

ACKNOWLEDGMENTS

Michael Levin provided extensive guidance as I got started. Anne Berggren's perspectives were then a big help. Peter Gelfan and Renni Browne, the experts at The Editorial Department, provided finishing critiques and editing that were first rate.

My wife, Mary Claire, bore the greatest burden, giving support, guiding me through the frustrating mysteries of the computer, and proposing many good changes in the text.

I was helped immeasurably on the family background by the genealogical material compiled principally by my cousin Pat Clarkson Welch, of Los Angeles, and before her by my uncle James Clarkson.

I have relied upon numerous primary and secondary background sources for the factual baseline to the story, including Brewster's classic *Rambles About Portsmouth*, and Richard Ketchum's superb history, *Saratoga*, which described the early, northern battles of the Revolution.

Valerie Cunningham could not have been more helpful. The book *Black Portsmouth*, co-written with Mark Sammons, and her constructive suggestions on the early drafts gave me assurance that I was adhering reasonably to the essence of the Black experience in eighteenth-century New England.

I received invaluable suggestions and encouragement from other family and friends including Janet Clarkson Davis, Leigh Clarkson Woodruff, Frank and Jocelyn Clarkson, Carmine DiAdamo, Jim Wade, Bill Hathaway, John Borgia, Bill Geoghegan, Bud Vieth, and Sidney Guberman.

Thanks to Chip Shand for his good map showing Will's route to the four battles in which he participated.

Thanks also to the gracious and helpful staffs at the Portsmouth (N.H.) Public Library, the Portsmouth Athenaeum, and the Library of Congress.

Last but not least, I am very grateful for the support and excellent product of my fine publisher, Peter Randall, his thorough copy editor, Doris Troy, in advance for the promotional and distribution work of Deidre Randall, Gordon Carlisle's cover illustration, and Grace Peirce's book design.

SOURCES

T he fine collection of resources available in the Portsmouth Public Library and the Portsmouth Athenaeum and visits to Portsmouth cemeteries and Rockingham County Registers of Wills and Deeds verified the historical base for the story. The books and documents included:

Births and Christenings, Portsmouth, N.H. (1795-1874).

Brewster, *Rambles About Portsmouth* (New Hampshire Pub. Co., 1859, 1873, and 1971).

Chipman, *Genealogical Abstracts from early New Hampshire Newspapers* (Heritage Books, 2000).

Index of Deaths in Portsmouth, 1808–July 1821.

New Hampshire Gazette—various issues as noted in the text.

Peabody, *History of the South Parish* (1859).

Records of St. John's Church, Portsmouth, N.H., 1795-1884.

Records of the South Church, Portsmouth, N.H.

Helpful background information was also provided in:

Berlin, *Many Thousands Gone: The First Two Centuries of Slavery in North America* (Cambridge, Mass., 1998).

Blatt and Roediger, eds., *The Meaning of Slavery in the North* (New York, 1998).

Bowen, *Miracle at Philadelphia* (Little, Brown, 1966).

Breig, *Finding Slavery in Unexpected Places* , in *Colonial Williamsburg Journal,* Winter 2006.

Craft, *The Bondswoman's Narrative* (Warner Books, Gates edit., 2002).

Cremin, *American Education: The Colonial Experience* (Harper & Row, 1970).

Dagenais, *The Black in Portsmouth, New Hampshire (1700-1861)* (University of New Hampshire master's thesis, 1970).

Dexter, *A History of Education in the United States* (MacMillan, 1911).

Du Bois, *The Souls of Black Folk* (Barnes & Noble Classics, 2003).

Ellis, *His Excellency: George Washington* (Alfred A. Knopf, 2004).

Emerson, *The Concord Hymn* (1837).

Equiano, *The Interesting Narrative of the Life of Olaudah Equiano* (New York: 1790, edited by Robert J. Allison (Bedford/St. Martin's, 1995)

Flexner, *The Traitor and The Spy* (Harcourt, Brace, 1953).

Flexner, *Washington: The Indispensable Man* (Mentor, 1979).

Fuess, *Daniel Webster* (Little, Brown, 1930).

Furneaux, *Saratoga: The Decisive Battle* (George Allen & Unwin Ltd., 1971).

Gates, Article, *Phillis Wheatley on Trial*, in *The New Yorker* (January 20, 2003).

Gates, Article, *Native Sons of Liberty*, in the *The New York Times* (August 6, 2006), p. WK 12.

Goldenberg, *Shipbuilding in Colonial America* (The Mariner's Museum, 1976).

Good, *A History of American Education* (MacMillan, 1956).

Haley, *Roots* (Dell, 1976).

Hammersley, *The Lake Champlain Naval Battles of 1776-1814* (Waterford, N.Y. 1959).

Harris, *The Improved New England Primer* (1690).

Henry, *Arnold's Campaign Against Quebec* (Munsell, 1877).

Hochschild, *Bury the Chains* (Houghton Mifflin, 2004).

Hochschild, *King Leopold's Ghost* (Houghton Mifflin, 1998).

Jenney, *In Search of Shipwrecks* (A. S. Barnes, 1980).

Johnson, *Battles of the American Revolution* (Roxby Press Ltd., 1975).

Ketchum, *Saratoga* (Henry Holt, 1997).

McCarter, *My Life in the Irish Brigade*, O'Brien edit. (Da Capo, 1996).

McCusker, *How Much is That in Real Money?* (Oak Knoll Press, 2001).

Mintz, *The Generals of Saratoga* (Yale University Press, 1990).

Morison, *History of the American People* (Oxford University Press, 1965).

Morison, *John Paul Jones: A Sailor's Biography* (Naval Institute Press 1959).

Mulzer, *Town and province in revolutionary New Hampshire: A stable political culture confronts change, 1765-1776* (Paper, University of New Hampshire 1987).

Nell, *The Colored Patriots of the American Revolution* (Wallent, 1855).

New Hampshire: A Guide to the Granite State (Houghton Mifflin, 1938).

New Hampshire: Years of Revolution, 1774-1783 (New Hampshire Profiles, 1976).

Parsons, *History of Rye, N.H., 1623-1903* (Rumford Printing, 1905).

Pate, *Amistad* (Penguin, 1997).

Piersen, *Black Yankees* (University of Massachusetts Press, 1988).

Pipes, *Property and Freedom* (Alfred A. Knopf, 1999).

Potter, *The Military History of the State of New Hampshire* (McFarland & Jenks, 1866).

Quinlan, *George Knox, a Black Soldier in the American Revolution* (Dartmouth College Library Bulletin, April 20, 1980).

Reisenberg, *Yankee Skippers to the Rescue* (Dodd, Mead, 1945).

Richmond, *John Stark, Freedom Fighter* (Dale Books, 1976).

Riker, *Democracy in the United States* (MacMillan, 1953).

Roberts, *March to Quebec* (Country Life Press, 1938).

Sammons and Cunningham, *Black Portsmouth* (University of New Hampshire Press, 2004).

Sammons and Cunningham, *Portsmouth Black Heritage Trail Resource Book* (1996, 1998).

Schama, *Rough Crossings* (Harper Collins, 2006).

Seelinger, *Buying Time: The Battle of Valcour Island* (The Army Historical Foundation, 2004).

Smith, *Arnold's March from Cambridge to Quebec* (Putnam, 1903).

Stowe, *Uncle Tom's Cabin* (Bantam Classics, 2003).

Styron, *The Confessions of Nat Turner* (Random House, 1967).

Thomas, *John Paul Jones: Sailor, Hero, Father of the American Navy* (Simon & Schuster, 2003).

Websites, as indicated in the Notes section.

Welch, *Tanning in the United States to 1850* (Smithsonian, 1964).

Wideman, *My Soul Has Grown Deep: Classics of Early African-American Literature* (Ballantine Books, 2002).

Wiencek, *An Imperfect God: George Washington, His Slaves, and the Creation of America* (New York, 2003).

Winslow, *"Wealth and Honour, Portsmouth During the Golden Age of Privateering, 1775–1815* (Portsmouth Marine Society, 1988).

Wise, *Though the Heavens May Fall* (Da Capo Press, 2004).

Zakaria, *The Future of Freedom* (W. W. Norton, 2003).

Zilversmit, *The First Emancipation: The Abolition of Slavery in the North* (Chicago, 1969).

For fictional treatments and styles of similar or related subject matter, see: Ball, *Slaves in the Family* (Straus and Giroux, 1998).

Deane, *My Story Being This* (University Press of New England, 2004).

Tademy, *Cane River* (Warner Books, 2001).

Wall, *A Child out of Place* (Fall Rose Books, 2004).

NOTES

Preface

All we actually know: The principal fragments are:

". . . our informant well recollects one Andrew Clarkson, an extensive tanner and public man, residing there (in Portsmouth, New Hampshire) since the time of the revolution. . . . He also recollects their slave, Will Clarkson." Brewster, *Rambles About Portsmouth* (New Hampshire Pub. Co., 1859, 1873 and 1971) ("Brewster"), p. 274.

"The slaves were permitted to hold their social meetings and had a mock government of their own . . . They elected a King (who was also a judge), a Sheriff and a Deputy. . . . They went up from town in procession, led by their King, Nero, the slave of Colonel William Brewster . . . Nero's viceroy was Willie Clarkson . . . Brewster, p. 212.

"The petition of Nero Brewster . . . Will Clarkson . . . (along with 18 other New Hampshire slaves), natives of Africa, now forcibly detained in slavery in said State (of New Hampshire) most humbly sheweth that the God of Nature gave them Life and Freedom upon the terms of the most perfect Equality with other men. . . . Therefor, your humble slaves most devoutly pray for the sake of injured liberty; for the sake of justice, humanity, and the rights of mankind; for the honor of religion; and by all that is dear, that your honors would graciously interpose in our behalf and enact such laws and regulations as you in your wisdom think proper, whereby we may regain our liberty and be ranked in the class of free agents and that the name of slave may not more be heard in a land gloriously contending for the sweets of freedom; and your humble slaves as in duty bound will ever pray." Petition for Freedom Addressed to the New Hampshire State Legislature, November 12, 1779. Sammons and Cunningham, *Portsmouth Black Heritage Trail Resource Book* (1996, 1998) ("PBHTRB"), p. 75.

In this fictional story, the names of Nero Brewster, king of the Negro Court; William Brewster, Nero's owner and mayor-equivalent of Portsmouth; and the actual owner of the ship

Exeter, John Moffatt, were changed. Those three men were, in real life, respected in the community.

PART ONE

Chapter 1

1   . . . the Isles of Shoals: Four of the islands, Lunging, Star, Seavey and White, were incorporated into New Hampshire in 1635 and are part of the town of Rye, New Hampshire.

1   The arrival of the *Exeter* with a large number of enslaved Africans is described in Sammons and Cunningham, *Black Portsmouth: Three Centuries of African-American Heritage* (University of New Hampshire Press, 2004) (*Black Portsmouth*), p. 17. The real captain of the ship, John Moffatt, is replaced by the fictional John Martin in this book; any resemblance is purely coincidental.While there is no documentary evidence that Will came from Africa on this specific ship, it is quite likely in that the dates match up. The African names of Will and the other Portsmouth black people at the time are fictional.

1   This stretch of North Atlantic seacoast: The earliest history of the area has been set forth in several books, including Parsons, *History of Rye, N.H., 1623–1903* (Rumford Printing Company 1905), pp. 1–19; Brewster, pp. 9–25; *Black Portsmouth*, pp. 1–74.

1   Over the intervening years: Notwithstanding the prosperity enjoyed by Portsmouth's wealthiest citizens, who were the slave owners, the lifestyles of the seacoast's general populace, in marked contrast, were quite humble. The book *New Hampshire: A Guide to the Granite State* (Houghton Mifflin, 1938) (*Guide*) states at pp. 37 and 45:

"The people in these times were a very plain people, dressing in homespun cloth. Every house had its loom and spinning-wheel, and almost every woman was a weaver. . . . For many years there was not a single wheeled carriage in town. People who owned horses rode them; and those who had them not went on foot. Husbands carried their wives behind them on pillions. More than one half of the church-going people went on foot. Sleighs or sleds were used in winter. I have seen ox-sleds at the meeting house. For years we had no stoves in the meeting-house

. . .; and yet in the coldest weather, the house was always full."
(David Sutherland of Bath, Maine) . . .

"Farmers hired their help for nine or ten dollars a month—some
clothing and the rest cash. Carpenters' wages, one dollar a day:
journeymen carpenters, fifteen dollars a month; and apprentices
to serve six or seven years, had ten dollars the first year, twenty
the second, and so on, and to clothe themselves. Breakfast
generally consisted of potatoes roasted in the ashes, a 'bannock'
made of meal and water and baked on a maple chip set before
the fire. Pork was plenty. If 'hash' was had for breakfast, all ate
from the platter, without plates or table spread. Apprentices and
farm boys had for supper a bowl of scalded milk and a brown
crust, or bean porridge , or 'pop-robbin.' There was no such
thing as tumblers, nor were they asked if they would have tea or
coffee; it was 'Please pass the mug.' " (from *The New Hampshire
Patriot* in 1821).

2   The type of ship and specifications of the *Exeter* are calculated
        from data in Goldenberg, Shipbuilding in Colonial America
        (Mariners Museum, 1976).

2   Twenty Men Slaves: *Black Portsmouth*, p. 17.

3   Even the wealthier families: See *Black Portsmouth*, p. 18, and
        Dagenais, *The Black in Portsmouth, New Hampshire*, 1700–1861
        (University of New Hampshire master's thesis, 1970), pp. 15–27.

3   All of Great Island is now known as New Castle.

4   This was Kwamba: See The Story of the Mandinka Epic, *www.
        si.umich.edu/chico/UMS/Drummers/oralmstory.html*.

5   The post of chairman of the selectmen was the equivalent of
        mayor of the city.

Chapter 2

7–11   *Black Portsmouth*, at pp. 19–22, describes the auctions.

8   James Clarkson: James Clarkson was born in Edinburgh,
        Scotland, in 1700, a Presbyterian Protestant of the Cameron clan.
        At age eighteen he had allied himself with the supporters of
        the Jacobite James Francis Edward Stuart, known as James VIII
        of Scotland and claiming to be James III of England, the first
        Pretender. Clarkson had enlisted as an ensign in Lord George
        Murray's Highlander Regiment and fought with Earl Marischal,

the Earl of Seaforth and a company of Spanish infantry at the Battle of Glensheil in 1719. When the English garrison under General Wightman defeated these insurgent Scots, Clarkson had become a prisoner in his own town. He escaped and fled in that same year to Portsmouth, bringing with him the Banner of the Thistle, the colors of his regiment. The flag was a testament of his adherence to the Jacobite beliefs in civil liberty and freedom from the English crown. Only nineteen years old and penniless, he took a job as a teacher in one of the public schools.

While teaching, Clarkson boarded at the house of William Cotton, a prosperous local tanner. Before two years had passed, Cotton died. Clarkson then romanced and won the hand of Elizabeth, Cotton's twenty-six-year old widow. Following a lavish wedding attended by more than a hundred of Portsmouth's leading gentry, he became the manager and owner of the profitable tannery. James and Elizabeth thereafter had three sons: James Jr., Andrew, and Walter.

Clarkson had served as Portsmouth selectman and assessor from 1722 to 1725 and in 1736. He was the town's moderator from 1741 forward and was also elected as a representative to the provincial legislature from 1734 to1748. When Elizabeth died, in 1746, he remained a widower. See Brewster, pp. 272-75.

Brewster was a bit off in one respect: *James* (Sr.) was the one who came from Scotland with the banner; James (Jr.) and Andrew were his two sons (along with Walter). [Research by Pat Welch held by the author ("Welch Research")] Brewster records that Clarkson "often spoke of the early transactions of his life with regret, but he said that he thought at the time, that his conduct was justifiable." Brewster, p. 273. The remnants of the banner are presently in the museum of the State Historical Society of Wisconsin in Madison.

11   Clarkson didn't hesitate. *"Forty"*: Based on a rough equivalent of the eighteenth-century pound in today's value, this price would be exceedingly high, but it is used for dramatic effect in the story. The pound in 1750 had the same purchasing power as $160 in 2002, and by 1790 the pound had the same purchasing power as 70 pounds in 2002. See Economic History Services,

eh.net/hmit, and McCusker, *How Much is That in Real Money?* (Oak Knoll Press, 2001).

Chapter 3

12   The handsome Clarkson house: Brewster says that the Clarkson house was "one of the most spacious old houses south of the south mill bridge. . . . [It] was gambrel roofed, facing the street and about a hundred feet back from it, leaving a handsome green spot in front, and a gravel walk to the door through two rows of trees." Brewster, pp. 272–73.

12   ...his son Andrew, Andrew's wife, Lydia, and: Brewster, p. 274 and Welch Research. In 1754 Andrew had been elected as a town selectman while doubling as surveyor, fire warden and auditor. Andrew also later served as an adjutant in Rogers' Rangers during the French and Indian War. Welch Research.

13   Pickering's Mille Pond is now known as South Mill Pond.

13–14   The description of the Clarkson tannery at pages 13–14 and 17–19 is derived from Welch, *Tanning in the United States to 1850* (Smithsonian, 1964). The Clarkson tannery may actually have been located next to their house (see Brewster, p. 285) with no access to the river (where most tanneries were located) to wash away the effluent and may have been more modest than is described here.

Chapter 4

No references.

Chapter 5

20   The imposing building: The historian Brewster, at p. 64, writes that the building was "between fifty and sixty feet in length, and not far from thirty feet in width,—its first story about eleven feet, and the second story about ten feet in hight,—the roof in an angle of about forty-five degrees, being somewhat elevated, gave the structure, in comparison with everything around it, a rather imposing appearance."

20   The reverend was born in Framingham, Massachusetts, in 1727 and graduated from Harvard College in 1749. He settled on South Church in 1752. Reverend Haven had resolved to join

the ministry at the age of thirteen upon hearing the preaching of George Whitefield, a revivalist of the Great Awakening of orthodox Calvinism in the American colonies. The Awakening gave great impetus to Americans' thirst for religious and civil liberty and spurred the American Revolution. The instigator of the movement was Jonathan Edwards, in Northampton, Massachusetts, who began in 1734 to fiercely attack the moralities of his day, particularly the transgressions of the young. Such antagonism toward God, he preached, assured man of eternal damnation unless true conversion, a radical change of heart, was accomplished and deemed adequate by a hard but benevolent Creator.

Reverend Haven's philosophy was to the center from Edwards' severity. Haven was a "moderate" Calvinist, more of the Arminian school—those who believed that good works alone could achieve salvation. The Arminian school became the Unitarian Church in the nineteenth century. Reverend Haven's background and description are taken from Andrew Peabody's *History of the South Parish* (1859) ("Peabody"), pp. 65–67.

Morison, *History of the American People* (Oxford University Press, 1965) ("Morison, History"), p. 151, states that the Awakening "descended like a whirlwind to sweep up lost souls. It stimulated a fresh interest in religion, caused hundreds of new churches to be founded, strengthened the movement for religious liberty, gave the common man a new sense of his significance, and thus indirectly contributed to the American Revolution." The Great Awakening and its significance in the Black experience in America are further detailed in Piersen, *Black Yankees* (University of Massachusetts Press, 1988), pp. 65–73.

21   " . . . *We're way outnumbered*": There were probably about one hundred and seventy Africans—one hundred and twenty men and fifty women, not counting about forty children, in Portsmouth at the time. There were about 4000 white men and women. This size and make-up of Portsmouth's African community during this period are estimated from *Black Portsmouth*, p. 19, Piersen, pp. 165,168 and Dagenais, pp. 15–27. *New Hampshire: A Guide to the Granite State* (Houghton Mifflin, 1938) (*Guide*) states: "When Governor John Wentworth assumed office in 1767 there were 633 slaves in the province. By 1773 the

number had risen to 674, but the returns of the Census of 1775 showed a decline to 626. Of this last number 533 were located in the two seacoast counties of Strafford and Rockingham."

21   . . . the other churches . . . Portsmouth's churches are described in Brewster, pp. 64–70, 326–332,and 349–353.

22   As he solemnly read: Haven was known to cite the words from the Book of Isaiah, ch 52, verses 9–10:

> Break forth into Joy, sing together ye waste Places of Jerusalem; for the Lord hath comforted his people: He hath redeemed Jerusalem: The Lord hath made bare his holy Arm in the Eyes of all Nations, and The Ends of the Earth shall see the Salvation of our God.

22   He guessed that the ten children: In all, Reverend Haven fathered seventeen children. See *The New Hampshire Gazette (NHG)*, Summer 2006, p. 2.

22   Reverend Haven was making it clearer: In a sermon Haven specifically expounded:

> The righteous sovereign, in whose hand the wicked are often the rod of his anger, has indeed suffered the Indian savages to shed much English blood, and sorely scourge the British colonies, even as the *Canaanites* afflicted Israel of old . . . . But a more dangerous enemy has been increasing and incroaching upon us. Canada has been the Carthage of New England; and the French have long endeavored both by artifice and arms to drive us from this good land which the Lord God gave unto our fathers. How they have fomented strife and sent forth their Indians on our frontiers! While they have been fostering new claims, and drawing a chain of forts around us. Together with these, they are incircling us with the chains of France and the superstitions of Rome.
>
> But in this review we cannot fail to observe the dispensations of divine providence towards this country. . . . When a cloud was gathering over England and began to discharge itself upon our father's, *hither* the divine hand of providence led them . . . *here* they sought an *asylum*, and took their abode among savage beasts and more savage men.
>
> They left their dear native country, their pleasant habitations, and indured a train of hardships, scarce credible to their posterity, that they might worship God according to

their consciences, and maintain the protestant religion *free* from those corruptions which the high-church party had introduced at home.

When we reflect on their design, it appears truly noble, becoming the disciples of Christ, who has taught his followers, "to call no man *master* on earth...." Adapted from Rev. Haven's Sermon on Joy and Salvation by Christ: His Power and Grace Displayed in the Protestant Church, 1763.

23   As he looked at the group: The prominent Portsmouth Black men are all described in *Black Portsmouth*, pp. 33, 52–55, although Nero's (Caesar's) reign as king may not have begun as early as 1755. See Piersen, p.174. See subsequent text showing realignment of officers of the Negro Court at the next election to accord with Brewster. Prince Whipple is described in *Black Portsmouth* at p. 87 as "a large, well proportioned and fine looking man, of gentlemanly manners and deportment."

Chapter 6

26   Two weeks later: Brewster, the city's principal historian, recorded in the middle of the nineteenth century:

There was in olden times not only a scarcity of carriages but also of wheels. Messrs. Clarksons' team might be seen passing frequently through the town, without any wheels,—two shafts attached to the sides of the horse, the ends dragging on the ground, made up the dray on which their hides and leather found conveyance to and from the yard. Brewster, p. 274.

26–28   See maps in pocket of Brewster.

27   Next they proceeded: See Brewster, p. 212, and *Black Portsmouth*, p. 53.

28   "... *from Maine*": Maine was actually still a part of Massachusetts until 1820, when it was established as the twenty-third state as part of the Missouri Compromise. The name is nevertheless used here for easier identification. The Missouri Compromise had two parts. First, Missouri was admitted to the Union as a slave state, with a provision that portions of the Louisiana Territory lying north of 36'30 north latitude would be free. (This limitation was later overturned by the 1854 Kansas-Nebraska Act and by the 1857 Dred Scott case.) The enabling

act also provided that fugitive slaves could be apprehended north of the compromise line and returned to their owners. The second part of the compromise was that Maine was admitted to statehood as a free state, thereby maintaining a balance of twelve free and twelve slave states. *http://www.pbs.org/wgbh/aia/part3/3h511t.html*

Chapter 7

31   Clarkson looked at Will: At least a few Africans in America in the eighteenth century did become educated, including most prominently Wentworth Cheswell, Benjamin Banneker, and Dr. James Derham.There was also Olaudah Equiano in England/America. It was not until the 1830s, in response to the abolitionist movement, in some southern states, that it actually became illegal to educate a Black person.

31   The books: These books, along with teaching techniques during the period, are described in Dexter, *A History of Education in the United States* (MacMillan, 1911), Good, *A History of American Education* (MacMillan, 1956) and Cremin, *American Education: The Colonial Experience* (Harper & Row, 1970). These and Harris' *The Improved New England Primer* (1690) may be found in The Library of Congress.

33   On one such trip: Randall & Caswell's fish store is pictured in Brewster; it may well have been established subsequent to the 1700s.

Chapter 8

34   When they reached the point: Shipwrecks were a frequent phenomenon on the New England coast in the eighteenth century. See Garvin and Grigg, *Historic Portsmouth* (Strawbery Banke, 1995), pp. 17–18. This particular wreck is fictional, but derived from descriptions in Jenney, *In Search of Shipwrecks* (A. S. Barnes, 1980), pp. 123–130, and Riesenberg, *Yankee Skippers to the Rescue* (Dodd, Mead, 1945), pp. 1–26.

Chapter 9

41   The native American Indians: See Who were the Abenaki Indians? Website. *http://scsc.essortment.com/abenakinewengl_rmru.htm*. It appears that the name is more likely to be spelled "Abenaki" in northern New England and "Abenaqui" in the

more southern parts. The "-qui" form may also reflect a French influence.

Chapter 10

46   On a bright Friday morning: The African elections for the Negro Court are described in *Black Portsmouth*, pp. 52–55, and Piersen, pp. 117–128.

47–57   Along the opposite side of the field: Piersen cataloged the unique aspects of Afro-American cooking, dancing, storytelling, dancing, and clothing at pp. 96–113.

49   Random gunshots: Apparently in New England some slaves were permitted to have guns, at least occasionally, notwithstanding any attendant fears their owners might have held. See, e.g., Piersen, p.120.

49–50   Psalms 1 and 21.

49–50   The religious aspects of the opening ceremony reflected fairly accurately the religious views and practices of the Africans in the New Hampshire colony: While perhaps twenty percent of the African population attended white Christian churches, principally at the direction of their owners, only one or two percent had actually converted.

For a detailed discussion of the religious views and practices of African and African-Americans in the eighteenth century, see *Black Yankees*, pp. 49–86. See also *Black Portsmouth*, pp. 48–52, 57, 61, 67, 73. Somewhat contrary to what Piersen indicates in *Black Yankees*, W. E. B. Du Bois's later experience toward the end of the nineteenth century was that the participatory emotional reactions of the Black congregations he had known in the North were very modest compared to those he discovered in the South. See Du Bois, *The Souls of Black Folk* (Barnes & Noble, 2003), pp. 134–35. Perhaps the enthusiasm of the evangelical movement in the North had somewhat waned by then.

53   *"Stuffed rags in our mouths"*: See Equiano, *The Interesting Narrative of the Life of Olaudah Equiano* (New York, 1790, edited by Robert J. Allison (Bedford/St. Martin's, 1995) ("Equiano"), p. 47.

Chapter 11

62–64   Haven's analysis is constructed, with apologies, from Richard Pipes' *Property and Freedom* (Alfred A. Knopf, 1999), pp. 4, 17, 63, 118–19, 130–33, 240–43, 283–91.

64   *"Be careful, Will"*: It is often thought that the breaking apart of African-American families did not begin until the twentieth century, when welfare laws gave greater benefits to unmarried women than to married women. In fact, this "singularity" practice began the breakdown as early as the colonial period.

Chapter 12

No references.

Chapter 13

69   Deacon Samuel Penhallow's house still stands, at Strawbery Banke.

Chapter 14

71–72   Compare *Brewster*, pp. 212–13, and *Black Portsmouth*, pp. 52–53, for variations of the Prince Jackson whipping scene.

72   In October 1762: Brewster, pp. 274–275, and Welch Research. Again, Brewster is slightly off: It was not James Sr., but rather James *Jr.* who married Mrs. Holland.

73   In November came: Morison, *History*, pp. 185-86. See generally Mulzer, *Town and province in revolutionary New Hampshire: A stable political culture confronts change, 1765–1776* (paper, University of New Hampshire, 1987).

73   Two days later: Brewster, pp. 179–80.

74   The reaction: Morison, *History*, pp. 189–99.

74   Then, in the fall: Brewster, p. 97.

Chapter 15

77   Abigail sat: See Brewster, p. 106.

81   *"It may be too late for an abortion. . ."*: The Website Abortion*facts*. com states:

"The colonies inherited English Common Law and largely operated under it until well into the 19th century. English Common Law forbade abortion. Abortion prior to quickening was a misdemeanor. Abortion after quickening (feeling life) was a felony. This bifid punishment, inherited from earlier ecclesiastic law, stemmed from earlier 'knowledge' regarding human reproduction.

"In the early 1800s it was discovered that human life did not begin when she 'felt life,' but rather at fertilization. One by one, across the middle years of the 19th century, every then-present state passed its own law against abortion. By 1860, 85% of the population lived in states which had prohibited abortion with new laws. The laws, preceding and following the British example, moved the felony punishment from quickening back to conception.

"Studying two hundred years of legal history, the American Center for Bioethics concluded: 'No evidence was found to support the proposition that women were prosecuted for undergoing or soliciting abortions. The charge that spontaneous miscarriages could result in criminal prosecution is similarly insupportable. There are no documented instances of prosecution of such women for murder or for any other species of homicide; nor is there evidence that states that had provisions enabling them to prosecute women for procuring abortions ever applied those laws. The vast majority of the courts were reluctant to implicate women, even in a secondary fashion, through complicity and conspiracy charges. Even in those rare instances where an abortionist persuaded the court to recognize the woman as his accomplice, charges were not filed against her. In short, women were not prosecuted for abortions. Abortionists were.'

"[But very few abortionists were prosecuted] because there were no scientifically accurate methods in those days to diagnose early pregnancy. The only absolute diagnose of pregnancy, medically and legally binding, was for the doctor to hear the fetal heart, and that was only possible after four and five months. Prior to that, the abortionist could claim that her menstrual period was late or that she had some other malady, and that all he did was to bring on her period. It is all but impossible to convict a person of murder unless the body can be produced, the corpus delicti. Since they were almost never able to obtain and examine the tissue removed from the woman's body, in a court of law it was almost impossible to prove (a) that she had been pregnant and (b) that the actions of the abortionist had terminated the pregnancy. In practice, abortionists, therefore, were typically only prosecuted when the woman had been injured or killed. It was not until the advent of x-rays in the early 1900s (fetal bones visible at three months) and later hormone tests for pregnancy in the 1940s that pregnancy could be legally confirmed in its earlier weeks."

Chapter 16

85   Tensions in the colonies: Morison, *History*, p. 200. Website: *http://cghs.dade.k12.fl.us/african-american/precivil/boston.htm.*

86   The Clarkson family: Brewster, p. 274.

Chapter 17

No references.

Chapter 18

91   *"Ran Away from . . .":* NHG, December 11, 1772.

Chapter 19

94   James Sr. died: Welch Research.

94   The citizens of Portsmouth: Brewster, pp. 332–333. Emphasis added.

95   This action, considered: Morison, *History*, pp. 203–204.

95–96   *"In looking over. . . ":* NHG, December 31, 1773. The quote from the *Gazette* is accurate, but the author has been unable to find the footnote in the Bible.

96   It didn't take Parliament long: Morison, *History*, p. 205–212, and *Guide*, pp. 17–20.

97   His attention became even more focused: For the Wheatley story, see Gates, *Phillis Wheatley on Trial, The New Yorker*, January 20, 2003; *Phillis Wheatley, Poet: A Brief Biography*, Website. *http://www.jmu.edu/madison/wheatley/biography.htm.*

99   *"Would it not be astonishing":* New Hampshire: Years of Revolution, *1774–1783 (New Hampshire Profiles*, 1976) (*Profiles*), p. 106.

Chapter 20

100   As 1774 progressed: *Guide*, pp. 19–20.

100   After much debate: Morison, *History*, p. 208.

100   But redress was not to be had: *Guide*, p. 22.

100   A month and a half later: *Guide*, pp. 22–24.

101   John Langdon: Langdon proceeded to have an illustrious career
       in New Hampshire. He served in the Continental Congress,
       as Speaker of the New Hampshire House, as a United States
       senator and as a six-term governor of the state. While a senator,
       he administered the oath of office to the nation's first president.

101   *"the mob triumphantly"*: *Guide*, p. 23.

101   *"in the British Annals"*: Brewster, p. 221.

102   . . . denied them access to the fishing banks: The historian
       Samuel Morison observed, on p. 210 of his *History*:

       To deprive the Yankees of their fisheries was like ordering
       Virginians not to grow tobacco. There might have been a
       revolution in the name of the "sacred codfish," had General
       Gage not made an excursion to Concord before news of the
       New England Restraining Act arrived.

102   On the night of April 18: Morison, *History*, p. 214.

102   A black slave: See Breig, *Finding Slaves in Unexpected Places*
       (Colonial Williamsburg *Journal*, Winter 2006). p. 20.

102   *"the embattled farmers"*: Emerson, *The Concord Hymn* (1837). See
       also Longfellow, *Paul Revere's Ride* (1861).

102   News of the dramatic clash: Morison, *History*, pp. 214–215.

102   In Portsmouth: *Guide*, pp. 29–30.

103   Further, many of the city's less fortunate: The *Guide* states, at p.
       29, that "trade had become stagnant; unemployment was rife."

103   Governor Wentworth himself: *Guide*, p. 26, 30–31.

105   Will's hopes: Morison, History, p. 217 and Website *http://www.
       blackfacts.com.*

105   *"My father, his father"*: In fact, both males and females
       participated in warfighting in at least some African tribes. See
       Equiano, at p. 40.

106   *"I hear the governor of Virginia. . ."* Lord Dunmore's proclamation
       offer to slaves was not issued formally until November 7, 1775,
       but Virginia slaves were fighting with him for up to a year
       prior to that point. Schama, *Rough Crossings*, pp. 66–77. See

Morison, *History*, p, 236. Undoubtedly the Governor Dunmore offer became well-known and widely discussed throughout the African communities in all thirteen colonies. Many did take up the offer, but the wisdom of Will's response was proven when the Virginia House of Burgesses reorganized itself as a committee of correspodence without Governor Dunmore and Dunmore's slave regiment was defeated. Id. at 221.

Chapter 21

108   Nathaniel Tracy's involvement is noted in Smith, *Arnold's March from Cambridge to Quebec* (Putnam, 1903) ("Smith"), p.62.

108   *"That's all in confidence"*: Smith also describes James Clarkson III's role as captain of the *Broad Bay* and commodore of the flotilla. See p. 287. See also Roberts, pp. 68–69. Henry Dearborn's participation is chronicled throughout Smith's book (beginning at p. 58) as it is in Roberts, *March to Quebec* (Country Life Press, 1938) ("Roberts"), and in Henry, *Arnold's Campaign Against Quebec* (Munsell, 1877) ("Henry"). Dearborn also kept his own journal of the proceedings of the expedition ("Dearborn"). Dearborn's life is summarized in *Profiles*, at p. 46.

108   To fit the story, General Washington's order to preclude blacks serving in the army has been moved from November back to August and his de facto rescission thereof from December back to September, a three-month switch. See Ellis, *His Excellency: George Washington* (Alfred A. Knopf, 2004), pp. 84, 291.

110   During the ride: See generally Smith, Roberts, and Henry.

110–12 Smith, pp. 61-63, 286.

111   The equipment supplied to each man is listed in Henry, p. 11.

111   Andrews was widely regarded as a first-class officer, as was Hutchins, who had served with Rogers' Rangers. During the expedition, Perkins also proved a stalwart. See Roberts, pp. 2, 37 ff.

PART TWO

Chapter 22

115–16 Arnold may well have addressed his officers and troops, but this speech is imagined.

116   Spring is identified as the chaplain at Smith, p. 62. The difficulties of the passage are described at Smith, pp. 65–73.

118   The next day: See Smith, pp. 75–83.

119   At Fort Western: See Smith, pp. 84–92 and 319.

119–20   See Smith, pp. 93–106, Roberts, pp. 45–46, Henry, pp. 13–15, and Dearborn, pp. 9–10.

121   See Smith, pp. 93–116.

122–23   See Smith, pp. 117-146.

123   Often they sank: Smith records, at p. 122, that "[we] sank 'half-leg deep' in the wet earth, and now and then, slipping in the mud, fell and brought [our] burden down with [us]."

124   The story of Natanis is set forth in Smith at pp.139–140 and in Henry at pp. 31–32.

124–25   The river and adjoining ponds: Smith, pp. 145–46.

125   The "Height of Land" was probably the main ridge of the Appalachian Mountains.

125–26   See Smith, pp. 147–195.

126   Colonel Enos's cowardly retreat and the effect it had on the rest of Arnold's troops is described in Smith, p 199, in Dearborn, pp. 13-14 and in Roberts, pp. 631-648. While Arnold's expedition was still underway, Enos was court-martialed and acquitted. Historians have observed that the result would probably have been different if Arnold and his officers had been present to testify. Ibid.

126–28   See Smith, pp.217–257; Dearborn, p. 21.

127   See Smith, pp. 196–217.

128   Miraculously some six hundred and fifty men had made it: Smith writes, at p. 254, "When all were mustered the sight was more pitiable than formidable. [Our] clothes, torn by thickets and bushes, hung in strings. Many had no shoes except the roughest of moccasins made of fresh hides. Many had no hats."

128   Roberts, p. 586, describes the scene as follows: "Quebec, the stronghold of Canada, stands in a commanding position on the north bank of the St. Lawrence, near the mouth of a small river, the St. Charles. It consists of an upper and lower town. The upper part of the city is a strong fortification, built upon a rock three hundred and forty feet above the lower town. Its harbor,

three hundred and fifty miles from the sea, is very spacious, and has a depth of twenty-eight fathoms."

Chapter 23

129–30 See Smith, pp. 247–252, 254; Dearborn, p. 20.

130 The colonel circulated a letter: General Washington's address is set forth in full at Henry, pp 5–6.

130–32 See Roberts, pp. 88, 90–93.

130–32 See Roberts, pp. 87, 93–94; Flexner, *The Traitor and The Spy* (Harcourt, Brace, 1953) ("Flexner"), pp. 83–84; Dearborn, p. 18.

130–32 See Dearborn, pp. 19–21; Flexner, pp.84–88; Roberts, pp. 90–95. The letter to Cramache is at Roberts, pp. 89–90.

133 Dearborn's arrival back in camp is noted in his own journal at p. 22.

133–34 See Dearborn, pp.22–23; Flexner, p.89.

134 In fact there had been no "draft" (conscription); the comment was inserted to set up the conversation with Will. That Dearborn's men were receiving shells and cannon balls is recorded in Dearborn, pp. 24–25.

135–38 The attack and its sad results are described in Dearborn, pp. 25–32; in Flexner, pp. 89–93; Henry, pp.107–115; and Roberts, pp. 102–106, 589–90.

135 *"Rush on, brave boys, rush on"*: Flexner, p. 91.

135 *"Come on my good soldiers"*: Dearborn's journal, p. 28.

139 On January 14 came word: Flexner, p. 95.

139–40 See Flexner, pp. 95–96.

140 One morning, looking across the frozen river: See Flexner's description at p. 95.

Chapter 24

141 See Flexner, pp. 95–96.

141–42 See Flexner, pp. 96–97.

143 Commissioner Carroll described the dinner in his journal: "[W]e were served with a glass of wine, while people were crowding in to pay compliments, which ceremony being over, we were shown into another apartment, and unexpectedly met in it a large number of ladies, most of them French. After drinking

tea and sitting some time, we went to an elegant supper, which was followed with the singing of the ladies, which proved very agreeable, and would have been more so if we had not been so much fatigued with our journey." Ibid. Carroll also commented on Arnold's deportment that "an officer bred up at Versailles could not have behaved with more delicacy, ease, and good breeding." Ketchum, *Saratoga* (Henry Holt, 1997) ("Ketchum"), p. 33.

144   The Sorel River is now known as the Richelieu River and St. Johns is now called St. John.

145   The remains of the army: One observer described the men as "not an army but a mob...the shattered remains of twelve or fifteen very fine battalions, ruined by sickness, fatigue, and desertion, and void of every idea of discipline or subordination. . . the very acme of human misery." In their report to the Continental Congress, Carroll and Chase wrote:

> We cannot find words strong enough to describe our miserable situation: you will have a faint idea of it if you figure to yourself an army broken and disheartened, half of it under inoculation, or under other diseases; soldiers without pay, without discipline, and altogether reduced to live from hand to mouth, depending on the scanty and precarious supplies of a few half-starved cattle and trifling quantities of flour. . . Your soldiers grumble for their pay; if they receive it they will not be benefited, as it will not procure them the necessaries they stand in need of. Your military chest contains but eleven thousand paper dollars. You are indebted to your troops treble that sum; and to the inhabitants above fifteen thousand dollars. Ketchum, pp. 33–36.

145   See Flexner, pp. 99–100.

Chapter 25

146   See Hammersley, *The Lake Champlain Naval Battles of 1776–1814* (Waterford, N.Y.:1959), pp. 1-2; Seelinger, *Buying Time: The Battle of Valcour Island* (The Army Historical Foundation, 2004) Website: *www.armyhistoryfnd.org/armyhist/research/detailz.cfm*, p. 1; Flexner, pp. 101–102.

146–48   See Millard, *History of Fort Carillon/Ticonderoga* (2004 webpage). *www.historiclakes.org/Ticonderoga/Ticonderoga.html.* Fort Ticonderoga. Website: *http://members.tripod.com/FortTic/Fort.html.*

148   Regarding Henry Knox, see Morison, pp.220, 233; and Ketchum, p. 5.

151   *"A declaration of independence was a fine thing. . ."* See Hammersley, p. 3. Skenesborough is now known as Whitehall.

151–53 See Hammersley, pp. 3–5; Seelinger, pp. 1–2.

Chapter 26

154–56 See Flexner, pp. 106–09; Hammersley, pp. 6–8; and Seelinger, p.3.

156–58 See Flexner, pp. 109–113; Hammersley, pp. 8–11; and Seelinger, pp. 3–4.

158   *"General Carleton was in a rage"*: Flexner, p. 110.

Chapter 27

161   Information about Colonel Atkinson and his home may be found at Brewster, pp. 107–08, 184, 192, and 217.

166   There he usually found the minister: Reverend Haven's patriotic contributions to the war effort are noted in Brewster, pp. 324,326.

166   *"Small islands not capable"*: Paine, *Common Sense* (Meridian, 1984), p. 43.

167–69 See Potter, *The Military History of the State of New Hampshire* (McFarland & Jenks, 1866) (*"NH Military History"*), pp. 315–354; *Guide*, pp. 81, 92–93; *Profiles*, pp. 39–41 and Flexner, pp. 125–133.

167   Stark was put in command of the Second Brigade and was the overall superior officer. He immediately turned to outfitting the new troops, a task in which he was greatly assisted by generous contributions of $3,000 in cash, a loan of another $3,000, and the proceeds from the sale of seventy hogsheads of rum, all from Colonel John Langdon of Portsmouth.

169   The horrifying scalping practice was graphically described by a contemporary surgeon:

   with a knife [the Indians] make a circular cut from the forehead, quite round, just above the ears, then taking hold of the skin with their teeth, they tear off the whole hairy scalp in an instant, with wonderful dexterity. This they carefully dry and preserve as a trophy, showing the number of their victims. And they have a method of painting on the dried scalp, different figures and colors, to designate the sex and age of the victim, and also the manner and circumstances of the murder. Ketchum, pp. 268–69 (from Dr. James Thacher)

169   The *New Hampshire Gazette* story actually appeared on August 16, 1777. See Ketchum, pp. 265–284. The date is changed here to fit the story. For more detail on the Jane McCrea story, see Furneaux, pp. 97–98, and Ketchum, pp. 274–77. Burgoyne and his officers fast became disenchanted with their Indian allies, whom why realized were quite uncontrollable, ineffective in organized combat, and downright embarrassing. The feeling was mutual. After the British losses at Bennington and Fort Stanwix, a large segment of the Indians, reading the signs that they were on the losing side, broke from Burgoyne and headed back to northern New York and Canada.

Chapter 28

170–75 See *NH Military History*, pp.317–354; Ketchum, pp. 285–328; Furneaux, *Saratoga, The Decisive Battle* (George Allent Unwin Ltd., 1971) ("Furneaux"), pp.114–32; Mintz, *The Generals of Saratoga* (Yale University Press, 1990) ("Mintz"), pp.167–75; Richmond, *John Stark, Freedom Fighter* (Dale Books, 1976) ("Stark"), pp. 62–68 and Johnson, *Battles of the American Revolution* (Roxby Press Ltd., 1975) ("Johnson"), pp. 78–79.

171   "Sancoick" is now North Hoosick, New York.

173   *"There is the enemy, boys"*: Stark's famous exhortation is worded slightly differently in various historical accounts, but the essence is the same. This is my favorite version. See, e.g., *Profiles*, p. 58, and *NH Military History*, p. 318.

175   "Fix bayonets! *Charge!*": Ketchum, p. 318. Ketchum's source for the quote was David Holbrook's account of the battle set forth in Dann, *The Revolution Remembered: Eye-Accounts of the War for Independence* (University of Chicago Press, 1980), pp. 87–91.

175   *"The Hampshire grants"*: Richmond, p. 69. Perhaps the general's aversion to fighting New Hampshire men contributed to the fact that New Hampshire was the only one of the original thirteen states not invaded by the British during the Revolution. *Guide*, p. 105. We took the fight to them.

Chapter 29

177 Prince had also obtained: General Whipple did not actually grant Prince his freedom until seven years later. The reason for the delay is not clear. That the general was sympathetic to the plight of the Black people in America is shown in a letter he wrote on March 28, 1779 to Josiah Bartlett:

> The last accts. From S. Carolina were favorable, a recommendation is gone thither for raising some regiments of Blacks this will I suppose lay a foundation for the emancipation of those poor wretches in that Country, & I hope be the means of dispensing the Blessings of freedom to all the Human Race in America. *Guide*, p. 215.

177–78 A significant number of Africans (at least one hundred and eighty from New Hampshire alone, according to *Black Portsmouth*, p. 70) fought in the Revolution, some in white companies and others in segregated black units. The seven African men described in the text were real individuals who actually participated in the war. Sampson Moore is described in *NH Military History*, p. 335. Jude Hall is mentioned in Nell, *The Colored Patriots of the American Revolution* (Wallcut, 1855) (*Colored Patriots*), p. 119. George Knox is described in Quinlan, George Knox, *A Black Soldier in the American Revolution* (Dartmouth College Library Bulletin, April 20, 1980) at pp. 54–62. Wentworth Cheswell's life is chronicled at many places, including Website: *http://www.gravematter.com/cheswell.htm*. See also Gates, *Native Sons of Liberty* (*The New York Times*, Sunday, August 6, 2006, p. WK 12).

Chapter 30

180 See Furneaux, pp. 164–80; Mintz, pp. 187–99.

180–81 See Johnson, p. 81; Ketchum, pp. 330, 337,341–43.

181 See Dearborn's journal, pp. 32–45.

181 Regarding Stark and his men, see Ketchum, p. 353.

182 The army pay levels are set forth in the *Guide*, p. 97. This book posits that Will kept his army pay for himself. *Colored Patriots*, at p. 121, states that the Rev. Dr. Jeremy Belknap reported in 1795:

> In New Hampshire . . . those blacks who enlisted into the army for three years, were entitled to the same bounty as

the whites. This bounty their masters received as the price of their liberty, and then delivered up their bills of sale, and gave them a certificate of manumission. Several of these bills and certificates were deposited in my hands; and those who survived the three years' service were free. It is believed that in many cases, however, white owners kept their slave's military pay for themselves and did not provide freedom for the slave in return.

182 The standard government issue for each New Hampshire soldier is described in *NH Military History*, p. 281.

Chapter 31

184–85 The events of early morning including the argument between Gates and Arnold are described in Flexner, pp. 170–71; and Ketchum, pp. 355–56.

185–86 The arrival of the troops from both sides and the opening of the battle is based on Ketchum, pp. 360–62. Flexner's sequence, at pp. 170–71, that the British arrived first, seems wrong.

186–87 See Ketchum, pp. 360–64.

187 *"riding in front of the lines. . . "* This is a real quote, but from Enoch Poor, who in turn purported to have heard it from one of Dearborn's men, which in this fictional account could have been Will. See Ketchum, pp. 362, 515, where that historian also points out that the extent of Arnold's direct involvement in this battle has been unclear and controversial.

187 The British regimental commander's (Riedesel's) charge is described in Ketchum, pp. 367–69.

187 As darkness fell: The definitive Saratoga battle historian Richard Ketchum concluded that "in four hours of hand-to-hand combat the Americans had held their own against some of the best troops in the world. Those four hours marked a turning point in the morale of both armies."Ketchum, p. 372.

188–89 The correspondence between Burgoyne and Clinton, Burgoyne's discussions with his staff, and the parallel dispute between Gates and Arnold are set forth in Ketchum, pp. 375–76, 383–89.During this respite after the battle at Freeman's Farm, as both sides patched up their wounded and strengthened their defensive fortifications, good news for the colonial troops arrived from Fort

Ticonderoga on September 25 that a force of 2500 men under Major General Lincoln and Colonel John Brown had successfully attacked a British post near the old fort, liberating one hundred and eighteen Americans and capturing more than one hundred and sixty of the enemy. See Ketchum, pp.376–379; Mintz, p. 200.

190   By October 4: Unknown to Burgoyne, in the interim Sir William Howe had ordered Clinton to the south to assist Howe in his confrontation with George Washington in Philadelphia. See Ketchum, p. 385.

190–91 See Ketchum, pp. 388–89, 393–96. What Ketchum describes as the battle of the "Wheat Field," the second battle of Saratoga, is referred to by some other writers as the battle of "Bemis Heights." See Furneaux, pp.222–67; and Mintz, pp. 200–27, for their descriptions of the battle and the subsequent surrender.

190   *"Well then, order on Morgan"*: Ketchum, p. 394.

192   See Ketchum, pp. 402–05, 408–416. John Stark's reappearance, Burgoyne's realization of the futility of his situation, and the subsequent negotiations are set forth in Ketchum, pp. 417–425.

192   The surrender ceremony is described by Ketchum at pp. 426–431.

PART THREE

Chapter 32

195   Abi and the children's exuberance: Events following the victory are described by many historians, including a reference to where Gates' troops went next by Ketchum at pp. 438–440.

197   Rising Castle Island is now called Badger Island. The outfitting of the *Ranger*, the embarking of her maiden voyage and Jones's relationship with Phillis Wheatley are detailed in Morison, *John Paul Jones: A Sailor's Biography* (Naval Institute Press, 1959) ("Morison, JPJ"), pp. 133–151, and Thomas, *John Paul Jones: Sailor, Hero, Father of the American Navy* (Simon & Schuster, 2003) ("Thomas, JPJ"), pp. 89–93. That the *Ranger* was the first American warship to fly the new Betsy Ross Stars and Stripes is stated in *Guide*, p. 41.

In addition to its role in building and harboring officially designated Continental Navy ships, Portsmouth was one of the most significant ports for privateers (vessels privately owned and operated but legally commissioned by the state to prey upon enemy commerce in wartime) during the American Revolution. See *Guide*, p. 41, and Winslow, *"Wealth and Honour, Portsmouth During the Golden Age of Privateering, 1775–1815* (Portsmouth Marine Society, 1988).

198   *"My freedom, as Master James agreed"*: Will's expectation because of his agreement with James was particularly justified, but even those slaves who fought and had no specific agreement with their owners shared the same hope. Breig wrote:

> When the war ended, the slaves who had fought on both sides expected freedom as their reward, a move that [James] Hamilton had anticipated in his letter to [John] Jay [both of New York]: "An essential part of the plan is to give them their freedom with their muskets."

198–99 There is no historical evidence that Will actually asked any of the Clarksons for his freedom and was refused, although it might be implied from his participation in the petition that he had first made such a request and was turned down. There is certainly no indication that any Clarkson reneged on a promise of freedom in return for Will's fighting in the war. The known facts are that he remained a slave of the Clarkson family until he was sold to Pierse Long after James Jr.'s death in 1779 and that he apparently remained enslaved to Long until the latter's death in 1789.

199   The biblical basis is found principally: Romans 8:29–30 states: "For those God foreknew He also predestined to be conformed to the likeness of His Son, that He might be the firstborn among many brothers. And those He predestined, He also called; those He called, He also justified; those He justified, He also glorified." Ephesians 1:5, 11 says: He predestined us to be adopted as His sons through Jesus Christ, in accordance with His pleasure and will. . . . In Him we were also chosen, having been predestined according to the plan of Him who works out everything in conformity with the purpose of His will." See also Romans 9:10ff and Matthew 24:22 and 31.

199-200 Haven's description of predestination and his responses to Will's questions are in large part based on the Website: *http://geneva. rutgers.edu/src/faq/predestination.txt.*

201   In July: No record of this marriage is available.

202   See Morison, *History*, p. 250.

202   See Morison, *JPJ*, pp. 152–202.

202–03 See Morison, *History*, pp. 254–57; Morison, *JPJ*, pp. 223–292.

Chapter 33

205-10 The petition of the twenty Portsmouth slaves is set forth in *Black Portsmouth*, pp. 66–67.

210   The signers listed in the text include the fictional "Caesar Bannister"; the real name on the original was Nero Brewster.

Chapter 34

211   *"The following is a copy"*: NHG, July 15, 1780, p. 1,col.1.

212   *"As you know, the legislature. . . "*: The New Hampshire House of Representatives Journal for June 9, 1780, states:

> According to the order of the day, the Petition of Nero Brewster [Caesar Bannister in this story] and other Negro Slaves praying to be set free from Slavery, being read, considered and argued by Counsel on behalf of the Petitioners before this House, It appears to this house, That at this time the House is not ripe for a Determination in this matter; Therefore ordered that the further consideration & determination of the matter be postponed till a more convenient opportunity.

Chapter 35

216   How could a man: The answer to Will's question appears to lie both in basic character defects—ambition, egocentricity, extravagance—and in Arnold's bitterness toward Congress for failing to recognize his accomplishments or to compensate him for expenditures of his own money he assertedly made on the Continental Army's behalf. He was also undoubtedly influenced by his new Tory fiancée, Margaret Shippen, and demoralized by the lack of improvement in his physical condition since his wounds at Saratoga. A biographer perhaps hit closest to the mark:

> A revolutionary soldier, Arnold had fought for *"freedom"* as he understood it: for motion without hindrance, for the right of the individual will—his will—to answer, light and jocund, the call of individual destiny. Where was his freedom now?

Strapped to a wooden box [a cast], he was imprisoned as he had never been. Flexner, pp. 218–19.

The freedom Will sought was very different from that pursued by Arnold. Will's objective was founded on principle; the General's was completely selfish and materialistic. See Morison, p. 259. See also Website: Henretta, *The Enigma of Benedict Arnold: http://earlyAmerica.com/review/fall97/arnold.html* ; Selling West Point: *http://www.si.umich.cdu/spies/stories–arnold-3.html* ; Benedict Arnold: *http://www.benedictarnold.org/* .

Chapter 36

218   See Inventory of James Clarkson Estate, p. 2, filed November 10, 1780, in New Hampshire State Archives, Concord.

218–19   Brewster, pp. 275–79, describes Pierse Long's career. See also *NH Military History*, pp. 290–91.

219   Walter sold both: While Will may or may not have been able to purchase his own freedom with money he had earned in the army, the historical fact is that Long became Will's owner after James Jr. died. See *Brewster*, p. 212.

219   The quoted Bill of Sale is a construct from similar documents during the same period. See, e.g., Dagenais, Appendix 9.

222   See Morison, *History*, pp. 257–65. 276–81. See Thomas JPJ, pp. 249–53; Morison, JPJ, pp. 381–92; and Brewster, pp. 367–372. The *America* never went into service for the Americans; in 1782, Congress voted to give the not-quite-finished ship to France.

222   . . . Jones moved next door to a house. . . . : The house is now maintained as a museum in Jones's name.

222   On the same day that Captain Jones: See Morison, *History*, pp. 261–265.

222–23   After a series of: The historian Samuel Morison described the scene that followed:
         One by one, the British regiments, after laying down their arms, marched back to camp between two lines, one of American soldiers, the other of French, while the military bands played a series of melancholy tunes, including one which all recognized as "The World Turned Upside Down." Morison, *History*, p. 265.

222–23   See Morison, *History*, pp. 266–69.

223   That evening, for the first time: Breig wrote:
        "African Americans viewed the war as an opportunity
        to break the bonds of slavery," said Martin Blatt, chief of
        cultural resources at Boston National Historical Park. "It
        signaled the beginning of freedom." Breig, p. 22.

Chapter 37

224   For more information on the economic decline of Portsmouth,
        see *Profiles*, p. 106; and *Guide*, pp. 132–206.

224   *"That infernal crew of Tories"*: *Guide*, p. 119. The suppression of the
        loyalists is described in Guide, pp. 118–131; and *Profiles*, p. 106.

225   Ibid.

227   The three members of the committee and Richards are fictional
        persons.

229–30 Abigail Adams: Mrs. Adams' husband was a delegate to the
        First and Second Continental Congresses and a signer of the
        Declaration of Independence, and was to become the second
        president of the United States. Breig reported that Mrs. Adams
        "wrote in 1775 that it had 'always appeared a most iniquitous
        scheme to me' to demand for ourselves 'what we are daily
        robbing and plundering from those who have as good a right to
        freedom as we have.'" Breig, p. 22.

230   *"I am going to. . . "*: There is no record of such a letter or even
        that Mrs. Adams had a cousin in Portsmouth.

233   . . . English abolitionist movement. . . : See Hochschild, *Bury
        the Chains* (Houghton Mifflin, 2004). The author knows of no
        relationship between the James Clarkson family and Thomas
        Clarkson.

233–34 Simes is a fictional person. The author borrowed the name from
        a colorful English lawyer who practiced in Portsmouth during
        the middle of the twentieth century.

243   *"Outrageous!"* blurted Simes: Simes' statements are supported in
        particular by a 1772 opinion by William, Lord Murray, Earl of
        Mansfield, Chief Justice of the King's Bench, *Somerset v. Steuart*,
        regarding a writ of habeas corpus filed on behalf of a runaway
        black man being held on a ship moored on the Thames River
        in London. See *Black Portsmouth*, pp. 64–65; Wise, *Though the
        Heavens May Fall* (Da Capo Press, 2004); and *Bury the Chains*,
        supra, note to p.226.

249   *"Whereas I, Abigail Clarkson"*: This recantation is similar to a
        standard form then in use. See *Guide*, p. 120.

250   Will took her hand: In 1812 a new state prison was constructed
        on Islington Road (see *Guide*, p. 213, and 1813 map in Brewster).
        Absent any available information to the contrary, it is assumed
        that the old provincial jail stood on the same site.

Chapter 38

251   Meechum is a fictional character; he is not based on any specific
        historical person.

Chapter 39

258   At the far end of the Plains: In the April 19, 1786, edition of the
        New Hampshire Mercury it was reported that:
           Died, on Monday last, at Colonel William Brewster's, NERO,
           late King of the Africans, in this town, aged 75.—A Monarch,
           who, while living, was held in reverential esteem by his
           subjects, his death is greatly lamented. See *Resource Book*, p. 59.

        In actual life the real Nero Brewster was indeed well respected.
        There is no evidence that he or his actual owner William
        Brewster ever engaged in the activities attributed to the fictional
        Caesar or the fictional William Bannister in this novel.

Chapter 40

259   Life was difficult: Naby was a real person, but there is no
        evidence that she ever married or had children. Will Jr. is
        fictional; there is no firm record evidence one way or the other
        as to whether Will ever had a son.

Chapter 41

263   From the political: See Morison, *History*, pp. 315, 317–323, and 336.

264   *Osborne's New Hampshire Spy*, October 20, 1789.

264   Reverend Haven did in fact meet with President Washington on
        November 3, 1789, regarding the corn dyes. See Brewster, p. 256.
        There is no evidence of Will's presence at the meeting.

Chapter 42

266–72 See Brewster, pp. 254–72, for a full description of President
        Washington's visit.

268   Then the judge . . . who with a magnanimity: Brewster, p. 259.

269   *". . . the State House on the Parade"*: Brewster, p. 262.

270   *"Mr. President, one in every seven soldiers in the war…"*: This ratio is often cited. See Website *http://www.americanrevolution.com/ LittleKnownFacts.htm*. It is difficult to ascertain the exact number of Africans who fought because of the absence of records, but it is apparently agreed that the number was in excess of 5,000. See website *http://wwwnps.gov/revwar/about_the_revolution/african_ americans.html*. If the total number of soldiers in the war was as high as 170–250,000 as has been estimated, the ratio was lower.

270–71   The considerations and events covered in President Washington's response to Will are described in Morison, *History*, pp. 276–81, and 305–16.

270   *"I did the best I could. . . "*: While Washington and others may have hoped that Federal supremacy over the slavery issue was established, it clearly was not. Witness the vituperative political battle leading to the Missouri Compromise of 1820 and the subsequent *Dred Scott* case.

271   Will would not have been the first to suggest to Washington that he free his slaves. Robert Pleasant, a Virginia Quaker, and the Marquis de Lafayette were among them. See Ellis, *His Excellency: George Washington* (Alfred A. Knopf, 2004) ("Ellis"), pp. 160–67.

270–71   The evolution of Washington's position on slavery, particularly on the issue of black Americans in the military, is described in detail in Flexner, *Washington, The Indispensable Man* (Mentor 1969) ("FlexnerGW"), pp. 389–398; and in Ellis, pp 84, 160–67, 256–65, 291. As late as 1796, a slave of Martha Washington named Ona Judge, a biracial housekeeper and seamstress, ran away to Portsmouth, New Hampshire, where she successfully eluded the Washingtons' efforts to persuade or force her to return. Ona purportedly said that she thought well of the Washingtons but her freedom was more important. See *Black Portsmouth*, pp. 71–72; and Ellis, p. 260.

272   *"We'd probably be better off back in Africa"*: This alternative might also have transpired to be an unhappy and even tragic one. For example, see Hochschild, *King Leopold's Ghost* (Houghton Mifflin, 1998), regarding the Congo.

EPILOGUE

273   The United States census: See Dagenais, p. 84.

274   They attended Matilda's church: In fact, Will, Matilda, and
        Naby were christened at St. John's in 1798. This point is
        deleted from the author's text because in this fictional story
        Will was christened earlier when he became a Christian while
        Abi was still alive. See *Records of St. John's Church, Portsmouth,
        N.H., 1795–1884*, Baptisms for January 21, 1798—"William
        Clarkson, Matilda Clarkson, 'his wife' and Naby Clarkson, 'their
        daughter.'" See also *Births and Christenings, Portsmouth, N.H.
        (1795–1874)* (Genealogical Society Computer Printout 1974), p.38.
        (perhaps erroneously listing "Matilda," "Naby" and "William"
        as two daughters and a son of William and Matilda).

274   Some African-Americans: Piersen emphasizes that it was still
        a very few. See *Black Yankees*, pp. 49–61. If Piersen is right, the
        wording of the 1779 petition, invoking Christian morality, surely
        reflects a canny shrewdness on the part of the drafters and
        signers.

274   The young nation mourned: Flexner GW, pp. 396–98, 399–406.
        Websites also describe the nation's mourning. *http://gwpapers.
        virginia.edu/exhibits/mourning/response.html. http://gwpapers.
        virginia.edu/exhibits/mourning/news.html.http://www.mountvernon.
        org/learn/meet_george/index.cfm/ss/2'*.

275   Benedict Arnold died: Flexner, p. 403.

275   Portsmouth records reveal that Will and Matilda: Chipman,
        Genealogical Abstracts from early New Hampshire Newspapers, vol. 1
        (Heritage Books, 2000), p. 127. (in turn from *The Farmer's Weekly
        Museum*, Walpole, N.H., Tuesday, Sept. 14, 1802). Matilda was
        an actual person who did marry Will. Abigail, Will's first wife
        in this story, is fictional; but it would appear that Will may have
        had an earlier spouse, whose real name we do not know, by
        whom he had Naby and perhaps a son.

275–76 Fuess, *Daniel Webster* (Little Brown & Company 1930) and
        Brewster, pp. 311–315.

276   Notwithstanding passage of the 1784 state Constitution: *Black
        Portsmouth* outlines the subsequent decline of slavery in New
        Hampshire, pp. 70–75, 77, 118–141. Throughout the country,
        while there were only 25,000 free blacks in 1776 (of a total black

population of nearly 500,000), the number was up to 60,000 by the time of the 1790 Census. See Website *http://encarta.msn. comencyclopedia_761595158_2African_American_History.html.*

277   As noted above, Henry Dearborn's subsequent career is summarized in *Profiles*, p. 46, as well as at two Websites: *http:// www.state.nh.us/nhdhr/warheroes/dearbornh.html* and *http://www. hampton.lib.nh.us/hampton/biog/henrydearbornl.htm.*

277   John Stark's life story is written in Stark (footnote to pp. 167–73).

277   Reverend Haven died: See Peabody, pp. 65–84.

277   James Clarkson lll died: Welch Research.

277   City records show that Will died: *Records of the South Church, Portsmouth,N.H.*, p. 31.

See also *Index of Deaths in Portsmouth, 1808–July, 1821*, p. 210. Will's actual age is difficult precisely to ascertain or rationalize from the records. He could not have been fifty-five in 1802 and seventy-eight in 1809, but it is clearly the same man. With no record of his birth, he may have given different dates at different times himself. For purposes of the story in this book and trying to fit all dates together most logically, the author has set his age at sixteen when he arrived on the Exeter in 1755, which would have made him seventy at death.

277   . . . but no burial marker has been found: In October 2003 workers installing a sewer main at Chestnut and Court Streets in Portsmouth uncovered two deteriorated wooden coffins that were apparently located in a "Negro Burying Ground" established in 1705 but covered over by 1815. See *http:// seacoastnh.com/arts/please101203.html.* While it is possible that Will was buried there, at present it seems that even with DNA and forensic tests it would be difficult to identify Will's remains at this juncture.

277   Matilda hung on: *Index of Deaths*, supra. That Matilda was eighty-eight at her death is calculated from the report of her marriage to Will purportedly at age seventy in 1802.

277   In 1782 General Washington had created: See Website: *http:// www.purpleheart.org/explanation.htm.* (9/10/2004).

MAP CREDITS

End leaves: A Plan of Piscataqua Harbor, the Town of Portsmouth, New Hampshire, in 1774. Courtesy of the New Hampshire Historical Society

Facing page 178: Will's Route in the Northern Theater. By Charles Shand, of Lake Barcroft, Virginia

ABOUT THE AUTHOR

STEPHEN CLARKSON is a direct descendant of Will's original owner in America. He graduated from Yale College and the University of Virginia School of Law. He practiced law in New York City and Washington, D.C., and was Vice President, General Counsel, and Secretary of Newport News Shipbuilding in Virginia. Now retired, he and his wife, Mary Claire, make their home in Rye, New Hampshire, where he lived as a boy. *Patriot's Reward* is his first novel.

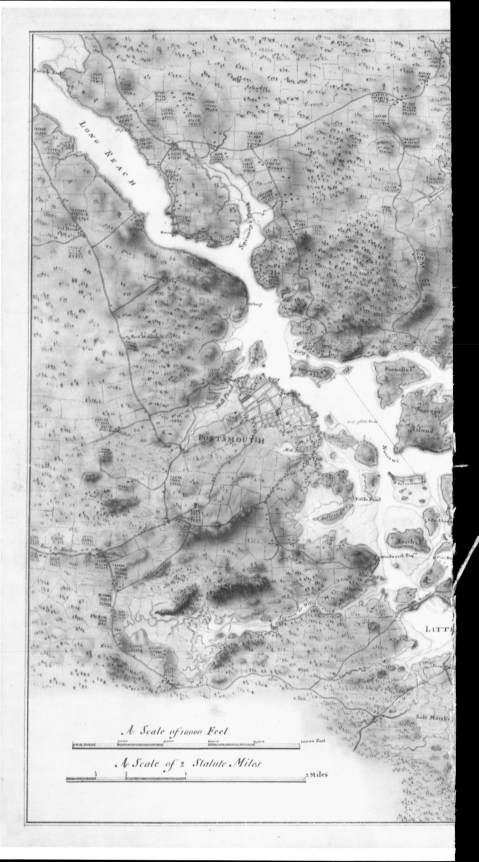

A Scale of 10000 Feet

A Scale of 2 Statute Miles

A PLAN

of

PISCATAQUA HARBOR

the

TOWN OF PORTSMOUTH &c.

References to the Town of Portsmouth

A. Episcopal Church
B. First Congregational Church
C. Second D.o D.o
D. Sandimans Church
E. Quakers Church
F. Town House
G. Assize House
H. Governor House

Surveyd and Drawn by
Ja.s Grant
1774

Spruce Creek

Salt Marsh

CUTTS ISLAND

M.r Cutt

Killery P.t

Battery Point

Fishing Rock

Sea Point

GARISHES ISLAND

M.r Cutt

Newcastle

Castle & Light House
Fort

Great Rock

Wood Island

Gorish Point

White Island

Battery

Jerry's Point

Frost Point